BOHEMIAN
GOSPEL

BOHEMIAN
GOSPEL

WITHDRAWN

A Novel

DANA CHAMBLEE
CARPENTER

PEGASUS BOOKS
NEW YORK LONDON

BOHEMIAN GOSPEL

Pegasus Books LLC
80 Broad Street, 5th Floor
New York, NY 10004

First Pegasus Books edition November 2015

Interior design by Maria Fernandez

Library of Congress Cataloging-in-Publication Data is available.

ISBN: 978-1-60598-901-3

10 9 8 7 6 5 4 3 2 1

Printed in the United States of America
Distributed by W. W. Norton & Company

For Greg,

who always keeps faith,

and for L and J,

who show me where the magic lives.

BOHEMIAN
GOSPEL

CAST OF CHARACTERS

Teplá Abbey

Mouse	Girl raised at Teplá
Father Lucas	Abbot, Mouse's mentor
Mother Kazi	Prioress and healer, Mouse's mentor
Brother Jan	Prior
Adele	Mouse's nursemaid
Brother Milek	Kitchener
Sister Kveta	Nun
Sister Ida	Nun

Ottakar and His Men

Ottakar	The Younger King of Bohemia
Vok	Lord Rozemberk, Ottakar's second-in-command
Damek	Knight
Evzen	Knight
Gernandus	Knight
Hartwin	Royal physician

Prague

Vaclav	Ottakar's father and King of Bohemia
Mother Agnes	Ottakar's aunt, sister to Vaclav
Prince Vladislaus	Ottakar's older brother
Lord Rozemberk	Vok's father and Vaclav's second-in-command
Lady Rozemberk	Vok's mother
Luka	Nephew of Lord Rozemberk
Bishop Bansca	Bishop from Rome
Bishop Miklaus	Archbishop of Prague
Lady Harrach	Wife of Damek
Lady Lemberk	Wife of Evzen
Lord Olomouc	Friend of Vaclav
Gitta	Maid in the royal court

Hluboka Castle

Ludolf	Master carver

Rozemberk Castle

Hanzi	Leader of the Romany clan
Margaret	Widow of Henry, Duke of Austria

Sušice

Enede	Cottager

Marchfeld

Vitek	Heir to the Rozemberk estate
Rudolf	Holy Roman Emperor

Podlazice

Bishop Andreas	Abbot at Podlazice monastery

ONE

The future king of Bohemia lay dying on the floor at her feet.

Silent stars burst at the edges of her vision, flattening the world into darks and lights as her eyes adjusted to the dim room.

She could see the shadowy outlines of the men packed along the walls of the abbey's infirmary; they looked like holes cut from the afternoon sun that filtered in through the windows behind them. The girl closed her eyes against the light and was too aware of how close they all were. Men pinned her from behind against the soldier in front of her, each of them panting from the hard ride, their axes and swords clinking as they shifted, pent up and pointless.

She had raced them from the river up to the abbey and was having a hard time catching her breath. She needed to breathe—to move. She stretched upward, arching her back and pushing against the chain mail on either side until she'd made a small space, a pocket of air that she sucked in quickly.

Her stomach heaved. The air was thick with the smell of leather soured with sweat and piss, mixed with the sweet pine of the forest, which still clung to the men's hair and clothes.

The man in front of her turned at the sound of her gagging and took a step away, shoving the men near him to make room. She bent, hands pressed against her knees, waiting for the burn to crawl up her throat and spew through her nose and mouth, but a bit of clear air slipped past the gap between men. She sipped it slowly, her jaw locked against the nausea.

And she saw him.

He seemed so small lying there, framed by the window, much more a boy than a king, except that strands of his tawny hair, disheveled and catching the sunlight, looked like they were on fire, a crown of flames. The Younger King they had named him, those lords of the land who had urged him to overthrow his father. At fifteen, he had done as they asked—besieged his father and usurped the crown—but then the pope had demanded a compromise, one that would let father and son rule together. And so they had ruled, until the father broke his oath and sent his son running for his life. Now here he lay, dying.

These knights, stinking and scared, crowded around the dying man they were meant to protect; they were the sons of those power-hungry nobles. Now, they watched their aristocratic futures writhe and suffocate on the cold stone floor, blood oozing past the arrow in their king's chest.

To these men, she was nothing. But to him, she might be everything.

Driving her shoulder through the gap, she burst into the light near him.

"Stop!" The command came from the dark corner on the other side of the king.

The girl took another step forward. The scrape of blade against sheath echoed around her as the king's guards drew their swords, but she dropped to her knees and laid her hand on the king anyway. The room closed in on her as if she had pulled the strings of a purse.

A man stepped out of the shadows, his sword at her throat as she turned her face up to him. She had seen this man at the river, driving his horse up the bank with one hand, the other twisted behind him, steadying the hunched figure at his back. Time had held them for a moment—the girl, the horse, the rider, and the wounded king. She had seen the cold anger in the rider's face as he looked down on her, had seen the king's bloody surcoat, the goose fletching on the arrow in his chest quivering with each pounding step of the charger. She had looked up and seen the king's face: pale, but eyes open and looking at her, not like the rider, but kindly, with the eyes of a man who knows he is dying and wants to leave the world gently.

Instinctively, she had reached toward him, the metal barding at the horse's flank slicing her palm as they rushed past her. She had turned to follow, but the rattle of tack and high whinnies of dozens more charging horses held her still. They crashed out of the woods on the other side of the Teplá and ran into the river, horses' bodies slapping against the water, pushing a wave forward with them as they pulled up the near bank where she stood.

"Run, girl! Out of the way!" the men had screamed at her, but there had been no time to run.

She shifted her body sideways, trying to make herself smaller. The horses' bodies, which were warm from the river water, steamed as they struck the chill air again. She had drawn a breath as the first tendril of mist touched her just before the horses' hooves slammed into the mud beside her.

And then she moved.

A few steps forward or back, twisting her body, the edges of her mantle swinging until the rabbit fur lining was covered in mud, her loose hair whipping and wrapping around her neck; she looked like she was dancing with the horses in some intricate and precise choreography set to music no one else could hear. Just by watching, she'd known how they would all move, which horse would bolt and which would stay steady, which rider would pull the reins and which would kick his mount, urging him forward and faster. She moved just seconds before them, this way and that, so close that their flying manes stung her face.

The horde had washed over her, breaking left and right around her like she was a stone in a stream. They left her shivering and wet from the river water and the sweaty froth the horses flung at her. The beasts' wild eyes had rolled in surprise; their riders had crossed themselves against her.

But she was used to people being afraid of her.

She gave chase as the riders took to the lane, but she was able to weave a shortcut through the dense woods. The abbey was home for her; she'd known where they would take him.

She had run into the courtyard as the last of them were dismounting. Forced to follow the slow ooze of men through the narrow archway, she had seen the trail of blood at the threshold, her own dropping steadily from the gash on her hand to land like islands beside the stream the wounded man had shed. She'd gritted her teeth and leaned hard against the man to her right, squeezing herself underneath his arm and feeling the metal hauberk bite into her cheek.

Now here she was, in the halo of space the frightened men had left around their king, a sword at her throat and dozens more at her back. The men were staring at her, some of them now whispering about what they had seen her do at the river. She heard one of them call her a witch. She'd been called that before.

Father Lucas called her his little *andílek*. Angel or witch, she didn't know what she was, but none of that mattered.

4

"Let me save him," she said to the man who'd emerged from the shadows, his sword scratching her throat as she spoke.

"He needs more than prayers, girl. Get away from him." He lowered his sword and turned his back on her.

"I am not—"

"Damek," the man called to one of the knights. "Deal with this."

"Yes, my Lord Rozemberk," came the response from behind her.

She was just turning to see who had spoken when she felt a hand twist into her hair, nails digging into her scalp, as she was lifted and pulled back, her head forced down like she was a puppet and he the master.

"The King must live until my man brings the surgeon," Rozemberk said to someone else in the shadows. "Get your healer."

"As I say, Brother Jakub is himself very ill and—" It was the voice of Brother Jan, the abbey's prior.

"Fetch him anyway."

"He cannot help you, Lord Rozemberk. Come, I will show you."

She heard the soft slap of Brother Jan's shoes against the stone floor in step with the quick, sharp pings of Lord Rozemberk's sabatons as they walked across the hall into another chamber.

The king groaned, and the girl instinctively tried to go to him, but as her feet moved forward, her head jerked back, still locked in Damek's grip. She lost her balance and fell, sliding against his hauberk, feeling it snag against her mantle until she twisted a leg under her and stood again.

She tried to speak, but the puppetmaster had her chin shoved against her chest. She could feel the rapid thud of her heart in her mouth, and she gritted her teeth again, angry at the time she was losing. She could see little more than her own muddy feet, but she rolled her eyes up hard until the muscles were burning and she was sure they would tear; she found the king's face again, saw the bloody bubbles at his lips.

"He is going to die," she growled through her clamped teeth. Damek shoved her head forward to silence her.

"There is no one else, then?" Lord Rozemberk asked Brother Jan as they returned. The girl could hear the fear in his voice.

"I am sorry, my Lord, but Mother Kazi, our other healer—she is gone to train some—"

"Do something for him!" Lord Rozemberk dropped to his knees, leaning over the king and wrapping his hands around the shaft of the arrow, pushing as he tried to stop the bleeding. The king arched in pain and sucked in shallow half-breaths, the bubbles of blood dipping and rising at his lips.

She had run out of time; the king would die because of her weakness. But as her eyes stung with frustration at her own helplessness, she realized what she needed to do; she'd seen children do it with their mothers. Of course, this was no mother who held her, shoving her face into her chest, but she had to try something.

She let her body go limp quickly, forcing Damek to lurch forward against the drag of her weight, and then she wrapped her leg around his and pulled. As he fell backward, he let go of her to catch himself, and she fell on the floor beside the king.

"Stop!" she yelled as she began prying Lord Rozemberk's hands away from the king's chest. "You make his breathing worse, see?"

Damek's arm wrapped around her throat, dragging her back.

Lord Rozemberk watched the king pant, trying in vain to get enough air, and then he pulled his hands away. "Let her go, Damek."

"Fetch wine, Brother Jan," the girl ordered as she yanked her mantle over her head and tossed it aside. She laid her cheek against the king's chest, then sat up again quickly. "Mother Kazi has a satchel in her cell underneath her cot. It has tools in it that I need." But Brother Jan didn't move. He was second only to Father Lucas, who was the abbot at Teplá, but the Father had been traveling for more than a year. Bloated with authority in the Father's absence, Brother Jan was not prepared to take orders from a girl. Especially not this one.

"Now! Or your king will die!"

"Do as she says," Lord Rozemberk ordered.

Finally, Brother Jan bowed and turned toward the door.

The girl was already loosening the small knife that hung from her girdle. "Help me get his clothes off."

The string of men that had tightened around her earlier now backed away, muttering. Brother Jan, just opening the door, spun around. "Nakedness is not permitted, especially with a—"

She looked up at him as she began cutting away the fabric of the king's surcoat; the fur lining was matted with blood and came away from the tunic underneath with a sick smacking. "How am I to tend his wound if I cannot see it?"

Lord Rozemberk's hand wrapped around her wrist, holding her still. She pulled against him, twisting her arm trying to free herself.

"What do you mean to do, Sister?"

"I mean to save this man's life. And I am not a nun. Now help me get his clothes off! And you," she said as she turned back to the prior, "get me that satchel and wine!"

Lord Rozemberk grabbed the king's tunic at the neck and ripped it, baring his chest; the skin stretched taut over the rib cage, sinking into the spaces between his ribs as he tried to breathe. The girl had only ever seen drawings of naked men,

7

but she did not blush as she slipped her hand under the king's bare back.

"I feel the tip here. It must have lodged between the ribs. How was he shot?"

"That is of no matter to you."

"If I know how he was shot, I will know how the arrow went in and what it might have damaged." She talked softly but held Lord Rozemberk's gaze, demanding an answer.

"It was an accident. The bow was not fully drawn. A man on the ground stumbled, loosed the arrow. The King was on his horse."

Her eyes closed as she pictured the scene in her mind. Certain she now knew how the arrow had penetrated, she laid her head down on his bare stomach, listening. She heard Brother Jan's hiss of disapproval as he neared, but she was already reaching for the wine and Mother Kazi's satchel. She untied the leather straps and unfolded the layers inside, the silver tools clinking against each other in her hurry. She slipped a tube and small knife out of the satchel, laid them on the king's chest, and poured the wine so it ran over the tools down to the wound and finally soaked into the pallet of straw beneath him.

As she picked up the knife, Lord Rozemberk's hand wrapped around her wrist again.

"What are you doing?" he asked.

"I must cut him so he can breathe." The king's blood dripped from her cheek.

"That is Ottakar, King of Bohemia." The hard look had returned to his face. He would not let some girl gut his king.

"He will be the dead King of Bohemia if you do not let me go."

"Who are you?"

"As Brother Jan could have easily told you,"—she looked up at the prior, who simply crossed his arms and clenched his jaw—"I am a healer. I have trained with both Mother Kazi and Brother Jakub, the abbey's infirmarians. I have read all the volumes of the *al-Tasrif*. I know Galen by heart. Now let me save this man."

Doubt rolled across Lord Rozemberk's face; he did not let go of her hand. "No, we should wait for the surgeon. He will be here soon."

"Do you mean Vilém, Teplá's barber-surgeon and butcher, too?" The girl laughed derisively. "Do you know what we call him? Happy Vilém. Do you know why? Knives make him happy—any kind. The big blades he uses to hack the meat. The smooth, small ones he uses to shave a pretty face. The long ones he uses to pierce a patient. Cut flesh, the smell of blood, these things make him happy." She spit the words. "The only time he is not happy? When his patients die and then the family blames him. Which is when Vilém gets drunk, and he is almost always drunk, Lord Rozemberk."

She waited for the truth of what she was telling him to sink in. Then she looked down at Ottakar's face. "We have no more time. Look, his lips turn blue. He has no air. Let me help him!"

The fear came back into Lord Rozemberk's face and he let her go.

She bent over the King again. "You must hold him still when I cut. He cannot move or the arrow will do more damage."

Lord Rozemberk nodded. "Damek. Evzen. Take his legs," he said as he grabbed Ottakar's arms. The men shuffled uncomfortably toward the King, stirring the thick smell of blood and sweat and wet furs.

Her hand shook a little as she pressed the knife against Ottakar's skin just below his last rib. Several short, sharp strokes of the knife and the cut was big enough; she took the wine-covered cannula and pushed an end of it into the opening she had made. A hot gush of blood poured over her hand, and Ottakar instantly drew a quick breath and then another longer, fuller one. He struggled to get air, but, at last, the King was breathing.

The girl crawled backward, leaving crimson handprints on the stone floor, pushed herself to her feet, and walked toward the wall of men.

"Let me pass. I need the shelves. There." She nodded behind the crowd of men, who parted for her like the horses had done at the river, only now she was the water moving against them, and they, the stones all clad in armor, were driven away from her. She took down a small bowl and some coriander and cloves and began crushing them with the heel of her bloody hand as she walked back to the pallet.

She dropped to her knees beside Ottakar, whose eyes were open again, his lips pink once more, his face still too pale. Gently, she brushed hair from his forehead with the back of her hand and leaned down to him.

"I must remove the arrow now."

He nodded.

"This will hurt, but you cannot move. Do you understand?"

He looked at her and nodded once more.

She sat up. "Lord Rozemberk, what kind of arrowhead was it?"

"Broadhead. Barbed."

She sighed as they looked at each other, both of them knowing what that meant. More pain. More blood loss. More danger.

She grabbed the shaft of the arrow, tensed, but then shook her head. "My hands are too slippery. Will you—"

Lord Rozemberk slid his hands over hers and snapped the shaft. Ottakar arched his back.

"Turn him to his side. That way. Careful and slow, so as not to move the arrow."

The men did as she ordered.

Ottakar cried out as she slid her fingers into the wound. She sang to soothe him. "'Oh Lord, give us thy love,'" she sang, placing her other hand at his back where the tip of the broadhead lay just beneath the skin. She put her forehead on his shoulder. "'Give us salvation and hear us.'"

She breathed as Ottakar breathed. She closed her eyes so she could visualize Galen's drawings of organs as she pushed against the shaft and threaded the arrow through the King's body, twisting it slowly so it could slide between his ribs until she felt it pierce the skin at his back. The blade sliced her fingers as she grasped it, pulling it slowly toward her. It slipped free of the skin with a wet pop.

Tossing the arrowhead to the floor, she pulled at the entrance wound, blood from her cut fingers mixing with Ottakar's as she tried to see what organs might have been damaged by the broadhead. Two ribs were broken and blood oozed from a small cut on the spleen.

She pulled an iron rod from Mother Kazi's satchel.

"Heat it in the fire," she said as she handed it to Brother Jan and then bent her face to Ottakar's again; he was moaning. "Shhh, shhh. Almost done now."

"Sing," he whispered hoarsely.

"'Oh, Lord give us thy love,'" she began again. She took the hot iron, not even wincing as her fingers burned, and looked back to Lord Rozemberk, who closed his eyes and held the King's arms once more.

With quick precision, she pressed the cautery against the arrow wound, searing the torn spleen and stopping the flow of blood. She bit into her lip as Ottakar screamed; he sounded like the horses that had burned at the market festival years ago. She was only seven, and Father Lucas had had to grab her arms, pinning her to the ground to keep her from running into the smithy's stables to save the horses. It was too late, he'd said.

Too dangerous. There was nothing she could do. Father Lucas was always shielding her, holding her back, telling her what she couldn't do. But she knew otherwise. She could have saved those horses. She would save this man.

"'Kyrie Eleison,'" she sang as she packed the wounds with strips of linen she covered in a paste of the ground coriander and clove mixed with a bit of wine. "'Kyrie Eleison,'" she sang as she washed his chest with more wine and wrapped it with more linen. She bent to speak to him again. When she stopped singing, she realized that the song went on, deeper, quieter.

She turned and saw the infirmary even more crowded now with Brothers who had come to watch and wait and pray. They—knights and Brothers alike—were all kneeling and singing to their king.

Ottakar laid his hand on hers. "What have you done?" he asked in a whisper.

"Saved you."

"God has saved you, my Lord," Brother Jan said, stepping close to the pallet, demanding notice. "It is a miracle. An answer to all our prayers."

"You," Ottakar said to the girl. "A miracle. Like Cosmas and Damien with the angels."

"No. It was just me," she said. "Just a girl. I saw no angels."

"And who are you?" he asked.

"I am Mouse."

TWO

"A right name for such a little thing," Damek said, and Lord Rozemberk chuckled. Mouse's cheeks burned.

"Get me something to drink," Ottakar said, but as she started to stand, he squeezed his hand around hers. "Not you. Vok." He looked up at Lord Rozemberk. "And send the men out. I do not need an audience for my sickbed." He tried to shift on the pallet and groaned.

"Go to the kitchener and tell him to brew some yarrow and comfrey tea," Mouse instructed Lord Rozemberk.

"No. I want ale. Strong." Ottakar drew in a quick breath and dropped her hand to push against the pain in his side.

"Ale will make you sluggish, slow your breathing. I need to see that the lung is working as it should. The comfrey will ease your pain and the yarrow will help stop the bleeding."

Vok did not wait for more discussion. "Out," he ordered as he spread his hands wide, corralling the king's guard toward the door. The din of mail and weapons echoed in the chamber as the men pushed themselves to their feet.

Brother Jan slipped into the space Lord Rozemberk had left beside the King, kneeling and muttering, "Let us give thanks to the beneficent and merciful God, the Father of our Lord, God and Savior, Jesus Christ, for He has covered us, helped us, guarded us, accepted us unto Him, spared us, supported us, and brought us to this hour—"

"Go pray somewhere else, Brother," Ottakar said.

"Yes, my Lord."

Hiding her grin, Mouse wouldn't look at the prior as he left.

"What is your real name?" Ottakar asked once they were alone.

"I have no other. Just Mouse."

"You were at the river. I saw you—" He closed his eyes. "You are an odd thing," he mumbled as he drifted off.

Mouse had been called that, too, when she was little enough that the things she could do were merely odd and not frightening.

At first, she'd thought she was like all the other girls who had been brought to the abbey because their parents didn't want them. Surnames were abandoned at the threshold, and the girls began a bleak journey to becoming brides of Christ. But even from the start, Mouse was different. She did not sleep in the dormitory with the other oblates; she slept in a private room with Adele, the nurse who had brought her to the abbey. Mouse was not allowed to go to Mass or to take the sacrament of the body and blood of Christ. She was not offered the salvation that came from such a union.

And Mouse never had any kind of name—first or last.

She grabbed at the bloody straw at the edge of Ottakar's pallet, pushing it along the pool that spread across the floor, but the straw was too wet to soak up more blood. She ran her finger through the streaks of red, which glistened in the dying light. *Anna*, she wrote. *Ludmila. Marie.* All names, but none of them hers.

It was an empty game she had played as a little girl, starting that day when Father Lucas taught her the sounds and shapes of the letters. He broke with custom—educating a girl not even meant for the Church—but he said that following God's path sometimes required breaking with Rome's rules.

Mouse had learned to read that day after morning Mass and, by Vespers that night, had taught herself to write. She was not yet five. Hiding in the empty guesthouse at the abbey, stretched out before the vacant hearth, she had traced the letters in the ash, raking her hand across them when they didn't look right and trying again until she could make them just as they were in the book. It didn't take long—such things came easily to Mouse—and soon she put the letters with their sounds together to make words.

She had started with the most important: *Adele. Lucas. Kazi. God.* Names of the people she loved, of the people who loved her—four in all the world. It was then she started her game, trying to make herself a name: Anna, Ludmila, Marie. But none of those names belonged to her; none of them fit.

So, with a sigh, she had written MOUSE—a nickname given to her by her wet nurse, Adele, when she was just a baby. *Quiet like a mouse. Small like a mouse. Helpless like a mouse,* she had thought, looking down on the word written in ash. It had made her feel sorry for herself, and she'd sucked in a breath and blew until MOUSE disappeared as the ash scattered across the hearth. She had cried again, for Adele, who had died, and for herself because no one had wanted her enough to even give her a name.

But that was ten years ago now, and she wasn't a child anymore. She snatched the handful of straw across the floor, slashing through the names in the blood. She was a young woman, fifteen come Hallowmas, and ready to make a place for herself in the world. But who would want a girl with no family, no dowry, no name? She had skills; she had just saved a king's life with her knowledge and steady hand. But they weren't the kind of skills that made a wife.

She had thought her skills would secure her a place at the abbey, but Mother Kazi had always been clear that the Church was not for Mouse. No one ever explained why the doors of the Church were closed to her, and Mouse never asked. She had seen what was either fear or awe in the faces of the Sisters. Even Father Lucas and Mother Kazi seemed afraid of her at times.

Because Mouse had more than just learned skills. She also had "gifts." That's what Father Lucas called them. All she knew was that she could do things she shouldn't be able to do. Things that scared even her.

She pulled the bloody straw to her chest and stood as she heard Lord Rozemberk sit the cup of tea on the floor next to Ottakar—and another of ale beside it. "Shall I wake him so he may drink?"

She kept her face down but shook her head. "Let him rest as he can."

"Can you leave him now?"

Mouse looked at him, confused.

"Another of my men is wounded."

Mouse followed him to the archway that led to the Mary Garden at the side of the infirmary. She could smell the man before she saw him, and she knew there was nothing she could do for him. They had laid him beside the dog-rose that climbed the stone arch; the last of its blooms, withered and brown, lay on the ground around the man's head. A low branch heavy with red hips hung near his face. The bush looked like it was shedding tears of blood. It was October, and the days were already growing cold. Mouse knelt beside the man and lifted the blanket someone had tossed on him. His intestines spilled from two large gashes.

"Who did this?" she asked.

"I did." If Lord Rozemberk was sorry, he didn't show it. "He shot the King."

"I thought you said it was an accident."

"He shot the King."

"I can do nothing for this man," she said.

Lord Rozemberk shrugged and went back into the infirmary.

Mouse ran her hand along the dying man's forehead, leaving behind smears of Ottakar's blood and her own. The man took a slow, ragged breath and then opened his eyes.

"Please." His voice was thick with pain. "The King?"

"He will live. Be at peace." Mouse knew what comforts to offer the faithful at the time of death. She had watched Mother Kazi.

But the man shook his head and grabbed Mouse's arm with surprising strength.

She tried again to give him comfort. "They know it was an accident. You are cleared."

He moved his mouth frantically until he had the air to speak. "No. A priest."

"I can get someone." She started to rise, but he wouldn't let go of her arm.

"No time. You, Sister."

When she was ten, Mouse had slipped into the sacristy and taken a wafer and a cup of altar wine and gone to the woods alone while the others went to Mass. She settled under a linden tree and uncorked a jar of holy water she had taken from the infirmary.

"'I baptize thee in the name of the Father, and of the Son and of the Holy Ghost,'" she'd said as she touched her forehead and chest and shoulders with one hand and poured the holy water over her head with the other, just like she'd seen Mother Kazi do to dying babies. "Amen." The baptismal water ran into her mouth as she spoke; it tasted like any other water.

Mouse had stolen her baptism. She was not among the saved, so she gave the dying man a lie. "I can take your confession."

"I took . . . money." Blood poured through his lips as he spoke. "To kill the Younger King."

Mouse shivered and tried to pull away.

"Absolve me. Quickly." His bloody spit splattered her face.

"Who paid you to do such a thing?"

"Absolve me!"

"I . . ." Mouse saw the dullness start to spread across his eyes, and she wanted to give him his peace, but the weight of his crime seemed too heavy to erase with another lie. "I cannot."

He was dead before she spoke.

She turned back toward the abbey to see if anyone else had heard, if anyone was watching, but she was alone.

"Eternal rest grant him, O Lord, and let . . . let perpetual light—" The words stuck in her throat. "From the gates of Hell, deliver his soul, oh, please God." But she shook her head because she knew. Mouse might not be part of the Norbertine life at the abbey, but she knew their rules and tried to live by them. She knew what her lie had cost this man.

She gathered two black stones from the path in the Mary Garden and, after closing his eyes, laid them on his lids and covered him with the blanket. There was no more to be done for him, and she had another man's life to consider. If there was a plot to kill Ottakar, who else among his men might be traitors?

Mouse took only the time to wash the blood off her hands and the evidence of crying from her face; she would wrestle with her conscience once Ottakar was safe. He was moaning and twisting on the pallet when she came to him. Lord Rozemberk was sitting on the floor nearby, firelight dancing across his face. "Do something for him."

"It is the ribs that hurt him. Only time will heal them. The pain should ease in a few days." She stood.

"Where are you going?"

"The blood has drained from his chest. It is time to stitch the wounds. I need light to see." She walked past him to shelves in the dark corner by the window.

"He is dead," she said as she gathered a handful of candles.

"What?"

"That man who shot—"

"Gernandus. That was his name."

"He said . . ." As confident as Mouse was that she could heal Ottakar's wounds, she did not see how she alone could keep him safe if there was another attempt on his life. Clearly the King trusted Lord Rozemberk, but Mouse didn't like him. Did that mean she shouldn't trust him either?

"What did he say?" Lord Rozemberk asked.

Mouse walked to the fire, her back toward him as she knelt to light the wicks, and she closed her eyes, shutting out the coughs and groans of the sick Brothers, the smells of burning wood, the feel of the heat on her face. She let her senses turn inward for a moment and then sent them outward toward Lord Rozemberk. She could see a silhouette of him glowing against the grainy blackness of her mind.

This was another of her gifts, the one that scared Mouse the most, this ability to see inside someone, to see their soul; it was the gift she had discovered first, the one that changed everything.

It had happened when she was only six and had gone into the woods with Mother Kazi. Small enough to move through the brush and saplings with ease, Mouse had followed a squirrel, wanting to share in the adventure and never thinking about needing to get back. But then the dense woods had grown shrouded with fog; the papery white trunks of the birches had looked like bones growing up from the ground, the rib cage of some massive, half-buried dead thing. The wet leaves and bracken stuck to her bare feet as she walked aimlessly through the undergrowth. Mouse was lost.

"Mother Kazi?" she'd called. The fog made everything look different, and it made the sounds of the forest ominous. She fought her panic as the rain grew hard enough to break through the canopy in sheets. She was drenched and cold within moments.

"Mother Kazi, where are you?" The tremor in her voice scared her—she didn't want to cry. Her breathing grew shallow and her heart raced. She sank onto the wet forest floor. Head in her hands, she rocked back and forth as the rain made a waterfall of the hair hanging in front of her face.

And then, something strange happened.

As she closed her eyes to wipe away the water, she realized she knew where Mother Kazi was. She could see her in her mind—not her exactly, not her body or face, but she could see an outline of Mother Kazi; it was glowing.

Mouse knew about souls; even though she was not allowed to go to Mass, Mother Kazi and Father Lucas had seemed intensely concentrated on Mouse's spiritual education. So little Mouse had reasoned that the glow coming from Mother Kazi must be her soul and that the unnatural vision, sent at this hour of need, must have come from God.

She had embraced the concept with the surety of a child, hopped to her feet and run in the direction that seemed so very clear now. She stepped into the clearing with a wide smile on her face just as Mother Kazi turned.

"Where have you been?" Mother Kazi's voice had been sharp with relief and leftover fear.

"I got lost, Mother." Mouse had cuddled into the stout woman's arms. "I was following a squirrel, and it went too far. And then the fog and the rain came, and I did not know where I was, but God sent me a vision, and I knew just where to find you." She had rattled the story out with the confidence of a loved child, never fearing rebuke, so she was shocked when Mother Kazi grabbed her by the arms and pushed her sharply away.

"What do you mean God sent you a vision?" Her face was stern, and the cold fear in her voice frightened little Mouse.

"I closed my eyes and, when I thought of you, I could see your soul, and I knew how to get to you," Mouse whispered. "Did I do something wrong, Mother?"

Forcing calm into her voice, Mother Kazi had asked, "How did you know you were seeing my soul?"

"I could not see your face or you, exactly, but there was something . . . glowing, and I knew it was you because it felt right, and it was what I wanted. That glowing thing was your soul, right? I read about—"

"Mouse, how do you know the vision came from God?"

"Who else would have sent it, Mother?"

Mother Kazi had pressed her lips together and said nothing else as she led the way back to Teplá Abbey. Mouse had to run to keep up with her. As they entered the door, she closed her eyes to help them adjust to the deeper darkness of the interior room.

Still only half seeing the shape of Father Lucas standing up from the desk, she'd heard Mother Kazi say, "It has started."

Mother Kazi would not look at her, but the girl could see the fear in the woman's eyes reflected in those of Father Lucas.

"Ah, my little Mouse, come to me." Father Lucas had invited her to sit on the bench beside the fire. "You are a very special girl, did you know?"

"Of course, Father. We are all special. Like the lilies, right?"

He bent to kiss her head, and she thought he looked so very sad but she could not understand why.

"Yes, andílek, my little angel, but you are even more special than the rest of us. The time has now come for us to try to understand *how* you are special."

"And *why* God made me this way?" That was what Mouse had really wanted to know, but Father Lucas had just looked at her.

Now, as Mouse looked at Lord Rozemberk, she could see his glowing shape in her mind, and she took his measure.

When she had first discovered her gift, Mouse had become fascinated with watching souls. She watched the Sisters as they prayed or ate or argued and the silent Brothers as they studied and worked the fields, and she learned that the size and brightness of the glow was different from person to person. Sister Kveta's was tight, like a rod running through her, and Mother Kazi's was yellow. Father Lucas's seemed almost overfull, his glow slipping past the shape of his body, and so bright Mouse could always find it anywhere in the abbey, even in the throng of people at St. Wenceslaus's feast day or in the dark night after she'd had a bad dream.

When she was younger and studying all those souls, she would measure them against Father Lucas's bright glow. Mouse used him as a standard again now for Lord Rozemberk. His was barely a glimmer.

"What did Gernandus say, girl?" Lord Rozemberk asked again.

Mouse stood with lit candles in each hand and walked back to Ottakar, her lips pressed in a thin line. "He said . . . he said he was sorry."

The King might trust this noble, but Mouse would not.

She sat on the floor beside the pallet and shoved the candlesticks closer to Ottakar's body. Her teeth were gritted against the guilt of having damned a man and her body was bent with the weight of responsibility for keeping a king alive, but neither was the reason for the shiver that went down her spine.

As a child, Mouse had spent days looking for her own glow, lying on the cot in her cell, refusing to eat, searching for so long that her little body would spasm against the strain, convulsing until she passed out. She wouldn't tell anyone what she was doing, not even Father Lucas; she had finally stopped looking because she was afraid he would figure it out.

But she couldn't stop herself tonight; she had to look once more, and now the truth settled again in her gut, cold and hard.

She could not find even a tiny spark in herself. As far as she could tell, Mouse had no soul.

THREE

S ing," he told her as she pinched the clean edges of the
arrow wound together.

"'Lady, wouldst thou save my life,'" she sang as she
threaded the needle. "'Give, give but one little look to me.'"

Lord Rozemberk knelt near the head of the pallet, hands
resting on the King's shoulders, but Ottakar did not need to
be held this time. He balled his fists into the straw and gritted
his teeth against the pain as she slipped the cannula from his
chest. Mouse worked quickly, pulling the wine-soaked silk
threads through the flesh in tiny, neat rows.

"I want ale," he muttered as she knotted the last stitch and
sliced through the thread, freeing him; he grabbed for the cup
Lord Rozemberk tried to hand him.

"Not yet," she said as she pushed him back down.

"How old are you?" Ottakar asked, throwing his head back
against the pillow. "Giving orders like . . . How old are you,
little Mouse?"

"Fifteen at Hallowmas. How old are you, noble King?" She
slid her leg behind her in an exaggerated bow.

"Ah, she bites back, this Mouse." Ottakar turned and smiled at Lord Rozemberk who was not smiling. "Eighteen," he said sleepily.

"Not quite," Lord Rozemberk added. "And you should address the King as 'my Lord,' girl."

Mouse didn't have to look up to see the sneer; she could hear it in his voice.

"Vok, go check on the men." The command was quiet and cold. For the first time, Mouse could see the king in the wounded boy.

"Yes, my Lord." Lord Rozemberk bowed as he left, graceful and quick, respectful. He caught Mouse's eye as he passed. She understood; if he was required to humble himself before the King, so much more so would she, a no-name girl living on the charity of the Church.

She turned back to Ottakar. "I need to listen to your breath again. May I?" She felt unsure of herself and wouldn't look at him as she lowered her head against his chest.

"You have blood in your hair," he said.

Mouse sat up. A strand of her hair curled in Ottakar's palm.

"It is your blood." She stood and walked to the cup of ale Lord Rozemberk had left near the fire. "And I will wash it out soon enough, my Lord."

"How long have you been at the abbey?"

"Since I was a little girl." She put her arm behind his back and held the cup to his mouth. "Here. Your breathing is better. You may have your ale."

He drained it and lay back quickly, grabbing at his side.

Mouse realized this was her chance to tell him about Gernandus's confession; he would know best how to protect himself and whom to trust. She leaned down and spoke quietly so no one would overhear. "My Lord, your man, the one who—"

"Your parents had many daughters and so gave you to the Church?" His eyes were closed.

"No. My Lord, I need—"

"Me, too. I mean my father had one too many sons and meant me for the Church until—" He ran his tongue across his lips. "Until my older brother died, and then—"

"*I* am not meant for the Church." It stung to say it out loud.

"Then why are you here? Who are your parents?" He half opened his eyes, blinking heavily.

"I do not have parents."

"Everyone has parents." He smiled, his eyes closing again.

"Well then, I do not know mine, my Lord. Please—"

"Do not call me that," he said weakly.

"Please. I need to tell you—" Mouse began again, but his breathing had deepened, and he fell asleep.

Mouse leaned her back against the wall near the window where she could see the rising moon making its way over the church tower. When Lord Rozemberk returned and lay down on the floor on the other side of the King, Mouse realized she would not soon get another chance to warn Ottakar. So she would keep vigil instead. His breathing was steady and deep, no signs yet of fever or rot in his wounds. This night, Mouse was not a healer but a guard. She liked the thrill that went through her. Tonight she had a purpose. Tonight she was where she needed to be, where she belonged.

And Mouse was no stranger to keeping watch for dangers in the night.

It had started at the baby cemetery; she was eight and had been in the woods searching for truffles in the dark hours of the morning. No one else could find the black mushrooms that hid in the dirt beneath the trees; you had to know which trees to search and then you had to smell the distinct mustiness of the truffle in the midst of all the other forest smells. Pigs could do it, but not people. Except for Mouse. Each time she came back from the woods with a basket nearly full, the Sisters crossed themselves.

On that particular truffle hunt, Mouse had gone farther up into the hills, searching. She had not meant to find it, the small plot framed by a wall of stacked rocks nestled in the soft spot just above a hot spring. But the soil was warm and wet, and Mouse could smell them—the truffles.

And the babies.

Her nose led her there in the dark; the moon had nearly set. She tripped on the first stone—not a proper headstone, just a large rock. Mouse crouched, her eyes an inch from the surface of the stone, her fingers tracing the crude carvings. A cross. A word stretched out in the thin, long lines of Old Church Slavic: BABY. Mouse reached her hand farther into the dark and found another stone and crawled toward it. A skull carved on this one and a name. PETER. And then another with three woven spirals, the three rays—a pagan this one was. When her fingers found the rock covered in carved butterflies, she wept. This mother or father had hope for their lost child even if the Church would not take the baby inside the sacred walls that guaranteed passage to Heaven.

This was a cemetery for the unbaptized, the unholy, the unwanted. Mouse felt like she belonged here.

She had heard it then, something sliding among the leaves at the edge of the wall. She'd seen it pull itself from the darkness into the shape of a child, same size as Mouse. "Hello," it said. Its voice was air whistling through the trees. "Come out and play?"

Mouse shook her head. Her hands wrapped around the nearest stone.

"Why not?" it asked.

"I do not want to," she whispered.

It started running along the outer edge of the wall. Mouse spun, following it with her eyes. She tensed as it neared the gate, but it stopped suddenly, turning toward her. The child-thing tilted its head and took a long breath in through its nose; then it smiled. "You smell different. Who are you?"

Mouse knew better. She'd heard the old women in town talk about giving away your soul when you gave a stranger your name. Mouse might not be able to see her own soul, but she would not give away the hope of it. She shook her head, trembling and waiting—for what, she didn't know.

The child-thing folded itself down to the ground, bouncing a little as it sat, legs crisscrossed. It leaned its forehead against the wooden gate, peering at Mouse through the slats. She couldn't understand why it did not come for her. They sat there like that for hours. Mouse pinched herself when her eyes grew heavy, pinched until her arms were covered in bruises. But she stayed awake.

At the first signs of light, the child-thing jumped to its feet, wiped a sleeve across the snot running onto its lips and dripping from its chin. "You might want to play another day," it said, and with a wave, it jumped into the dark between a cluster of trees and was gone.

Mouse sat there until the sun was fully up and there were no shadows. She saw the symbols then, carved into a stone at each corner of the wall and along the back of the gate. Crosses. The Church might not consider this sacred ground, but clearly someone did. Mouse could not walk to the gate without stepping on a baby, buried in the soft soil; she could feel the crunch of the dried bones beneath her feet.

She'd run all the way back to the abbey, her basket empty this time, and had spent the afternoon dipping wicks in the hot suet to make candles. She had filled her cell with them that night to drive away the shadows.

❧

Ottakar coughed and Mouse crawled to him, lightly running her fingers across his lips. No blood. She laid her head against his chest. No sounds of rattle or fluid. Firelight flickered against the stone walls, but it was quickly eaten by the dark.

Silently, she rose and went to the shelves near the fireplace and gathered what candles were left. Brother Jan would be angry, but Mouse didn't care. She made a circle of them around the King and Lord Rozemberk and herself; they would bring light until the morning, though they offered little protection against assassins. That would be Mouse's job.

Near dawn, Ottakar woke, trying to push himself up.

"Wait," Mouse said through her teeth as she bit at the thread she was using to stitch the gash in her hand. It was already healing, the flesh starting to knit itself closed; she wouldn't even have a scar after a few days.

That was another of Mouse's gifts. She never got sick; she healed quickly. Too quickly. No one at the abbey would notice now; they rarely even looked at her anymore—pretend like she didn't exist and maybe she wouldn't. But if Lord Rozemberk or Ottakar noticed . . . Mouse didn't want to lie, but she wanted to be normal, at least in someone else's eyes. The King had already called her odd. Odd she could handle, but the idea of him looking at her in fear, crossing himself against her, had sent Mouse searching for the needle and silk. She was pulling the last knot tight and edging closer to the King when the nearest candle flickered.

She crouched, grasping the needle like some tiny sword, as shadows in the dark swayed and a figure moved into the murky light.

"Who are you?" she asked as the man neared.

He ignored her and tried to move past her toward the King. Mouse stepped into his stride, forcing him to stumble, and then put her hand against his chest.

"No farther until I know who you are and why you are here."

From behind her, she heard Ottakar's soft laughter. "Looks like I have a new guard, Vok."

Lord Rozemberk pushed her arm from the man's chest. "Finally, you are here, Hartwin."

Mouse turned as Lord Rozemberk moved to let the man go to the King. She started to take a step forward when a hand wrapped around her arm.

"You are no longer needed. Get out," Brother Jan hissed in her ear.

"Who is—?"

"A real physician from the court. Lord Rozemberk sent for him last night." The prior pulled her back as the physician knelt beside the King and pulled something from his robes.

"Stop!" she cried as she lunged forward, but Lord Rozemberk was on her too quickly. He took her by the shoulders and pushed her into the dark interiors of the infirmary.

"No! Ottakar. He might be—" Mouse stumbled, turning back toward the King, and again, Lord Rozemberk shoved her, his long strides bringing him on top of her so she had to keep backpedaling until she slammed into the wall at the far edge of the hall. He slid his hand between her head and the stone, grabbing a handful of hair with one hand as he reached for the door handle with the other.

"You will address the King as 'my Lord,' girl." He pressed his iron sabaton into the crook of her knee and pushed, buckling her leg. "Now get—"

"He is in danger! The King is in danger," she said as she wrenched her head free of his grip, words spilling out in her haste.

Lord Rozemberk jerked her to her feet. "What are you saying?"

"Gernandus said . . . something before he died. The King is in danger. I know it."

"Why should I believe you?" His voice was steady, cold.

"Why would I lie?" Mouse looked him in the eyes.

He took a step toward her, speaking quietly. "Tell me exactly what Gernandus said."

"I do not trust you. I will tell the King."

Mouse thought he was about to strike her, but he just stood there, staring at her. She took advantage of the silence. "How well do you know this physician who is with your king? They are alone but for Brother Jan, and he could not stop a—"

Lord Rozemberk grabbed her wrist and pulled her after him, back toward the King.

"Hartwin, leave us," he barked as he neared the pallet.

The physician had just finished unwrapping the wound; he gathered the bloody dressing as he stood.

"And you." Lord Rozemberk nodded at the prior. "Go."

Brother Jan bowed as he backed away from the alcove, but the King did not see; he was watching Mouse.

"Tell the King what Gernandus said, girl," Lord Rozemberk said as soon as they were alone.

Mouse started to take a step toward Ottakar, but Lord Rozemberk kept his grip on her wrist. "He knew he was going to die. He wanted a priest. But there was only me. He said someone had paid him to kill you." She saw Ottakar's pupils dilate as if a shadow passed over him, and then she felt Lord Rozemberk's fingers dig into her skin. "My Lord," she added through gritted teeth.

Ottakar was silent. He laid his head back, closing his eyes.

"Who paid him?" Lord Rozemberk asked her.

"I do not know."

"You did not think to ask?" He nearly choked on his disdain.

"I asked. He died."

"Why should we believe you? Did anyone else hear Gernandus?"

"You left me alone with him."

"Why not tell us immediately after Gernandus confessed? Instead, you waited to tell us when you were no longer needed. Maybe you made it up in the hopes you would get to stay near the King."

Mouse felt the heat in her face; she worked hard at focusing on Father Lucas's lessons about controlling her anger. *He who is slow to wrath is of great understanding. You want to understand, do you not, little andílek?* he would say. *And you, who can do so much, must take extra care to do little in anger.*

Mouse would not let Lord Rozemberk bait her. She looked down at the floor, following the dark line of a crack in the stone until it disappeared in the shadows, and she held her tongue.

"Why not tell me this last night?" Lord Rozemberk yanked her arm, spinning her to face him.

"I . . . I thought . . ."

"She could not trust you, Vok." Ottakar's voice was sure and sad. "For all she knew, you were part of the plot against me."

Mouse looked up to find him watching her again.

"She took a great risk with your life, my Lord. You were unguarded. The men bedded down in the stable and me asleep. It would have been easy for—"

"Mouse kept guard. Did you not?"

"Yes . . . my Lord."

Lord Rozemberk let go her wrist. "And Gernandus said nothing else?"

"'I took money to kill the Younger King' was all he said. And 'absolve me.'" Mouse hoped they did not hear the catch she felt in her throat, but Ottakar's eyes narrowed.

"And did you? Absolve him?" he asked.

She shook her head but said nothing more.

"So who is trying to kill me this time?" the King asked as he looked down at the naked wound in his side. Mouse walked to the basket of clean linen on the shelves. She gathered a bowl and herbs and went to kneel beside the pallet.

"You believe her?" Lord Rozemberk asked.

Mouse poured wine over the wound and focused on the row of neat stitches and the skin already beginning to pucker as it healed.

"Yes," Ottakar said. "And so do you."

Lord Rozemberk sighed with resignation. "Just as you know who wants you dead, my Lord."

Mouse squinted as the morning sun broke over the tree line and burst through the window; it brought with it a sudden awkwardness as she was too aware that she was rubbing crushed herbs and wine along Ottakar's naked rib cage, which was now bathed in the light.

He must have felt it, too; he flinched and put his hand on hers. "Let Hartwin do it. Vok, go get him."

She snatched her hands back.

Ottakar saw the flash of anger in her eyes. "You misunderstand, Mouse. Clearly you know your craft. I owe my life to your skill. But you have also been up all night; you should sleep. Surely we can trust Hartwin to dress my wound."

"He was once your father's physician," Lord Rozemberk said, his voice laced with disapproval and doubt.

"What does that matter? My father has summoned us to Prague to reconcile, Vok. I am his only son. His only heir. He does not want me dead."

Lord Rozemberk crossed his arms over his chest. "As you say, but the girl does well enough. Let her finish the job."

"Do you think you can sit?" Mouse asked Ottakar, fully focused now on being a healer and not a girl.

"Gladly," he said as he started to push himself up, wincing with the pain.

"Wait. You might pull the stitches loose inside." She slid her arm beneath his back. "You." She nodded at Lord Rozemberk.

"Put your arm behind him on the other side. Lift when I say. But gently."

Ottakar let go the breath he was holding once he was upright. "Vok, get a chair. I am done with the sickbed. And bring me a shirt."

"You must move slow and easy or your lung will fold again," Mouse argued as she wrapped the linen around his chest. She was tying it off when Lord Rozemberk returned with the chair, a shirt, and Brother Jan and Hartwin following behind him.

"Put the chair by the fire," Mouse directed as she slipped herself under Ottakar's shoulder and waited for Lord Rozemberk to do the same on the other side. They moved as one to lift the King, bearing most of his weight as he took the few shuffling steps to the chair and sat. Mouse lifted the shirt, helped him thread his arms through the sleeves, and let the linen fall to the seat, making mounds of white against his black woolen chausses. She slipped the pillow from the pallet behind his back.

"My Lord, I was told you needed my services," Hartwin said as he stepped forward, clearly irritated.

"It seems I already have a physician, Hartwin."

Mouse could not stop the smile that played at the corners of her mouth.

"My Lord, I think you have been misled. This girl might offer you certain . . . comforts, but she is no physician." He sneered with his insinuation.

Mouse froze; she willed her eyes to find the crack in the floor again, made herself breathe, but the sting of embarrassment grew hotter still.

Ottakar shifted in his chair. "Lord Rozemberk, pay the man for his trouble. And, Hartwin, be sure to let my father know I am in good health when next you see him."

Mouse turned to pour a fresh cup of wine, looking for anything to do that would hide her face long enough for her to regain her composure. She handed the cup to Ottakar without looking.

"I am hungry. Am I free to eat?" Ottakar asked her abruptly.

"No meat. Start with a simple soup and bread. It is the feast day of Mary's birth. Brother Milek will have fish soup for the poor in Teplá." She turned to Brother Jan. "Bring only the broth." Her voice was as flat as she could make it, healer only, no woman to be ashamed of being made an object of some stranger's scorn, no self to be offended at Ottakar's failure to defend her honor.

Brother Jan waited for a nod from the King before he turned to leave, looking past Mouse as if she weren't there.

"You may go," Ottakar said.

Mouse thought he was talking to the prior.

"I said you may go, Mouse." Ottakar's dismissal of her was sudden, though not unkind. She gave a stiff bow and a mumbled "my Lord" anyway. She passed Lord Rozemberk on her way to the door. He did not look at her.

She heard the King as her hand closed around the latch. "Prepare the men to leave."

FOUR

Mouse ran down to the Teplá River and along the bank until it grew shallow. She was afraid of the water and could not swim, but here her feet would stay on the bottom, toes curled around the smooth rocks, anchored against the current. As she lowered herself into the water—made warm by the area's hot springs—strands of her hair floated in front of her; she saw trails of red pull away from her and disappear in the river. The water loosened the King's blood in her surcoat, and pools of it swirled at her chest as if she were bleeding. But they, too, slowly vanished.

And then she was as done with the King as he seemed to be with her.

She tossed the surcoat onto the bank and laid her head back in the water, playing with the idea of letting the river carry her away to a future she couldn't figure out for herself. Surely it would be better than going back to the abbey.

Mouse stood up instead, the weight of her wet hair pulling at her neck, and her linen undershirt clinging to her body.

When she heard the sound of something in the tree line, she dropped back under the water, wrapping her arms around her chest, waiting.

Huffing and snarling, a pair of pine martens tumbled out of the dwarf cherry at the edge of the woods, fighting over the shredded remains of a squirrel. The marten in the front dropped his piece of the flesh and launched himself against his enemy, tearing a gash in its golden fur. The injured marten bared its teeth and coiled, ready to strike back.

"Stop!" Mouse yelled.

In an instant, both martens sat back on their haunches, lips still curled with fury, their bodies quivering with the desire to move, but they just stared at her, waiting unwillingly for her next command.

Mouse shuddered.

This was another of her gifts that she hated and one over which she seemed to have little control. It didn't matter what she said or even how she said it, but sometimes, especially when she was angry or afraid, she seemed to be able to compel living things to obey her. She felt so powerless in her own life, following Church rules and trying to mold herself into every-body's expectations, that the last thing she wanted was to play master over some other creature.

"Go on then," she whispered.

The wild things obediently turned and disappeared into the brush, leaving their bounty behind.

Mouse pressed her fist against her stomach; she felt ill, though some part of her thrilled with her use of power. She'd been so careful these past years—never looking for souls, until last night, walking barefoot like Father Lucas or St. Norbert himself, using the pain of her damaged feet not as penance for what she had done but as mindfulness against what she might do. She kept as busy as the Sisters and silent as the Brothers.

Mouse might not be a Norbertine monk, but she lived like one, which meant that until yesterday, she had not spoken more than a dozen words to another person in nearly three years.

Except for Father Lucas. They broke the vows of silence together, reading and talking in the scriptorium, in the library, even as they walked in the Mary Garden. But he'd been away for more than a year now, and in those months of silence, she had almost tricked herself into believing that she was normal. But it was all a lie. No normal person could see a body's soul or command the animals with a word.

Andílek, Father Lucas called her. An angel. With special gifts.

Father Lucas had taught her to hide those gifts and never to use them, telling her how people are afraid of what they do not understand. And when she argued that Jesus warned against hiding talents or when she cited the saints who used their gifts for God, Father Lucas told her somberly, *We live in an age of doubt, little Mouse, blind to the wonders of God. The people would condemn you.*

But Father Lucas was also blinded—by his love for Mouse. He wished to keep her safe above all else, but she was not his "little Mouse" anymore; she didn't need protecting. If she could save a king all on her own, what might she do if she let loose her power and let herself be who and what God made her to be?

She took a full breath, tasting the metallic cold of the air, and pulled herself out of the river. She walked over to the bloody corpse the martens had left behind. It looked like a torn rag. Only its head, the face partly peeled away from the skull, named it as God had made it—a squirrel.

She tore a slender branch of green wood from a beech sapling in front of her and ran her fingernail along the end, smoothing it to a fine point. She knelt between the mangled squirrel and the river and began drawing in the mud, sketching the image of a squirrel she'd seen in a German bestiary Father Lucas had brought home from one of his trips when she was a child. She remembered every detail, every line in the fur on the tail, the shape of the eye, the scale of the nut held in the tiny front paws. There beside the river, she drew an exact copy of the image with a bit of stick and some soil.

Mouse never forgot anything. An image. A text. A word spoken. She remembered all. Father Lucas also called this a gift, but when Adele died, Mouse learned the truth.

She could still paint Adele's face as if her nursemaid were sitting for her; she could hear her voice just as it had been, soft and high and thick with French. Mouse could replay every moment she had spent with Adele, but she couldn't make her live again, couldn't make her answer the questions Mouse had never thought to ask at five but which were so vital to her now: Who were her parents? What happened to them? Where did she belong? And yet, Mouse's perfect memory kept the grief sharp, always, never dulling as it did for others when faces of lost ones faded. This wasn't a gift but a curse.

And so it would be again with these hours she had spent saving the Younger King of Bohemia, being part of something bigger than herself, connected to someone if only for a few moments. He could dismiss her, she could wash away his blood, and Ottakar could be gone, but the memory of it would all still be there in her head.

As she finished her drawing, she looked over at the ravaged squirrel and wondered about a resurrected Jesus. Had he smelled like something dead? Had his heart beat? Thomas had stuck his hands in the wounds, so clearly Jesus's body hadn't healed. She sucked in a sharp breath as she imagined Adele risen, her flesh rotted and bones gnawed by things in the earth, her teeth clacking together as she tried to answer Mouse's questions.

And then the squirrel twitched.

Mouse pushed herself back from it, watching as pieces of skin and muscle started to knit back together. Bits of the creature's face stretched taut over the skull and reached for the other half that must have been lost somewhere in the woods; tiny claws pawed at the dirt. And then it started to scream, high and quiet.

"Stop," Mouse whispered, but nothing happened. The squirrel kept writhing and screaming. "Oh, God, stop." Turning away from the squirrel's suffering, Mouse saw the image she had drawn, and with a sudden hope she dug her fingers in the mud and raked them across the picture. The squirrel fell still and silent. With shaking hands, Mouse pulled the bits of flesh apart again, snapping the small bones in her haste, until the carcass lay mangled and dead once more. "Oh, God, what have I done?"

She thrust her hands, bloody again, into the river. They sank into the silt at the bottom as she leaned on them to retch, bile and saliva dripping from her mouth as the dry heaves shook her body.

As she slowly made her way back to the abbey, Mouse tried to understand what had happened. She had not meant to bring the squirrel back to life. Maybe the pine martens hadn't actually killed the squirrel but just wounded it, and what she had seen were its last signs of life, not a life she had given it. Mouse wanted to believe this, but she had seen the flesh weaving itself together. Somehow she had made that happen.

It scared her—what she had done and the thrill of power it sent through her.

She needed Father Lucas; he could explain it. But he was gone, and there was no one else who would help her, no one she could trust, nowhere to turn for answers. Except Father Lucas's books—she might find answers there.

At Father Lucas's alcove in the cloister, Mouse crawled under the desk to a small cupboard in the far back corner. She sat for

a moment, running her fingers along the carvings on the cupboard doors, trying to quiet her guilt for betraying the Father's
trust. The books he kept in these cupboards were the ones he
had traveled far to collect; these were the books he did not
want the Brothers to see, the books he had never let Mouse
read. She should be patient and wait for him to come home;
she wasn't going anywhere and the questions would certainly
still be there.

But she was tired of not having answers.

As she snatched one book and then another, racing through
them, leather latches squeaking as she yanked them open,
Mouse realized that the real answer she was looking for was
how to rid herself of these gifts, how to make herself normal.
She and Father Lucas had discovered many texts explaining
how to exorcise demons; she wondered if such a book existed
for exorcising gifts from God. But when she had emptied the
shelves, not one of the books had offered answers or comfort.

Disheartened, Mouse was sliding the books back into place
when her hand ran up against something hard lying flat against
the back wall like it was part of the cupboard. She curled her
fingers around the edge and pulled; a book slapped down on
the shelf. She laid the small codex in her lap, hunching over
it, her fingers trembling a little with the sense of foreboding
that crawled up her spine.

Like many of the Brothers, Mouse knew several languages—
it was helpful in reading and copying manuscripts—but when
she lifted the wooden cover to the title page of the little book,
she couldn't read it. She bent close to study the faded script and
saw even fainter lettering at the top of the page. Someone had
written FRATRES PURITATIS—"Brethren of Purity." Was it a translation or a mark of ownership? If it was a translation, Mouse
might use it to decode the text. The book was old, maybe older
than any she had seen. She carefully turned the leaves, studying

41

the illustrations and then turning back to the title, trying to piece together words with the unfamiliar symbols and the context of the pictures. Some of the images in the illustrations were familiar—numbers, astrological symbols, animals—but none of it made sense to Mouse.

She jumped when the hand slammed against the table over her head.

Brother Stefan ducked his head down beneath the table and made the sign for her to stand. Growing up in the silence of the Norbertines, the canon's sign language was the first Mouse learned; all the Brothers and Sisters used it to communicate simple needs and wants. And Brother Stefan clearly wanted Mouse to stand. Now.

She started to put the strange book back in the cupboard—manuscripts never left the cloister—but she felt drawn to it. More willing to break the rules than part with the book, she slipped it quickly into the leather bag that hung from her waist. Brother Stefan stomped his feet and motioned to her again. As soon as she crawled out from under the table, he put his hand to the top of his head, fingers sticking up. A crown. The King. And then he gestured toward the door at the end of the cloister walkway.

Mouse ran to the infirmary.

The pallet was empty, bloody straw strewn across the floor. She spun, heading for the door again, when one of the sick Brothers called out to her from his bed. "They have gone to the guesthouse."

Breathless from running, she found Damek standing guard at the guesthouse door. He opened it for her without a word and Lord Rozemberk met her in the front hall.

"Where have you been?"

"Is it the lung again? Or fever?" Mouse asked as she slipped her mantle over her head, silently chastising herself for letting her pride make her neglect her patient.

"See for yourself."

The King was in bed, propped on pillows. "Finally! Would you tell Vok that I can have something besides fish piss to eat? It is already well past midday. I want real food."

Mouse smiled as she bent to listen to his breathing. "Have you passed water today and—"

"Yes, yes, everything is working."

"Then I will go get something from the kitchen for you."

"No. Vok can go."

"Eggs, vegetable porridge, bread," she said, looking over her shoulder to where Lord Rozemberk stood by the window, keeping watch.

"While I fetch your food, you might ask your physician whether or not you should ride tomorrow as you intend, my Lord." The way Lord Rozemberk slid over the word *physician* made Mouse's skin crawl and her temper rise. But the martens and squirrel served as an uncomfortable reminder of what could happen if she let her discipline slip. She let Lord Rozemberk carry her anger with him as he left.

"You washed away the blood." Ottakar was looking at her hair. It had dried in wavy strands; she had not taken the time to brush it. She fought the urge to comb her fingers through it now, imagining what it must look like, disheveled and unkempt.

"Yes," she said.

"But you do not look like you slept."

"I had tasks."

"Other sick and wounded?"

"No. I am not the healer here. I only help when—"

"What tasks?"

Mouse could not understand why any of this would matter to the King, but she knew she must answer. An image of the squirrel's paw clawing the ground made her shudder.

"I was . . . in the cloister studying."

"The Sisters have a cloister here?"

"No, I was—" She had answered without thinking. In trying to avoid one truth, Mouse had revealed another, and by the look on Ottakar's face, a shocking one.

She knew the Church rules, of course. Even the Sisters were not allowed in the Brothers' area of the abbey, but this place was the only home Mouse had ever known. She might not belong to the Church, but she had always belonged in the abbey. She knew it better than anyone—the best places to hide, the loose stones, where the herbs would come up in spring—this place was hers as much as anyone's, and she never thought to question why she alone had free reign to go where she wanted. She was like a ghost haunting the place, the Brothers and Sisters aware of her but looking through her, past her.

"But you would not be allowed in the Brothers' cloister," Ottakar said.

Mouse couldn't understand why he sounded so sad, and then she realized that he thought she was lying. If he thought her a liar, he would likely assume that she had also lied about Gernandus's confession, just as Lord Rozemberk had suggested.

But if she told the truth now, that Father Lucas allowed her to go where she pleased, it would put him in jeopardy.

"I sometimes slip in while the Brothers are at prayer." She stared out the window as she spoke. Mouse wasn't used to lying; she discovered that she was uncomfortably good at it. "How would I get the knowledge I want if I had no access to books?" She turned to him as she asked the question because that part of it was true, and she wanted him to see it in her face; it would help hide the lie.

Ottakar pushed himself more upright against the pillows at his back. "Thank you for telling me the truth, Mouse, but the law of cloister is the foundation of the abbey. You have defiled the space."

She flinched but nodded, wondering what he would think if he knew that besides being a woman and vow-less, she was unbaptized, unholy in the eyes of the Church.

"If the abbot knew . . ." he said.

Mouse's stomach squirmed. She could not let Ottakar tell anyone. She could imagine Brother Jan's glee at confessing to the King that Father Lucas actually took her into the cloister to study with him. If the opportunity presented itself, Brother Jan would surely make the most of it; he was next in line to become abbot. And the Church would certainly strip Father Lucas of his title. He would also face punishment. Mouse had seen the Brothers flog themselves, ripping the flesh on their backs as acts of righteousness. She didn't want to imagine what they did to one of their own who had broken the law.

Mouse began to wonder if she could make Ottakar keep silent like she had stilled the pine martens.

She had compelled a person once before, but it had been an accident, and there'd been something wrong with the boy. An "idiot," people called him, laughing at him or ignoring him. Mouse had always felt sorry for him until that day she had gone to the village on an errand for Mother Kazi. She was twelve. The boy, who was as big as a man, saw her. He wanted what he wanted. As he shoved her into the stall out back of the smithy, she had screamed at him to go away. And he did. He walked out of the stall into the pasture, and he kept on walking. His parents started looking for him when he didn't come home for the night. The town searched for him for days, but no one ever saw him again. And Mouse said nothing. On that day, she swore to herself and God, if he was listening, that, except with Father Lucas, she would speak only when necessary. She hadn't broken that vow until yesterday with Ottakar.

"I know I am in the wrong, and you have the right to—"

"I will not tell anyone, Mouse, but you must swear that you will not enter the Brothers' cloister again."

Mouse thought of the books and the days of study with Father Lucas she would be giving up when he came back—if he came back—but she would not put his life at risk.

"I promise," she said.

"So have you convinced him not to ride?" Lord Rozemberk called out as he turned the corner into the room with several lay brothers carrying food behind him.

"Not yet," Mouse said, taking a quick step back from the King's bed, startled by the sudden intrusion and hoping Lord Rozemberk had not been listening. "Did you walk here from the infirmary?" she asked Ottakar, happy to slip back into the role of healer.

"No. We carried him," Lord Rozemberk said.

"And how did that feel?" Mouse asked the King.

Ottakar opened his mouth to answer, but again Lord Rozemberk spoke for him. "He groaned like a woman about to—"

"Vok!"

"Excuse me, my Lord." Lord Rozemberk bowed to the King but his eyes were on Mouse, and he was smiling.

"Can you sit up, feet on the floor?" Mouse slipped her arm behind Ottakar's back for support. He bit his lip as he moved, clearly determined not to groan. "Good," she said. "Now take a deep breath."

She already knew what would happen when he started to suck in air. He grabbed at his broken ribs, crying out at the pain.

"You are not fit to ride. Not tomorrow. Not for several days."

"We leave in the morning. Now bring me my food." He motioned to the lay brothers, who picked up the small table and brought it to the King's bed. Ottakar grabbed the bread.

"If you ride, the ribs might push against the lung and make a hole. Do you remember how it felt to not be able to breathe?" Mouse asked.

Ottakar chewed silently.

"If you ride, the cut in your spleen might open again and fill your gut with blood before you even know it. And you will die."

Ottakar dipped the bread in the porridge.

"If you ride, you will sweat and get dirty. Your wounds will fester. You will rot. Have you seen someone die of rot? The flesh swells and turns black and oozes—"

"Enough," Ottakar said as he put the bread back on the table.

"Pretty picture she paints for you, my Lord," Lord Rozemberk said. "I can protect you from a killer, but I can do nothing to stop rot or a bloody gut."

"She can," Ottakar said. "We will bring her with us."

FIVE

M ouse didn't know what to do.

She waited outside, listening to Ottakar argue with Lord Rozemberk, until Damek came with the order that she be ready to leave at dawn.

It was beginning to get dark. Mouse slipped into the abbey's cellar, gathered an armful of candles, and headed to her room at the back of the Sisters' dormitory. She had to go down the dark stairs into the even darker hallway with only a small cresset for light. She held her breath, listening for other noises, but there was only the creaking of the door as she entered her tiny room, windowless and pitch black.

Mouse laid the candles on the floor by the door, lighting one with the cresset flame. Shadows danced along her walls. She had painted murals over the plain white plaster, mostly images she'd seen in books—animals, dragons, the saints—and on the ceiling she had copied in perfect detail a summer's night sky over the abbey.

The most elaborate picture was on the wall opposite her small cot. It looked like Mary holding a baby Jesus, but Mouse had not painted an aura or a crown—just a mother cradling her child. The woman's mouth was slightly open; she was singing. The baby's mouth was at her nipple ready to suckle. They lay on a bed; carvings in the headboard swirled about their heads.

It was beautiful—except for the blood seeping through the bedclothes and running onto the floor. And a dark figure that faded into the edge of the picture.

This was Mouse's first memory, though she had told no one about it. Who would believe that she could remember her birth? But she did. Being trapped in such a small space, squeezed over and over until she couldn't move, couldn't breathe, arms pressed too tightly against her chest. Mouse took a quick full breath as even now she panicked at the close space.

She remembered her mother, too—her smell, her touch, and her voice. She'd sung a few lines of a lullaby before Adele had come and taken Mouse away into the night.

Mouse bent quickly to light the other candles, filling the tiny space with a warm, yellow glow, but it wouldn't be enough. She would have visitors tonight . . . visitors drawn by the use of her power.

The shadowy thing that found her at the baby cemetery had kept its promise to find her again; that same night, an eight-year-old Mouse had woken with its breath on her face. It had come to play. But its games had frightened Mouse—changing its face from boy to serpent to snarling wolf to demon with rows of bloody, ragged teeth. That first night, Mouse had screamed, and Mother Kazi had come running. The creature had slid back into shadows, so that Mouse could see only its eyes as they followed the old woman through the door. Mother Kazi had said it was just a dream.

After that first night, the dark thing had brought others with it. When Mouse stopped being afraid of the shifting figures, they had started making themselves into Mother Kazi or Father

Lucas. In the light of day, Mouse knew that none of it was real, but in the night, the things toyed with her mind. In the night, Father Lucas pierced her with long, sharp fingernails, and Mother Kazi scalded her with boiling wax. In the night, the two of them did terrible things to each other. In the night, the two people she loved in the world called Mouse unnatural and unwanted, a burden, a curse. The creatures pulled her from terror to rage to despair like a needle through cloth, over and over again.

Mouse remembered how the creature had fled the cemetery at the first signs of light, and she started spending her days dipping wicks into the hot suet to make candles so that she could keep them burning through the night in every corner of her room. If there was even a bit of dark, they could come. She kept vigil through the nights so she could light fresh candles as one would begin to flicker and the shadows would start to grow.

Becoming herself a creature of the night, she was always awake when the Sisters stumbled down to the chapel at Lauds. For months, Mouse slept only during the day in a few clustered minutes, huddled with her back beside the church wall, listening to the drone of the Brothers at prayer. She hoped that the prayers would cover her like a second skin, camouflaging her so the dark things would lose her scent and leave her in peace.

Father Lucas had been gone during that time, taking the salvation of the Lord to the Carpathians. He was shocked to come back to a hollow-eyed ghost of a Mouse.

"Have you found trouble, little andílek?" he'd asked, holding her hand as they walked in the Mary Garden among the foxglove and wild thyme.

"It has found me, Father."

He had cried a little as she told him about her nightmares.

"They are not just dreams, are they?" she'd asked. "God is testing me. He does that to his people."

Father Lucas buried his face in his hands. When he looked up, he said, "I will show you what you must do."

No one had ever been in her room, and Mouse blushed as he studied her paintings. She worried that he might ask about the paints and gold leaf she had stolen from the scriptorium. Instead, he had shaken his head in wonder and said, "Why, you are an artist, my little Mouse."

And then he taught her a protective spell. He showed her how to make a shape of power with the salt they had taken from the cellar. Many shapes would work, Father Lucas had said—circles, a pentagram, a cross. But the first shape he taught her was of a fish like the early Christians used to identify each other in secret, though Mouse learned that the shape was far older than Christ and meant many things to many people, which is what gave it its power. Father Lucas drew the salt fish around her bed then sliced his palm as she gasped and let his blood drop at the fish's mouth and at each fan of the tail. He read from a book as he walked the salt line. Mouse memorized the words as soon as they spilled from his lips, like a cat stealing a baby's breath.

Doubting the spell, Mouse had sat awake, waiting. Nothing came. The second night, her faith growing, she lay on the cot, arms crossed on her chest like a body ready for burial, and she closed her eyes. As she began to slide into sleep, she'd heard them, like cloth tearing as they pulled themselves up through the dark.

Mouse sat up. There was but one candle still lit within the salt-line fish. Dozens of the child-things pushed up against each other as they neared the cot, but they froze at the salt and screamed at her. Mouse had laughed. They could not touch her, body or mind.

She had given Father Lucas a picture as an act of gratitude, a portrait of herself small enough to fit in his breviary so he could carry her with him on his travels. So he would not forget her, she had told him. So he would always come back to her.

She had been a child then, waiting for Father Lucas to save her, but now she was nearly a woman and must learn to take care of herself.

Mouse took the bag of salt she kept in her room and shaped a cross with her cot at the center. She slid the knife across her forearm and let the blood drop at the four ends of the cross as she muttered the words of the spell. Let the dark creatures come, one by one, as the candles sputtered and died, but they would not be able to reach her—not to sink their teeth into her flesh, not to play with her mind.

With a sigh Mouse threw herself onto the cot, wrapping her arm with a piece of linen. She needed her mind clear tonight. She had much to decide. She knew she couldn't go with Ottakar. A young, unmarried woman traveling alone with a group of men would be prey to gossip and worse. But if she let Ottakar go, the chances were high that something would go wrong with the lung or the wound. The King would die, and it would be her fault.

She needed to talk to Mother Kazi; she would know what Mouse should do. But Mother Kazi was at the nunnery in Chotesov. Mouse sat up quickly—she could get there by morning if she left now. But then she saw the salt sparkling in the candlelight. Mouse wouldn't be going anywhere tonight.

She lay back down and took a deep breath. Smiling at the sweet smell of honey, she realized that some part of her must have already decided to go; without thinking, she had taken the beeswax candles instead of the tallow ones. Brother Jan had bought them from the Prague candle makers especially for Michaelmas. He would have her skin for it if she stayed. Literally.

Mouse was flooded with the wish to be free of the ritual and regulation of abbey life. That life would never be fully hers anyway. Surely there was somewhere she belonged, but how would she ever find it if she never left Teplá?

She pushed herself to the end of the cot and reached into the small box on the floor, pulling out a handful of coins, a small statue of an angel with a silver Hungarian denar embedded in its chest, and a bracelet—all that she owned besides the clothes she wore. The coins she had earned over the years helping Mother Kazi, and the angel was a christening gift from Father Lucas after Mouse confessed her stolen baptism. He had carried the clay figure over the Carpathian Mountains wrapped in layers of wool and strapped to his chest so not even the fragile tips of the angel's wings had broken. The bracelet had belonged to her mother.

It was the only proof Mouse had that her memory of being born was true, and it was her only link to whatever past or family she might have. She ran her fingers along the braided gold circlet and traced the engraved swallow; its claws held a red stone overlaid with gold bars so that it looked like a banner striped in red and gold. Mouse didn't understand what it meant, but she was sure it would lead her to her family someday. Adele had never said anything about her mother's family, but surely some of them still lived. They might know her father, too. Mouse didn't know if he was dead or not. Adele never talked about him.

Mouse had imagined meeting him many times. She wasn't naïve; in none of her imaginings did he scoop her up with joy in finding her at last. She knew she had been sent away and forgotten. But now that she was grown, maybe she would have some worth. People had told her she was pretty—Adele, of course, but also strangers at the market festivals in town. Maybe her father would find some value in her now.

But not if she damaged herself by traveling with Ottakar and his men.

Mouse slipped the bracelet around her wrist. If she had any hope of reuniting with her family, she must take care to protect not only her virtue but also the perception of her virtue.

Startled, Mouse looked up as one of the candles in the far corner near the door sputtered and went out. She tensed, waiting. Her eyes watered as she watched the shadows stretch long and thin and sharp until a long-nailed hand took shape. The tearing sound sent a shiver through Mouse. She knew what was coming.

They tumbled over each other, clawed their way free of the dark into their own shapes as children of different ages, dark-eyed and gaunt and naked. Even now Mouse wasn't sure if they were real or not; maybe they were hallucinations brought on by lack of sleep and stress or maybe they were the ghosts of all those unholy babies trapped forever in Limbo like the Church taught. Mouse only knew they were hungry and mean.

But tonight, they could not touch her. They crowded around the salt cross, soot-covered toes jammed a hair's distance from the ragged white line. The creatures seemed different tonight, less playful, more watchful. Their silence was unnerving; no restless fidgeting of normal children, no sounds of breath. With her gifted hearing, Mouse could usually pick out the heartbeats of people near her. Here, there were none. She had never noticed before because the dark things were usually laughing or taunting.

Finally, one of the children ran its tongue across the clear dribble of snot running from its nose to its lips and spoke. "What did you do?"

Though its mouth moved, the voice came from all around the room like a whisper.

"What do you mean?" Mouse asked.

"We felt you, but it was bright and we could not see."

"I do not—" she said.

"It felt like fun," another child-thing said, shoving its head over the shoulder of a child in front.

"You played without us."

"What did you do? Tell us." They were all asking now. The tiny room filled with hundreds of whispered questions that sounded like snakes hissing.

Mouse started shaking; she knew they were talking about the resurrection of the squirrel. If they thought it fun, then it was surely evil.

"Teach us your new game," they said.

Mouse shook her head and pulled her knees to her chest, wrapping her arms around them. She remembered her own joy at her use of power that morning by the river.

The children threw their heads back as one, opening their mouths and exposing rows of black and bloody teeth filed to jagged points; they screamed with rage.

Mouse covered her ears with her hands and pushed herself back farther on the cot, though the creatures were only an arm's reach from her still. "I will not!" she screamed back at them.

"Teach us!"

"I will not," she said, weeping.

In an instant, they went quiet, just children again. They turned and began sliding through the dark at the corner of the cell where another candle was dying. One of the hollow-eyed children stayed at the salt-line cross watching Mouse until the others had disappeared.

"You will teach us," it said.

"No, I—"

"You have tricks," it said, pointing to the salt. "But others here do not."

"What do you—?"

"You will teach us," it said again and then disappeared into the shadows.

The first scream came from a room down the hall from her own. Sister Ida. Mouse took a step toward the door, her foot hovering at the line of salt.

Another scream. She bent her head listening; she heard fear, not pain. No one was hurt. She sat back on the cot. At least now she knew the dark things were real. If others could see them, they must live somewhere else besides Mouse's mind.

If she crossed the salt, she would be unprotected. She didn't know what powers the creatures had, but she knew they could play with her mind. They could take what they wanted. Could they take her power? Learn what she had done to the squirrel? Do it to other dead things? Mouse couldn't take the risk.

She pulled her knees to her chest again, laying her head against them, rocking. It was her fault the Sisters were suffering. Her tears darkened the stain of Ottakar's blood on her surcoat.

Mouse knew dawn was coming when the screams finally stopped.

Her body ached as she stood, but her mind was clear. She would leave the abbey today.

⁓

Lord Rozemberk met her at the guesthouse door.

"Where are your things?"

Mouse pulled her mantle back and pointed at the leather sack hanging from her waist.

"We do not need the other horse," he said over his shoulder to one of the men.

Mouse reached for the door handle, and Lord Rozemberk grabbed her arm. "Where are you going?"

"I need to speak with the King."

"No, you need to mount your horse. We are leaving."

"I am not going with you."

"What?"

"I need to go somewhere else first and then I will catch up with you," Mouse said as she pulled her arm free of his grasp.

"As much as I would love to leave you behind, the King wants you with us in case he has need of you." He made no effort to hide the innuendo. "You have no say in the matter. You go where he says and when. Which is now."

Lord Rozemberk moved to grab her arm again, but Mouse anticipated him this time, turning just as he reached out and then shoving him hard in the chest. She pulled the door open, smiling as she slipped into the guesthouse, and closed the door behind her.

He was at her back by the time she reached the King's room. "My Lord—"

"Did you sleep well?" she asked as she approached Ottakar, who was sitting in a chair by the fire.

"No." He certainly sounded tired.

Brother Jan came in carrying a cup of warm mead. "It was a strange night, my Lord." He bowed as he approached the King, who took the cup.

"And how did you sleep, Mouse?" Ottakar asked.

She simply shook her head.

"Seems it was a bad night for everyone, then," he said. "Good enough reason to start the new day." He sat the cup on the table and pointed to a hauberk at the foot of the bed. "I am ready, Vok."

"Can you not ride without the mail? The extra weight will worsen the pull on your ribs," Mouse said.

"He is safer with it on," Lord Rozemberk said.

"Not if it makes the injury worse."

"That is why you are going with us."

"No I am not, I must—"

"The King said you are—"

"Enough!" Ottakar said. "What do you mean you are not going?" he asked Mouse.

"I must get permission from my guardian, Mother Kazi. She is training the Sisters at Chotesov. I can walk there by midday prayers, and, if she gives her blessing, I will catch up with you by tomorrow." Mouse had crafted her plan last night. "If you ride slowly, stop frequently and change your dressings often—"

"I must get to Prague. My father waits for me. By your own word, I need a physician to manage my wound." Ottakar winced as he raised his arms for Lord Rozemberk to slide the hauberk over his head.

"And what will happen to me when we reach the castle with your court, including your own physicians? You will have no need of me then. How will I seem to others, a woman, neither wife to man nor Christ, who has traveled alone with men?" As she spoke, Mouse fiddled with the bracelet in the bag at her waist.

Ottakar walked to her. "You will be under my protection, Mouse." She kept her eyes on the floor. He bent his head to speak more quietly to her. "Will you not feel safe with me?"

Her heart raced—too aware that she was arguing with the King and too aware of how close he stood. "I would feel safe with you, but can you also keep me safe from what others would think? Others like Hartwin?" *Or your own men*, she wanted to add.

"I will grant you guardianship, then. We will draw the papers here. Bring someone to—"

"My Lord, this is ill done! You know nothing about this girl," Lord Rozemberk said.

"What say you, Mouse?" Ottakar asked.

Mouse didn't know what to say. She had never expected such a response. "I am . . . deeply honored, but Lord Rozemberk is right, I am no one and have no family. My only connections are here. I cannot imagine that your friends would advise—"

"I am the King of Bohemia. Or one of them, at least. I need not heed the advice of anyone. Will my guardianship suffice to shield your reputation as well as your virtue?"

Mouse nodded.

"You will need the signature of her current guardian to make it legal, my Lord." Brother Jan spoke softly from the corner where he had been quietly observing. Everyone turned to him. He smiled, and Mouse could see his intent. Though he wanted her gone from the abbey, he did not want Mouse to go at the favor of the King. "And I am sad to say that Father Lucas is away. We have not heard from him for some months."

"Mother Kazi is also my guardian. She may sign," Mouse said.

"You have papers to prove this?" Lord Rozemberk asked.

Mouse was about to answer that the papers were in the library when she realized that she would be stepping into Brother Jan's trap, revealing to the King and Lord Rozemberk that she had been in cloistered space. They would have little choice then but to punish both her and Father Lucas.

"I am sure Brother Jan knows where they are," she said.

"Fetch them," Ottakar ordered. "And someone to write the new guardianship papers. Quickly! Seems we will need to stop at Chotesov anyway."

"I can write them," Mouse said.

Ottakar startled them all with his laugh and then he grabbed at his side and sat back down on the edge of the bed. "You are most certainly an odd Mouse," he said, looking at her.

"Surely you know women who can read and write," she said, stepping over to a table already scattered with parchment. The King had been working.

"Read a little, write a little, but not draft a legal document." He chuckled more lightly.

Mouse was nearly done by the time Brother Jan returned with the papers. He handed them to the King.

"Thank you, Prior," Ottakar said. "We are also in need of a chaperone. A Sister. To leave with us immediately."

"Yes, my Lord."

Mouse gave Ottakar the document she had written. Her script was beautifully even and smooth, her hand steady, but her head was swimming. She was about to become a ward of the King of Bohemia, and as astounding as that was, Mouse understood that it had simply been the easiest means for Ottakar to achieve his ends. His protection would end when they reached Prague, and she had written the document to show that she understood this. What unsettled her was his request for a chaperone though she hadn't asked for one. Chaperones were for people of value.

Sister Ida was already mounted when Ottakar, Lord Rozemberk, and Mouse stepped out into the courtyard. The Sister looked ill. Mouse wanted to go to her, echoes of her screams reigniting Mouse's guilt, but Lord Rozemberk, hand around her arm, pushed her toward a horse. She was suddenly astride it and tugging at her mantle and surcoat as the line of horses began trotting toward the gate. They were headed down the hill toward the river so quickly that Mouse had not had a chance to say good-bye to the only place that had ever been home for her. She turned to look back, but all she could see was the tip of the church tower against the dusky pink sky.

SIX

"V ok! The King!" Mouse cried out. She had seen the subtle slump of Ottakar's shoulders as the horses were reined to a stop at the nunnery steps, but she was too far behind to do anything. Lord Rozemberk had just dismounted to speak with the abbess. He now turned quickly toward the King, catching him as he started to slip from his horse.

By the time Mouse reached them, the abbess was directing them to the infirmary.

"No, he will be more comfortable in the guest rooms," Mouse said. She motioned for Lord Rozemberk to follow her to a smaller entrance at the corner of the front wing. She'd spent much time here over the years with Mother Kazi training healers. Mouse spoke over her shoulder to the abbess, "Mother Marta, would you please bring Mother Kazi?"

When she recognized Mouse, Mother Marta crossed herself, nodded and left; she had been a Sister at Teplá when Mouse was a child.

The guest rooms at Chotesov were small but elaborate with carved wooden panels along the walls and heavy tapestries in rich colors. The ceiling was painted with murals of Bohemian saints: Cyril and Methodius, who fought Rome to bring Christianity to the Slavs in their own tongue; Ludmila, who was strangled with her veil for keeping faith; and Eurasia, who lost her limbs and her head to save her virtue.

It was the image of Eurasia, hands severed and bleeding, that had caught Mouse's attention as a child and made her wonder what she believed in enough to be willing to make such sacrifice. A Church that rejected her? A faith she wasn't sure she had? It was people who anchored Mouse. Father Lucas, Mother Kazi—for them she would give up anything.

Mouse looked at Ottakar's face, milky gray, his eyes closed as they laid him on the bed, and she felt a visceral draw to this man she had known for only two days; it frightened her and thrilled her all at once.

"Take his surcoat and hauberk off," she said to Lord Rozemberk as she unfastened her own mantle and tossed it aside. And to Damek, who had helped to carry the King, "Get me cool, clean water and wine."

She frowned when she saw the blood staining Ottakar's tunic, dreading what she might find under the dressing. He was beginning to stir by the time she pulled the linen wrap away from the wounds. She sighed with relief; it was oozing at the edges, but the stitches had held. She laid her cheek against his chest, listening.

"How is he, child?"

Mouse nearly wept at the feel of Mother Kazi's hand on her shoulder. "The breathing is good, but he has a fever." Her voice broke.

"Tell me what we do for a fever," Mother Kazi said, teacher to pupil.

Damek was there with the water and wine. "You bleed him," he said.

"No," Mouse answered, calming now that Mother Kazi was there and settling into her healer's training. "He bled too much with the wound. He is weak and has pushed himself too hard. Look." She pointed to the thin line of stitches. "No signs of festering." She laid her hand on his abdomen. "No swelling in the gut."

"Mother, will you check him?" Lord Rozemberk asked.

"There is no need," Mother Kazi said. "Mouse is a better healer than I. She knows what to do."

Mouse took a piece of clean linen from the bag at her waist. She soaked it in the water, washed the sweat from his face, and then laid the cool cloth on his forehead and another at the back of his neck.

"For a fever, you give coriander seed," she said to Mother Kazi. "And honey and warm ale. Can you bring those?" Mother Kazi nodded and disappeared down the hall.

While she waited for Mother Kazi to come back with supplies, Mouse washed Ottakar's wounds with the wine and dressed them again.

"What happened?" he asked.

"You overtired yourself, made yourself feverish. Nothing I cannot manage."

Ottakar smiled. "We are at Chotesov then?"

"Yes"—she turned at the sound of steps—"and this is Mother Kazi. Mother, this is—" Mouse stumbled, not sure of the proper way to introduce a king.

"I know who he is, child. My Lord." Mother Kazi bowed.

Mouse could see Lord Rozemberk shaking his head. Embarrassed, she bent her head to the task of crushing the coriander and mixing it with the honey and ale.

"Drink this. It will help with the fever." Mouse held the cup to his lips.

"Bring the papers. And then we will eat and be gone," he said after he drank.

"No," Mouse barked, but she softened her tone after a look from Mother Kazi. "If you rest today and tonight, you will be able to travel farther tomorrow and make better time."

"I have already told the men to set camp out back near a pond. Should I revoke that order, my Lord?" Lord Rozemberk asked.

Ottakar closed his eyes again. "No. We will ride at daybreak. Let me sleep."

Mouse changed the cloth on his forehead. She and Mother Kazi moved to a table at the far side of the room to give the King some quiet. Lord Rozemberk went to check on the men.

"I left you to help tend the sick Sisters," Mother Kazi said as she poured a cup of wine for each of them. "How did you manage to find a king?"

"He came to me, Mother." Mouse told her everything, except for what happened at the river and last night's terror in the abbey.

"I cannot decide if I should chastise you for recklessness and overconfidence or be in awe of what you did."

"You would have done the same, Mother. That was how I knew what to do, imagining what you would do." Mouse laid her head on the table.

"You are tired. Let me have them ready a room for you."

"No. He may need me in the night if the fever worsens." Mouse yawned. "There has been little time for sleep these past two days."

"I understand there was trouble at the abbey last night?"

Mouse sat up.

"Sister Ida talked about terrible nightmares, not only hers, but for all the Sisters."

"The Brothers, too," Mouse added, tensing.

"And you? Did you also have nightmares?"

"I did not sleep." Mouse would not tell the rest.

Mother Kazi was quiet for a long time before she added, "Sister Ida's description of what happened sounded much like the dreams you had not many years ago."

Mouse laid her head back on the table, and again there was silence.

"Why have you come here?" Mother Kazi asked. Mouse could hear the edge in her voice; Mother Kazi was afraid.

"The King wants me to go with him to Prague. I said I needed your permission first."

"Go."

Mouse sat up again, startled by the naked answer. "And leave the abbey?"

"The abbey is not your home, Mouse. It never has been."

Anger welled in Mouse. "It is the only home I have ever known."

Mother Kazi sighed. "I know, and I am sorry for it. I warned Father Lucas when he took you in and again when you—"

"You did not want me?"

"Oh, Mouse. I did want you, but I also saw the complications to come—for us and for you. The world offers little chance of happiness for most women and for someone with your . . . circumstances. . . . I just . . . I tried to tell Father Lucas, but he loved you from the first, like you were his own, all he could think of was protecting you, even—"

"*He* loved me . . . but not you?"

"Of course I love you! Have I not taken care of you, taught you—"

"Then why can I not return to the abbey with you and Father Lucas?"

"You have no future at the abbey."

"How do you know? Does God seek your counsel?" Mouse hissed.

"Mind your tongue, child."

"No." Mouse leaned closer to the woman. "I am tired of being told what I can and cannot do. You are quick enough to close doors, but what other future waits for me?"

"This is what I tried to talk to the Father about before he left for this trip, and now—" Worry darkened Mother Kazi's eyes.

"Have you heard from him?" Mouse felt uneasy, her emotions swinging from sadness to anger and now fear for the Father.

"No. Have you?"

Mouse shook her head.

"I wanted us to craft some plan before he left of what we meant to do with you, in case he . . . but now, it seems you have found your own way." Mother Kazi nodded toward Ottakar. "You will have a great adventure, full of possibilities." She meant to sound encouraging, but Mouse heard the relief in her voice; Mother Kazi was glad to rid herself of this burden. Perhaps the taunts of the hollow-eyed children had not been all lies.

Hurt, Mouse pushed back from the table, chewing at her lip. "I understand. You have fulfilled the obligation that was purchased on my behalf." She meant the words to be icy daggers, and they hit their mark.

"Mouse, please, I—"

"I need to sleep," Mouse said as she turned away. She sat leaning against the stone face near the fire, her back to Mother Kazi. She didn't want the old woman to see her cry.

∞

Mouse woke to the sound of voices. She held herself still, listening.

"I am sorry, my Lord," Mother Kazi said quietly. "I can tell you little about it."

"How did she come to the abbey?" Ottakar asked.

"Her nursemaid brought her."

"And did the nursemaid say nothing about her family?"

"Nothing."

Mouse could hear the lie in Mother Kazi's voice and heard her heart skip as she told it.

"She . . . she came from somewhere in France," Mother Kazi added. "And she had several pieces of a woman's jewelry to offer the abbey. She said it belonged to Mouse's mother."

Mouse heard the chair scrape the floor as Ottakar shifted. "What kind of jewelry?"

"Necklaces, rings, bracelets, clasps. Mostly gold. Some silver."

"Gems?"

"Yes." Mother Kazi gave her answer reluctantly.

"Then she does come from a noble family."

"My Lord, there is no way to know that. The nursemaid might have stolen the jewels. The girl might have been hers all along." Another lie.

"What do you believe, Mother?"

"What I believe is of no consequence, my Lord."

Mouse moved, letting them know that she was waking. Lord Rozemberk was asleep by the window. A faint light shone through it. Dawn. She had slept through the night. No dreams. No screaming. Some part of her uncoiled a little at the hope that the dark things had lost her scent, but she feared that they might still be haunting the Brothers and Sisters at the abbey.

"Vok, it is time to ready the men," Ottakar said as he walked toward Lord Rozemberk.

Mouse moved stiffly to the table, her muscles sore from yesterday's ride and sleeping on the stone floor. She grabbed a piece of bread and a cup of wine.

"Good morning, little Mouse," Mother Kazi said, her voice full of conciliation.

Mouse took a bite of bread.

"Sleep well?" Ottakar asked, coming back to the table and reaching over her to take a piece of bread himself.

"Did you?"

"Quite well."

Mouse laid her hand on his forehead. "No fever." She smiled.

"Permission to ride then, physician?"

"Permission granted."

"May I take Mouse for a little while before you leave, my Lord?" Mother Kazi asked.

"Of course. It will take the men an hour or so. And I must ready myself."

"You will be able to ride longer if you do not wear the hauberk," Mouse said over her shoulder as she left the room.

Mother Kazi led her to the outer parlor and wasted no time. "I know you are angry with me, Mouse. But I do want to help you."

"I do not need your help."

"Yes, you do. You cannot go to court like that."

Mouse looked down at her stained surcoat and muddy mantle.

"I have laid out some clothes from a girl who has just come to us. Her family is often at court in Prague, so these should be fashionable." Mother Kazi lifted a deep blue gown from a stack of clothes on the chair. "And you must wear shoes. Here." She handed Mouse a pair of soft leather slippers and some wooden pattens.

"No. I bare my feet for penance like Father Lucas."

"You are not a monk, Mouse. You are part of the King's court. You will be expected to wear shoes and dress properly."

Mouse looked down at the elaborate clothes. "I do not know how to put them on."

"I will send a Sister to help you dress." Mother Kazi stood to leave.

Mouse ran her fingers along the fine gold ivy embroidered along the collar and cuff of the gown. Still hurt and wanting to lash back, she grabbed Mother's Kazi's arm. "What do you know of my parents?"

"You know I know nothing," Mother Kazi answered warily.

"You are a liar."

"Mouse! You should—"

"Do not tell me what I should do. You no longer have that right. And I can hear your lie here." Mouse reached out to touch Mother Kazi's chest, but the old woman flinched. Mouse pulled her hand back. "Why are you afraid of me?"

It was more a plea than question; Mother Kazi's fear wounded her. Mouse balled her fists defensively.

"You are not supposed to use your . . . gifts. Father Lucas has told you, has taught you—"

"I cannot help what I hear or see or smell. That is part of who I am. Why does that frighten you? I love you, Mother." She sat down on the chair, crying.

"I love you, too, child. And I am not afraid." She winced, knowing that Mouse would hear that lie, too. She knelt in front of the chair and pulled Mouse to her. "This will be very difficult for you. Court is different than anything you know. Watch what others do. You learn fast. You will be fine." She was trying to reassure herself as much as Mouse.

Mouse nodded, tears still rolling down her cheeks. "Will you—" She pressed her hand against her lips, trying to get the words out. "Will you tell Father Lucas where I have gone? When he comes back and I am not there?"

Mother Kazi stood. "Let the abbey go, Mouse. Do not look back. Do what is right. Father Lucas and I have worked hard to fill you with goodness, and you are . . . you are a good girl, Mouse."

The telltale skip in Mother Kazi's heart exposed the last as a lie, too. But Mouse didn't have the courage to ask what she was if she wasn't a good girl.

SEVEN

They had been on the road for three days when it happened.

Mouse was sore from riding; they were mounted each day by sunrise, and they made camp not long after noon. The King would never call them to a stop so Mouse did. Reading the pallor of his face and how he held himself, she knew when the pain of his ribs was too much. The men assumed it was she who slowed them down, and she let them think it. She was surely glad to be off the horse anyway, and the quiet moans every time she moved her legs were real enough.

The men thought other things, too, when she lifted the talon of the massive eagle embroidered on the front of Ottakar's tent and followed him inside each afternoon. That she came out reeking of mint and chamomile did not alter what they imagined. She could hear their whispers, lurid enough to make her feel the shame even if she never committed the sin. She could see the lust in their eyes as they followed her from the King's tent to her own.

Mouse spent her time inside the claustrophobic space, pacing. She felt like a bridled horse in the clothes Mother Kazi had given her; the wimple pulled so tightly at her chin that she fought to eat or speak. Fortunately, she felt little desire to do either except when she was with Ottakar. They talked about stories and science, Ottakar full of plans for bringing new ideas to Bohemia, Mouse often referring to something Father Lucas had said or some book he had shown her.

"It seems an unusual relationship for a Norbertine canon to have with a girl," Lord Rozemberk said one night as they ate. Lord Rozemberk was nearly always with them.

"What do you mean?" Mouse spat back.

"I understand that the Norbertines are not allowed familial attachments so that they may give their whole heart to the Church."

"How could his kindness to me weaken his love for God?"

"Perhaps you have mistaken charity for kindness."

Mouse bit back her anger. "He is the only father I have ever known or will likely know."

"I envy you the father you have, Mouse," Ottakar had said quietly.

She'd cried herself to sleep that night, feeling very alone in the world and sure that, given the way Mother Kazi behaved, she would never tell Father Lucas where Mouse had gone. Mouse doubted that she'd ever see him again.

She had woken later, swallowing a scream from a nightmare—the squirrel was crawling after her in disjointed jerks like some lost golem looking for its master. She sucked in a breath of stifled air heavy with the scent of mint and dead squirrel. The smell came from the new mantle Mother Kazi had given her; it was lined with squirrel fur.

Mouse tossed the mantle out of the tent and yanked at the wimple tight against her neck. Afraid she would never be able to get it back on right, she had left it alone, even sleeping in it. But now she was free, the cool air brushing against her bare neck, soothing her.

And so it was the next morning, as they mounted to ride the rest of the way to Prague, that Mouse wore only a simple veil pinned in her hair, leaving her ears open to the birdsong, the clack of the hooves, the sounds of the forest. Her unnatural hearing no longer muffled by the layers of scratching cloth, she heard everything. And it saved them.

⁂

"Protect the King!" she screamed. The horses nearest her shied, and the men just stared at her. But Mouse kicked her horse, racing the sound of the coming flight as she tried to reach Ottakar first.

"Shields!" Lord Rozemberk commanded, and the ring of men around the King tightened into a circle of flaming eagles as wooden shields clashed. The other men kept riding, confused and squinting as they searched the sky.

"Down!" one of them yelled as he spotted the first arrows. But it was too late. A couple of men dropped from their horses, grabbing at their necks.

Just as Mouse reached Ottakar, one arrow sank into her horse's flank and another in its throat. The horse tumbled with a scream, throwing Mouse over its neck as it fell. She rolled, slamming against a large linden tree, and scrambled behind it, trying to catch the breath that had been knocked out of her.

"Ride! Ride!" Lord Rozemberk ordered. As the horses surrounding the King took off with him nestled safely in the center, Lord Rozemberk swung his mount toward Mouse, his arm stretched out to her. "Get up!"

She ran to him, grabbing his hand and jumping to the back of the horse just as a new flight of arrows descended, one piercing Lord Rozemberk's arm. She threw her arms around his waist as the horse raced down the slope after the others. Mouse could see towers in the valley and knew it must be Prague. She looked behind her but could see no one in pursuit.

Froth hung from the horse in white streaks by the time they rode under the arch of the gatehouse. The huge wooden doors rammed shut behind them, and the horse reared as it ran up against the others just inside the courtyard. Lord Rozemberk nearly kicked Mouse in his hurry to dismount, but she wasn't far behind him as he ran toward the center of the melee.

"Move!" he shouted. "Let me pass."

Mouse wove herself through the gaps Lord Rozemberk made until he stopped abruptly. She heard Ottakar but could not see past the men.

"Just a race, guardsman, a bit of fun to see who could reach the castle first, right, lads?" Ottakar's men hooted assent, ready to follow his lead.

Lord Rozemberk turned a little toward Mouse and whispered, "Pull the shaft before the guard sees."

She wrapped her hand around the fletching and yanked; it slipped free easily, as she knew it would, leaving the arrowhead imbedded in his arm.

"Vok, it seems you owe us all a wager." Ottakar said it heartily enough, but Mouse could hear the strain in his voice. "What kept you?"

"The girl lost her seat, my Lord." Lord Rozemberk stepped aside, leaving Mouse exposed. "I thought you would want me to fetch her."

The men laughed. Mouse chewed at her cheek and clenched her fist tightly around the shaft she kept hidden at her back.

"She is hurt," Ottakar said, and Lord Rozemberk turned to look at her, too.

Mouse looked down, studying her body for injury; she seemed whole, but then she felt the stinging and raised her hand to her forehead. It came away bloody.

"Get her to a room," the King ordered, and Lord Rozemberk grabbed her arm, pulling her with him as they cut through the men toward a large stone building that turned into a dark alcove and then a black wooden door.

"Take her to my chambers. Go the servant's way," Ottakar hissed as they stepped into a hallway with stairs leading to the right and another doorway to the left.

"Where are you going, my Lord?" Lord Rozemberk asked.

"I want to be seen in the Great Hall, robust and healthy," he barked and then headed up the stairs.

Mouse followed Lord Rozemberk though narrow halls and up some stairs that finally opened at the end of a larger corridor. They went in a door opposite the small stairwell. The room was as large as the whole of the women's dormitory at Teplá. A massive bed rested against the wall across from the fireplace, a table and chairs stood nearest the door and another seating area was at the far end of the room. It was cold, with no fire lit, and dim with sunlight filtering through the slats of the shutters on the windows. Mouse blinked as Lord Rozemberk opened them.

"Bring water and wine and get a fire started for the King."

Mouse thought he was talking to her, but as she turned back to the door to go fetch his water and wine, she saw a tall young man standing behind her. He bowed and left. Lord Rozemberk sat down heavily in a chair near the table, grabbing at his arm.

Mouse pulled out a small leather case from her bag as she knelt beside him.

"Leave it," he muttered, jerking away from her.

"By the saints, you are a stupid man!" she said. "This will come out. Now hold still."

She tore at his shirt to get to the wound.

"Shall I call for the King's physician?" The young man had come back with a pitcher in each hand.

"No," Mouse and Lord Rozemberk said in unison.

"Just hand me the wine," Mouse added.

She poured it over the wound and then over what looked like a metal spoon with its handle split and curled to either side; it had a hole at the top. She took her knife, cutting across the wound to widen it, and then slid the spoonlike tool past the arrowhead until she felt its tip slip into the hole. She pulled slowly, easing the arrowhead out until it clanked onto the floor by her knees.

Ottakar came as she was finishing her stitching. He poured himself a cup of wine and dropped into a chair on the other side of the table from Lord Rozemberk. Mouse looked up briefly to find him staring at her.

"My enemy is watching us closely to know our travels so well, or else there is a traitor besides Gernandus among us," Ottakar said.

"Or both," Mouse mumbled past the needle she held in her mouth.

"And how was your father?" Lord Rozemberk asked the King.

"Not here."

"What do you mean? He summoned us to Prague. Where has he gone?"

"To Austria. The nobles are not happy with Rome's choice of a duke for them."

"What do they want with your father?"

"I imagine one or the other of them has his own claim and wants my father's aid in taking it."

"Surely they are not interested in him as duke?"

"I do not know, nor do I care. What I want to know is who is trying to kill me."

Lord Rozemberk grunted. "Luka, is Evzen here?"

"No, Uncle," said the young man who had brought the wine.

Ottakar pushed himself back in the chair, shifting his weight from the wounded side. "Vok, you did tell Evzen to come to Prague once he had questioned Gernandus's family?"

"Yes, my Lord."

"They live in Plzen—less than day's ride away. So why is Evzen not here already?"

"Dead, most likely," Mouse said.

"A pretty picture you paint," Ottakar answered.

"Better than him being a traitor," Lord Rozemberk added.

"Yes, except that we must look to our men for another," the King said bitterly. "Unless you have something to tell me, Vok?"

Lord Rozemberk jerked around just as Mouse finished tying the dressing.

"What say you, my Lord?" he asked hotly. "You question me and not this girl?"

Mouse sat back on her heels and kept her eyes on the floor.

"What do you mean?" Ottakar asked.

"It was she who called out the warning, long before there was any sign of attack."

"So I have Mouse to thank, again, for saving my life?"

"She could have been signaling the attack. It was she who wanted you to go without armor."

"If Mouse wanted me dead, she could have done her job less well the other day and faced no blame."

"Well, then Gernandus must have told her when and where to expect another attempt on your life." Lord Rozemberk sounded flustered. "How else can you explain how she knew the attack was coming when none of our men did? They have been in battle. She is just a girl."

"Mouse?"

She looked up and sighed. She had no answer but the truth, and she knew how ridiculous it would sound. "I heard them."

"You what?" asked Lord Rozemberk.

"I heard the whistle of the arrows."

"And how would you know the sound of a volley of arrows? Have you been to war, then?"

"I may not have been to war, Lord Rozemberk, but I am not a stupid girl. I heard something that did not fit. It only took me a moment to understand what it meant."

"You cannot have heard them from so far away and before my men," he growled at her.

She looked at him calmly though her heart was thudding. "I have good hearing, Lord Rozemberk."

Ottakar laughed. "And I am glad you do!" Mouse turned, smiling; his eyes trailed up to the blood streaking her face, and he lost his mirth. "Is it deep?"

She had forgotten about it, used to letting her body mend itself as it always did. She ran her fingers along the gash. It was a finger long and had most likely gone to the bone, but Mouse could tell it was already closing. She shook her head.

"Luka, show the lady to a room and send a girl to see that she has what she needs," Ottakar ordered.

"Yes, my Lord."

Mouse was about to argue that she needed to change his dressing and apply a poultice, but she bit her tongue. Clearly the King did not want anyone at Prague to know that he was being hunted. She would keep his secrets. And, anyway, he had the court physicians to use now.

"You did not mean to call me traitor, my Lord," Lord Rozemberk said coldly as Mouse followed Luka out of the room.

"Of course I did not mean it, you ass," the King spat back. "But I gave you one order, Vok. Protect my ward. And yet here she is bloody and—"

The heavy chamber door closed with a thud behind her.

"This way, my Lady."

"I am . . ." *Not a Lady*, Mouse started to say, but what would she have him call her? Girl? Mouse? She looked up to the high arched ceilings, the rich wood polished to a shine; her leather slippers crackled on the rush mats covering the stone floor, and the sweet smell of pennyroyal followed her. "Mouse" didn't seem to fit here.

"Grateful," she finished meekly.

∽

Mouse was looking under a bed three times the size of her little cot at the abbey when the girl surprised her.

"Been sent to help you bathe and dress, my Lady."

"Dress for what?" Mouse asked.

"To go down to the Great Hall for supper with the rest, my Lady."

"Oh, no I am not." Mouse knew she was breaking some protocol by the look on the girl's face. "Not well," Mouse added. Her head still hurt, though the gash was now little more than a scratch. But she felt ill at the idea of facing all those people and their questions. She wasn't ready yet.

After the girl helped Mouse bathe and brought her a borrowed tunic and silk mantle, Mouse sent her to tell Ottakar that she wouldn't be coming down for supper. But Mouse knew she couldn't hide in her room forever. She needed answers for the questions that would inevitably come about who she was and what she was doing here. She ran her fingers in her hair, rubbing at her scalp, sore from braids and pins as much as from slamming her head on the ground.

78

The knock on the door startled her, and again she was faced with not knowing what to do. She wrapped the mantle around her more tightly and moved toward the door, but it opened before she got there.

"My Lady, my Lord the King of Bohemia." The girl bowed slightly and Ottakar swept into the room.

"They said you were unwell. Your head?" he asked as he stepped close, looking down at her forehead.

She meant to answer, but she couldn't stop looking at his scarlet cloak fanning out behind him, lined with golden fur, and the silver belt at his waist and the pearls stitched into his surcoat. The crown on his head caught the candlelight. It was all too much for Mouse who was more aware than ever how much she did not belong here.

Embarrassed, she finally managed to mutter "No," and stumbled backward to the chairs near the fire.

"Can you tell me what is wrong? You are my ward, after all." She heard the smile in his voice.

Mouse tried to laugh, too. "And you, my wise old guardian." But then she second-guessed the tone of familiarity; he seemed far more a king now than a boy or her patient. "I am sorry, my Lord. I should not—"

"Did you know I had an older brother, Mouse?" he asked as he lowered himself into a chair opposite her. "Vladislaus."

"You told me . . . that first night."

"I was never meant to be King." He pulled at the gold belt, reached up and took off the crown. He sighed. "Vok and I were foster brothers. I lived with his family part of the year and he lived with mine for the other. He is a younger son, too. We hunted together. Trained together. I was just Ottakar to him when I was the second son. I lost that when my brother died."

Mouse looked up at him.

"I know I am King, Mouse. And you know I am King," he said, smiling. "And there is a level of formality we must follow at court, but here"—he waved his hand at the room—"I would like it if I could just be Ottakar."

Mouse wanted to say yes, but she wasn't sure what she was agreeing to—calling him by his name so he didn't get lost in his title, so someone in the world knew him as himself? She could understand that, trying to hold on to who he was. She could help him do that. But was he asking for a different kind of intimacy?

"Mouse?"

She had never thought much about boys. Her mind had always been on God and books. When Ottakar said her name, her body betrayed her.

"But who am I supposed to be?" she asked.

"What do you mean?"

"Am I your physician? I am no longer your ward. The papers grant guardianship only until we reached Prague."

"Mother Kazi insisted I change that. I am your guardian still, wise and old or not."

That Mother Kazi would still look out for her surprised Mouse, but it did not solve her problems. "So what am I, then? They are calling me 'my Lady,' but you and I know—" She hesitated as she looked over at the servant girl. Ottakar followed her eyes.

"Ah, Gitta knows how to hold her tongue." He turned back to Mouse. "And you and I know nothing about your lineage. In fact, based on what Mother Kazi could tell me, I am more convinced than ever that you are from a noble family, most likely in France. And as soon as I have settled the matter of who is trying to kill me, I mean to find out just where you come from and who your parents were."

Mouse wasn't sure if she wanted to find those answers or not; they might close more doors than they opened. "In the meantime, who am I to be?"

"Lady Mouse?" He chuckled, and Mouse shook her head. "Lady Dusana? No. Lady Ester." He laid his head back against the chair. Mouse smiled, thinking that she had someone to play her name-game with now. "I know. There was a woman my mother spoke of." He was oddly quiet. "From Austria. She helped people, the poor and sick, anyone she met who needed her. They say she will be made a saint. Her name was Emma. You shall be Lady Emma."

It wasn't hers any more than the ones Mouse had tried on as a girl, but it would do for now, until she found out who she really was.

EIGHT

M ouse stood at the threshold of the chapel but did not go in. Sts. Wenceslaus and Ludmila stared down at her from the stained glass windows flanking the altar. This was as close as she had ever been to Mass. Mouse chewed at the corner of her veil as she tried to summon the courage to enter. Lady Emma would have to go to Mass. And take communion. And make confession. But not today.

She slipped out into the courtyard unseen. A light rain was falling, but she didn't mind getting wet if she could find some solitude and fresh air. But the rattle of carts on stone, the squelch of feet in the mud, stifled coughs, and shouted greetings shattered her hopes of being alone. The air hung in a thick mist and carried the smells of people and animals crowded into an enclosed space. Mouse wanted the woods and the riverside. Surely if she followed the wall, she would find a way out and down to the Vltava River, to the trees and the sound of the animals—they might give her the courage she needed.

"Where are you going, my Lady?"

She spun around. "Luka." She sighed with relief.

"My Lord the King sent me to look for you when he did not see you at morning Mass, my Lady."

"Oh," Mouse scrambled for an excuse. "I meant to take a short walk outside the walls, but I could not find the way out."

"At the South Tower, there." He pointed back the way they'd come. "And at Black Tower, here at the back of St. George's. But my Lady should not walk outside the walls without an escort. May I take you back now? They will have set the hall for midday meal."

Mouse held her tongue and gave him a quick nod, but all the way back she was thinking of how soon she might slip away for that walk in the woods despite what Luka said. She was not accustomed to being told where she could walk nor that she must accept unwelcome company.

When Luka left her at the entrance to the Great Hall, Mouse's hoped-for courage went with him. She arched her neck to look up at the ceilings, impossibly high. Stone columns grew like trees and then branched out in smaller arches along the ceiling, interlacing like the limbs of the ironwood trees out back of the abbey at Teplá. Brightly colored murals filled the space between the arches so that the ceiling was a canopy of pictures, animals like she had seen in bestiaries, castles, scenes of jousting and battle, people she did not know. The artist in her marveled at the skill and beauty. Without thinking, she raised her hand wanting to touch them. A servant brushed past her carrying dishes and cups, drawing Mouse's attention back to the lords and ladies who filled the Great Hall.

Mouse recognized some of the men—Damek and others who had been with Ottakar—but it was the women she watched. They seemed to glide across the floor, their long gowns trailing behind them but never twisting, the women never laying a hand on the skirt to lift or shift it; Mouse had been tripping on hers. The women held their necks stiff, their hands posed. They all wore wimples pulled tight against their chins, their heads covered by veils capped with embroidered fillets, their hair bound by knotted nets of gold thread. Mouse shook her head a little at the feeling of being tied and tethered. The ladies lifted and lowered their eyes as they were approached by this man or that woman, clearly some unreadable awareness of social place and politics at play. Mouse felt her stomach flip at the idea that she would have to learn the game, and then she remembered Mother Kazi's parting words that all she need do was watch the others and learn.

And so Mouse settled against the wall, shielding herself from view by the door, her skin prickling as she focused all of her unnatural senses on studying the ladies. She realized that she could anticipate how they would move, like the horses at the river, though this felt far more dangerous.

It was the music that finally drew her in, a high lilt against thrumming drums and the haunting pull of a rebec. Mouse wanted to see the musicians, but the people were in the way. With a shake, she stretched her body, mimicking the posture of one of the women who looked like someone had threaded a string through the top of her head and was pulling her upright. The woman seemed impossibly straight, but Mouse managed to make her body do the same. She positioned her arms correctly and then with a subtle kick of her knee against the long gown and a swish of her foot forward, Mouse entered the Great Hall.

She kept her eyes on the floor in front of her and followed the music, but by the time she reached the far corner where the minnesingers played, her cheeks flamed with embarrassment. She could feel everyone in the room looking at her. She tried to focus on the music, but all she could hear were the whisperers wondering who she was.

And then the man began to sing. Mouse had been surrounded by the voices of the Brothers and Sisters lifted in
prayer, and they were beautiful, but she had never heard
anyone sing like this—clear, alone, telling the tale of a dis-
honored knight working for redemption to win the hand
of a lady.

"The King wants you," Luka whispered in her ear, startling
her. As she turned to go, the singer opened his eyes for the first
time; they were clouded and rolled wildly.

"He is blind," Mouse said, starting to turn back to him
as if there were something she could do, but Luka held her
arm, guiding her toward the high table, and she realized that
everyone else was already eating. They stopped when they saw
her take the seat beside the Younger King, a place of honor.

"You like the music?" Ottakar asked, smiling.

"Very much, my Lord," she said. Lord Rozemberk, sitting on
the King's other side, turned his head slightly in her direction,
apparently approving of the change in her decorum.

The approval was short-lived as Mouse grabbed the King's
arm excitedly. "Oh, look!" She pointed at the tapestries hanging
on the walls—one full of dark mountains with a man, stitched
in gold, looking down to a land of green, and another, bright
with reds and blues, showing a woman wearing a crown and
taking the hand of a ploughman who held the tethers of two
oxen in his other hand; they looked onto a great city. They were
the history of Bohemia—Father Czech coming down the Carpathians and discovering the land; the prophetess Libuse mar-
rying the first Premsyl and foreseeing the building of Prague.
Each of the dozen tapestries around the hall gave some piece of
the story of Bohemia straight from Cosmas's Chronicle, which
Mouse had copied many times at the abbey.

She tore a piece of bread from a loaf and dipped it in the
cup of wine nearest her, but she was much more interested in

the room and the music than the food. She lost herself in the spectacle until Ottakar interrupted her reverie.

"There is someone I would like you to meet," he whispered to her and then leaned forward, speaking more formally to the person on Lord Rozemberk's right. "Lady Lemberk, allow me to introduce you to Lady Emma, my ward." Mouse turned in time to see the surprise on the woman's face; it was the woman whose posture and movement Mouse had mimicked. "Lady Emma, this is Lady Lemberk," Ottakar continued, looking now at Mouse.

"I did not know you had a ward, my Lord," Lady Lemberk said as she glanced at Mouse's face and then let her eyes slide down Mouse's body.

"I am sure Lady Lemberk will help guide you around the castle and show you how to manage the day-to-day of court life," he said. "Lady Emma has been recently at the abbey in Teplá."

"I see," Lady Lemberk said. "I would be most happy to help, my Lord."

"Thank you." He bowed slightly as he stood.

And suddenly, everyone was standing and then bowing as Ottakar left the room, dinner officially done. As the rest of court bustled out of the Great Hall, Mouse was left with Lady Lemberk.

"You must tell me all about yourself," Lady Lemberk said as she motioned for Mouse to follow, but Mouse kept quiet as she trailed the lady's train up the stairs. She counted them in her head, trying to ease the growing sense of dread—seventy-nine steps up to the landing and twelve kick-slide steps to the large wooden doors. The solar hummed with women's voices. Mouse instantly isolated them, consuming bits of their conversations and piecing them together again, learning what she could about each of them. She knew many of their names before Lady Lemberk had made the actual introductions and settled Mouse near the fire.

"Do you play?" Lady Lemberk asked as she moved a small table with a chessboard closer to Mouse.

Mouse nodded. She had played with Father Lucas when she was a child.

"Are you any good?"

Mouse shrugged.

"The ladies here have no head for it. They are all music and stitchery and gossip." Lady Lemberk put the pieces in their places; she gave herself white.

Mouse kept her eyes on the board, but her attention stayed on the women in the room. The woman seated near the window was pregnant; Mouse could hear the baby's heartbeat.

Lady Lemberk moved her pawn.

The girl plucking at a lute in her lap had a rattle in her chest. Mouse shifted, about to go offer to make the girl a poultice, when she heard the whisper of one of the women huddled over an embroidery hoop.

"A girl her age as ward and him unmarried?"

Mouse moved her pawn.

"How long have you been the Younger King's ward?" Lady Lemberk asked as she moved her knight.

"Some time." Mouse slipped out her bishop.

"Is she family? She must be family," muttered the other embroidery woman.

"Maybe the Old King's bastard daughter," came the reply.

The heat from the fire licked at Mouse's face.

"Is the King's mother here?" Mouse asked.

The room went silent. She didn't need to look up to know that they were all staring either at her or at Lady Lemberk, waiting to see what she would say.

"I should think that you would know," the Lady said wistfully. "But then, they do not like to speak of it. Understandably."

She crossed herself, and Mouse heard the scratch of silk as the other women did the same.

"Oh, I am sorry," Mouse said. "God rest her soul." And she, too, made the sign of the cross, her hands shaking a little.

"She would not be with God, my dear. She was a . . . suicide." Lady Lemberk whispered the last. But the other women took up the story, pale and quiet from the shock, but their eyes alive with the excitement of telling the gossip to someone who had not yet heard.

"It was when the Younger King came up against his father and them still so heartbroken over Prince Vladislaus."

"My Lady the Queen was out of her head with grief. And then to have her other boy join up against his own father—"

"Now be careful what you say. We all know there was a right to what happened. For a father to hate his son so—it is surely a sin. And there were other things, an oddness that grows even yet in the old King," said the pregnant woman.

"You should mind your own tongue, Lady Harrach, or you will lose it should that get back to my Lord, the King."

"Enough!" said Lady Lemberk. "His Holiness has himself commanded that we make peace and let the father and son rule together. We should—"

"She cut herself up, the Queen," the girl at the lute blurted out. "To the bone down both arms. Run through the floor and dripped down into the Great Hall, the blood did. Can still see the stains of it."

"And no one would mourn her, not father nor son." A feverishness filled the voice and spread through the room.

"But the Younger King did cut her free from the straps as the people started to drag her. He would not let them have her to defile. He carried her to the Sisters at Agnes himself. I saw. Made them take her, he did. Shameful."

Mouse's chest tightened.

"They say the reason the great King hates the younger is because she—"

"No more." Lady Lemberk's command was cold and certain. The women pressed their lips together and turned back to their entertainments, including the whispered gossip, much of which centered on the late Queen, but some of it turned back to Mouse.

She tried to focus only on the game, but unlike looking for souls, she had no control over what her gifts let her see or smell or hear.

"And where are you from?" Lady Lemberk asked as she moved her next piece.

Mouse's heart raced but she held her voice steady. "My family is from France." She sacrificed a rook and could hear Lady Lemberk's heart flutter as she slid her bishop to take the offering. The lady thought she was going to win.

"And they are?"

"Checkmate, my Lady."

"Oh!" The Lady looked sharply down at the board, angry and trying to make sense of what had happened, but she recovered quickly; she might have lost one game, but she was intent on winning the other. "It is so nice to have someone who can really play, Lady Emma. Now what were you saying about your family?"

She gave Mouse an embroidery hoop and moved her basket of thread to the table. Mouse took it absently, her mind a swirl of the story of Ottakar's mother and the hissing of the women.

"Did you see how the Younger King looked at the girl? And she him? What he calls a ward others would call a—"

Mouse stood quickly, tossing the embroidery hoop on the table, knocking over several chess pieces. "I am sorry, my Lady, but I am unaccustomed to the warmth of the room. We do not have such grand fireplaces at the abbey. Please excuse me while I get some air."

Mouse lifted the front of her skirts as she hurried down the stairs; there was no one to see, and she was glad of it. She needed to be alone. She thought about going to her room but was afraid Gitta would be there. She decided to make good her promise to disregard Luka's warning and slip through one of the gates and out into the woods around the castle, but when she reached the bottom landing, she saw the door to the chapel slightly askew, a few rays of light scattering through the stained glass visible in the opening. Mouse wanted the quiet of home; she felt unclean after listening to what the women thought of her and sorrowful for Ottakar and his mother. Mouse knew well how it felt to be outcast. A flicker of rage tinted her sorrow, and she pushed the heavy door open and walked into the chapel, fed up with being shut out.

Her leather slippers slapped against the stone floor and echoed in the quiet. *Who are those women to condemn Ottakar or his mother?* Mouse thought. *Who is Mother Kazi to tell me what I can and cannot do?*

She stopped where she was in the middle of the aisle and tried to pray. She knew hundreds of prayers, the common ones in the Book of Hours, forgotten ones she and Father Lucas had discovered in some old text. She started with the thirty-seventh Psalm. She did not mean to smile at the idea of those women's tongues withering and cut like grass. Mouse did not mean to wonder if she could make it so, but she felt the power in her scratch at her chest, ready, waiting.

"'Cease from anger, and forsake wrath; fret not thyself in any wise to do evil,'" she muttered over and over.

And then the door opened. She started to move toward the cover of the benches along the side, but she was seen already.

"I suppose I should not be surprised to see a church-Mouse in a chapel." Ottakar put out his hand to help her stand, wincing a little at the pain in his ribs as he pulled her up. "Why are you not with the other women sewing and gossiping?"

"It was hot, and I do not much like sewing." He was taking them closer to the altar, but Mouse was pulling a little at his hand, her stomach still twisting as she fought her anger. "Or gossip." The last word came out as a hiss.

"Ah," he said, turning to her. "What secrets did you hear?"

"You look tired," she said instead. "You need to rest. Shall I make you a poultice to draw out the pain?"

"You have not answered my question."

She sighed. "I am not familiar with women's ways."

Ottakar laughed. "You have spent your life in a covey of Sisters, Mouse! How can you not—"

"But they are not women. They are Sisters, and they do not talk much." She shook her head. "These ladies, they say . . ." She didn't want to tell him what she had heard. "But it matters little. I should leave and let you—"

"I came to clear my head before going back to the afternoon's business. I must tend to the growing crowd of people who have matters they need managed. My father left much undone." It was his turn to sigh.

"You do not like to manage your people?"

"Most of the time I do, but, as you say, I am tired and my mind turns to the problem at hand." He touched the arrow wound. "I would like to know who is trying to kill me."

"I will let you have your quiet, then." She turned to go but he grabbed her arm gently.

"No. You help me clear my mind, Mouse."

Her breath caught in her throat, but this time the warm tickle in her chest did not come from anger or a thirst to use her power. She thought about the intimacy he encouraged last night—her, just Mouse, and him, just Ottakar. What did he want from her?

"How can I help?"

"Come pray with me," he said after a moment.

And Mouse found herself kneeling before the altar with the King.

"Now tell me what the women said that sent you hiding in the chapel," he said after a while.

Mouse kept her eyes closed. "They called you the Younger King." She heard him choke back the chuckle.

"I have been called that many times, and though I know they mean it as an insult, it is true. I am young. I am King. I am not my father." Mouse could hear his teeth grind as he looked back to the altar. "What else?"

Mouse would not lie to him, but she did not want to confess what she had learned about his mother; she was sure it would hurt him, and if he told her himself one day, she would take it as a sign of real trust, the promise of something more.

So she gave him another truth instead.

Mouse took a breath. "They ask questions I cannot answer. About where I am from. About my family. They do not believe I am your ward. They think that I am . . . that we . . ." The warm tickle flamed in her face now. "Like Hartwin thought," she finished.

"I see." His voice was tight, and she turned to see if he was laughing at her again, but his face was unreadable. "And they said this to you?"

"No. I overheard them."

"Ah." He sat back on his heels. "I am sorry, Mouse. I cannot stop them from thinking what they will. If they accuse you of such things, then I can . . ." He reached over and took her hand. Much like the Sisters, Mouse had never really thought of herself as a girl, a woman, except for when the village boy tried to rape her, and then, because of her careless use of power, she felt like a monster. Her head was swimming now with feelings she couldn't understand.

"Does it matter what they think, Mouse? You and I know—"

The door opened and a priest shuffled into the chapel. Ottakar stood quickly, pulling Mouse up with him.

"Oh, my Lord, I am sorry. I came for afternoon prayers, but I can—"

"No, no, your Excellency. Lady Emma and I were just about to pray for an ease to her homesickness. She misses abbey life, I fear." He smiled down at her. "Bishop Miklaus, this is my ward, Lady Emma. You will find her quite educated. The Sisters at Teplá did well."

"Ah, Teplá. Who is abbot there now?" Bishop Miklaus asked.

"Father Lucas," Mouse answered.

"Oh? I understood from Brother Jan that the Father had been lost, not come home from his last mission. I assumed Brother Jan had—"

"No, your Excellency. Father Lucas is not lost. He is the abbot at Teplá. He will return soon," she said, her voice unnaturally even in her effort to convince herself as well as the bishop that what she said was true.

"I see." Bishop Miklaus's eyes slid over her and back to the King. "My Lord, as you were about to pray anyway, perhaps you would join me? It might offer Lady Emma the comfort she needs."

In answer, Ottakar led Mouse to a near bench as the bishop took his place behind the altar. Mouse knew what to do, what to say and when to kneel, but her heart raced each time she joined in response to the bishop. By the end of the short service, though, she felt a growing sense of liberation. There was no one here to bar her from the Church, no one to know that she was unholy, unbaptized, an infidel.

No one but her.

NINE

Ottakar let her stay with him in the Great Hall throughout the afternoon as Luka led in those waiting for an audience with the King. Some of the disputes were over land and taxes, some between the lords themselves, but Ottakar seemed most interested in hearing the complaints of the farmers who rented and worked the land. While listening to him mediate, Mouse had an idea, and she motioned to Luka.

"Can you bring me parchment, ink, and a quill?" she whispered.

By the time the last person made his case and accepted the judgment of the King, Mouse had filled several pages, which she presented to Ottakar.

"What is this?"

"A record of the disputes you heard today and your decisions in settling them."

"Why?"

"You listened so well to each of them, even the old man arguing about his goat, and then took such care in explaining why you judged the way you did. I thought others might learn from it and that there should be a record in case there was a misunderstanding later, if someone accused you of changing your word or of ruling differently out of favoritism. The record would serve as witness for your integrity."

Ottakar was studying the pages. "You have written every word, Mouse. Exactly as it was said."

She could hear the awe in his voice and she didn't like it.

"Yes," she said quietly.

"This is wonderful. We could make a book of laws." He smiled and tapped her on the head with the stack of parchment. "Would you be willing to do the same tomorrow?"

She didn't need to imagine a thread pulling her up straight and tall as she nodded.

Mouse was still beaming when she entered her room a little later to rest before dressing for supper. She felt like she was beginning to see a place for herself here with Ottakar. She was on the bed dreaming about her future when Gitta came in carrying an armful of clothes.

"A fresh gown for you, my Lady."

"From whom?" Mouse was wary of obligating herself to any of the women at court.

"Lady Harrach's maid came to me saying her ladyship thought you might not have another dress as you just came from the abbey. She cannot wear this one seeing that she is heavy with child, so she sent me to give it to you."

"Lady Harrach . . . she is Damek's wife, yes?" Mouse remembered her; she had defended Ottakar that morning in the solar. Mouse ran her fingers down the gown trying to figure if it was meant as a gesture of friendship or as a trap. She shook her head; she would not let herself start making decisions based on assumed plots and politics.

An hour later, Gitta smiled and clapped her hands, happy with her work. "You look beautiful, my Lady."

Mouse looked down at the sheen of the green silk; pearls lay at the center of embroidered red flowers that ran at the neckline and along the outside curve of her breasts down her sides to where the fabric trailed behind her. She absently rubbed her finger against the skin exposed at her chest.

"Have you no jewels, my Lady?"

Mouse shook her head, the veil tickling her cheek, but then she remembered. "Oh, wait!" She turned to where her bag lay on the bed and pulled out her mother's bracelet. She had never worn it before, never felt like it really belonged to her. She slipped it over the tight sleeve on her wrist.

"There you be!" said Gitta as she bowed.

Mouse didn't hesitate at the doors to the Great Hall this time but kick-swished her way to her place at the head table, pausing only to bow to Lady Harrach, who smiled at her. As she sat, Mouse tilted her head, letting her hair and veil slide to the side so she would not sit on them; Gitta had only partially braided her hair, leaving the back loose to curl at Mouse's hips. The King was not yet at the table. With a flicker of worry at how tired he had seemed earlier in the afternoon, Mouse instantly reverted from pretend-lady to healer, but just when she stood to find Luka or Lord Rozemberk, Ottakar stepped in the room as servants with platters of food streamed past him.

"Lords and Ladies, I am delayed a moment, but I insist that you begin." He gave a nod to the minnesingers and then left the hall.

Mouse chewed at her lip, unsure of what to do; he looked tired, his face pale and drawn. She wanted to check on him, but everyone would see her go, and she could imagine what they might think. She kept her seat, looking down the table past the empty places to the next lord in ranking—Olomouc, she remembered someone had called him; he was not one of Ottakar's men. She watched as he knifed through the feathers of a swan seated in the center of a gold platter. The bird almost looked like it had just come up from the water to nest; someone had sewn its feathers back on in tidy rows, but its eyes were flat and dead.

As Lord Olomouc gouged out a slice of the roasted swan, Mouse overheard him whisper to his neighbor, "Seems trouble stirs in court for the Younger King."

She turned back to her own plate, pretending to focus on the cup the servant filled with wine, but Mouse had her mind trained on the conversation down the table.

"I worry that this patched-up peace will not hold," said Lord Olomouc.

Mouse took her knife from her waist and reluctantly cut a small piece of swan as the bird was brought to her. She had eaten no meat in her life, fasting like the Norbertine Brothers and Sisters on fish and eggs and what they could grow from the land, but she didn't want something else to mark her as different in this strange place.

"I think the Younger King may discover that he has more enemies than he knows." The voice came from the man on the other side of Lord Olomouc. Mouse turned, trying to see his face, but she could not see past Lord Olomouc's girth.

As she sampled the unfamiliar food—snails and oysters and meats she did not know—she worked to overhear more of their conversation, but the men kept their mouths too full for more talk. Then the minnesingers stopped playing, moving farther back in the hall, and a handful of lords and ladies took the center floor in a round.

Barrump-barrump.

The drum started so deep that Mouse could feel it in her chest. The men and women stomped in time with the beat. When a higher drum countered with a *tadum-tadum, tadum-tadum,* quick and light, the women lifted the front of their skirts slightly and hopped on one leg and then the other, moving toward the center of the circle and then out again while the men kept stomping to the heavy drum.

Mouse had seen some visitors to the market fair at Teplá dance like this around a lindenwood tree, but she had been with Mother Kazi, who had frowned and muttered something about old pagan ways; they had not stayed to watch. Mouse felt a thrill now seeing the men and women bounce lightly on their feet as the flute and rebec picked up the tune.

"Would you like to dance?"

She turned to find Damek at her side.

"My wife sent me. She knows I love to dance and she is not able. She thought you might be a willing surrogate."

Mouse found the Lady Harrach, who was smiling and pointing to the circle of dancers.

"I do not know the steps," Mouse said even as she stood and let Damek lead her onto the floor. She found the rhythm easily enough, but it took her several steps to figure out how to manage her skirts. After a few turns, though, she spun and twirled and stomped like she had been dancing all her life. Mouse felt like a little girl again, Adele holding her skyward and spinning. She threw her head back, laughing.

And then the music stopped, and the room was spinning though Mouse was not. Damek took her arm, steadying himself as much as her. The minnesingers started playing again but a quiet tune this time, slow and pensive. The dancers held hands, stepping and leaning to the right, bending down gently at the waist and back up again, another step, closing the circle tight and sliding it open, in and out, over and over.

And then they began to sing.

> Truelove, come O come to me,
> I am waiting here for thee:

I am waiting here for thee,
Truelove, come O come to me!
Sweetest mouth red as the rose,
Come and heal me of my woes;
Come and heal me of my woes,
Sweetest mouth red as the rose.

The tune and the weaving of the dancers and the bodies and the voices cast a hypnotic calm over the room. As the circle turned so that she was facing the royal table, Mouse saw Ottakar watching her, but she could not read his face. He seemed so very serious. And only then did Mouse think to look for the man on the other side of Lord Olomouc, but he was gone.

She was flushed and out of breath when Damek escorted her to her seat. Ottakar stood to meet them, his hand at her back, his mouth held in a tight line.

"Are you ill?" she whispered to him as they sat. "Your wound?"

He shook his head, his face relaxing a bit, and took a slice of venison as the platter came to him. Mouse reached for her cup of wine.

"What is that?" Ottakar asked, taking her arm and fingering the bracelet.

"It was my mother's. It is all I have of her."

He ran his thumb along the engraved sparrow. Mouse grew uncomfortable with the quiet. And that he had not let go of her arm.

"Where is Lord Rozemberk?" she asked finally.

"On an errand. May I have it?"

"What?"

"The bracelet—just for a little while. This"—he pointed to the red stone crossed in gold bars—"looks like a crest and this bird might be a sigil. If so, we might learn something about your mother's family."

She didn't know if it was the excitement of maybe getting answers to her past that made her throat tight, or if it was Ottakar sliding his thumb along her palm as he slipped the bracelet from her wrist.

But when he laid his mouth near her ear to say, "The men cannot keep their eyes off you, Mouse," she knew what had made her lightheaded.

⁂

Mouse woke with vomit burning her throat, barely enough time to sit and lean her head over the side of the bed before it spewed from her mouth and splattered on the floor. Gitta, who fortunately slept on a pallet on the other side of the bed, was ready by the second wave with washbasin in one hand, pulling Mouse's hair back from her face with the other. Mouse had never been sick before; she was exhausted and sore by the time she emptied her stomach.

"Ate something not right by my guess, my Lady," Gitta offered as she knelt to clean up the mess on the floor.

Mouse agreed; most everything she ate last night was "not right." Today she would fast, but first she wanted some mint to settle the nausea.

The sun was not yet fully up when she slipped through the Black Tower gate and into the fog-covered woods near the castle. Her bare feet stung against the cold ground; Mouse stopped, bent her head, and let herself focus on the pain—pain as penance for yesterday's indulgence. She laid her hand against a tree as another wave of queasiness took her, but it was more than just her stomach that caused it. She was embarrassed as she recalled what Ottakar had said; she didn't want all the men looking at her, but she very much liked that he had been one of those who couldn't take his eyes off her. She had heard the desire in his voice, and it had called to her own.

Mouse wrapped the mantle more tightly around her and walked farther into the woods. For the first time in days, she relaxed, whistling back to the birds, running her hands along the smooth bark of the trees. She heard a small creek in the distance and made her way toward it, stopping to grab a handful of mint on the way. She squatted near the water, more careful than usual to keep her knees up and hem clear of the mud as she rinsed the leaves in the water and then put them in her mouth, chewing to release the sweet coolness that would calm her stomach.

She was cresting a small hill when she saw the men hunched back against an outcropping. A deer was strung up from a tree and another two lay on the ground.

Mouse wondered why she hadn't smelled the blood. Even now her nose burned with mint though she could see the men covered in red, see the blood pouring like a waterfall from the deer's slit throat. Two of the men steadied the hanging carcass as a third hacked at the thin tissue between flesh and skin. At first Mouse thought they were Ottakar's men, but then she noticed their worn clothing, ragged hair and beards, haggard faces—peasants or thieves poaching the king's deer.

They'd be strung up for the crows to eat if they were caught. Mouse didn't care about the law, actually thought it unjust and cruel, but the men wouldn't know that if they saw her; they would be sure she meant to turn them in.

Mouse eased back from the crest of the hill. She made no sound.

But one man turned his face up anyway.

Mouse bolted, pulling her skirts up as she could, and ran toward the castle. She heard the crunch of the fallen leaves and bracken as the men gave chase.

"Catch her before she brings the king's men down on us!" one of them yelled.

She wove between the trees and underbrush easily except for her gown, which kept snagging and slowing her. She paused to rip the silk free, and as she turned to run again, Luka stepped out from behind a fir.

"Ah, I found you. The guard said you had come—"

"Go, go!" Mouse was pushing him, trying to turn him back toward the castle, but then she jerked backward. One of the men had grabbed a handful of her hair and yanked. She landed hard on her back, her head slamming into the ground, and for a moment she could not see. She heard sounds of fighting, but she was being dragged away from them. And then a knee was pressing on her chest and a hand closed around her throat.

"My lads Belch and Toad'll gut Master Pisspants back there while I wet my cock. Maybe I slit your throat before they take a turn." He reeked of deer blood and sour breath. Mouse tried to turn her head, but the weight of him was crushing her. She couldn't breathe.

He shifted, clawing at her skirts with one hand and digging his fingers into the skin and cloth at her chest with the other. As he moved, Mouse twisted hard to the side away from him and then pushed up, throwing him off balance. She scrambled to get her footing, but she was too slow, and he was on her again. She planted her feet and threw herself back against him, but he was ready for her this time. His arms clamped around her, and he used his weight to shove her facedown into the dirt.

Mouse spit blood and bracken from her mouth and let her body go limp. He was too big. She could not fight him. Not with her body. She turned her focus inward. Her nostrils flared as she reached deep and loosed the tickle of power in her throat.

And then the man let her go.

As she spun, she could see him scrambling off into the woods, and she put a hand to her mouth. She had not said a word. Was she able to command with a thought? And then she heard something behind her. Crouching, she turned and saw Luka, holding a sword covered in blood, running to her. He must have scared the man off.

"My Lady, are you hurt? Did he—" Luka knelt beside her.

She shook her head, running her hand along her face down to her chest, and realized that her gown had torn, exposing a breast. She fumbled at the cloth, trying to cover herself, but Luka kept grabbing at her arms as he tried to help her up. She couldn't stand his breath on her face. His nearness. Him touching her.

She pushed him away and pulled at her gown again. "You must not see!" The scream burned her throat.

And then Luka's sword was falling and he was clawing at his eyes, a high whine of panic slipping from his mouth as he dropped to his knees.

"What is it?" she cried as she crawled to him, her body shaking with shock.

She pulled at Luka's hands, trying to see where he was hurt, but he fought her, spittle dripping from between his own hands as they shielded his face.

She finally managed to wrestle one of his hands away for just a moment, and she saw his opened eye.

It was covered in milky white like someone had poured hot wax over it.

Mouse shoved herself away from him, wrapping her arms over her head as she cried. "What did I say? God, what did I say?"

And then it came to her, loud and shrill—*You must not see!* That's what she'd told Luka. But she didn't understand. She hadn't said it as a command. They were just words spoken out of fear—like when she had told the town boy to leave her alone. The boy who had left and never come back.

"No," she whimpered as she bent again to the ground, weighted with guilt. "It cannot be. I never meant—"

A branch snapped.

Snot and tears and blood dripped from her chin, and she raked her sleeve across it, leaving a nasty grin in its place as she looked into the face of the man who had tried to rape her. Mouse had never hated anyone before, but she let it run through her, burn her. "You came back."

"Heard a bit of trouble, I did," the deer-slayer said as he took another step toward the curled and writhing Luka. "Sounded like a chance to come back and rid myself of some worry. If you two be dead and poor Belch and Toad, who's left to talk of me?" He started to reach toward the knife at his waist, but Mouse was faster. She grabbed Luka's sword and stuck it in the man's gut, letting go of the hilt as he fell backward. She watched him shred his hands as he tried again and again to pull the blade free. And then he was still.

Mouse crawled back over to Luka and laid her head on his back, trying to stop him from shaking, but she was shaking, too.

She didn't know who it was who lifted her from the forest floor. She didn't care.

Mouse had killed one man and blinded another.

TEN

Mouse rolled herself into a ball on the bed. She would not speak, not even to Ottakar. She was too afraid of what might happen.

She wanted Father Lucas.

It had been three days since the attack, and she had not eaten nor slept. Her tongue swelled from where she had chewed at it, bitten it until the blood poured down the back of her throat. She was too frightened of Hell to kill herself, but she must pay penance for what she had done. She had often treated cuts left by the whips the Sisters flung across their backs, or salved the inflamed, raw skin left from the hair shirts worn for weeks until they stuck in the blisters they made and crusted over. Mouse had learned the lesson well: Pain was penance and the righteous must not forget that they lived in a state of sin as well as a state of grace. She might not ever reap the grace, but Mouse certainly sowed the sin.

The door opened. She knew who it was. She had learned the sound of his footfall in the hall; it was always accompanied by the tinkle and clank of armed guards, four if Mouse's ears could be trusted. She wondered what the new danger to him might be, but when the question rose in her mouth, she sank her teeth into her lips. She was far more dangerous than anything his guard might shield him from; she could kill him with a word.

"My Lord," Gitta said quietly from the other side of the room.

Ottakar laid his hand on Mouse's shoulder. "Will you please talk to me, Mouse?"

She lay still until he left.

She must have fallen asleep. It was dark outside, the fire in her room nothing but embers and a flicker now and then as the air stirred. Something had woken her.

Mouse sat up quickly, scanning the room for the dark creatures but saw nothing. She looked over to Gitta's pallet, but the girl was not there. And then she heard the scream.

She snatched her mantle and jumped to her feet; stars exploded in her eyes and the room spun. She put her hand out to the bed, steadying herself until the dizziness passed—consequences of a lack of food and days spent in bed. She needed to move more slowly. As she took a step toward the door, it opened. Ottakar was there in the hall, holding a candle, but it was Damek who came to her.

"Please. My wife . . . she needs you."

Mouse could feel his fear. She nodded, grabbing her leather bag from the table and following him as he rushed down the hallway.

The room sweltered with heat from the fire and candles. Lady Harrach lay still on the bed. Mouse went to her, putting a hand on her forehead. Gitta closed the door, leaving the men in the hall.

"The baby?" Lady Harrach asked.

"He lives," Mouse said. She could hear the baby's heartbeat. It raced and then slowed to a near stop with the contractions. She turned to the midwife.

"Turned wrong, it is," the old woman said. "There is no hope."

"I will get it out," Mouse whispered.

She gave Gitta and the midwife quiet orders for what she needed as she took her tools from her bag, laid them on the bed, and cleaned them with wine. Mouse climbed over the footboard and straddled Lady Harrach's legs while the other two women held the Lady's arms. Mouse hesitated as she looked down on the smooth, creamy skin. She had seen the bloody effects of Happy Vilém's attempts to cut out a baby; no one lived.

Mouse shook herself and then made the cuts quickly, first the skin in a widening red line down the stomach and then the muscle underneath, until she saw the womb, which tightened like a squeezing fist. Lady Harrach screamed and writhed.

But as the contraction passed, the baby did not move. Mouse could not hear its heartbeat.

She cut through the uterine tissue quickly; a tiny blue hand popped out as Mouse slid her own through the opening and under the baby's shoulders, gently pulling him out. His lips were blue, his chest still, and the knotty cord wrapped twice around his neck. Mouse ran her fingers behind the slimy rope and eased it over his head until he was free.

It was too quiet in the room. Lady Harrach had passed out from the pain.

Mouse crawled back down the footboard, cradling the bloody infant against her chest and trailing the umbilical cord behind him. She crouched on the floor, laying him in her lap on his side; his limp arms flopped against his chest. She slid her finger in his mouth, dragging out thick fluid, and rubbed his back with her other hand.

She waited.

He did not breathe.

Mouse shook with anger and grief. She would not let this happen. She needed this baby to live.

"Breathe," she whispered in the baby's ear, letting her power lace her words.

But nothing happened.

Mouse's hands closed around the baby's chest, holding him to her own. She didn't know she was crying until the salt burned her tongue as she licked her lips.

A guttural moan built in her chest as she rocked the baby.

"You will live." The power erupted in her throat, and the words spewed out in a gasp.

The baby wailed, filling his lungs, and his hands and feet and lips slowly turned the same dusky pink that had blanketed Teplá the day Mouse left. After tying and cutting the cord, she stood slowly and handed the crying baby to the laughing midwife.

Mouse had more work to do. Pulling gently at the cut cord as she watched the womb contract, she delivered the afterbirth, and then bent over the incision. Her fingers were stiff and aching by the time she tied off the last stitch, but she refused to let the other women take over the cleaning and bandaging. *Penance,* she thought, the muscles in her back spasming as she stood.

The midwife gave Lady Harrach sips of chamomile and comfrey tea; Gitta cleaned the baby and laid him beside his mother. The bedclothes were soaked in blood, like in the mural on Mouse's wall at Teplá, like at her own birth, but this time both mother and child lived. Mouse wondered how different her life might be if this had happened for her, too; she wondered if saving this mother and child might somehow give her another chance for a happy ending.

"Come see the baby," Gitta said.

Mouse shook her head. The picture was too full of joy, the baby too new and clean, innocent. She walked out of the room, tears in her eyes.

"Oh, God, no," Damek said as he saw her bloody mantle.

"You have a son. Your wife lives." She let him throw his arms around her. "Let the midwife clean up and then you can go in."

"Thank you, my Lady."

"Thank God," she said as she pulled away.

Ottakar had been leaning against the wall behind Damek with guards on either side of him. As he turned to walk beside her, he glanced at Mouse but said nothing. She stopped after a few steps. Her teeth chattered as her body shook from exhaustion. She buried her face in her hands, turning toward Ottakar, who pulled her to him.

She only cried a little. "I am tired," she mumbled into his chest.

"Sit," he said. And so they sat on the floor near the landing of the stairs. The hall was dark except for a flickering candle on a sconce in the wall.

Mouse laid her head against her knees as she pulled them to her chest. They were sticky with blood, but she didn't care.

"I killed the man," Mouse said. The confession she really wanted to make was what she had done to Luka and to the baby and to the squirrel, but she was too afraid.

"You saved Luka," Ottakar said softly.

"No. Luka was brave." She ran her fingers in her hair. "He told me not to go walking in the woods alone. I thought I . . . it was all my fault."

"It was the dead man's fault," he said angrily. "A thief and a . . . Mouse, did he—"

She shook her head.

One of the guards shifted, reminding Mouse of the question she'd wanted to ask earlier and giving her a chance to change the conversation.

"Why the extra guards? Someone else try to kill you?"

Ottakar chuckled. "No. But someone did try to kill my father."

"Your father is here?"

"No. On his way back from Austria, he stopped at Rozemberk Castle. Vok's father is a friend to mine. It was there that it happened—poison. But my father still lives. Now Vok insists on making a servant taste my food and drink."

"Lord Rozemberk is back?"

He nodded. "Yes. I had sent him to Plzen to talk to Gernandus's family and to look for Evzen. He found him. You were right. Evzen is dead. Vok was returning to Prague when he found you in the woods. He heard the—"

"Lord Rozemberk found me? I owe him my thanks, then." She was not pleased with the obligation, especially since she also bore the guilt for blinding his nephew. "Where is Lord Rozemberk?" She laid her head back against the wall, closing her eyes.

"Interrogating Lord Olomouc, I imagine. He has been at it for days. It seems that it was Olomouc who tried to poison my father and paid Gernandus to kill me. But he has yet to admit it. He is secretly a Slavnik, a family that has been long-time enemies to mine. We thought we had killed them all. We will finish that task soon enough. Vok wants to get names of any other conspirators first."

Mouse shuddered again. She imagined what methods of torture Lord Rozemberk used, and she doubted that his sole ambition was to garner information.

∽

Mouse still kept mostly to her room the next day, letting Ottakar's visits and Gitta's chatty gossip ease her back into the world. She missed the public torture and eventual beheading of Lord

Olomouc, though everyone still seemed festive at week's end when she went down to the Great Hall. Mouse got her chance to thank Lord Rozemberk, which she did quickly. Trying to apologize for what happened to his nephew hurt more.

"How is Luka?"

"He is resting with the Brothers at Strahov."

"And he is recovering?"

"Why? Are you so great a healer that you can recover him his sight?"

Mouse felt the sting. She deserved it and much worse. "He was very brave."

"And you were very stupid."

"That is enough, Vok," Ottakar said. He took Mouse's hand, turning it so that her arm lay on his. "It was not your fault," he said, leaning toward her.

Mouse wanted to argue with him, but she was still afraid of herself, of accidentally unleashing her power with the wrong words, so she kept quiet, laid her head back against the chair and focused on the soft, warm pulse of Ottakar's wrist resting against the underside of her forearm.

Since the attack, she had not wanted anyone to touch her, flinching when Gitta helped her dress, holding herself tightly like a coiled snake, but the rawness of Ottakar's skin on hers, simple and safe, made her hungry for more.

"I sent your bracelet with one of the Brothers from Strahov," he said. "He was traveling to the university in Paris. I asked him to have someone there look at it. He should be there by now. Soon enough we will have answers about your family." She wanted to ask questions, but her words got caught in the tightness of her throat. All she could think about was how Ottakar was running his thumb along her wrist. The future that spilled out in her mind danced with her desire and left her breathless.

ELEVEN

During those early days of waiting, Mouse practiced patience and penance and tried not to imagine what it would be like to finally have answers about who she was, to have a family, to know her mother; she especially tried not to hope for finding her father.

Most mornings she spent transcribing the record of land disputes and Ottakar's rulings. Wanting to avoid sleep and the dreams that came, she worked late into the night stitching the pages together to make a book; she painted the wood cover blue with wild hyacinths on the spine. The artist in her sighed a little when Ottakar gave the book its mundane title—*The Land Tables*—but she filled with pride at his reverence as he laid his hand on the book, naming it before the court.

Every day, Mouse walked the two miles there and back to Strahov. She wanted to see Luka, but the Brothers would not permit her. She refused to give up until the guard assigned to escort her muttered to himself once too often that she ought to learn her place. She didn't know what she would say to Luka anyway, though the guilt lay heavy on her. She had nightmares when she did sleep, waking just as the scream started to build in her throat.

But just before Hallowmas, she woke to someone else's screams.

Mouse had heard it before. Lady Harrach. She ran through the hall to the Lady's chambers, sure she would find the Lady consumed with fever. Mouse had checked on her often; she seemed to be healing well, but such wounds could turn bad quickly.

Lady Harrach sat on the bed rocking her son. "He is not dead," she whispered over and over. Damek sat at her side.

Mouse swallowed hard, but then she heard the rapid *whirr, whirr, whirr* of the baby's heart.

"No, my love, he is not dead. It was just a dream," Damek said. "See, here is Lady Emma. She will make sure the little man is well."

Mouse took the baby, who seemed perfectly fine and ready to go back to sleep.

"But it was so real, Damek. I was awake. I am sure I was. I had gone to feed him, and he was lying there, not breathing, and then he opened his eyes and . . . oh, Damek! They were sunken and dark and dead. He was dead. I know he was," she sobbed. Mouse handed her the baby as comfort. She had just sent Gitta to make some lavender tea when she heard a second scream from farther off in the castle grounds. A shudder of dread went through Mouse. Had the child-things followed her here, drawn by her use of power?

No one said anything about nightmares the next day, but Mouse nevertheless filled a bag with salt, and, when she went to visit Lady Harrach, she sprinkled a cross with the bed and cradle at its head and foot as she pretended to pace the room. The salt rattled as it settled into the rush mats; it would stay put there. Mouse paused at each spoke of the cross to let blood drip from a cut she'd made in her palm, waiting as it slid through the woven rushes to meet the salt below. She mumbled the spell quietly as Lady Harrach talked about her rosy-cheeked baby, the brightness of his eyes, his hearty appetite—anything to wipe away visions of the dead thing from last night.

Mouse crafted a protection spell in her own room also, but she could not go to Ottakar's chamber to do the same without raising questions. So she prayed for him instead and hoped that her fears were unfounded, that the dark creatures had not found her again. But the hollow-eyed things had so salivated over the squirrel; they would surely be delirious over a resurrected infant.

More than ever, Mouse wished that she knew where Father Lucas was. He was long overdue. When he returned—if he returned—Father Lucas would be expected to stop at Strahov to make a report of his mission, but Bishop Miklaus still had heard no word from him. Mouse would not let herself think about what might have happened to Father Lucas, an emissary of the Church among pagans, but she resolved herself to having to deal with her problems alone.

If the dark things from the baby cemetery had followed Mouse to Prague, she needed to be prepared.

She grabbed the leather bag that had carried all her belongings from Teplá and went to the private garden that once belonged to Ottakar's mother. No one else would go there, tainted as it was by the woman's sin. It was the perfect place for what Mouse needed to do.

Closed in by the chapel and the outer castle wall, the garden offered Mouse solitude; it was her own cloistered space. Even overgrown and untended, the place was beautiful. The roses that climbed the trellises along the walls readied themselves for winter, last shriveled blooms clinging to thorny branches as the leaves curled back from them and dropped to the ground. Mouse followed the maze of head-high hedges until they opened on a small fountain surrounded by tall grasses and shrubs that had once bloomed. Moss crept up a stone bench on the far side of the water.

Mouse sighed as she sat down. Guilt hung heavily on her as she pulled a book from the bag. It was the small codex she had taken from Father Lucas's cupboard. She'd meant to return it, but when Ottakar insisted she come with him to Prague, she couldn't help but bring it with her—the mysteries of the unreadable book overcoming her shame at being a thief. What language was it written in, and who wrote it? What secrets did it hold, and why did it make the back of her neck prickle with unease?

But as she opened the book now, the sun glaring against the parchment and the old pages crackling in the breeze like the dead roses, desperation quieted her guilt and curiosity. She only hoped that the book had the answers she needed: how to shield the castle from the dark creatures.

Because, if they weren't already here, Mouse knew they would be coming for her.

She spent the afternoon trying to decipher the text, at first working to see if the lightly inked BRETHREN OF PURITY correlated to letters in what seemed to be the title. She tried to identify the images of plants so she could translate the words beneath the drawings into Latin or German or French or any of the other languages she knew, but, despite the herbal knowledge Mother Kazi had taught her, Mouse could not label a single plant in the whole manuscript. Frustrated and bleary-eyed, she gave up.

That night, the screams came from outside the palace.

∞

"It happens every year at Hallowmas," Lady Lemberk said dismissively the next day as the women settled into their places in the solar. "Simple people have little control over their own minds. Scared of the dark, they are, and every little creak or groan."

"And for all their churchgoing, too many of them still believe in the old ways," another woman added, laughing. "They probably thought some tree spirits had come out of the woods to get them."

But Mouse knew too much to be comforted, and she skipped the midday meal to go to the garden again. The shadows stretched from wall to wall by the time she slammed the book closed and buried her head in her hands. She felt more convinced than ever that it held the answers she needed, but it would not give up its secrets. She would have to face those dark creatures alone and with nothing more than the handful of protective spells Father Lucas had taught her. It would not be enough. She could not protect the whole castle.

Leaving seemed to be her only choice, for if she did, the dark things might leave with her. She did not mean to cry, but the thought of never seeing Ottakar again pricked at her eyes and squeezed her throat.

And then she heard the footfall. Someone was coming through the maze.

There was no other way out. Mouse moved toward the opening on the far side of the fountain, slipping behind the hedge, so she could see the intruder without being seen herself. But the man found her eyes through the thick hedge without pause. She almost didn't recognize him. It had been over a year.

"Come, my little andílek. I have missed you so."

Mouse was in his arms before he finished speaking, her face scratching against his white habit; she breathed in the smell of him—exotic scents she could not place, sweet, rich, the tang of saltwater mixed with the familiar. A different Father Lucas, but Father Lucas all the same.

"One of the lady's maids told me I would find my little Mouse here in the garden. And so I have." He stroked her hair as he held her to him.

"You are thinner," she said, finally pulling back enough to see his face.

"I find I do not like travel by water."

"Where have you been? We thought you—"

"I went across two seas, fell ill and had to recover so I could come home to you. Imagine my surprise at finding you here instead." He ran his thumb across her cheek. "But why are you crying?"

"Because I am happy you are here."

"Hmmm." He knew her well enough to catch the half-lie, but he let it go. He took her hand in both of his as they sat on the bench. "So, where did we leave off, little Mouse? It was my turn, I believe. Ah, I know . . . 'And the human stands erect and looks toward heaven so as to see God, rather than look at the earth, as do the beasts that nature has made bent over and attentive to their bellies.'"

Mouse smiled. It was their own kind of chess, a game Father Lucas had crafted to challenge himself and her—name the author, book, and quote the next line.

"Isidore," she said. "Book Eleven of the *Etymologie*. And the next line is: 'Human beings have two aspects: the interior and the exterior. The interior human is the . . . is the soul and the exterior is the body.'" She stumbled on the line not because she had forgotten it, but because it hurt more now to say it than when she read it for the first time years ago, just after she had stopped looking for her own soul.

Father Lucas sighed. "Ah, you still do not read it as I would have you read it. Isidore tells us next the soul is like the wind. Can you see the wind?"

"No, Father, but I can see your soul. It glows so bright it hurts my eyes. I am dark inside, and now . . ." She swallowed hard against her guilt and fears about the dark creatures. Father Lucas looked so tired, and Mouse just wanted to revel in the joy of him being here.

"Have you found trouble, andílek?" His question was so like the one Mother Kazi asked, but Mouse knew he would never send her away, no matter what trouble she'd found. "Is that why you are not at home where you should be? Have you become a king's Mouse now?"

"No, Father!" Embarrassment flamed in her face, but she looked away quickly so he could not see the rest of the truth in her eyes, the truth that she would very much like to belong to Ottakar. She bristled defensively. "I could not stay at Teplá. And besides, it was Mother Kazi who bid me come with the King. He needed a healer."

"Mother Kazi sent you? But why could you not go back once the King—" As he moved his hand down to the bench, he brushed against the book that Mouse had left laying there. "What is this?"

She wanted to slide it under her skirts and give him a lie, but she wouldn't. "I . . . I took it from the cabinet in your alcove. I needed—" She shook her head. "That does not matter. I took the book even though I knew you did not want me to read it. I am sorry, Father."

"And did you read it?"

"Are you angry I took it?"

"Ah, little Mouse." He bent and kissed her on top of the head. "When have I ever been angry at you? I meant for us to study those books together, true enough; they tell dark and confusing stories. But I have been more absent than not these past years, looking for more books like those, and I have had little time for study with you. It is right that you should read them on your own and make of them what you can. Perhaps you can offer new insights seeing them fresh and without someone else's prejudice." He picked up the book. "But you did not answer. Have you read it?"

"I cannot. I do not know the language. Can you teach me, Father?" She turned toward him smiling and feeling like herself again, eager to learn from him, to discover something new with him.

"I do not know the language, either."

She felt herself sag as the weight of her worry settled on her again.

"And over the past several years, in all my travels, I have found no one else who can read the language," he added.

"How is that possible?"

"Either it is a lost language, one so old we have not even a trace of it, or the book is not written in a language at all but rather in a code."

"Why would someone write something no one could read?"

"People will do anything to keep their secrets. And to uncover the secrets of others."

"But there must be a key. Some way to understand the code."

"I agree," he said.

Mouse sat straighter, studying his face. She had heard something in his voice, in his heartbeat. "You have the key."

Father Lucas laughed. He lifted his hand, gently sliding it down her face, closing her eyes. "Andílek, if you look at me any more closely, I am like to shatter and be spread on the wind."

Mouse pulled away sharply, too unsure of what she was capable of—if she could blind the sighted and raise the dead, might she not also shatter a man?

Father Lucas put his hand under her chin, lifting her face. "I will show you, and maybe we can unlock the secrets together."

"I would like that very much," she said. "But first I have someone I want you to meet."

TWELVE

Mouse made the introductions much more gracefully than she had with Mother Kazi, bowing low and "my Lord-ing" in all the right places; she was disappointed that Ottakar seemed stiff and regal and Father Lucas distracted.

Ottakar quickly excused himself for a meeting with Lord Rozemberk and Father Lucas went off to report to Bishop Miklaus. Mouse walked with him as far as the South Gate, but she would not go beyond the castle walls.

A cold rain misted down as she turned back toward the keep, and as she crossed the bailey toward St. Vitus's, Mouse caught the taste of metal in the air. It was slaughter time. She heard the bellows of the sheep and cows that were waiting for their turn at the knife, but she would not turn the corner to serve witness. Her stomach heaved, and she walked blindly into the dark of the basilica's portico just as the rain fell harder, running down the church façade.

Mouse leaned against the wall, letting the steady beat of the rain drive out the sounds of the panicked animals. She lifted her skirts and held her foot under the falling water, digging her fingers between her toes to loosen the caked mud; she had adopted St. Norbert's bare feet again as penance after what had happened with Luka. Her feet were raw and tender, and the water felt good.

"I love the harvesting days. The smells of summer gone fill the air as the women thrash the grain. But I hate slaughter time."

Mouse spun toward the dark corner. How could she not have heard him there? It was the blind minnesinger from that first night in the Great Hall.

"Smell of death, it be. And not a right one, no. Not like the old star what slips away in the deep dark, peaceful and quiet. Or a martyr's death who dies for the good, fierce and noble." He spoke like a poet, Mouse thought, like the songs he sang. "This time of year, death steals what it wants, too impatient to wait. Those poor beasts out there are but some of its bounty."

"Their flesh will give life to many this winter," Mouse offered quietly. "Like Christ's body slain."

"True enough, I suppose, but not your truth, I think," the blind minnesinger said.

"What do you mean?" she asked sharply.

"You would not have them slaughtered. You will not take the life stolen from them."

Mouse's head was spinning. "No. I mean, I do not know. I would not have the living ones watch the slaughter."

"It is better if they do not know what is coming?" he asked.

"I think I would not want to know until I felt the knife at my throat."

"Death would be easier?"

"Maybe," she said. "I am sure at least that living would be easier if I could not see too far down the path."

"I wonder if knowing what waited for you would make life sweeter. If I had known that I would lose my sight, I think I would have seen more—more colors, more faces." He sighed. "I miss faces and watching how they change while people listen to my music."

Mouse ran her sleeve across her cheek, crying for what the old man had lost and for what she had taken from Luka. She put her muddy hands on either side of the minnesinger's face, her thumbs sliding down his forehead over his eyes, which closed as she touched them. "I wish you could see again," she whispered as she bent to kiss his forehead.

She turned and stepped out into the rain, headed back to the castle.

"What have you done?" he said hoarsely.

Mouse stood for a moment, frozen, before turning to look back at the old man. He was standing just on the other side of the curtain of rain, looking at her.

Looking at her with clear, blue eyes.

"No," Mouse muttered, the rain running in her mouth as she leaned toward the old minnesinger and watched his pupils dilate with the shift of light. Something quivered in her stomach.

"What are you?" He was reaching for her, grabbing her wrist, his face and voice full of awe. "You are beautiful! Dark hair, skin so smooth." His other hand slid through the rain toward her face. "Your eyes, green as a yew tree. Are you a saint? An angel?"

"No. I am nothing. A girl." She tried to pull her arm free. "Only a girl. Please, I did not do this." But the thrill of what she had done started to overcome her fear. She had given the man his sight. She might do the same for Luka.

The minnesinger kissed her hand. "Come. We must tell my boy, Matthias. Oh, my son, I have not seen his face since he was a babe." He stepped out into the rain with her.

Like lightning, Mouse saw what would happen if the minnesinger told his strange tale and laid the miracle at her feet. At the very least, it would be Teplá all over again—people crossing themselves against her, staring at her with awe or fear, but she wouldn't be shielded by the abbey, by people who had known her since she was a little girl. These strangers were as like to call her witch and strap her to a stake and burn her this Hallows' Eve.

Then an image came of herself surrounded by the sick and wounded, healing them; maybe this was what God meant for her. Her life fell into place, all the disjointed or missing pieces now so clear—not part of the Church, but rather part of the world, sharing her gifts and her training as a healer. She would be a saint. But not yet. Not now. Not until she was ready.

The minnesinger pulled on her arm. Mouse caught him off balance and shoved him back under the portico, her arm pressed against his chest, her face inches from his own.

She laughed as the tickle of power ran up her throat. "It was the blessed Ludmila who came to you and restored your sight, a gift for all the joy you bring to others."

His eyes went blank for a moment and Mouse was scared she had undone the miracle, but then he saw her, embraced her. "I can see! The blessed Ludmila has given me my sight!" And he went dancing into the rain.

❦

"You are soaked!" Gitta said as Mouse spun around the room minutes later, spraying rainwater everywhere. "Why so happy, my Lady?"

"It is my birthday and Father Lucas has come back to me!" She grabbed Gitta's arms and swirled with her.

"Today is your name day? All Hallows'?" Gitta asked breathlessly as she started to remove Mouse's wet clothes.

"Not a name day—I do not have one of those—but my actual birthday."

"Well, God bless you, my Lady. And glad I am that it is a happy one. You deserve a bit of happiness after all that trouble in the woods."

"Thank you, Gitta." But the gift that filled Mouse's mind was the one she meant to give Luka as soon as she figured out how to get the monks to let her in at Strahov.

Later, at the feast before the All Hallows' vigil, she asked Ottakar once more to get her admittance to the monastery.

"No," Ottakar said again. "I told you I will not interfere with the Brothers." But he was smiling. How could he not? Mouse beamed with joy in a way he had not seen since the attack on her in the woods. Her playfulness and confidence drew him in like a song, like that night he had watched her dance.

"But it is my birthday, my Lord." Her eyes sparked.

He leaned in closer, turning his back on Lord Rozemberk and oblivious to the crowd in the Great Hall, who all talked about the minnesinger's miracle.

"Then tell me something I might give you."

Mouse felt his breath slide across her cheek and down the back of her neck. She saw herself in his eyes. She knew what she wanted. And what he wanted.

But then he looked over her shoulder and straightened. "Welcome, Father Lucas."

The older man bowed. "Thank you for inviting me, my Lord," he said and then turned his attentions to Mouse. "May I have a moment with you?"

"My Lady Emma," Ottakar said. "Be quick. We leave for the vigil at St. George's soon."

"Of course, my Lord." Mouse bowed.

Father Lucas led her down the hallway and into the chapel, guiding them to a bench at the back.

"I heard about the minnesinger. What have you done?" he asked.

"I do not know what—"

"The girl I left at Teplá told no lies and no half-truths either. The woman I find at court has told me little else."

Embarrassed by how easily he saw through her and shamed by the truth of his accusations, she felt her cheeks flame, but rather than confess her sins, she lashed out. "Reap what you sow, Father. Is that not what you teach your flock?" She felt the power, fully awake since her afternoon miracle, purr and stretch in her chest.

"I do not understand. What have I sown? And are you no longer part of my flock?"

"I never have been, according to Mother Kazi," she spat back.

"Ah, I see. You turn the knife on those who hurt you. But I have taught you to do better. And when have I ever hurt you, Mouse?"

The gentleness of his voice and the care in his face swallowed up the angry words she meant to fling, and something inside her uncoiled just a little so she could breathe.

She hid her face in her hands. "I am sorry, Father." And she told him everything, everything except about the baby; that secret was hers alone. "I did not mean to do any of it, Father. Not the lies. Not Luka. Not giving the old singer his sight. But that was a good thing, was it not?"

"Oh, little andílek—"

Mouse sighed, sorry for the disappointment in his voice. "You call me that, your little angel, is that what I am?"

"Have I not told you that you are God's creature? Is that not enough? To live by his will? To do good?"

"But I did good, Father. Even Christ restored sight to the blind."

"Even Christ? Is that what you think of yourself now?"

Mouse blushed. "No, I did not mean it that way. I meant that others have done miracles. St. Wenceslaus gave a blind woman her sight. St. Procopius drove out demons. St. Ludmila—"

"Ludmila was driven from her homeland and then strangled. Wenceslaus's own brother hacked him to pieces." His frustration and fear sharpened his words. "Is that what you want? I would not have it for you." He shook his head angrily.

Mouse thought about the sheep and the cows waiting for slaughter in the bailey.

"But if it is God's will? He gave me these gifts, should I not use them?" she asked quietly.

This time, Father Lucas lowered his head into his hands. "It is not safe, Mouse. You saw how the people at Teplá treated you, and they had only seen your oddness as a child with no idea what you were truly capable of doing. And, besides, your arguments are hollow. You know the danger already. According to the minnesinger, it was St. Ludmila who gave him his sight. I am quite sure she was not at St. Vitus's this day, was she?"

Mouse shook her head, and they sat in silence.

"Father, do you know who my parents were?"

The old man showed no surprise at the question. "God made you. Like he made all of us. Nothing else matters."

"It matters to me. And it matters to Ottakar."

"You mean to say 'My Lord, the King.'" He lifted his head to look at her, his eyes dark. "Beware, Mouse. Court is as dangerous as the Church, both steeped in politics and power-mongering and filled with ambitious people. Will you not come back to Teplá with me?"

"I am not wanted there, Father. And you will not stay there long anyway."

"I think my travels may be close to done." He sounded tired. "I have something for you." He pulled a book from his leather bag and handed it to her.

It was smaller than most, the cover cracked with age. She opened it. It smelled of saltwater and sand. *The Book of Enoch* scrolled across the top of the opening page. "It is in Hebrew," she said with some relief, glad to have a book she could actually read.

"Yes, but it is like the others in my cabinet. Not everyone would understand why we would want to read such a book."

"What is in it?"

"Stories you will not have heard before, but I think you might find the book most helpful for other reasons."

Mouse thumbed through the pages, thinking about what he said. She looked at him sharply. "It is the key! To reading the other book!"

He nodded. "I traveled a long way on the hopes that it was, but I confess I can find no answers to breaking the code in it. I hope you will be able to see something I cannot. But for now, take it up to your room and then we will go back among the wolves. I imagine we have overtaxed the King's patience."

Heavily scented smoke swirled around the ceiling frescoes in the Great Hall like clouds waiting to descend on the handful of revelers below. As Mouse entered, Ottakar beckoned to her, then stood, pulling her to him and kissing her cheek; he smelled of sweet wine and fatty meat.

"I sent the others on to the church," he said as they stepped out into the night.

Only a few people remained in the courtyard, and they formed a straggly line toward St. George's Basilica. The air had gone cold, the day's rain now scattered flurries and the clouds thick enough to shutter the moonlight. A fuzzy circle of candlelight emanated from the lanterns hung from hooks on either side of the open doors to the church. They looked like eyes glowing beside a fiery mouth, and the dark spires of the Adam and Eve towers shot up into the night sky like horns; it looked like a waking dragon filling its belly with people before taking up battle.

Tomorrow the faithful would feast in the church for All Saints, but tonight they would keep vigil against the darkness of All Hallows' with a night of prayers for the dead.

"Soul cake," a child's voice called out over the courtyard.

People looked around, confused.

"Soul cake!" another child's voice echoed, until all through the courtyard from palace to church, the high, plaintive whine of voices clamored. "Soul cake, soul cake, soul cake."

Mouse looked past the thinning crowd and saw them, dozens of children wearing masks, their gaping mouths painted red on white faces with black eyes—masks of the dead. They closed in from the deeper shadows near the walls.

"Be you town children?" someone asked.

"Soul cake," came the answer.

"Soul cakes come on the morrow with All Saints as you well know. Be off with you. Come back tomorrow and you shall have your soul cake. Go on!" someone shouted and waved his hand at the children encircling the crowd.

And then the bells began to ring.

The people lifted hands to cover their ears as the bells of St. George's and St. Vitus's clanged from either end of the bailey. The town bells rang from across the river. The people shuffled forward toward the church, bumping into each other in their hurry.

"No one rings the bells in Prague," Ottakar muttered, letting go of her hand and pushing through the crowd.

"Why would they not?" Mouse asked. Ringing the bells for the dead had always been part of the vigil at Teplá. But Ottakar was gone.

Mouse made to follow, but the children closed around her, their heads cocked as they said as one, "Soul cakes!"

And she knew that the dark creatures had found her at last.

THIRTEEN

Mouse watched as the church doors closed, shutting Ottakar inside with the last of the stragglers and leaving her alone in the courtyard with the children who were not children.

The masks they'd worn morphed into the hollow-eyed, sharp-toothed faces of the dark things from the baby cemetery. They laughed liked normal children—high and playful—but Mouse knew that whatever they may have been once, these things were anything but innocent.

One of the child-things reached out and tugged her hand. "Play?" it asked.

And then Mouse saw the church. Flames danced at the windows, bright backdrops for the dark silhouettes of people burning. Fire licked up the outside of the basilica.

Ottakar was in there. And Father Lucas.

Mouse ran toward the church doors.

She could smell her flesh burning, feel the heat searing her as she grabbed the iron pull. The doors would not open. She fell to her knees, clawing at the bottom of the door trying to find leverage to force it open, splinters driving beneath her fingernails. The screams inside the church grew higher until they sounded just like the screams of the horses that had burned in the smithy's stables at Teplá.

Exactly like the horse's screams.

She jerked her head up. The hollow-eyed children were playing with her mind, feeding her the vision of the burning church. The screams, the smells—none of it was real.

"No more," she said as she walked down the steps toward the creatures that now huddled close and stood unnaturally still. She ignored the sounds of wood cracking in the heat and focused on the sound of the bells. "Go away."

Mouse's hands clenched at her skirts as she let the angry, squirming power build in her throat. "I said to go away!"

The children laughed and suddenly the clang of bells stopped.

"Will you come and play?" they asked as they held out their hands.

Mouse turned slightly at the sound of footsteps behind her. Someone had come out of the church.

"The King is asking for you. Will you come inside?"

Mouse took a step in front of Father Lucas as he came to stand beside her.

"I will be there soon. Will you go tell him for me?" She wanted him back in the church. One of the hollow-eyed children reached its hand toward Father Lucas.

"Is there trouble, andílek?"

"Be careful, Father!" She pulled him out of the thing's reach. "These are not children as they seem. They are—" But Mouse did not know what to call them.

"I know. These are the things that haunted you as a child, yes?"

She nodded.

"But these are not the lost souls of the unbaptized, Mouse."

"What are they, then?"

"Corruptors." Mouse shivered at the chill in his voice. She wanted to ask him what he meant, but it would have to wait. The hollow-eyed children had started to sidle closer, bit by bit.

"I tried to command them to leave, but they did not obey. I can try again—"

"No!"

Mouse jumped at the sharp order.

"I do not think that will make a difference," he said, softer this time, but Mouse could hear the fear in his voice. "Step back slowly. We will be better able to protect the people when we are inside the church."

The creatures followed them step for step like shadows. Mouse made Father Lucas slip through the open door at the church first, and she slammed it shut as she crossed the threshold.

"I do not think doors will stop those things," Father Lucas said.

"We could shape protections but we have no salt."

Father Lucas nodded.

Screams came from the nave. Mouse listened closely, isolating the chaos of noise with her unnatural senses.

"They see the crucifix bleeding," she explained to Father Lucas. "Those creatures can make you see anything, believe anything. Father, if we do not do something, these people will suffer. Someone will get hurt."

"We can use blood to make the charms, Mouse. The salt is only a channel; it is the blood that holds the power," he said as they stepped back into the vestibule.

"That is a lot of blood, Father."

"We have no choice. I will move along the side aisle to the left and up to the choir. You start here and take the right aisle.

I will cover the north transept and you, Ludmila's Chapel. Our blood will form the cross."

Without hesitation, Mouse took the knife tied at her waist and sliced into her hand. But when she laid the blade against Father Lucas's outstretched arm, she could not cut.

"Let me do it alone, Father. It is my fault those things are here. It is my responsibility to—"

He put his hand over hers and pushed the knife into his flesh.

They parted, each walking slowly along the outer aisles leaving a trail of blood, each murmuring the protections as they went. They kept their backs against the wall, hiding their bloody palms as they slipped past the people in the nave, who bowed as the bishop began the prayers for the dead.

"'Out of the depths have I cried unto Thee, O Lord: Lord, hear my voice,'" came the whispers of the faithful in response. They shuffled and shifted, spreading out as they could to make room to kneel.

As Mouse stepped up into Ludmila's Chapel, she searched the crowd until she saw Ottakar's crown flickering in the dim candlelight, and she sighed with relief. At the back corner of the chapel where no one could see, she opened a gash on her other palm, the first already beginning to knit closed. She waited until her hand filled with blood before she began tracing the wall again. As she reached the end of her side of the cross, a wave of dizziness overcame her, and she leaned against the wall near the steps leading up to the choir, letting herself slide down to her knees. She bent her head.

"'My soul waiteth on His word: my soul hopeth in the Lord,'" she mumbled with the others.

A cool breeze touched her face. She opened her eyes and saw the mouth of the crypt. They had forgotten the crypt.

Mouse started to crawl toward the steps when Father Lucas fell heavily to his knees beside her. His eyes were closed, his face too white. He had lost too much blood, and he sagged against her, driving her into the wall. She tried to catch him, but he was too heavy. The bishop stopped praying, and everyone was looking at her.

Then Ottakar was at her side. "Let us move him to the crypt for the cooler air," he said, slipping his arm under Father Lucas's shoulder and looking up to Bishop Miklaus. "Your Excellency, the people seemed disquieted. They are in need of your guidance."

The bishop bowed, taking up the prayer again as Ottakar and Mouse guided Father Lucas down the lower steps into the crypt. Mouse looked up, the gold in the ceiling mural drawing her eye as the candlelight wavered with the bishop's swaying; the painting showed John's vision of the Heavenly Jerusalem, streets of gold, a city made of glass. From Mouse's view, it looked like the city hung there, held by the artist's thin strokes, waiting to come shattering down on them.

After settling Father Lucas on a bench, Mouse knelt beside him. He rested his head against the column at his back, his eyes closed; she slipped her hand inside the hem of his habit, ripping away a piece of the linen tunic underneath. She tried to shield the blood-soaked sleeve from Ottakar's view as she wrapped the cut, but he saw and grabbed at Father Lucas's arm.

"He is bleeding."

"It is not what you think, Ottakar. Stop." She put her hands on his without thinking and then pulled them away with a sticky smack.

"And you, Mouse?" He held her hands, bloody palms up. "What is this?"

"Let me tend him first, then I will tell you what I can."

He nodded and let her hands go. He walked up the steps a little, motioning to someone in the nave. "Fetch some bread and wine," he ordered.

"No!" Mouse said. "No one can leave the church. It is not safe."

"Why not?" Ottakar asked angrily.

Father Lucas moaned.

"Please, Ottakar, just trust me," she said.

"They have already brought some of the food for the feast tomorrow, have they not?" the King asked the servant, who crouched at the top step, the praying masses at his back.

"Yes, my Lord. It is in the north transept."

Ottakar turned to look at Mouse. She nodded.

Folding his arms across his chest, he paced the dark edges of the crypt until the man returned with bread and a cup of wine. While Mouse tied off the makeshift bandage, the King tore small pieces of wine-soaked bread and fed them to Father Lucas. Despite the crown and jeweled mantle, nothing about him seemed stiff or regal. Mouse kept her head bent where she could watch him unseen. His face was soft, kind, his voice gentle as he encouraged the old man to eat.

As she lifted her face, she realized that she had also been watched unaware. A look of sadness flitted across Father Lucas's eyes before he could mask it.

"You must finish, andílek," he said.

She nodded as Ottakar turned to look at her, too.

"What does he mean?"

Mouse opened her mouth, but it was Father Lucas who gave the answer. "Evil spirits are among us, my Lord," he said weakly. "This night it is easy for them to torment the living, and they seem particularly bent to vengeance on people in this church."

"How?"

"They play on the minds of your people, make them see things, hear things that are not true."

"The bleeding crucifix?"

"Yes, my Lord."

Ottakar crossed himself. "Is it a tainted soul seeking revenge on someone?" Mouse saw the anguish pull at his face. Ottakar almost sounded like a child needing reassurance—a child sure his damned mother had come back for revenge. Mouse laid her hand on his arm, wanting to offer comfort, to tell him it was not his dead mother harrowing his people, but he did not know she knew about the Queen's suicide.

And Father Lucas was too quick.

"Yes, my Lord," he said, lying in order to feed the King's misunderstanding. "We must pray for the dead, my Lord, pray to ease their suffering, but we must shield ourselves from their wrath. We were using the *vade retro satana* like St. Procopius himself to protect those inside the church." Father Lucas closed his eyes again as he gave the lie; the spells he and Mouse used were not sanctioned by Rome.

"But why the blood?"

"It strengthens the exorcism," Mouse said, fumbling for her knife and holding to Father Lucas's lie. "A shedding of life to preserve life."

"Like a beast at the altar," Ottakar said.

She nodded. "We covered the perimeter of the church but not the crypt."

"Finish," Father Lucas said again. He sounded strange. Mouse looked first to his face and then followed the line of his sight. He was staring at a statue of Mary nestled into one of the alcoves along the crypt walls. She was flanked by angels about to crown her. Mouse could see nothing unusual about it, but when she turned back to Father Lucas, she felt his terror.

And then she saw the shadows move, slowly stretching toward them.

"Stay in the light," she said to Ottakar as she pulled her knife across her hand.

"No!" He grabbed for the knife too late but held her by the wrist.

"The worst is done, Ottakar, now let me finish."

He pushed her hand away and spun toward Father Lucas as Mouse moved quickly to the edge of the light, trailing blood.

"You let her do this? You taught her to mutilate herself? This is your purview, Father, your vocation. Not hers! She is just a girl," Ottakar hissed.

"You are right, of course, my Lord, but we both know that she is not just a girl." Father Lucas closed his eyes again until Mouse sat down heavily beside him. He looked warily toward the statue again and, smiling, laid his head back. "I think I will rest a little now."

Mouse pressed her thumb into her cut palm to stop the flow of blood.

"You are pale. Drink." Ottakar held the cup of wine to her lips. Mouse drank.

Then he held out his hand. She took it. He led them to a bench on the other side of the crypt, grimacing at the barrier of her blood behind them as they sat.

"You will not do that again, Mouse."

She stiffened at the sound of command; this was her king and not Ottakar talking. "Would you order your men thus, my Lord? To preserve themselves at all costs even if there are others in jeopardy? I do not think so."

"You are not a soldier," he said more gently.

"I can be."

He turned her hands over. Mouse was glad of the thickening blood to hide the nearly healed gash. "Yes, I see that." He kissed the underside of her wrists. "But I do not want to see you . . . I do not like to see you do harm to yourself." Only when she saw his jaw tighten did Mouse remember how the queen had killed herself. Mouse turned her hands over quickly and laid her head against his shoulder.

"Will you pray with me, Mouse? For our mothers. Yours . . . and mine."

Mouse nodded, and they slid to their knees on the cold stone floor of the crypt, hands entwined, heads bowed, both whispering the first of the vespers for the dead. They faltered at the third verse when they heard the screams bounce along the castle walls and sift down into the crypt. The hollow-eyed children had found others beyond the protected church to torment. There was nothing Mouse could do for them. Not tonight.

"'The sorrows compassed me, and the pains of Hell gat hold upon me,'" Father Lucas joined in, steady and calm.

"'I found trouble and sorrow,'" they all said together. "'Then I called upon the name of the Lord; O Lord, I beseech Thee, deliver my soul.'"

Mouse mouthed the last words but could not give them voice.

They prayed through the night. At the sounds of the people stirring in the nave and the first signs of light softly glowing against St. George's rafters, Mouse and Ottakar and Father Lucas pushed themselves up stiffly. Father Lucas steadied himself with a hand on the bench.

"'On those living in the shadow of death a light has dawned,'" he quoted as he walked up into the nave.

After Mass, as the others crowded around tables set with food, Ottakar quietly led Mouse out into the courtyard and through the gate at the Black Tower. He did not speak. He did not need to, and Mouse wouldn't either, although when he stopped abruptly in the middle of the Judith Bridge, the morning mists of the Vltava crawling over their feet, she almost spoke, wanting to wipe the horror from his face.

She was sure he was remembering; she could see the scene in her mind—him, at fifteen, struggling with the weight of his mother's body in his arms, nose flared at the smell of death, grief and despair at her lost soul tearing at him. Mouse wondered if he had also paused here that day, thinking of tossing the body over the bridge, letting the water take his mother like Mouse had tempted the Teplá to do for her. But she did not speak; she waited until he was ready, and then they crossed over the river and silently through the streets of town.

He knocked at the door of the convent but did not ask admittance when it was opened. The nun simply stood aside. Mouse could see the family resemblance in the woman's square jaw and high forehead. This was Ottakar's aunt, Mother Agnes.

But Ottakar made no introductions. He gripped Mouse's hand as they wove through a hallway and into a darkened room. He left her a moment and came back with a candle. Its light deepened the circles under his eyes. He walked past her toward the back of the room.

It was a plain room. No furnishings, no tapestries, no statues. Just windowless, cold stone.

Mouse stood quietly at the doorway until the candlelight on the wall shook with his weeping. When she put her hand on his back, he dropped to his knees like she'd cut some invisible string. She took the candle from him and sat it on the floor as she knelt beside him. She saw the marker then, flat and thin, not even a name, just an etched flower carved into the stone. She traced her finger along the curves of its petals; it was a bellflower like the ones that, in spring, covered the meadows purplish blue. She understood; this was where the Queen had been buried.

"No." Ottakar pulled Mouse's hand away. "None here would mourn her."

"I will."

"It is not right. She did it to herself. My mother. With my father's hunting knife, I am told." He ran his palm along his bearded jaw and would not look at Mouse. "She did it in the room we stayed in as children until they took us away to school. Not Vlad, of course—my father wanted my brother close. But my sisters and I were groomed as pawns he could sacrifice as he wished." Bitterness laced Ottakar's words, but then he sighed and his voice softened. "When we were young, though—what fun we had. Mother loved to dance and to draw. She spent as much of her day with us as she could. She read us the German stories of knights and their honor, and we played out their adventures. She made a fearsome dragon for my brother and me to battle as we saved our sisters." He looked down at Mouse with a half smile that turned into a grimace. "She did it, right there where we wrestled and laughed as she tickled us."

He bent over, his hands dug into his hair, pulling at the crown. "She killed herself as my army stormed the city and my father fled for his life. It was her last reprimand for me, her worst. She wanted me to know how ashamed she was of me." His voice broke.

Mouse laid her hand on his head and waited for his weeping to ease before she said, "I wonder if your mother chose that place for a different reason."

"What do you mean?" He sat up, looking at her.

"It was a place of joy for her, you said."

"What does that matter?"

"It tells us something about her mind at the time she died. She wanted to be somewhere that reminded her of happier times. She could leave this world with the images of her children playing in her mind and the echoes of their laughter ringing in her ears. I do not think this sounds like someone who was angry with her son. I think it sounds like someone who was very sad and was trying to run away from more sadness to come."

"Yes, sadness I brought to her by betraying my father."

"Why did you?"

"What?"

"Turn against him?"

"You have not met my father," he said quietly. After a moment, he stretched his hand out to trace his mother's flower as Mouse had done.

"Ottakar, if your mother sided with your father, why would she not have gone with him when he fled?"

He turned to look at her. "I had not considered that. The siege was chaos. Perhaps he could not reach her, but surely his guard would have—"

Mouse could see the doubt growing in his eyes; she had more questions as she tried to piece together what might have happened. "Was your mother distraught after your brother's death?"

"Of course she was. Her heart broke. My father's, too. But she could find no relief from her sorrow. Her women forced her to eat, forced her from the bed where she would lay, soiling herself, no will to move until they made her. They took away the knives after she cut away her hair. It was growing back white and soft as a lamb's." He stretched out his hand as if he were touching it.

"Her mind was twisted with grief?"

He nodded.

"The Church makes allowances for people disturbed of mind. Even the Talmud distinguishes between those who are sane and not. If you press the bishop for an inquest, your mother can have her burial rites. We can offer suffrages to ease her pain through purgatory. She can be saved, Ottakar."

Mouse saw the hope in his eyes and kept the rest of her speculations to herself. If his mother was in such jeopardy of mind, how had she gotten her husband's hunting knife, and what had urged her to action after a year's absence of self-will? Someone else's will was at work, and Mouse thought she knew whose.

"God has sent you to me," Ottakar whispered, pulling her from her own thoughts as he lowered his mouth to hers.

Mouse felt like she was floating in the warm Teplá River; it was taking her to her future just as she had asked.

FOURTEEN

The streets were hushed and somber, the people dark-eyed and wary, as Mouse and Ottakar made their way back to the castle. The smell of fresh rolls led them to Celetna Lane, where they stopped at one of the bakeries.

"A bad All Hallows', my Lord, was it not? Bodes ill for the coming winter, do you think?" the baker asked as he handed the King a roll.

"Every All Saints, I hear tell of the long Eve before, haunts and strange happenings. Why was last night any worse than others?" Ottakar's voice was bold and comforting, but Mouse could hear the fear behind it.

"You speak true, my Lord, but it is not every All Hallows' that a man cooks himself in his own oven."

"What do you mean?" Mouse asked.

"Was old Delf, it was. His wife—now widow, I guess—heard him crying out for his boy, crying like his heart would break. She run out to the kitchen in time to see him crawling into the fire like he was grabbing at something. He turned when she

142

screamed for him. 'O wife, it is our boy, our poor boy. Someone's done pitched him in and stoked the flame,' he told her. And then the fire took to his hair and clothes and she could not get the water fast enough."

"What of the boy?" Ottakar asked.

"My Lord, his boy done died years back with the fever. But if that be not strange enough, his wife says she saw something moving in the fire, and old Delf was right, too. Someone had stoked it up fresh and hot 'cause the wife and he had it cooled to embers for the night."

They walked in silence the rest of the way to the castle—Ottakar tearing at the bread absently, Mouse unable to eat. The King took his leave of her just as they entered the gate; he was anxious to meet with the bishop to talk about his mother. Mouse's thoughts had already turned to the coming night. How many more would suffer or die as the hollow-eyed children played their games? Mouse might appease them, offer herself in exchange for leaving everyone else alone, but she only knew spells to keep them at bay, not to draw them in. And so, instead of sleeping, Mouse read.

Father Lucas had told her that the stories in the book he had given her, *The Book of Enoch*, were less important than what he hoped she would find—an encoded key to decipher the book Mouse had taken from the abbey. But she found herself fascinated by Enoch's tale of the angels—the Watchers, he called them—who wanted lives like men; they wanted children and so they left Heaven to beget them. Enoch called the children giants; God called them evil spirits. There were no illuminations in the manuscript, only text, so Mouse imagined for herself what the children of the angels might look like. The only visage she could picture was pasty, waxlike, and hollow-eyed like the dark creatures. Maybe they were the children of the Watchers.

Enoch wrote about binding them all in deep pits so they could not corrupt the lives of men. That meant it could be done, if Mouse found a way to bind them.

She pressed the heels of her hands against her eyes. The sun was stretching to the far side of the room, the day passing. Fighting a growing desperation, Mouse grabbed both books and headed to the Queen's garden. She wanted the sun on her back and fresh air to help clear her mind.

She sat on the ground near the fountain with the books spread out in front of her. As interesting as Enoch's story about the Watchers had been, he had also written visions and histories. He spoke of secrets, which the Watchers had given to men, hidden knowledge about plants and charms and the way the heavens worked.

Mouse felt the pricking of something at the back of her mind.

The other book contained images of plants and the heavens and detailed drawings of circles in differing patterns. What if they were descriptions of charms? What if the language of that other book, unknown to man, was the language of the angels?

Mouse ran her hand lightly over the opened pages of the mysterious book. Could this be the book of the Watchers?

She shook away the questions as she remembered her task at hand—finding a way to protect the people of Prague against the torments of those dark creatures. Regardless of whose children they were, Mouse knew they were here because of her. She turned back to Enoch with a renewed focus on finding the key. There would be time later to unlock the book's other secrets.

Mouse had decrypted several texts for Father Lucas over the years, mostly letters hiding information about apocryphal writings he wished to acquire without the scrutiny of the Church. All the codes she'd encountered were based on mathematic formulas. The formula should be in Enoch's book since that was the key.

She spun around onto her stomach and tore at the dying grass until she had a clear patch of dirt. She broke off a branch of lavender, stripping its leaves and spilling the soft scent into the air. Her hand shook a little as she began to write in the dirt, remembering her drawing that resurrected the squirrel, but she pushed the image away, emptying her mind to let it race through Enoch's words, thumbing the pages as she looked for the numbers: *Six portals, twelve windows, thirty mornings, ten parts day to eight parts night, seven great islands.* She played with the figures in the dirt, first one way and then swiping her hand across the soil to try them all again another way. Was movement west, toward the setting sun, a subtraction or an adding of days as we neared our death? Her mind ran through the possibilities until the equation lay there, stark and absolute, scribbled in the earth.

She pulled the unreadable book to her and began looking for patterns that fit the formula, looking in the leaves of the plants, in the number of roots crawling along the bottoms of the pages. She found her first code in a flower that looked like a mountain upturned, blue and green and white petals circling out around its open mouth, red flowing down its sides broken by tongues of white.

The pattern of them mirrored the mathematical equation.

Her heart pounding against her chest, Mouse looked to the words scribbled above and around the flower, letting her eyes lose focus so her mind could see through the lens of the formula. The first word started to take shape as the pattern of letters was revealed.

Mouse rubbed at her eyes. The letters would not stay still on the page; they swirled and darkened.

"Have you found something, then?"

Mouse sat up quickly, surprised that she'd not heard him coming.

"Yes, Father," she said breathlessly. "I think I have found the key, but it will still take time to decipher the text." She looked up to the sky where the bright stars and moon glowed against a deepening blue. "But we have no more time," she said, pulling the book nearly to her nose as she tried again to decode the first word.

And then she had it. A name—one of the Watchers Enoch had listed.

Suddenly the letters ran together like wet ink on the page. By the time Mouse understood what new image they shaped, it was too late. Thousands of spiders poured out of the text, crawling up her arms and face. She dropped the book, screaming, but still they came. Down the neck of her tunic. Under her veil. She clawed at her hair, hands coming away covered in the black things. As they sank their teeth into her, their bodies liquefied and seeped under her skin, running dark along her veins.

"Let her be!" Father Lucas cried out as he kicked the book closed and knelt beside her, sweeping the spiders off. But she was rolling and beating at her body, trying to stop the searing pain of the ones under her clothes biting her.

Father Lucas slid his arms around Mouse. "Be still, child. Let me take you." He lifted her up and into the water of the fountain, her skirts billowing around her. He cupped the water in his hands and poured it over her head. As soon as it touched the spiders, they dissolved. He did it again and again until the fountain ran inky black.

Mouse crouched on her hands and knees in the water, heaving.

"Mouse?" Ottakar called out as he rounded the last corner of the hedge maze, running. He had heard her scream. "What have you done?" he spat at Father Lucas as he shoved him aside to get to Mouse. She whimpered as he gathered her in his arms, black rivulets rolling from her hair down her face.

"She was attacked by something, my Lord. Some kind of insect, it seemed." Father Lucas laid a shaking hand on Mouse's forehead, wiping away the watery remains of the spiders.

"Show me!" Ottakar demanded.

"They have all gone. Disappeared, my Lord," he said as he gathered the books.

"Semjaza," Mouse whispered.

"What is this she says?"

"I do not know, my Lord," Father Lucas lied. He, too, had read the *Book of Enoch* many times since he purchased it from the man in Tunis, and he knew the names of Enoch's Watchers. Semjaza had been a leader among the rebel angels; he had taught men secret enchantments and plant lore.

Mouse's teeth chattered as tremors shook her and her head fell against Ottakar's neck.

"She is burning with fever!"

Night had fallen by the time they had her dry and covered in her bed. She lay shivering, her eyes closed, silent except for quiet moans as aches coursed through her body.

Father Lucas grew more worried the longer she lay there. He had never seen Mouse sick and he knew how her body healed itself, but clearly her power would not work against the spiders' poison.

"You must fetch someone to bleed her, to draw out the venom," he said hoarsely to the King as Mouse arched in pain. "Please, my Lord. She worsens."

Ottakar left and came back minutes later with the court physician. After examining Mouse, he looked gravely at the King. "I will do what I can, my Lord, but her fever is very high and her heart runs too fast."

He slipped his hand into a jar he had carried with him and pulled out a long, slimy leech, which he laid against Mouse's wrist. It began slowly undulating as it sucked her blood. He affixed another dozen on her arms and neck.

"By the saints," he gasped as he looked back at the leech on her wrist; it lay blackened and curled like a dead worm. One by one, the others shriveled and died as they ingested Mouse's tainted blood.

Her breathing came shallow and fast.

"Try something else!" Ottakar commanded.

"I can fetch a barber-surgeon, my Lord, to let her blood," the man stammered.

"There is no time. I will do it," Father Lucas said. "Bring a knife."

"But Father, the Church will not allow you to do such a thing anymore than I can," the physician argued.

"And I will not allow this girl to die." Father Lucas held his hand out, waiting for the knife.

Ottakar took out his own knife, dousing it with the wine they had tried to get Mouse to drink earlier. "She did it before she cut me," he explained, handing the blade to Father Lucas.

Ottakar held her arm while Father Lucas drove the blade into the vein in the crook of her elbow. A gush of black spewed forth.

"God save us! What manner of illness is this?" the physician exclaimed.

"Get out," Ottakar said. "And if you speak of this to anyone, you will no longer have a tongue to speak at all."

"Yes, my Lord," the man muttered as he backed his way to the door.

Father Lucas cut the other arm and Gitta placed a bowl to catch the inky fluid. Ottakar watched Mouse's face go from flushed to pale. "Enough," he ordered.

"No, my Lord, not until her blood runs fully red again," Father Lucas said.

"The bowls are nearly full and she is such a little thing. You will drain her dead."

"She is stronger than you may realize, my Lord, and we must get all the poison out."

Ottakar's arm shot out, grabbing the Father's shoulder. "What do you know of this?" He nodded to the black that now mixed with red as it oozed from Mouse's arms. "More of your evil spirits?"

As if he had been heard, the first screams of the night rang out through the castle bailey.

"The evil came when you came, Father," Ottakar said coldly.

"No." Mouse stirred, trying to push herself up. "This is all my fault," she whispered.

"Lie still, little andílek, while I wrap your arms." Father Lucas took rolls of linen from Gitta and pressed them into Mouse's elbows.

"How is this your fault?" Ottakar asked her as he bent to kiss her on the head.

"I—"

"The scripture tells us that evil is the consequence of all men's sin. It is no one's fault," Father Lucas interjected.

The high screams of a panicked child pierced the quiet, and Mouse turned to Father Lucas. "We must do something, Father." She started to roll to the edge of the bed, but Ottakar pushed her gently back.

"No, Mouse."

"I will go and do what I can, child," Father Lucas said. "You must rest."

"The books?" she asked.

"I do not think you—"

"You know I must."

With a sigh Father Lucas took them from his bag and laid them on the foot of the bed. "Not now, though. Rest. There will be time later."

Mouse started to argue that there was no more time—night was here, the screams already begun, and some child might drown himself or some mother jump to her death because of the tricks of those dark creatures—but she could not move without her muscles spasming and her head spinning. She could tell from the look on Ottakar's face that he meant to keep her there.

As Father Lucas closed the door behind him, fresh cries floated up from outside the castle. Mouse regretted letting him go.

"Will you stay with me?" she asked Ottakar, slipping her hand in his.

"I do not think—"

"Gitta will be with us."

He nodded and then sat on the bed beside her. They both startled at more screams, from inside the castle this time.

"Talk to me," she said, wrapping her arm around his and laying her head against his shoulder. He was safe here with her.

After telling her about his meeting with the bishop—His Excellency's willingness to order an inquest and his assurances that the Queen would be allowed full burial rites—Ottakar talked about his plans to build a church at Mother Agnes's convent. His head was full of ways he could ease his mother through purgatory.

"When Bohemia is mine alone to govern, Mouse, I will build cities for the people. And grand churches. And schools. I will make laws to shield the weaker from the power of the nobility. I will honor my mother thus." His voice sounded dreamlike as fatigue finally took him.

"It will be a golden time for Bohemia, and you, its Golden King," Mouse said, listening to his breath grow deep and steady in sleep.

But as tired as she was, she wouldn't let herself sleep, easing down instead to the foot of the bed.

Her hands shook as she opened the cover of the book, waiting for it to once again defend its secrets. She flipped to the section she'd been reading in the garden and found another image that fit the pattern, an image of intricate medallions whose spokes pointed to strings of letters in the unknown language. Using the formula, she pulled words from the text carefully, watching the letters for any sign of malice, but they stayed still and on the page. Perhaps the protective spell she'd cast in the room, the blood and salt cross that shielded her from the dark things, also inhibited the power in the book. Or maybe the spiders had been the book's only defense besides its encryption. A defense meant to kill made any other defenses unnecessary, and the spiders' venom would surely have killed a normal person.

Mouse read through the night—at least some of the book's secrets now open to her. Near dawn, she curled up beside Ottakar again and let silent tears roll into the sleeve of his tunic. She knew now what she needed to do.

Tomorrow she would leave him.

FIFTEEN

Ottakar kissed her as he left in the morning and told her to stay in bed. She waited until she could no longer hear his steps in the hall. She groaned as she stood, her body taut and sore from the fever.

"Gitta, can you help me dress?" she said as she held the bedpost waiting for her legs to steady. "The blue one—you mended it, yes?"

"I did, my Lady, but then I gave it to Lady Moravec's girl. Never thought you might want it again after what happened in the woods. Besides, this green draws out your eyes. Though pale as you are, the red would be better."

"I need something sturdier, plainer. Something for travel."

"Are we going somewhere, my Lady?"

"Not we. Me."

"But—"

"Please, Gitta. No more questions. Just get me a dress I can wear."

By the time Gitta came back, Mouse had braided her hair and packed the books and her small satchel of medical tools in her bag.

"Lady Harrach's riding dress," Gitta explained as she tossed the clothes on the bed. "Says she doubts to ever fit in it again, and I daresay I agree, broad as she got with the baby. But worth it, he is, with those lovely cheeks!"

Mouse was out the door as soon as the last lace was tied. The guard, who attached himself to her at the gate, watched her warily as she walked slowly down the path to Strahov, her arms wrapped tightly across her chest as she trembled with the remains of the fever. She felt sure Father Lucas would be at the monastery.

The monk who opened the door was not happy to see her. "Lady Emma," he said, letting his aggravation seep into his voice, "I have told you that you are not permitted here. Nothing has changed. Nothing will change. Go away."

She put her hand on the door as he was closing it. "I do not want in. I want Father Lucas to come out."

"He is down at town, my Lady."

She found him leaning against the wall near the moat.

"Father," she said as she gently shook him. She saw his bloody palms and an empty bag on the stone beside him with a small trail of salt trickling out of its mouth, and she knew how he had spent his night.

"Get a roll of bread, please." She handed her guard a coin. "Go on. Surely I will be safe here with the Father."

"We will need help tonight, Mouse," the Father said as soon as they were alone. "We must think of something to tell the bishop so he will order the people into the churches. We can go from place to place today to—"

Mouse shook her head. "I found something in the book. A binding spell, I think."

"You can read it now?"

"Not all of it. I think there are different codes in Enoch that must be worked against different sections of the book. I only

153

had time to decipher one piece, the Semjaza section, but it spoke of tethers crafted by enchantments, chains to bind, and instructions for what seemed to be spells."

"What do you need?"

"Simple tools, really. Gathered stones of blue and green, a mother's milk, roots of what the book calls the Breath of Life, but it sounds like angelica to me, the juice from another plant, I think it is chicory, and blood." She sighed at the last. "Always blood." She ran her finger along Father Lucas's palm and turned at the sound of the guard returning. "You can go back to the castle. Father Lucas will see after me," she said as she took the roll.

The guard waited a moment and then reluctantly headed back over the bridge.

"So you can bind them but to what, andílek?" Father Lucas asked between bites.

Mouse shrugged as she swallowed her own bite of bread. "Me, I guess."

"No." He shook his head sharply.

"What choice is there? Enoch's descriptions of the pits of fire and darkness, where God meant the evil spirits to be cast, are shrouded in vision. They seem to me more story than not, and anyway, I do not think the angel Uriel likely to come show me the way. But if I can make the dark creatures come to me, then I can lead them away, take them somewhere with no people to taunt and torture."

"And what of you?"

Mouse looked off toward the castle. "If I know he is safe, it will be enough." She turned back to Father Lucas. "It is my fault anyway. I drew them here."

"But they will be bound to you, Mouse. You will not be able to protect yourself from them. They will torture your mind until it breaks." He grabbed her arm, fear for her thick in his voice.

"Maybe this is my purpose, Father; maybe God made me this way so that I have the power to siphon off some part of the evil in the world and keep men free of it." Water slapped against the moat's stone wall like listless clapping.

"We will gather what you need and then we will leave." His words were firm, determined like a battle call, and his eyes shined with fervor as he leaned close to her. "But we will not bind them to you. There is a pit, Mouse, just like in Enoch's story." A smile pulled taut across his face. "And I know where it is."

They went different ways—Mouse to collect what they needed for the spell and Father Lucas to get horses and a few supplies for the trip. It took most of the morning to find the stones and plants, but the milk came easily enough when she asked Lady Harrach for a jar of breast milk to make a tincture for someone ill. Mouse carefully nestled the jar, covered with hide, into her bag.

Then she went to find Ottakar. When she thought she had no hope of returning, Mouse had meant to slip away with no good-byes, but now, there was at least a chance she might come back—if there was a pit as Father Lucas said, if it was actually a binding spell she'd found in the book, and if nothing went wrong.

Ottakar was watching his men at swordplay in the south bailey, the midday sun fading as a biting wind pushed heavy clouds in from the southwest.

"I thought I told you to stay in bed today," he said, smiling as he took her hand, kissed it and kept it in his own. "I am beginning to think I should have ordered my men to do the same. They are sluggish."

"It was a bad night for everyone, my Lord," Mouse said.

He cut his eyes toward her, no longer smiling. "I suppose it will be again."

"I want to talk to you about that. Will you walk with me?" She pulled him up and led him toward the gates of the South Tower.

"Where shall we go? It looks like a storm is coming so we ought to stay close." Their mantles billowed and snapped in the wind.

"Into the woods a little, then?"

He nodded and then waved off the guards who tried to follow them as they left the castle. As soon as they had cleared the first line of trees, he pulled her to him. "I want to kiss you, Mouse. A real kiss."

She gave a soft nod, not trusting herself to speak, and as his mouth closed on hers, as she felt his arms slide around her, heard his heart beating fast with hers, she thought she was as surely bound to him now as any spell might do. Even as she laid a hand on his chest to ease him back so she could tell him good-bye, she swore to herself and God that she would come back to him.

"I need to tell you something, Ottakar," she said as he pulled his head back slightly, his breath still on her cheek. "I have to go away for a while."

"What?" He took a half step back, his hands on her shoulders.

"Not for long. Days, maybe a few weeks."

"Why?" Mouse knew by the way he asked that he already suspected the answer.

"We, Father Lucas and I, we think we can—" she stammered.

"No."

"Let me finish, Ottakar." She wanted to talk to the man, not the king. "We can drive out the evil that has come to Prague."

"Good. Let the Father do it. It is his work to do, not yours."

"It is mine also."

"You are just a—" He stopped short, remembering the Father's rebuke. "What will you do that the Father cannot do alone? Let him bleed, Mouse, not you." He pulled her against him again. "I want you here with me. I need you." His face rested against the top of her head as he breathed her in. "I am afraid I will lose myself here, Mouse—become what they want me to be. But you—I cannot say it well—you make me feel like my *real* self or at least who I want to be, and if you leave—"

"I will come back to you, Ottakar. I promise. But Father Lucas cannot do this alone. I must go with him."

A rumble of thunder broke across the hills and wind shook the trees. "Come back to the castle. The storm is here." Ottakar grabbed her hand as they wove through the trees toward the tower.

The rain broke just as they reached the gate, and they stood trapped under the stone archway. Mouse could see Father Lucas leading two horses across the muddy courtyard. Ottakar saw him, too.

"No, Mouse. I do not allow it."

"I have no choice, Ottakar. I must—" At first, she thought the sound she heard was another peal of thunder, but as it grew nearer she caught the gaited rhythms. "Horses," she said. "Someone is coming."

Ottakar spun looking up to the archers on the wall. "You, Konrad, do you see horses?"

"None, my Lord. But it is hard to see in this rain."

Ottakar turned to Mouse. "Can you tell from which direction they come?"

"With the storm. From the south."

"Look south, Konrad. Look hard."

"I see them, my Lord!"

"Shut the gate!" a guard called out.

"No, wait! I see a banner," Konrad said. "It is the eagle, my Lord! It is King Vaclav come home!"

Ottakar changed in an instant; his body grew rigid, his face stony, as if he had slipped into some kind of invisible armor.

"What is wrong?" Mouse laid her hand against his back, but she could not reach him. He stared blankly toward the gate until the first of the horses thundered through it. They bore the King's banners, which were dripping with rainwater. As more horses streamed through the gate, Mouse and Ottakar were pushed back against the wall. Then King Vaclav rode in, his charger flinging water and froth as it stamped and reared.

Mouse saw the King in profile—very much like Ottakar, sharp jaw, high forehead, deep-set eyes, though his eyes were dark where Ottakar's were the color of the wild hyacinths that grew in the fields behind the abbey.

"Welcome home, Father," Ottakar said. "I am pleased to see you recovered."

Vaclav turned to look down at his son, and all similarity melted away for Mouse. A long scar ran down the left side of his face and through the socket where his eye should have been, though it wasn't the disfigurement that startled her. The pull of his mouth into a thin line and the cold, dead stare he settled on Ottakar made her catch her breath. There was something not right about the man.

And then he turned his eye on her, and she felt the coldness of him pierce her.

"Father, may I introduce you to my ward, Lady Emma, lately of Teplá Abbey. Lady Emma, my father, King Vaclav."

"My Lord," she said, bowing.

"Lady Emma." His voice was smooth like metal. And then he was done with her. "I am glad you are still at Prague. Your men, too?" he asked Ottakar.

"Yes."

"Good. Well, let us get out of this cursed rain. I want a fire and warm ale and a fleshy pair of legs wrapped around me." His eyes flicked to Mouse again, but she looked down quickly. Then he stormed off into the sheets of rain toward the keep.

Ottakar turned to follow, but Mouse caught his arm and nodded toward where Father Lucas was waiting just beyond the archway.

"The horses are ready. I must go," she whispered.

"Ottakar!" King Vaclav called.

"As must I." Ottakar looked down at her. "I do not wish you to go, but I will make no demands of you."

Mouse felt shredded under his gaze as Father Lucas looked on, but she had no choice. "I must go, Ottakar. I will come back as soon as I can."

His eyes flashed with temper, but all he said was, "Be well, then." And he turned his back to her and followed his father.

∞

Mouse's horse followed Father Lucas's without direction from her, cantering when his horse did, slowing to a walk when it was sure it wouldn't be left behind. Mouse held the reins loosely and kept her head down, the rain stinging first and then running in a slow curtain down her face. Her mind was on Ottakar and the finality of his good-bye.

The heavy clouds and steady rain shrouded the sun and made it impossible to tell the time of day, but something in Mouse sensed the closing sunset. She couldn't decide if it was a growing dread or a sense of thrill that made her urge her horse to go faster.

"How much farther?" she asked.

"There," Father Lucas said as he pointed toward some gentle hills.

"This is nowhere." Mouse could see no signs of home or village, no rivers or ponds, just wildness all around. As they moved down the rise, the woods grew up before them, tall and old, but unlike most old forests, this one was thick with underbrush and bracken, until finally they were forced to stop.

"We must walk from here," Father Lucas said as he dismounted. He tethered the horses while Mouse slid down and untied the goat strapped to the back of Father Lucas's horse. It bleated softly to her as she lowered it to the ground.

"I am not your friend," she said to it as she draped the satchels carrying their supplies over her shoulder and began pushing her way into the dense elderberry, heedless of the branches that tore at her clothes and face. Mouse did not need Father Lucas to guide her now; she could feel the place, like a magnet drawn north.

Father Lucas hoisted the goat onto his shoulders and followed her. It was slow going. They had to stop and find ways around the carcasses of huge fallen oak and linden trees. The tangle of vines and ferns tripped them as it grew so dark deeper into the woods that they could not see. Father Lucas kept his eyes on Mouse as she let herself be reeled in by what was waiting for them.

She felt the night push down the last of the sunlight. But as she tried to quicken her step, she heard the dry rustle of dead branches in the dark to her right. She took a step toward Father Lucas then froze as a massive bear broke free of the shadows. Mouse crouched, preparing for an attack, but despite the deep growl rolling in its throat, the bear kept its head lowered submissively.

And then a howl came from behind them. Mouse spun. Two large gray wolves were pacing a few feet away, moving eerily as one. They stopped suddenly and looked at her, heads cocked.

"Why do they look at you that way?" Father Lucas asked in awe. "Like they are waiting for something?"

Mouse shuddered and then shook her head. "It does not matter. We have work to do."

She took a step forward cautiously, her eyes on the bear and her ears tuned to the wolves behind her. With an odd lurch, the bear moved in step with Mouse. The wolves fell in behind them.

Mouse led them through the undergrowth, feeling her way from tree to tree until her hand ran along something barkless and smooth—a wood post. She felt the wall reaching out on either side; they were standing at the corner of some structure. She looked up, but the trees ran so close to the wall that they were still under the forest canopy.

She slid along the wall to her left, Father Lucas following and the animals flanking them. She stopped when the posts gave way to a gate with iron rings facing her. Mouse was confused. The rings should be on the inside of the gate so that a piece of wood or an iron rod could be run through them to bar intruders, to protect the people inside the walls.

This was designed to keep something inside from getting out.

She pulled on one of the iron rings and the gate creaked open. As she stepped inside, she could make out the shape of a building a few feet away. She squinted as she looked up, waiting for the rain on her face, but in the absence of trees, she saw a clearing sky—a few thin clouds still passing between her and the moon. With that bit of moonlight, she was able to make out more of the details of the place. The trees looked like giants trying to reach over the dark line of the wall. Large spikes jutted inward from the top of the wall; severed bits of rope dangled from other pieces, which were tied to the spikes and ran across the courtyard like a massive spider's web.

Mouse inched her way toward the building looking for a door. Something crunched and snapped under her foot. She crouched, feeling along the ground until her fingers closed around something hard. She held it up in the moonlight; it was the skull of a bird.

"Father, what is this place?" She whispered like a child in the night, frightened but also excited.

"An old fort. It is called Houska."

"Whose fort?"

"It was built more than a hundred years ago, though I imagine that there was one here before this."

"Who built it?"

"Many people have claimed it for a time, but they always leave—one way or another. Even the Church has been here and left many times over the years. It seems to be abandoned now."

"Why?"

"I do not know why they would leave."

"No. I mean why build it?"

"Why does anyone build a fort?"

"There is nothing here to protect. No road to watch over, no village to guard. There is nothing of value here. We are surrounded by thick forest and bog."

"You will see once we go inside."

"I can hardly see anything at all," she said as she dug her hand into one of the satchels and pulled out a candle.

"No," Father Lucas said. "Wait until we are inside." He moved toward the door.

She waited until he was far enough away and then wrapped her hand around the top of the candle. She glanced warily at all the wood—fence and tree and fort—but she was determined to see what was waiting for her before she got there.

She laid her mouth against the opening at the top of her hand. "Burn," she whispered. She jerked her hand back as the wick caught fire. The wolves ran circles around her as they snipped at each other, and the bear snorted and barked almost like it was laughing.

Mouse held the candle up, scattering a pale light over the near courtyard. It was covered in thousands of dead birds, some already bone, some rotting, others still feathered and fresh as if they had just fallen from the sky. Hawk and sparrow, owl and finch.

"What is this place?" she asked again.

"Come see," Father Lucas called from the doorway, the goat bleating in the background.

Mouse walked to the door and stepped inside.

SIXTEEN

T hough it was huge, the room had nothing in it. No furniture. No windows. No doors but the one they came through, which Father Lucas closed as the wolves neared the threshold. Mouse could see a second floor but no means to reach it—no stairs, no ladder. There was a fire pit in the center of the room but no signs that a fire had ever burned there. A single bird's skeleton rested in the middle of the pit; it had fallen through the smoke hole in the ceiling.

Mouse jumped as the door groaned with the weight of the bear pressing against it, trying to get in.

"This way," Father Lucas said from the far corner. He looked like a ghost, his white habit catching the candlelight. He had the goat on his shoulders again.

Mouse only saw the spiral staircase when her foot was on the landing. The opening was as narrow as a coffin and masked by the wall. As small as Mouse was, she could walk easily down the narrow stairs, but Father Lucas had to turn sideways. Dark smears ran along the walls, but Mouse could not tell what they were. As they descended, the air grew dry and cold. They could see their breath by the time they reached the bottom.

They were standing on a slab of limestone. As far as she could tell in the halo of candlelight, the stone followed the subtle curve of the hill they were on, part of the earth, immovable. She could see the posts holding up the fort along the shadowy perimeter.

Mouse could stand in the space. Father Lucas hunched his head and shoulders.

The place felt unnatural. No spiders' webs in the flooring above them, no dirt or animal droppings, no signs of the kind of life that sought out dark underbellies to live. Nothing lived here.

And yet, Mouse could feel a presence, the thing that had been drawing her here, that was calling to her even now. She walked slowly toward the gaping dark at the summit of the rock.

"Careful, andílek." Father Lucas put the goat down and took Mouse's hand.

"What is this place?" she asked again.

"A gateway to Hell, according to the Church."

"How do they know?"

"There are stories of unnatural things coming out of the pit."

Mouse eased up to the edge of the pit, sliding her feet slowly along the limestone. The crack was uneven, jagged and higher at the lip of the stone, not like natural weathering or shearing of the rock but like something had pushed its way up from the earth and broken free through the stone. It wasn't very large, as long as a tall man and as wide as heavy one, but she could see only darkness when she peered into the opening.

"What is down there?"

"No one knows."

"No one has gone into it? To see what is there?" As uneasy as she felt, the unseen presence tickling at her consciousness, Mouse was more curious than afraid.

"Legend tells of many men who have been lowered into the pit, but none were ever able to speak of what they saw when they were pulled back up."

"You believe the stories?"

He squeezed her hand a little tighter. "One of the men was my father."

"Your father?"

"My family lived near here. He was a knight for the grandfather of your young King. He was good at killing and so won his king's favor and an estate near here. He was also good at drinking and gambling. One night, someone dared him to come up here and go down in the pit. They lowered him laughing. He went down a young man, but when they heard him screaming and pulled him up, he was old, withered and white and out of his head."

"I am sorry, Father." Mouse pulled his hand to her cheek.

"We all have sorrow, little Mouse. It can break us and sour us or by God's good grace it can temper and drive us. I have studied this place, read the stories and talked to the people who live near here. There is an ebb and flow to the evil that emanates from the pit, periods of time when it seems quiet and the stories almost die out, and the people grow complacent, no longer watchful. I believe this gateway has been sealed at times and then forgotten until the evil that lives here starts to slither back into the world of men. I want to seal it again this night and be diligent about guarding it."

"And we will lock my dark things into the pit as we seal it."

"*Your* dark things?" he asked, an edge in his voice.

"They haunt me. They follow me where I go. I woke them at the baby cemetery, and now they want something from me. They hurt others to try to make me give it to them. They are here because of me and I will get rid of them." She spat the words into the pit almost like a dare.

"What do they want, Mouse?"

She shook her head. "You will see soon enough. It is the sugar that will draw them here." She moved away from the pit and lowered the satchels and began pulling out the supplies for the spell she had learned from the book.

"We need the other candles, Father." Her voice echoed against the stone, hollow and cold.

While he lit the candles and placed them around the pit, Mouse mashed the angelica root into a shallow bowl she had brought. She poured in the small vial of chicory juice she had gathered and then added Lady Harrach's breast milk. She put the blue and green stones she had collected into the bowl, coating them with the mixture, and laid aside another set of stones, gray and dull. Then she crawled back to the pit.

At one end of the fissure, just where the stone began to split, Mouse pressed the point of her knife against the limestone and pulled, scratching a thin line as the rock screeched. When she finished, she stood looking down on the pentagram she had drawn, the pit situated at its center.

"Move this here," she mumbled more to herself than Father Lucas as she adjusted the candles, positioning them just outside the spokes of the pentagram. "And now the stones."

Father Lucas handed her the bowl, which she took absently, her eyes closed as she pictured the image from the book, the pattern and placement of the stones. She stepped in and out of the lines of the pentagram, laying a blue stone here, a green one there. Her fingers grew sticky with the mixture that coated them and dripped onto the limestone.

"What about these gray ones?" Father Lucas asked, holding out the handful of leftover rocks.

"They must be made red," she answered as she reached out to take them.

"Ah," he said, knowingly, and pulled at the sleeve of his habit. His arm was still bandaged, a thin red line staining the linen.

But Mouse shook her head. "The blood must be of one source." As she bent to place the rocks carefully along the lines she had scratched into the rock, she looked over at the goat, which stood shaking near the bottom step of the spiral staircase. "Bring it to me," she said hoarsely as she walked to the top spoke of the pentagram and sat down.

Father Lucas laid the goat in her lap. Mouse ran her fingers along its head, and it lifted its face to her, bleating, asking for more petting. In doing so, it exposed its throat. "I am so sorry," she whispered, and, with a shaking hand, plunged the knife into its neck. She held the goat over the pentagram and laid her head against its face. As the blood poured from the goat's neck, it eerily followed the pattern of Mouse's scratches perfectly, flowing left and right, up and over the gray rocks as it ran, leaving them marked with red, until it joined and stopped at the lower spoke. Finally, the goat's head lolled against Mouse's knee, its life spent.

"So now it is time to draw the evil spirits here," Father Lucas said. "How did you plan to accomplish that?"

"I will tempt them with what they want."

"And what is that?"

She lifted her head, but could not look Father Lucas in the eyes. "The gift of life after death."

"What do you mean, child?" Mouse could hear his heart racing; he was afraid.

"I am not a child anymore. Watch."

He shook his head, but she did not see.

"Live." The word bounced between the stone and wood. "Live," Mouse said again.

The goat kicked its legs and lifted its head sleepily, its eye rolling to look up at her for a moment.

"Welcome back, little one," she said as the goat scrambled to its feet, its mouth moving in silent bleats, its eyes as wide as the hole in its throat.

"What have you done?" Father Lucas whispered hoarsely.

She started to answer, but then the sound of whimpering came from the outer edge where the wood of the fort sank into the dirt. Mouse took a candle and peered into the dark, expecting to see the shadows take shape and the space to flood with the hollow-eyed children. She saw claws instead, digging at the dirt. The wolves were trying to get in.

"Where are the children?" she asked, turning to Father Lucas, confused.

"How long have you known you could do this, andílek?" He still held his arms against his chest tightly and looked at her with a face full of fear, but he was clearly working to accept this new gift of hers. His pulse calmed as he took slow, even breaths.

Mouse told him the story of the squirrel and the visit from the dark creatures, and then, teeth gritted and hands balled, she told him about Lady Harrach's baby. "He lives because of me," she said boldly, defiantly.

"But, Mouse, God gives life. God takes it away. It is his will to do, not yours."

"I thought of that, but he tells us to heal the sick, tend the wounded. And if he gave me this gift, is it not his will that I use it?"

"Oh, Mouse." The sadness in his voice frightened her; he acted like he had more to say, but he laced his hands together and raised them to his head, turning away from her.

Mouse chewed at her lip and stepped into the pentagram, kneeling near the fissure and looking over the edge into the abyss. She could see nothing. Smell nothing. Hear nothing.

"Why will they not come?" she asked again, pushing herself up.

"They want you to teach them this new gift, yes?" He joined her near the pit.

She nodded.

"The squirrel was your first resurrection and they came to you, but they did not follow you to Prague until you . . . until the baby." Father Lucas sighed. "They will want something more than a goat to draw them here."

Mouse froze as she saw the conclusion he was drawing.

"I will not," she said.

"You must."

They both jumped at the bone-rattling bellow as the bear joined the wolves to paw at the dirt and wood.

"Mouse, think about what those things are doing in Prague. Right now they could be leading a mother into the river, making her think she is saving a drowning child. Or tricking a child into the flames of a fire like that baker. Or tormenting your young King until his mind breaks." Fervor laced his words and brightened his eyes as the spiritual warrior in him over-powered his worry about her ability to resurrect the dead. "You must do what is necessary to draw the corruptors here so we can seal them in the pit where they belong."

Mouse ran her hands through her hair, which had been torn loose from her braid in the journey through the woods. "But I cannot do it. I love you."

"More than all those innocents suffering even now in the city?"

"Yes."

"And what of the King? What of Ottakar?"

"Do not make me choose," she begged. "I will not."

"Then I have failed you. I meant to teach you Christ's love so that you might learn to sacrifice for the good, even when it goes against your own wishes."

"And I have, Father." Mouse was weeping now. "I would die for them. I would claim their suffering. But how can I take your life? You alone, who have loved me?" She lifted her hands to cover her face.

"Then I will do it myself."

"No!" She was beside him instantly, stilling his hand as it reached for the knife at his waist. "If you take your own life, you might go someplace where I could not call you back, and if I failed, you would be lost forever." Her mind was too full of Ottakar's anguish over his mother; she would not let Father Lucas take such a risk.

"Then you must do it, andílek. To protect my soul."

Mouse nodded and lifted her face, smeared with tears and the goat's blood that had been on her hands. She kissed him on the cheek and then took him by the hand and led him to the top of the pentagram where she had slaughtered the goat.

They both knelt facing each other, and then Father Lucas lifted his chin so she might slit his throat.

"No, not the throat." She looked over at the goat, which stood at the edge of the circle of light farthest from Mouse; its mouth was still working to bleat, but a wet gurgling noise was the only sound it made. Fresh blood trickled from the wound in its neck.

Mouse ripped strips of cloth from her underskirt and dug needle and thread out of the bag at her waist. "To tend your wounds—after," she explained. Then she rolled back the sleeves of his habit. As she slid the blade into the skin at his wrist and sliced the flesh up the forearm, she thought again of Ottakar's mother. When she had finished both arms, Father Lucas turned to let the blood flow onto the pentagram. Again it slipped perfectly along the scratched lines until the pentagram glistened red in the candlelight.

The blood poured out of him. "I am afraid," Father Lucas said as he slumped forward.

Mouse caught him, laying his head in her lap. "I am here, Father. I will save you. I promise." She tried to sound confident, comforting, but she was sobbing as she spoke.

"Child, there is something I would tell you," he said weakly, his face graying. "Before I—"

Mouse brushed strands of his hair from his face. "Not now, Father," she said, swallowing hard so she could speak. "Wait until later. After I . . . after you come back to me."

"It is about your . . ." He took a shuddering breath. "Your father."

"You can tell me later." She laid her fingers against his lips. She wanted him to keep his secrets as a promise that he would not leave her. She saw his eyes start to cloud.

"I love you, Father." She kissed his forehead, leaving her lips against his skin until she heard his heart stop.

With trembling hands, Mouse threaded the needle and bent over first one wrist and then the other, stitching together the interior flesh and then the skin; she had to remind herself to breathe. She stole glances at the still chest, the dead eyes, which she would not close. When at last she had finished her stitches and tied the linen to bind his wounds, she leaned down to his ear, her forehead pressing against the limestone.

"Come back to me," she whispered. "Live." She turned his head so she could watch his opened eyes for signs of life.

Mouse watched and waited.

"Live, Father," she said more forcefully. She buried her face in his hair which spilled out onto the floor.

She strained to listen for a first breath, a first beat of his heart.

Nothing.

"Oh, God, what have I done? Please let him live, please. I swear I will never do it again, not after this. Never kill, never give life to the dead, never compel another person. I swear it!

I understand now—those are for you to do or not. Please, God, let him live."

She sat up and straddled Father Lucas, grabbing him on either side of his head, lifting it from the floor. "Live, I say!" she screamed at him. She let his head fall back as she put her ear down to his chest, listening.

Silence.

Whimpering with panic, she tried to think what to do. She had been angry when she had brought the baby back, angry with God and herself. She let that fury fill her again now. She put her face inches over Father Lucas's, her tears and snot splattering him.

"*I command you to live.*" The voice was not hers. She felt it shredding her throat, tasted the blood in her mouth. She tried to hold back the guttural scream, but it would not stop and tore through her chest, leaving her gasping for air.

She fell to the side of Father Lucas's body. And then he sat up. His mouth opened and shut, like a fish out of water, until finally he sucked in a wheezy breath. Mouse laid a hand on his back, but he jerked away from her, holding his hand up as she tried to come near him again.

"Please, Father. I need to see that you are well." It was a half lie. She could hear his heart and lungs, steady and strong. But she needed him to talk to her so that she could be sure that he was fine, normal, *her* Father Lucas come back to her.

"Father?" she said tentatively as she walked toward him again.

She was pleased to see his face beginning to color, but still he did not speak, and he looked past her as if she weren't there.

"Father?"

He pointed. She turned.

The shadows were growing.

"They are coming! Father, please, we do not have much time." Mouse moved to the top of the pentagram again, ready to recite the words of the spell. A single, gaunt, hollow-eyed child took a step from the deep shadows to the edge of the light. Mouse clenched her fists and reached out, snatching Father Lucas's arm and pulling him behind her.

"Ready to play?" the child-thing asked.

"Where are your friends?" Mouse asked in turn.

"They are busy having fun with the others. They will come when I call."

"Call them now."

"You will teach us your game?" The child-thing shifted its gaze to Father Lucas.

"Yes, when the others get here."

It smiled and clapped its hands. The shadows at the edge of the fort rippled until dozens of empty eyes were staring out at her from the dark.

"We have come to play," they said as one.

"The secret is down there." Mouse pointed at the pit.

They craned their heads toward the fissure but not one of them took a step.

"You have to go down there to learn how to play my game," she said again.

The child-things turned to look at the one who had come first, the one brave enough to stand nearest the light. It cocked its head at Mouse. "You first."

Mouse had known it might come to this. She took a step toward the pit.

"No." Father Lucas grabbed her hand.

"You know I must." She held out the end of a length of rope to him; she had cut down a piece hanging from the net over the fort's courtyard. The other end she tied around her waist.

Mouse sat down, her feet disappearing into the dark fissure. Small arms circled around her neck from behind as the child-thing climbed onto her back.

"I will come with you." It spoke into her face but she felt no breath brush her cheek.

"What about the others?" For the plan to work, she needed all of them to go into the pit.

"We travel in the dark. They will meet us there." And as Mouse watched, the child-things pulled back into the shadows and disappeared. She turned, lifting the nearly weightless burden on her back, and held herself against the edge with the sharp rock cutting into her fingers, her feet feeling for purchase against the wall of stone, the rope growing taut and pressing on her ribs.

With a last look at Father Lucas, Mouse lowered herself into the mouth of Hell.

SEVENTEEN

The darkness was absolute. Not even a flicker of candle-light from above filtered into the crevice. But what unnerved Mouse was the absence of sound.

She knew Father Lucas would have started reciting the spell she taught him, the words encoded in the book that would seal the gateway and trap the creatures in the pit, but she could not hear him, not even a mutter, even with her heightened senses. She knew that the hollow-eyed children were here in the dark with her, but she could not hear them. When she realized she could not even hear her own breath or heartbeat, she pulled her hands away from the rock and pressed them against her chest. Her body spun as the rope took her weight. She sighed when she felt the regular rhythm of her heart, but still she held a hand to her nose and mouth so she could feel the air pulled in, the breath pushed out.

She swallowed the bile rising in her throat and fought the urge to tug on the rope, to scramble back up into the light. She made herself turn back to the rock face, groping until she found foot- and handholds. She inched farther into the abyss; it seemed to go on forever.

The thing on her back buried its face in her hair.

Moments later, the rock beneath her hands grew soft; it squirmed under her grip. At first she thought it was the hollow-eyed children, but then she felt the spindly legs and fat bodies.

Spiders. Swarming along the crevice walls. It was too dark to see, but she imagined larger versions of what had poured out of the book and attacked her in the garden.

Mouse jerked her hands away, which sent her spinning on the rope again. She slammed into the rock with her back. Frantically, she turned and planted her feet against the wall, and then, convinced she could feel them crawling up her legs, she swung one leg free, shaking it violently and then the other. The creature slapped at the spiders crawling on it as it pulled itself around to Mouse's chest.

Mouse squirmed and spun, imagining thousands of them scurrying along the walls around her. She shook her head, ran her hand through her hair, sure they had dropped onto her from above.

She kept up the battle against the unseen spiders for what felt like hours until her heart thrummed and her muscles quivered with fatigue. Surely Father Lucas must have finished the spell. Why had he left her down here in the dark? Exhausted, she wept as she bounced limply against the rock face, forfeiting herself to the swarm.

When she reached out to steady herself, she realized that the rock was just rock once more.

"No more tricks!" she hissed into the face of the creature, their foreheads touching, though she could see none of it, not even a glint of wetness at the eyes.

She wasn't sure if it heard her, but then it crammed its mouth against her ear. "Not me. This place," it said, the words barely whispers by the time her mind registered them. It wrapped cold hands around Mouse's face; it sounded tired, too. "Teach us your game and let us go."

They must have been in the pit for hours, maybe days. She couldn't understand why Father Lucas hadn't pulled her up yet. Had something happened to him? Had the life she summoned to resurrect him fled once she went in the pit? She craned her head trying to see the surface. It was all darkness.

"Teach us and let us go back," the creature said again, laying its head against her chest.

Mouse was beginning to have doubts about imprisoning the child-things in such a place. They seemed so frightened; how could she shut them up forever in the dark?

"I cannot teach you what I did because I do not know how I did it." She had not meant to tell them the truth, but she would not condemn them without first trying to reason with them.

The black nothing ate the snarl before the teeth sank into Mouse's cheek.

"You tricked us!" it screamed, spitting blood in her face.

"I am sorry," she said tightly, trying not to move the torn flesh as she spoke.

She heard a hiss come near and then another and another, and she tensed, waiting for the others to bite or tear at her, too, but nothing happened.

Mouse was shocked when the creature instead took her hand and laid it gently against its chest. "We forgive you if you forgive us," it said. "Just give us what you gave the others." It tapped a rhythm softly against her hand: a heartbeat.

Mouse understood. The hollow-eyed children wanted to live. They had been abandoned in a world that had no place for them, and they longed to be human.

Just like her.

Mouse could give them what they wanted, but at what cost? Maybe they would be like normal children, and she could love and care for them. Or maybe they would use the life she gave them to move in light as well as darkness so they could torment more people, grow more powerful.

"Please," the child-thing whispered at her ear.

Sorrow and hope and fear welled up in her; in an act of faith, she leaned her head down and laid her torn cheek against the cold, dead cheek of the creature. Her eye caught an odd glow of light below her. For the first time she could see how the pit grew the deeper it went; still she could not see the bottom. A heavy mist, glowing in the eerie light, rose slowly toward them.

The air grew frigid, so cold it burned her skin. The inside of Mouse's nose hardened and cracked with the cold, dry air; it licked at the moisture in her eyes until every blink felt like sand scraping under her lids.

Mouse looked up again, hoping to see the opening of the pit and Father Lucas's silhouette. But it was all darkness above her and the icy mist coming from below. When Mouse finally saw what was behind the icy cloud, she screamed, but the silence swallowed it.

They looked mostly human but they were misshapen—arms disjointed, flesh bulging in places and pulled tight against bones in others, skin a bluish white and hairless. They moved wrong, scuttling along the wall in jerky motions, legs bending in the wrong places. They were huge, and like the hollow-eyed children, their mouths were full of jutting, ragged teeth. These must be Enoch's begotten giants, the Anakim, the consequence of the Watchers' lust for the daughters of man.

Mouse felt frozen, unable to move, unable to look away. Time froze, too. What felt like years passed as she waited, in horror, for the monsters to reach her. When they did, they feasted. In the ghostly blue glow, Mouse watched as they snatched one hollow-eyed child after another. They sank their teeth into bellies and sucked as the children arched their backs, screaming—not alive enough to die but living enough to feel the pain of being eaten.

It was her fault. She had lured them here, had misunderstood their want as malevolence. And she would die for it. The brutal truth settled in her like cold stone: She was trapped in the pit with the hollow-eyed children and would never get out. Her secrets—her willingness to kill, her ability to resurrect—would die in here with her.

Mouse closed her eyes and looked inside herself. It was all darkness.

EIGHTEEN

Mouse waited as the monsters moved closer; they were horribly slow and purposeful as they gorged themselves on body after body. Her mind grew numb from the violence, everything emptied by the hopelessness until all she wanted was for it to be over.

She hardly noticed when the rope dug sharply into her chest; her lower ribs snapped, but she did not cry out. She did not move. She only watched as she was pulled farther and farther away from the monsters and what was left of the hollow-eyed children.

Father Lucas gasped as he dragged her over the lip of the crevice. He picked her up, carrying her beyond the border of the pentagram, and laid her gently on the limestone before turning back to the pit. He walked the perimeter of the blood-soaked symbol as he muttered the final passage of the binding spell. The last word came as he stopped at the top spoke. Flame shot up from the blood-covered stones and raced down the etched lines, forming a fiery pentagram with a black crack at its heart.

And then just as quickly, the fire died and with it the raging screams of the creatures in the pit. The howls of the bear and the wolves fell silent.

Mouse was silent, too, and unmoving, her eyes open, the pupils gaping and the bright green grown dark.

Father Lucas lifted her again carefully, her body just bone and skin, and carried her up the staircase. He built a fire in the center pit of the great hall, tossing the dead bird to the side. Mouse's tongue was withered, her lips cracked and pulled back from her teeth. He held a canteen to her mouth, but most of the water ran down her chin and neck, with just a few drops trickling down her throat. He heated more water in the bowl Mouse had brought, and he soaked strips of his ripped habit and wrapped them around her hands and feet, which were blackened by frost-bite, the nails on her fingers and toes grown so long they twisted and curled. Her body showed the weathering of decades, just like the stories about the others, like his father, who had gone into the pit young and come out aged, dying.

Father Lucas pushed back matted hair from her face; her hair was still dark, her face smooth, but she was older—nearer to twenty than her fifteen years. He bent to kiss her forehead. She didn't blink. "Oh what have I done to you, my little andílek?"

He fed her sips of water, shifted her from back to side, worked her arms and legs, talked to her. When the food ran out, he left her to find more, the nearest place a tiny village nearly a day's walk away. When he got back, Mouse had not moved.

He stripped her soiled clothes, rinsed them with what water he could spare and laid them out in the sun. He bathed her, cut her nails. He prayed.

She screamed as her dried muscles and leathered skin came back to life; her body writhed and trembled as it healed.

"You left me," she said between swallows of mashed bread and berries when she was finally ready to speak.

He sobbed with relief. "I did not. I never would."

"You left me."

He could see the pain of betrayal in her eyes. "On my soul, I swear it, Mouse. What passed as years for you was only minutes for me. What happened down there?"

Mouse just stared at him and did not answer.

Father Lucas woke one morning and Mouse was not in the great hall. He went to look for her in the courtyard, where she had started taking walks and picking up the dead birds and making a great pile of them, but she was not there. The gate was still closed.

He knew where she was.

She had not moved any farther than the last step of the staircase; she sat there, her head resting on her knees as she rocked back and forth. He sat down behind her.

"We cannot ever let it open again. They are hungry." Her voice was still dead, like her eyes.

"Who are, child?"

"I am not a child."

"What did you see down there?"

"Evil."

Knowing that she had stopped its escape had been the one consolation Mouse had clung to during her recovery. Guilt gnawed at her. Nightmares woke her, mouth opened in a silent scream like in the pit, her body rigid with seizures. She wrestled with images of Father Lucas dead in her lap, of the fear in the hollow eyes of the child-things, of the monsters eating them. But even as she shouldered the responsibility for all those deaths, Mouse knew her purpose. She had seen evil, not just the vileness of humanity, but primal, original evil; it was the enemy.

Angel or saint or witch or just odd, noble-born or not, God had made her a soldier, despite what Ottakar had said. No one else could have decoded the book. No one else could have gone into the pit and lived.

"I must keep guard here. Like you said, we must be diligent and not forget like the others before us." She sounded old.

"How long will the binding spell last?" Father Lucas asked.

"I do not know. Maybe it only lasts as long as someone remembers it, like a sentry keeping watch for the enemy. It does not matter." She sounded tired. "Someone must keep watch here at Houska. But before I start my vigil, I have a promise I must keep. I will go back to Ottakar. To say good-bye."

"You are not alone, Mouse. It is my burden, too." Father Lucas laid his hand on her head, grieving for the girl he had lost in the pit. "We will make a life here. You and I. Watching. But we will need supplies. You go to Prague. I will write a letter to the bishop telling him what to send. It will help if you can get the support of the young King."

Mouse sighed, letting go of the dreams she had dared to imagine for herself and Ottakar. She resigned herself to what her life would be; she felt too damaged to dream anymore. Prague and Ottakar seemed such a long time ago. Wearily, she pushed herself up. "Write your letter. I will go."

<hr>

Days later, in the dark hours of the morning, she came to the castle gate. She was so tired she could barely stand, her body stiff with cold. Like a ghost, she had wandered out of Houska and back into the world and none of it seemed real. Squinting at the colors and flinching at birdsong, she had walked until she couldn't anymore, and then she huddled in the hollow at the base of a linden tree, dropping like rain into a deep sleep, waking only a few hours later, sore and cramping, to push herself up and do it all again. She avoided the villages, all of the people too bright, too bold, too alive.

Despite her soiled and torn clothes, the guards knew her and let her pass at the castle gate. She went straight to the bishop's house, holding the letter Father Lucas had penned in berry ink on a page he had torn from his breviary. The monk, too, recognized her when he opened the door. He beckoned her in, pressing his hand to his nose as she passed.

Bishop Miklaus sat at a heavy table near the fire of his receiving room. "You do not seem well, Lady Emma. Sit." Mouse was already leaning heavily on the chair. "Brother," he said to the monk, "fetch some wine and bread."

"Thank you," Mouse said.

"And where is Father Lucas?"

"He is at Houska still. Here, he explains everything in his letter."

She studied the bishop's face as he read. Father Lucas had written only a few vague details about unnatural beasts and forces of evil at work as he called for the Church to take arms at Houska, but even these seemed to unsettle Bishop Miklaus, whose eyes widened as he read. "I must write to Rome," he muttered to himself.

The bishop looked up with relief when the monk entered with food and wine.

"Here, my Lady, you should restore yourself. Brother, ready the west guest room for Lady Emma. She will want to rest after her journey."

"Thank you, your Excellency," Mouse replied, "but I mean to go see my Lord King Ottakar. He is still in Prague, is he not?"

"He is here, my Lady, but . . ."

Mouse's senses fired at the sound of fear in the bishop's voice; it pierced her fatigue. She slid to the edge of her seat. "But what?" she asked.

Bishop Miklaus cleared his throat and watched until the monk closed the doors behind him. "Much has changed in the weeks since you left, Lady Emma."

"What do you mean?"

"King Vaclav has returned."

"I know this."

The bishop flinched. "King Vaclav and his son have not always lived in peace."

"I know this, too." Anxiety hardened Mouse's tone. "By the saints, tell me what has happened!"

"King Vaclav claims that it was the Younger King who plotted to poison him."

"That is a lie." She read his face. "And you know it."

"With all respect, my Lady, who are you to question the truth of the King?"

"It makes no sense, Bishop. Someone plotted to kill Ottakar, too. Paid off one of his men. He came wounded to Teplá, nearly dead. Whoever made the attempt on Ottakar is likely the same person who tried to poison Vaclav." The bishop chewed at his finger. The man stank with fear, and Mouse felt the same emotion sink its teeth in her. "What has he done with Ottakar?"

The bishop would not look at her. "I am not sure I am supposed to say. It is no business of the Church."

Mouse saw the politics at play in the man's mind; they were the same as among the ladies in the solar. Ally with the wrong king, the losing king, and you could find your privilege gone or your head on a stake at the Judith Bridge—right and wrong didn't matter.

"Where is Ottakar?" she asked.

"It is no business of yours, either." She could see the wall go up around him; he was protecting himself. He would not take sides. "It will be difficult under the circumstances, but I am sure we can manage to send some supplies back to Houska with you. We will talk more tomorrow after you have had time to—"

Mouse stood and leaned over the table. The bishop swallowed his breath at the smell of her and glanced nervously toward the door.

"Look at me," she said with a voice that was quiet and controlled. He turned his face to hers. She had commanded him not with her power but with her desperation. "Is Ottakar dead?" She steeled herself for his answer.

"As far as I know, not yet." He sighed as he settled back in his chair. "The King is afraid of an uprising. So he waits." He lowered his eyes again, picked up a quill, shuffled some parchment on his desk. "Now I must finish some work, Lady Emma. The Brother will show you to your room."

"Thank you, your Excellency." Mouse tried to bow but her legs were shaking with exhaustion. "Would it be too much trouble to send for my maid, Gitta? I imagine she is still at the keep."

"Of course, my Lady. Just instruct the Brother."

∽

Mouse fell onto the bed in the room she had been given and curled into a ball.

"Am I Job then, for you to test me so?" she whispered. "Does this mean you love me, too?" She closed her eyes, searching for an answer from God, but she saw only darkness inside her still.

"I did not think so," she said bitterly.

She pushed herself upright, resting her head on her knees as she worked through the problem like a chess match. The game to be played here was a dangerous one. First, she needed to understand the pieces at work and how they moved. Ottakar and Vaclav she knew about; she needed to see who else was playing.

Soon, Gitta arrived, bringing some of what she needed—fresh clothes and information. Mouse was pleased to see her again despite the news she told: many of Ottakar's men were imprisoned with him in the Black Tower. Others had fled, along with their wives, for home. Mouse would find no allies here at court.

When Mouse went down later for morning Mass, she was prepared for the unfamiliar faces. She felt the burning of curious eyes on her as she approached the bishop after the service. "Your Excellency, I am afraid that my return to Father Lucas will be somewhat delayed. I have matters to tend to here first." She held her smile at his raised eyebrows and spoke loudly enough for others nearby to hear, wanting to make it as difficult as possible for him to refuse her. "You will be able to send a Brother with the supplies, will you not?"

"My Lady, I think it would be best if you—" Bishop Miklaus stopped short, looking over Mouse's shoulder and bowing. "My Lord."

Mouse turned to find King Vaclav behind her. "My Lord," she said as she too bowed. She wondered if he would remember her from the brief encounter at the gate that rainy day, and, if he did, if he would see her as an ally to his son—and a threat to him.

The King took her hand. "It is Lady Emma, is it not? You were Ottakar's *ward*." His mouth lingered on the word, lips puckered like a kiss and then pulling back in a sneer.

"Yes, my Lord." She searched his eyes for news of Ottakar but saw nothing besides lust.

"May I introduce you to my good friend, Lord Rozemberk?"

"I already know—" She stopped as she saw the man who had been standing behind the King. He was indeed familiar to Mouse, but he was not the Lord Rozemberk she knew.

"I am confident we have never met, my Lady," the man said smoothly. "You mistake me with someone else."

"She must know your son, the youngest—Vok," the King said.

"He is no son of mine. He is a traitor and deserves the wheel."

"Now, now. He is a younger son, like mine. Their place makes them desperate to grasp at power whenever they can, however they can. We will humble them soon enough."

As this other Lord Rozemberk turned toward the King and Mouse saw his profile, she knew where she had seen him before. He had been the man on the other side of Lord Olomouc that night at supper, the night she had danced. In her memory, she replayed his words—"*I think the Younger King may discover that he has more enemies than he knows.*" It was another piece of the puzzle and this man another player, but she could not fit it all together.

"You look pale, my Lady," King Vaclav said, lifting her face with a finger under her chin.

"I have been ill, my Lord. It was why I was away."

Bishop Miklaus, nervously watching the tense exchange, interceded. "I will take her back to her room at my house and let her rest. She must return to Father Lucas tomorrow."

Mouse could see he was trying to slip her neck free of the noose closing around it, but she was prepared to hang herself if that's what it took to free Ottakar. "Thank you, Your Excellency, but I—" she started, and then the King interrupted.

"Send someone else to your Father Lucas, Bishop. Lady Emma will stay with us." King Vaclav offered his arm. "Let me assist you to the hall. Some food will do you good, I think. Now where to settle you? The keep is quite full." Mouse kept a taut smile even as she imagined the rope tightening around her throat.

"I am sure your sister, Mother Agnes, will have room for me at the convent."

"No," Vaclav said sharply. "Ottakar's chamber is empty. You can stay there. You will find comfort in the familiar, I think, and restore yourself more quickly."

"And where is Lord Ottakar?" she asked innocently, ignoring his insinuation that she had spent much time in his son's room.

"Not here," he said simply.

The smile Mouse wore felt carved, unnatural, as she lowered herself into her usual chair beside the King's seat. *Ottakar's seat,* she said defiantly to herself.

"He seemed to like you," Vaclav muttered, leaning around her side from behind. "Very much, I think." She could see him calculating her value as she found herself a piece now in play in his game. "I like you, too," he said.

She held herself still against the shiver as his one eye traced her body. Vaclav was already talking about Ottakar in the past tense.

Mouse had little time, and she needed help.

NINETEEN

L ater, when Vaclav and his men had ridden out to hunt, Mouse slipped out of the keep and across the Judith Bridge, which was covered in a swirly, dusty snow. Panic had driven her to the only person she could think of who might be willing to help. She tried now to calm herself as she paced in an unfamiliar room, her heart racing as the minutes passed. She started when the door opened.

"Mother Agnes." Mouse bowed.

"I know you." The Mother squinted her eyes, studying Mouse, but she would not come farther into the room. "You came with my nephew to see . . . *her.*"

"Yes," Mouse said, relief flooding her. "I need your help."

"For what?" Her eyes lowered to Mouse's belly.

"Not what you think," Mouse answered briskly. "We must save Ottakar."

"From whom?"

"Your brother, the King."

"Vaclav is teaching Ottakar a lesson in obedience," Mother Agnes said, turning to leave. "But the King will not harm his only heir."

Mouse crossed the floor quickly and grabbed the woman's arm. "You are wrong. I have word that he means to kill his son."

"I do not believe it." Mother Agnes pulled her arm free. "And besides, I can be of no help to you. I no longer have any sway over Vaclav. Once, he counted me among his closest advisors but not since the Queen . . . died."

"He is afraid of you." Mouse had heard the fear in Vaclav's voice when she'd suggested staying at the convent; something about Mother Agnes frightened him. Mouse needed to know what that was so she could use it against him.

"He is afraid of many things."

"Tell me."

"Why should I betray my blood to a stranger?"

"I am no stranger. You saw me here with Ottakar. I cannot imagine that you want harm to come to your nephew."

Mother Agnes took a step back toward the door. "I must prepare for prayers."

Mouse reached out again, gently touching the Mother's arm this time. Her voice trembled with pent-up fear as she made a final plea. "Please, can you at least help me find a way to see him? To see if what you say is true—that he is unharmed and this only a father's chastisement? I will leave it be then. But I cannot rest until I know that Ottakar is well. Please. You took his mother despite Church rules. You have watched him grieve. You must love him, too. Please help me."

Mother Agnes sighed. "There is a guard—Havel, the smith's son. I helped his family through a hardship. Tell him I sent you to check on my nephew."

"Thank you, Mother."

"I want to know what you find," she said quietly as she left the room.

✏

Mouse sent Gitta to find out the guard rotations while she went down for the evening meal and entertainment in the Great Hall as expected. The plan was for Gitta to come to the hall if Havel was on guard; Mouse would plead ill and leave. But she had not anticipated King Vaclav's attentions. He pulled her chair so close it touched his own; he cut the best pieces of meat for her, though she ate none of it.

"Dance for me," he ordered when the minnesingers started the carol.

"My Lord, please do not make—"

"I heard you danced for Ottakar. It was quite . . . enjoyable, I understand." He turned slightly toward the old Lord Rozemberk, who chuckled; he had been there that night with Lord Olomouc.

Something pricked at the back of her mind. "You were friends with Lord Olomouc, were you not?" Mouse asked Lord Rozemberk.

"Oh, yes, they were old friends," the King answered for him. "The two of them caused their share of—"

Mouse turned back to the King. "But it was Lord Olomouc who poisoned you, yes?"

Lord Rozemberk leaned forward. "When we were younger, my Lady, circumstances often brought Olomouc and me together, but Olomouc and I had not seen each other for many years. I could not have known that he had turned traitor."

Lord Rozemberk was a cool liar, but his heartbeat gave him away.

"What kind was it?" she asked.

"What?"

"What kind of poison?"

"Belladonna is what the physician said." Vaclav tipped back his cup and then motioned the servant for more. "Said he could smell it in the wine."

"How did you survive?" Mouse was more suspicious than ever; if the belladonna had been strong enough to smell over the sweet wine, it would have been lethal no matter the treatment.

"The physician acted quickly," interjected old Lord Rozemberk. He was lying again.

"What did he do?"

"Why so many questions?" Lord Rozemberk's eyes narrowed as he studied her.

"Simply curious. I was trained as a healer, my Lord," she said sweetly.

"I might like being treated by you." The King's one eye twitched oddly as he spoke, and his words slurred.

Mouse saw Gitta standing at the doorway. She pushed her chair back and started to make her excuses. "My Lord, I am not feeling—"

"You are a beautiful woman, Lady Emma." The King took her hand.

"Thank you, my Lord. I think I—"

"I understand that you were raised at an abbey?"

"Yes, my Lord." She tried to pull her hand free, but he wouldn't let go.

"And your parents?"

"I know nothing about them."

"But you came to the Sisters with some wealth."

"Did I?" Mouse meant to give him nothing more than he already knew.

"You were allowed to keep a trinket of your mother's, I believe? A bracelet?"

The smile slid a little from Mouse's face. Surely Ottakar would not have shared this with his father, but there was no point in lying since Vaclav clearly already knew the answer. "Yes, my Lord. It was all I had of her."

"Some weeks ago, I received a letter from France suggesting that your bracelet was engraved with a crest and a sigil—a sparrow, as I understand it."

Mouse's mouth went dry. He had taken the letter meant for Ottakar. Vaclav likely knew more about her than she did herself.

"I know the family who claims the sparrow. It is the Crown of Aragon."

"Crown?" She had meant to hold her tongue, to not give him the satisfaction of sharing news that was not his to share. She wanted to hear this from Ottakar. But she couldn't help herself.

"Yes. The Crown of Aragon is a collection of kingdoms along the Mediterranean Sea ruled now by James. 'The Conqueror,' they call him."

"My mother?" The hope of something cracked her voice.

"I do not know. The letter only says they continue to trace the bracelet, but I have a mind to send a courier to Aragon myself. Like as not, your mother was one of Alfons the Chaste's girls and you her bastard child. But by whom? Have you nothing of your father's? Were there no jewels or trinkets of his?"

"No, my Lord." Mouse closed her eyes a moment; she could see her father's silhouette in her memory, hear the low rumble of his voice, smell him—there was something different about him she couldn't place, all of it strangely vague—but none of it gave her anything she could use to identify him. That flash of memory of him at her birth was all she knew of him.

"I cannot imagine any of the Aragons sinning with someone less than noble." He laughed as he put his hand under her chin again, lifting her face to catch the candlelight. He leaned in, his drunken breath on her lips "And I see nothing common or crude in your making."

Mouse pulled back, trying to hide her disgust, and saw Gitta again, pacing in the doorway.

"My Lord, it is time to select your bird." Lord Rozemberk nodded toward two men who stood in front of the table holding beautiful roosters, feathers rich brown and gold. The men stepped forward to show them to the King.

Vaclav chose one and, with an unsettling giggle, turned to Lord Rozemberk. "My cock is bigger than yours."

Mouse stood. "I am sorry, my Lord, but I am not fully well. I think I must rest."

"I might retire early myself, have a private cockfight in my chambers." Vaclav lurched forward, grabbing at her.

"My Lord, I think you have had a good deal to drink." Lord Rozemberk took the King's arm, holding him back in the chair.

"No, not enough! Where is that boy of mine? Now he can hold his drink."

Mouse watched a bead of sweat roll down Vaclav's face. Was he so drunk that he had forgotten he had Ottakar imprisoned in the tower?

"Where is Vladislaus? He loves a good cockfight. He knows how to keep up with me. Not like his whelp of a brother."

Mouse shook away the chill that ran through her. The King was talking about his eldest son, the dead one, as if he were still alive. Surely this was more than drunkenness; the King was mad.

The paleness in the older Lord Rozemberk's face deepened her suspicions. "My Lady, I apologize if you were offended. Drink has loosed his tongue and addled his mind."

"Of course." She bowed stiffly and headed toward Gitta. The low warning warbles and louder squawks of the birds, the frantic flap of wings as they went at each other, and the King's cackle of glee followed her to the door.

She pulled Gitta quickly into the courtyard. Gitta tossed a dark cloak over Mouse's shoulders and then went back to the keep as Mouse made her way through the bailey, keeping to the shadows along the wall. The air was biting cold, snow still falling. As she neared the first guard, she kept her face pulled back into the hood of the cloak and spoke softly. "I need to see Havel, the smith's son."

The guard pointed to a heavy door behind which Mouse found a set of stairs. Havel was standing sentry at the top landing. Convincing him to let her see Ottakar was far easier than she'd expected; one mention of Mother Agnes and he was opening the door to a dark room.

"The others have gone to watch the cockfights. But be quick," he said as he shoved her inside and locked the door behind her.

In the sudden black, where she could see nothing, Mouse felt the panic rise; she was back in the pit, had never left it and would be trapped there forever. She threw her hands out in front of her, touching nothing, and sucked in a breath. The smell of piss and shit and blood and unwashed bodies brought her back to the moment, and the sounds—guttural moans and childlike whimpers—drew her forward. Ottakar was here and she must find him. There was just enough light from dying embers at the center of the room for her to make out figures along its periphery.

She came to Damek first, left taut on the rack, ribs protruding from stretched skin. One arm stuck out from the socket at an odd angle, dislocated, but his flesh was whole.

Then came a voice—raspy and weak—from the other side of the fire. "Get out of here."

Mouse turned in the direction of the voice. She took a step forward but paused at another sound: Water dripping. She took another step. Eyes narrowed, she could make out the shape of a man.

"Who is there?" she whispered.

"Go away, I said." It was Lord Rozemberk. Vok.

He was naked, like Damek, and his body was covered with cuts and bruises, his feet and arms bound and pulled tight. A vise ran across both toes and thumbs, screws twisted so that the nails had split and bled, the flesh flayed out beneath them.

As she came to his side, she saw the source of the water. A large copper pot with a long, slender spout hung over him. Lord Rozemberk's head was trapped in an iron mask and latched to the table with just his forehead and face exposed. Mouse watched as a drop of water formed on the end of the spout, growing until it slipped free and fell onto Lord Rozemberk's forehead, splattering and then running down the sides of his head. She heard his heart race and skip as the water fell; his body spasmed as it hit.

At the sound of the next drop pulling away from the copper tube, Mouse thrust her hand out, catching it. It was icy cold.

"No. Let it fall." He was weeping now.

Mouse laid her hand against his forehead; he cried out in pain.

"The hole. Is it large? Deep? Will it be over soon? I want it to be over."

"There is no hole. Only water."

"But my head hurts so. The water eats through the skin, digs through the bone, like it hollows out stone." A sick laugh bubbled in his throat, but he closed his eyes and then sank his teeth into his lips, which were already bloody and swollen. "No. I will not break."

"There is no hole, Vok."

His eyes snapped open. "You must get out of here. If they find you, they will kill you. Or use you. Do you understand?"

Mouse hadn't thought about that—being tortured to break Ottakar. "Where is he?" she asked.

"There." She followed the line of his sight. "In the box."

On the other side of the room sat a metal box. Fingers of orange and yellow crawled across its surface, reflections from the fire. Mouse ran across the room and knelt beside it. The box seemed impossibly small to hold a man. How could Ottakar be in there and still be alive?

Mouse pressed her face against the iron grill and tried to see in through the tiny openings. She gagged at the smell but refused to pull back.

"Ottakar. Can you hear me?"

She waited.

"Please, Ottakar, make a noise."

With the silence, she began frantically pulling at the iron latches to open the box. "I have to get him out." Her voice trembled in the dark.

"Stop. It will only make things worse. Even if you got him out, where would you take him? Stop! Mouse." Lord Rozemberk had never called her by her name; it stilled her.

"I have to try." She was crying now, digging her hands into her hair as she tried to think of a way to free them.

"You will get him killed."

And then, from the box, there was a sound. "Mouse."

She barely heard it, but it was enough.

She pressed her face against the grill again. "Ottakar?" Her throat was so tight it was difficult to speak.

"Mouse," he breathed again.

She thought she saw his eyes open, but it was so dark she couldn't be sure. Then the door behind her opened and Havel's hands were on her shoulders, pulling her away.

"I will get you out. You must live," she yelled as she was pushed out to the landing. "Do you hear me, Ottakar? You must live! All of you. You must live."

Havel slammed the door shut. "You must go, my Lady. It will be my head and yours if you stay any longer."

Mouse nodded, too afraid for Ottakar's life to argue, but as she descended the stairs, her anguish over his suffering shifted to a twisting rage and the power in her trilled in answer. She had made a promise at Houska never to use that power again, but it vibrated in her with a lust to act. She could make Havel help her free Ottakar.

She stopped on the stairs, shaking her head. Ottakar would not leave the others. And besides, Vaclav would come after his son. Mouse might command a man to do her will but not an army.

She swallowed hard as she passed the guard at the tower gate; she counted her steps as she crossed the Judith Bridge in the cold dark, lulling the power to sleep despite the sense of urgency that quickened her pace.

The snow had stopped but lay thick on the ground, crunching under her feet and shining in the moonlight as she approached the abbey. The Sisters must have been at Matins; it took a long time for someone to admit her. Once inside, she prowled the room again as she waited for Mother Agnes. When Mouse finally heard approaching footsteps, she moved to the wall beside the door; she meant to make the woman come all the way into the room this time, to listen and to act. She closed the doors behind Mother Agnes as she entered, leaning against them.

Mouse wasted no time. "He is torturing them. They will die if we leave them there. You must help me."

Mother Agnes had jumped as the door slammed shut, but she quickly composed herself. "Vaclav might torture his son—he has always hated the boy—but I tell you, he would not kill his only heir. He is too ambitious."

"He is young enough to sire another heir."

Mother Agnes scoffed. "He has no wife and is not likely to find another at his age—at least not one noble enough to satisfy his thirst for power."

"He certainly seems to be in the market for one, and I think his mind is . . . he seems not right. He spoke as if his other son, the eldest, still lived."

Mother Agnes sank into a chair. "It has been too much for him, these last years. The constant fighting with the emperor. Vladislaus's death—so unexpected—and then Ottakar's uprising and the Queen's death. Enough to break the strongest of us, and my brother has never had a strong mind.

"It is my mother's fault," Mother Agnes continued. "She hated him. She blamed him for my older brother's death. Vaclav was only a baby when Vratislav died, but Mother's mind was addled, and she was sure Vaclav had stolen Vratislav's breath, killing him so that he might one day be king. Whenever the church bells rang, she would do harm to Vaclav. Twist his limbs, pinch him, hold his feet to the fire, dunk him in his bathwater. The sound of the bells covered his screams, you see."

"Was there no one to stop her?"

"Only the nursemaids and my sisters and I. But we were too afraid of her to act. When he was older, almost eleven, she broke his arm, and not long after that, he and I were sent away to Austria. Vaclav's arm healed, but his mind never did." She looked into the fire. "To this day, he cannot stand the sound of bells. Have you ever noticed that they never ring in Prague? No, nor anywhere the King travels. A guard goes before and warns the people."

"I am sorry for the King's suffering," Mouse said, "but he must be stopped. He is not fit to rule."

The words were a mistake. Mother Agnes turned on her. "Who are you to deem him fit or not? My brother is a good man. A great man. He protected Bohemia against the heathen Tartars and lost his eye for it."

"He has his son shut up in a metal coffin rotting in his own shit," Mouse spat back.

Mother Agnes sat back again, the fire squealing and snapping in the silence. "Do you know he writes music? Love songs." Her voice broke. "My mother did, too." She puckered her lips and whistled; the sixteen-note tune bounced eerily against the vaulted ceiling and echoed in Mouse's head.

"What is that?" she asked gently.

"A song of hers. She was always whistling it." The woman looked up, her eyes filled with tears. "People think that shame of a broken betrothal chased me to the Church, but I tell you it was fear. Fear of becoming like her. Fear of ever having a mother's love for a child because I know how easily such love can be turned to cruelty."

Mouse knelt by her side, a hand on the woman's back.

"What do you want of me?" Mother Agnes asked. "I tell you I cannot touch him. He will not even see me in private. Not since the Queen died. His mind has grown worse since then. I think he thinks I am my mother. I look just like her."

And then Mouse knew what needed to be done: a plan played out in her mind.

"Will you come to him and try to talk to him? Make him see you. For Ottakar's sake."

Mother Agnes nodded wearily.

"Thank you," Mouse said as she stood.

"I tell you it will do Ottakar no good."

Mouse shrugged, but she knew her plan would work. King Vaclav was already standing at the edge; all he needed was a little help to go over it.

It was still dark as Mouse crossed back over the Judith Bridge, whistling.

TWENTY

S he spent the early morning of the next day walking along the riverbank working out strategy. Mouse needed the first assault on the King's fragile sanity to be dramatic, jarring enough to fully unsettle him. She knew the weapon she would use, but she needed to think of a way to wield it without getting caught, and she refused to put someone else in the path of Vaclav's mad wrath.

Rounding a river bend, she walked into a flock of griffon vultures feeding on the bloated carcass of a deer. "Calm," she said as they hissed and spit at her, shoulders hunched as they skirted around the body. "Be calm." As they grew still, Mouse felt a flare of remorse at using the power she'd sworn to abandon. She appeased her guilt by reminding herself that they were not human; they had no will to manipulate, only instinct to overcome.

"Fly," she ordered. "Fly to the belfry." As she tried to hold the image in her mind, to share it, she realized the flaw in her plan. The vultures knew *fly* and *calm*; they would know *eat* or *mate* or *fight* should she command it, but they did not know belfry. And so they flew, not to the belfry, but over the hills at the edge of Prague, headed toward the mountains. Since she could not command an unwitting ally, Mouse would have to take the risk herself.

And so she wound silently up the stairs of the Eve steeple at St. George's just after noon. Once she'd reached the belfry, she wrapped her arm around the thick rope and waited. Victory depended on her timing. Her life depended on it, too. Too soon and she would miss her mark. Too late and she would surely get caught.

When she heard the whinnying as the horses were led out into the bailey, she pulled, letting her full weight hang on the rope, feeling it slip along the wheel above her until it grew taut, and then she let it up again. On the second pull, the clapper slapped a low dong against the bell, and Mouse started the count of seconds she would have to get the bells fully ringing and still have time to slip into the sanctuary of St. Ludmila's Chapel to avoid being caught. After a few more pulls, the bells clanging, she ran down the stairs, not pausing as she caught a glimpse of a crowd gathering around something in the bailey. She heard the footsteps as she reached the bottom landing and pulled herself into a small alcove just as someone ran past, heading up the stairs two at a time.

By the time they were able to stop the bells, Mouse was kneeling before the altar in the chapel, seemingly deep in prayer, her breath even and slow though the veins in her neck bounced with the quick thud of her heart.

"I am sorry to bother you, my Lady." A guard stood in the doorway, a nervous Bishop Miklaus not far behind him. "But did you see anyone else in the church?"

"I have been at prayer all morning. Why? Has something happened?"

"Someone rang the bells."

"Yes? At Teplá, we rang them all the time."

"She is new to Prague," the bishop offered as explanation.

The guard sighed. "But you saw no one? Heard no one?"

"I am sure there have been people coming and going, but my attentions have been here." She nodded to the fresco of St. Ludmila beside the altar. She reached out to the guard, who helped her stand. "You act as if something is wrong."

"The King is ill, my Lady," said the bishop.

"I shall pray for him then." She knelt again, bowing her head as they left.

Later, as she made her way back to the keep, she heard the people talking.

"The King went stiff as a board and fell off his horse. A fit, it was."

"I seen it before. When old One-Eyed was a young man, just back from Austria, we rang the bells for his homecoming. It was the bells that did it to him," an old lady said as she beat a rug in the crisp air. "Slather from the mouth like a sick animal, his body jerking like he got a demon in him."

◦◦◦

Mouse's heart still thrummed as she entered the solar where the other ladies were spending their afternoon. She sought the safety of numbers and the appearance of normalcy. Despite the bishop's unintentional validation of her, she felt exposed. She'd hoped to ring the bells more than once over several days, but she knew now she couldn't take the risk. She had more covert ways of attacking the King, but she needed more allies, willing or not.

The women quieted as she crossed the room to pay her respects to a black-veiled Lady Lemberk, Evzen's widow. Next to her was an older woman. Mouse guessed who she was before the introductions; Vok had his mother's features.

"Lady Rozemberk, this is Lady Emma, *Prince* Ottakar's ward," said Lady Lemberk.

Mouse gritted her teeth at the slight to Ottakar.

"His ward?" Lady Rozemberk asked, eyebrows raised.

"Yes. My Lord King Ottakar took me under his protection when I left the abbey." As she spoke, Mouse quickly calculated the risk of her next move. "In fact, I tended him when his men brought him to Teplá with an arrow in his chest. Some thought it an accident; some suspected intent."

She honed her senses on their reactions.

Lady Lemberk's pulse and breathing stayed steady, calm. "You *tended* him?" she asked, a smirk pulling at her face.

"I am a trained healer, my Lady." But Mouse had little interest in defending herself against accusation. She was too busy studying Lady Rozemberk. The woman had paled at the news of Ottakar's accident, her eyes darted down, heart racing.

"I thought perhaps your son might have told you, Lady Rozemberk. He was there."

"My son?"

"The younger Lord Rozemberk, I mean. Vok."

"You know him?" And here the Lady's heart skipped and jumped. She was anxious about him.

"Yes, my Lady, I know your son." Mouse laced the words with as much meaning as she could without seeming obvious to Lady Lemberk, who smirked still.

Something dark slid across Lady Rozemberk's face. "If you know him, then you should know he is no longer claimed by the Rozemberk house, whatever he may call himself. He is no son of mine." She shifted in her seat, turning her back to Mouse. It was a clear dismissal, but Mouse knew it had been played for show. Lady Rozemberk was a mother who cared very much about her son whether the father claimed him or not.

Mouse took a seat at the far side of the room and gathered an embroidery hoop and some thread. At first, she chatted amiably with some of the women near her; they seemed eager to please, no doubt due to the favor King Vaclav had shown her. But soon, Mouse let the conversation drop and turned her attention to her needlework. While she pulled the thread up, eased it down through the silk, and pushed it up again, she began to hum: the same sixteen notes, over and over again. All afternoon, she hummed or whistled until her lips quivered with the strain. She kept the tune low and quiet, just part of the background, so that no one really noticed.

But then the woman at the harp began playing it.

"That tune is beautiful. Where did you learn it?" someone asked.

"I just made it up. Do you like it?"

Affirmations were offered from the other ladies, and Mouse was pleased that several of the women were whistling quietly when they all retired to dress for supper.

∽

When the King appeared in the Great Hall that night, he looked ill and moved stiffly as if he were sore. Mouse pretended to focus on her food but kept her attention trained on him. When she saw him cower suddenly, she looked across the room, searching for the cause of his discomfort. Mother Agnes had entered the hall and sat down at a lower table. Mouse could see the fear on the King's face. She knew that, in his addled mind, he saw not his sister but his mother. Mouse's plan was unfolding more quickly than she'd thought.

If she felt guilty, Mouse abated it by letting the smells and sounds of the tortured men surface in her perfect memory. She watched the King closely. Anytime his eyes fell on his sister, Mouse would whistle or hum softly as she smiled and looked out over the hall. She heard other ladies humming it, too.

Vaclav paled at the sound, pulling at his ears. He ate little and drank much. Finally, he clamped his hands over his ears, sending his crown crashing to the floor. Lord Rozemberk half carried him from the hall.

Mouse caught Lady Rozemberk's eye to let her know that she was leaving; she wanted to give Vok's mother the opportunity for a private conversation. She waited near the door to the Queen's garden, and, as expected, Lady Rozemberk joined her minutes later. They walked together to the bench near the fountain.

"It is terribly cold out here."

"I am sorry, Lady Rozemberk, but it is the only place I know where we will not be overheard. I thought perhaps you would appreciate the discretion."

The Lady sat heavily beside Mouse. "The King is mad."

"I know."

"My husband is very loyal."

"So is your son."

"I wish they were loyal to each other, but crown politics and their own ambition destroyed any chance of that long ago. I lay the blame at the feet of our one-eyed King and his sick, twisted mind. I hate him for what he has done to my family," she hissed, then sighed. "Ottakar is a good boy. He lived with us during much of his childhood, did you know? He and Vok were foster brothers."

Mouse nodded.

"I was quite pleased when he offered land and title to Vok. A mother's love should spread to all of her children regardless of whether they were born first or last, girl or boy."

Mouse remembered what Mother Agnes had said about mothers; she thought she would approve of Lady Rozemberk's approach. An unexpected twinge of regret pulled at Mouse as she realized that a life at Houska with Father Lucas meant no hope of children for herself.

"But my husband saw the honor to Vok as a slight to himself," Lady Rozemberk continued. "And then when the other nobles stirred up the revolt and Vaclav came running to us, he swung the axe that finally severed the bond between my husband and son." Lady Rozemberk wrapped her arms around herself, shivering. "I am not allowed to even speak his name. I am not supposed to have any contact with him." She took a slow breath and let it out in a rush. "I could live with this loss if I knew Vok was happy and safe, but to have him locked up in the tower . . . I know they must be doing unspeakable things to him. He may even be dead already. My husband presses for it. How could a father hope for such a thing?" She couldn't hold back a sob.

"I once saw a wolf eating its own pups," Mouse said. "The winter ran long, and he was starving. It seems to me that an ambitious man will do whatever he must in order to achieve his ends." She paused. "I have seen your son. He is not dead yet."

Lady Rozemberk looked up quickly.

Mouse described the smells, the dripping water and thumb-screws, the state of Vok's mind.

"I will not leave my boy there to die," Lady Rozemberk said through gritted teeth. She sat up straighter. "My husband plotted with Vaclav to kill Ottakar. They bought some of his men—Lord Lemberk I know for certain. But my husband killed him after he brought word that the second assassination attempt had failed; Vaclav did not want anyone left who could speak of it."

The news was hardly a surprise to Mouse, but the vileness of it angered her all the same. Gernandus and Evzen bought by the father to kill the son; it must have been Evzen who had planned the attack on them as they neared Prague.

"And then they staged Vaclav's poisoning," Mouse said, working out the plot. "They wanted to throw off any suspicion Ottakar might have against his father, to encourage him to lower his defenses and relax here in Prague with his men, all of them vulnerable. But why have they not killed them? Why wait?"

"The King fears the people. He is afraid of revolt, should he execute his son. If Ottakar were to die in a hunting accident or be assassinated and my son with him, no one could connect it to the King, though some might suspect him. But he cannot afford Ottakar's blood on his hands."

"Then why imprison Ottakar?"

"It was not the plan. The King got angry about something Ottakar said and in a fit of rage ordered them to the tower. Now that they are imprisoned, he must find some way to lay treason at their feet so he can hang them. My husband works even now to craft evidence to prove that they tried to poison the King."

"Then we must act quickly."

"I have a few resources to get them out of the country, but how do we free them from the tower?"

Mouse shook her head, her eyes full of rage. "We will not run. Ottakar never would. Nor your son, either. No, I will break this King. And you will help me."

❧

Lady Rozemberk knew the women Vaclav took to bed— servants, maidens, wives, and widows. She sought out the ones who were biddable, bribable. She taught them the tune, paid them to hum it while the King slept. Meanwhile, Mouse spent the next several days walking the grounds whistling, infecting smithy, farmer, washerwoman, soldier with the tune. The bailey was full of it by the time the King's physicians allowed him to ride again.

As the King prepared to mount, Mouse watched from the shadows.

Vaclav stuck his foot in the stirrup, then stopped, glancing wildly around the stable. "What is this? That noise?" he shouted. The startled horse reared, knocking him to the ground.

Lord Rozemberk was instantly by the King's side. "I hear nothing, my Lord," he said, helping him up. Anyone nearby who had been whistling had stopped to watch, ready to witness another of the King's fits.

Vaclav shoved his friend away. "Leave me be! I tell you I heard something. A tune. I know that tune." He hummed it, his eye growing wide. "But it cannot be!"

"Here, my Lord, I have hold of your horse. Let us go."

"No! I do not want to ride. I need a man to go to Porta Coeli for me. Now!"

"Why, my Lord?"

"Now!" Vaclav screamed again. The horses shied and reared.

"You, smithy. Fetch a courier," Lord Rozemberk called out.

"No, I do not trust them. They might give me a lie."

"A lie about what, my Lord?" Mouse could hear the growing panic in Lord Rozemberk's voice. "Please, let us ride together out in the hills."

"No. You must go. Go see that the old woman is still dead— still buried at Porta Coeli."

"But my Lord, the morrow is Christmas. I cannot be back by then. And the sky darkens with more snow."

"I said GO!" He grabbed Lord Rozemberk by the back of the neck and pushed him toward his horse.

Lord Rozemberk had no choice. "I do your will, my Lord. Always." He mounted and rode through the South Gate, snow already beginning to fall.

Mouse was glad. The King would be easier prey in the absence of his friend. It was better fortune than she could have hoped.

But Mouse could not have imagined the dark turn that fortune would take.

The screams started not long after Mouse had reached Ottakar's room to rest and dress before supper. She hurried to the window to look down on the bailey. People were running toward the north side of the castle toward the Black Tower.

A chill slid down her spine.

Mouse nearly fell as she raced down the stairs. She had to fight the crowd once she reached the courtyard, squeezing herself between people. Some of them pressed hands against their mouths and looked away. Others stood staring as if they couldn't move. Her stomach in her throat, Mouse worked her way to the edge near the wall, slipping forward until she could see.

Damek was strapped to a large wheel. The King stood before him, swinging an iron cudgel at his immobilized limbs.

The bones sounded like branches breaking under the weight of ice after a storm. Damek threw his head back, mouth open, as a warbled, high whine built in his throat and grew, bouncing off the stone tower and back down on the people.

The crowd screamed for the King to give mercy. But Vaclav wasn't listening.

"Quiet!" he yelled, pulling his arm back for another blow. Damek's legs jutted at odd angles, broken above and below the knee; the shattered end of a bone pierced his thigh, and blood spewed from it, spraying the King's face. Huge snowflakes fell like goose down onto the splatters of red as Damek shrieked in pain like a dying animal.

"Stop that noise!" the King screamed again. He swung the cudgel against Damek's neck, and the bailey fell silent.

Damek was dead.

Vaclav stood for a moment staring, his arms limp by his side, and then he spun, flinging the iron cudgel behind him. "Move!" he spat at the people near the front of the crowd.

As the crowd parted, Mouse saw her own hatred for the King reflected in their faces. These people knew Damek. They knew he was a good man—kind, always eager for a bit of fun. He was a new father. He didn't deserve to be treated like this.

Mouse turned and walked slowly toward Damek. She thought about the night they had danced and the night she had delivered his child and given him the good news. She wondered what would happen to him now and who would write to Lady Harrach to tell her what had become of her husband. Mouse dropped to her knees, retching.

King Vaclav had done the killing, but she had driven him to it.

TWENTY-ONE

Only hours later, Christmas settled in Prague like an unwelcome guest, ushered in at the midnight Mass— the Angel Mass, the faithful called it. Mouse sat among the people. They were still angry, still unsettled by what they had witnessed their king do in the bailey. Their heads were too full of Damek's screams to hear stories of joy or salvation.

They met again for the second Mass at dawn. Few had slept. During the Christmas play, while the shepherds listened to the angels on high sing of the coming of the Lord, Vaclav began pulling at the thick, grisly scar over his eye socket. At first, he just ran his fingers along its crooked line, but by the time the shepherds had followed the star to the manger, Vaclav's head was bent, both hands digging at his flesh.

Lady Rozemberk, sitting beside him and softly humming those sixteen notes, leaned over, whispering. "Is there something the matter, my Lord?"

"My eye," he said, nearly weeping. "Someone has shut up my eye."

"No, my Lord. Do you not remember? You lost it at the—"

214

"Help me! Help me pull it open so I might see!" he yelled.

The monks acting out the shepherd's play looked to the bishop, unsure of what to do. Bishop Miklaus motioned the monks to continue, but Vaclav jumped up and stumbled out of the church.

After the dawn Mass, Mother Agnes summoned Mouse. This time, when Mouse arrived, the old woman was waiting for her.

"The man from yesterday. What was his name?" Mother Agnes asked.

"Damek. He and his wife just had their first child. He was a good man."

The Mother nodded, staring into the fire. "Damek," she said as if it were a command, an answer. "His blood is on my hands." She shook her head now, the wimple stretching and creasing. "No more. You have some strategy, I suppose? To free my nephew and those other men?"

"You will not like it, Mother."

Mouse explained the plan, and when Mother Agnes lowered her face into her hands, she felt sure the woman would take back her offer to help. Mother Agnes had spent much of her life protecting her little brother—shielding his fragile sanity, pitying the boy who had been so misused. To ask her to aid in driving him fully and finally over the edge so they might declare him unfit to rule and release Ottakar and his men was cruel. And Mouse felt the pain of it.

But Mother Agnes knew it had to be done. "No more innocents must die, no more good men tortured at the hand of my brother."

Though Mouse felt more certain of success, she grew more frightened as well. The assault on the King's mind would be relentless, and what had been Damek's fate yesterday could belong to Ottakar or Vok or Mother Agnes next.

After the final Christmas Mass, everyone headed to the Great Hall. The scent of cedar boughs and mint and the smell of the meat roasting on the fire began to work its magic on the people, lifting the gloom that had settled on them at Damek's execution. The holly glistened in the candlelight, the red berries shining like pearls. The Yule log crackled. The minnesingers played. The people grew festive.

Mouse watched from her usual place beside the King; Lady Rozemberk sat at his other side. Servants brought in wood planks and stones and started to construct a barrier in the center of the hall for some Christmas entertainment to come. But Mouse was more interested in what was happening around the edges of the room.

Several of the servants—agents of Mother Agnes, Mouse assumed—hummed quietly as they brought food and drink. The general roar of talk and laughter blanketed much of their efforts, but every now and then, a piece of the tune would lift above in the lull and pierce the King; his body jerked and shuddered as if he had been struck by arrows. Wide-eyed, he scanned the hundreds of faces in the hall.

Then a woman entered the room. Most of the people were too busy eating and already half drunk to pay her much mind, but Vaclav saw her. His face sagged and drained of color as he watched the woman meander along the edge of the wall, until she neared the dais, stopping a few feet from the guard.

A beastly roar echoed in from the courtyard, startling some and bringing eager smiles to others. Even the King turned his eyes from the woman to the door, waiting. He giggled as a man led a bear into the room on a leash. An iron muzzle circled its snout and an iron collar wrapped around its neck. As they reached the center of the room, the man tapped the animal with a stick, and it reared on its hind legs, letting out a fierce bellow.

Bile burned Mouse's throat. She had not anticipated a bear-baiting. Sick about the coming violence and sick with worry about how it might affect the plan to expose the King, she could do nothing but wait. And watch.

Two other men entered the hall, pulled by four snarling dogs flinging thick strands of slobber as they shook their heads, trying to free themselves of tether and master. They wanted to kill something. They wanted the bear.

Mouse bit into her lip as the man removed the bear's iron muzzle.

The King leaned over the table, resting his chin in his hands, ready for the show.

And then the men loosed the dogs.

They tore at the bear's snout, ripping chunks of its flesh. It tried to swat at one of the dogs, but the other three sank teeth into its arm and haunches. The bear screamed and threw its head to the ground, pulling the man holding its leash off balance. It covered its face with its front paws, trying to protect itself.

"No, no, no!" the King cried. "Make it fight! I want to see it fight."

The bear's master prodded the animal with the stick, trying to make it rear again.

"Make it fight!" the King yelled so shrilly he did not sound like himself. The people turned to watch the King, and Mouse could see the disgust return to their faces as they witnessed his bloodlust; it was clear they were thinking about what he'd done to Damek.

The King stood, screaming for the bear to fight.

And then the bells of Prague began to ring, clear and high in the cold Christmas air.

Fractures spread through the King like he was made of glass; Mouse watched his sanity slip from his eye just as she had watched the life drain from Father Lucas's. She followed the line of his sight. He was staring at the woman against the wall. She was looking back at him, smiling.

Mother Agnes did not wear her habit. She had found a dress, a wimple and veil, chin strap and hat, all a deep red. She pursed her lips and whistled.

The pain in her eyes seared Mouse.

"Mother." The King growled the word, low and slurred as if his tongue was too thick.

And then he launched himself at her.

The King rushed past the guard and threw himself on Mother Agnes, hands around her throat. His lips pulled back from his teeth like an animal, fangs bared.

The bells chimed.

In the center of the room, the bear's master let go of the leash. The creature stood on its hind legs, arms stretched wide, and threw its ravaged head back. Finally freed of its constraints, it roared and dealt a swift revenge against the dogs, swiping first one and then another, slamming them into the barricade, breaking their backs. It towered over the others and then came crashing down, its weight crushing one dog, its mouth closing around the neck of the last. With one shake, the dog hung limp.

No one had been watching the King. With a primal howl, he hurled himself and Mother Agnes into the center pit. "You will die, once and for all, Mother. You will torture me no more," he yelled in her ear, spit splattering her face, as the bear came running toward the new threat.

"Help her!" Lady Rozemberk stood and screamed. "That is Mother Agnes, the King's sister. Do you see? His mind is broken. He is going to kill her! Help her!"

The guards slid over the table and drew their swords as they moved toward the bear, the King, and Mother Agnes.

But Mouse had already made her way from the dais to the floor. She pushed a section of the barricade open and came at the bear from the side, slowly. The bear turned to look at her. She was ready, the power summoned.

"Be still," she commanded. "Be at peace. No one will hurt you."

Instantly, the bear lowered itself to all fours and then lay down on the floor, panting, exhausted.

Mouse was aware of the sucked-in breaths, the flutters of heartbeats, as the people watched her.

One of the guardsmen ran up to the bear, sword raised, but Mouse stepped in front of him. "You will not hurt this animal. It is docile, see? No longer a threat. Leave it be." The guardsman lowered his sword and backed away.

A palpable calm settled over the hall for a moment. And then the King shrieked, shoving Mother Agnes to the ground only inches in front of the bear. It did not stir.

Vaclav turned to his guards, pointing at Mother Agnes, trying to tell them something, but the sounds that came from his mouth were guttural, slurred, not language at all. He lurched toward the nearest man, grabbing at his sword. The guard caught him, trapping the King's arms behind his back.

Mouse helped Mother Agnes to stand. "Now is the time," she whispered to the woman.

Mother Agnes pulled herself upright, but her voice shook still. "My brother the King is ill. My Lord Chamberlain, please escort the King to his chambers and make sure that he is well tended and guarded constantly. He must not be allowed to leave his room. As you all have seen, he is a danger to himself and others. We must protect the King and pray that God will heal his mind." Her face twisted with pain. "And, Your Excellency, Bishop Miklaus, as chancellor, it is your purview to release my nephew, King Ottakar, and the other good nobles unjustly imprisoned in the Black Tower."

The bishop looked hard at Mouse for a moment, but then bowed to Mother Agnes. "I will order the release at once."

As the King was escorted from the room, it was as if tethers had been loosed. People clamored for the door. The bear's master cautiously sidled up to his ward.

"May I have him back, now, my Lady?" He would not look at her nor come near.

Mouse decided to use the fear to her advantage. "He has earned an easy life. No more fighting. Food and comfort, do you hear?"

The man nodded.

"I will know if you break your word, bear-keeper. And I will come for you."

He nodded again, stooping to hook the leash to the bear's collar. Mouse knelt, her hand on a patch of fur not ravaged by the dogs. "Go gently. Heal and be well," she said.

And then only Mouse and Mother Agnes remained in the Great Hall.

"We broke him, my little brother." Mother Agnes put her face in her hands and wept.

Mouse put her arm around the Mother's waist. "Come, let us go see your nephew. See the good that came of what we did."

But Mother Agnes lifted her face, which looked much older, and said, "I am going back home to the sick and the paupers. There is joy among those of us life has rejected. You would be welcome there, as well, should you wish it."

Mouse shook her head. Another life of isolation and rejection awaited her at Houska, but first she had a last task to do as the King's healer.

"Thank you for the invitation, Mother, but my duties call to me from the Black Tower. Ottakar needs me."

TWENTY-TWO

Ottakar learned to walk again slowly. His muscles, weakened by starvation and atrophied by weeks of disuse, gradually grew back under Mouse's careful watch. She ordered his food, fed him, treated his wounds. His hands had been bloody pulp when they opened the box, bits of bone showing at the tips of some of his fingers where he had tried to claw his way free. Despite Mouse's care, the scars would be with him always.

But at least his body was healing; Mouse still worried about his mind. At first, Ottakar had spoken little. He had asked once about his father, but, reassured that Vaclav was no longer a threat to him or the country, Ottakar had receded into a silent melancholy. Mouse understood; her weeks of muteness after Father Lucas pulled her from the pit were still fresh in her mind, so she had not tried to make Ottakar talk. She read to him, told him stories; his eyes had followed her as she paced the room, finding tasks to do while she talked herself hoarse.

By Ottakar's birthday near the end of January, he was able to walk a little in his room and sit in a chair. Barons and dukes, many who'd been loyal to Vaclav and now clamored for the son's favor, sent well-wishes on slick vellum, sealed with colorful wax and stamped with elaborate crests. But their gifts of horses and hunting dogs only reminded Ottakar of what he couldn't do. He spent the day staring wistfully out the window.

By St. Valentine's feast day, though, he managed to attend Mass and walk in his mother's garden. As they sat on the bench near the pool, Mouse handed him a book.

"What is this?"

"A gift. I did not have it ready by your birthday."

He looked through the book, pausing at the brilliantly colored illustrations—a man bathing in the blood of a dragon, his body covered in crimson but for the linden leaf on his back; a couple swearing vows in the dappled sunlight of a forest; a first night together, the woman's round white thigh slipping free of the linens as the man lowered his face to hers; his corpse at her feet and her face buried in her hands. Her holding the head of another man, lifted high in revenge.

"It is *The Song of the Nibelungs*," Mouse said. "The story of brave Siegfried and his wife, Kriemhild. I read it once when I was a young girl. It helped me dwell less on my own troubles as I saw how terrible life might be."

Ottakar ran his finger along the edges of the picture of Siegfried and Kriemhild's wedding night. "And beautiful. Life can be beautiful, too."

"Yes, beautiful, too."

The story had come back to her not just as a way to help Ottakar, but also as a way to heal herself. With the urgency of freeing Ottakar gone, the horrors of the pit had come back, as had a pressing sense of obligation to return to Houska and

Father Lucas—and, with it, the despair of what her life would be and what she would be leaving behind.

"You copied this? Drew the pictures? All of it?" he asked.

Mouse nodded, though it wasn't quite true. She hadn't copied it like he meant; she had written it from memory and the pictures were all her own.

"You have a gift, Mouse."

She winced at the word.

"I am sorry," he said, and Mouse looked up, ready to explain, but realized that he hadn't seen the wince; his face was turned away.

"Sorry for what?" she asked.

"Being weak. I let him—" He shook his head, trying to clear away the emotion. "I let him take me. I let him torture my friends." He swallowed hard. Mouse took his hand. "Damek is dead because of me. He was a good man. How could—"

He let go of her hand, clenching his fists together, his head dropping slowly to his knees as the anger and guilt finally broke free. "I was helpless, listening to them laugh as they . . . I would have ripped their throats out." The words shot through his mouth. "But it was my fault. I brought my men here and let my guard down like a stupid little boy wanting his father's love. I was trapped in the dark, pissing myself like a baby, and then you . . ." His body shook.

Mouse held him as he wept. She wept with him.

"You are not weak, Ottakar," she said when he finally sat back, dry-eyed. "You lived through that torture. You were not broken."

He scoffed and held his bandaged hands as evidence of his failure.

"Wounded, yes. But not broken. You are here. You live. You never gave in to him." She slid her arms around his waist, laid her head against his chest. "You are strong, Ottakar. Like iron.

The Iron King they should call you. And you are good." She closed her eyes and let herself see his soul, bright and steady. "Like gold," she whispered. "The Gold and Iron King."

∽

He had gotten better after that—talking, telling stories of his own, even managing some necessary business of ruling, but he kept to his rooms still. Mouse liked the isolation; she knew how the people would look at her after having seen her calm a raging bear with words. She wasn't ready for the averted eyes, the signs of the cross, the looks of awe and fear.

She'd had taste enough of it when Lady Rozemberk and Vok came to visit Ottakar. When Vok's father had returned to find Vaclav locked away and himself implicated in the assassination attempt on Ottakar, he'd fled beyond the borders of Bohemia. He meant to take his wife with him, but Lady Rozemberk elected to stay with her son, who, though less injured than Ottakar, still needed time to recover.

Mouse had actually been pleased to see them on their first visit to Ottakar's chambers, hoping they could draw him out in conversation, but he'd had little to say, and Vok had seemed oddly deferential, almost shy, with her. Lady Rozemberk kept her eyes down and said nothing, but Mouse had heard the muttered prayer from the woman's lips as they entered: "Holy Father, keep us from evil."

After that, Mouse left when they came to visit.

But the whispered gossip followed her through the keep, some of it about what she'd done at Christmas, some of it about what she was doing at night in the King's room.

Of course, none of the gossipers could know that Gitta slept there as well. Or that they kept candles lit all night. Mouse even trained herself to hear the quiet sputter in her sleep, to sense

224

the shift of light behind her closed eyes as the last candle began to flicker and die so that she would wake and light another. For Ottakar.

Though Mouse wrestled her own demons in the dark, sure she was back in the pit, frozen and waiting for the beasts to sink their teeth into her belly, it was Ottakar's screams that woke them; he was often still asleep but ripping the bed linens as he tried to free himself in his nightmare. Mouse would lie beside him, talking to him gently until he woke. She wanted the room lit so he could see instantly that he was no longer in the box. And then she would sing him back to sleep.

Mouse tried to armor herself against the gossip when she and Ottakar made their first appearance in the Great Hall after Mass in early March. The celandines had started to spread a carpet of yellow as they chased away the snow, but there was still a chill in the air. Mouse held back at the door, letting Ottakar enter alone. The hall was full, noisy with greetings and conversations, but all grew silent, standing and turning to watch him cross the floor and ascend to the high table.

"My Lord King Ottakar," the chamberlain said as he bowed. And all in the hall bowed with him.

"My Lord King Ottakar," they said. And so it was that Ottakar became the sole King of Bohemia. Vaclav might still hold the title while he lived, but the people, all of them, would look to the son to lead them now.

Mouse slipped quietly to her seat beside him, the whispers already reaching her ears.

"You look ill," Vok said as he came to stand beside Mouse's chair. Ottakar, who had been talking to Lady Rozemberk, turned and looked at Mouse.

"Just a little tired." Mouse smiled reassuringly at Ottakar. "It has been a long winter."

"True enough, but spring is all but come," said Vok. He turned back to Ottakar. "We should ride out, my Lord, as soon as you are able."

Ottakar shook his head. "There is much business here that needs tending. Bohemia and Margrave have suffered enough neglect. I will not be a lazy king. I will do my duty first above all else."

Mouse fought the little shiver that ran up her back.

"Could you not manage affairs from Hluboka, my Lord?" Vok said. "I was there just a week ago. Those German craftsmen you set to build your castle are truly artists. You should see the progress they have made."

"Is it an easy ride, Lord Rozemberk?" Mouse asked, thinking about the King's still weakened condition.

"Yes. Not far and level terrain."

Mouse could see the light growing in Ottakar's eyes and the question he asked her silently. "It seems a good plan, if you wish it," she said.

The King nodded, smiling. "Make the preparations, Vok. I want to be there by Cyril and Methodius's feast day."

But Mouse could not share Ottakar's joy. She had sent a letter to Father Lucas with the caravan of supplies that Bishop Miklaus had ordered soon after Ottakar's release. She had explained her absence and promised to return to Houska as soon as Ottakar was recovered.

She had not yet told Ottakar.

She finally found the courage the day before they left for Hluboka. They were walking in the woods, not far from where she had said good-bye to him the first time. He held her hand now as he had then.

"Ottakar, I must speak with you." She kept her eyes on the ground.

"You can tell me anything, Mouse."

"You will not like what I have to say."

"Have out with it, then."

"After you are settled at Hluboka, I must—"

"If you are about to tell me you plan to leave, to go back to the abbey or to that Father of yours, you can stop now. I need you."

"I do not mean to leave right away. Not until I see that you are fully out of danger. But your body grows stronger every day." She ran her hand along his arm. "And the nightmares come less."

He let go of her hand. "Is that all I am to you now? A patient? A man ill in body and mind?"

"You know that is not what I meant. You are . . . " She shook her head, unable to tell him how she felt, but she pulled his head down and kissed him. He was breathless when he drew back.

"Can you tell me why you must go?"

Mouse sighed. "I cannot tell you everything that happened there." She shuddered at the memory of the beasts in the pit, the screams of the hollow-eyed children. "Like you cannot speak yet of those weeks in the tower. Maybe someday. For both of us?"

He nodded.

"But I can tell you there is a great evil that lives at the heart of the wilderness at Houska. There is a wooden fortress built on the ruins of another fortress built on the ruins of another. For hundreds of years, people have stood guard over the evil in that place."

"I have heard stories, but—"

"They are true. But over time, we forget. We think they are just stories, made up, and we stop watching."

"And what happens then, Mouse?" he asked in a whisper.

"The evil slips out. Just a little at first, testing the strength of its prison, the fortitude of its guards. Sometimes the people renew their efforts and trap the evil again before it is fully free. But sometimes . . . sometimes horrible things happen."

"Is it now trapped or free?"

"Father Lucas and I have it bound."

"We must keep vigil, then."

Mouse nodded. "Which is why I must—"

"No."

Mouse started to argue, but he gently put his hand over her mouth. "I know you are more than just a girl . . . a woman. You are a healer. A soldier. My savior time and again. I do not doubt your ability to do anything, Mouse. But it is arrogance to think that you and only you can save us from evil. You see that?" He lowered his hand, freeing her to answer.

"Yes," she said, though in her mind she knew what he did not—that she had gifts no one else had. "But I—"

"Before we make any decisions, let us talk to Bishop Miklaus. He knows the situation?"

"Mostly. He has not been there."

"Well, he can go if needed." He was sounding more like a king. "Let us go see him now."

&

"I agree, my Lord. Houska is no place for the girl," Bishop Miklaus said as he poured more wine in the King's cup.

"We are not talking about her place. Her place is anywhere I will it," Ottakar said sharply.

Mouse squirmed. "The issue is what Father Lucas needs," she said. She knew she ought to go back; she had promised to go back, and she would as soon as Ottakar no longer needed her.

"What I want to know, Bishop," said the King, "is if you are fully aware of the danger Houska poses. Have you been there yourself?"

"I have been rather busy here, my Lord. But I sent a caravan of supplies along with Brothers Ales and Marek, and I have written to my friend, Bishop Bansca, who is in Rome. I received a letter from him saying that he himself would be coming. He seemed singularly interested in what was happening at Houska. And, particularly, in Father Lucas's involvement."

Mouse straightened, about to ask what he meant, but Ottakar commanded the conversation.

"It is well that Rome involve itself in protecting my kingdom from enemies I cannot engage in battle. I do not have the means, I think, to fight the dangers lurking at Houska. But I will do what I can. We will build a proper fortress of stone with ample battlements designed to keep the enemy contained. I will draw the plans for the castle myself and send a garrison of knights to oversee its construction. I will write to the Holy Father and request a schedule of holy men, trained against such forces of evil, who will hold constant vigil at the fortress." He turned to Mouse. "Surely with such reinforcements, Father Lucas can manage without you?"

"I—"

"Bishop Bansca writes that he means to be at Prague by Easter and will travel on to Houska soon after," Bishop Miklaus added.

"You see," Ottakar said, taking Mouse's hand. "Father Lucas will have help from Rome by the time you would be free to join him. There is no need for you to go at all."

Mouse blinked back sudden tears; Ottakar was fighting to keep her with him, not just for a little while but for always. As a girl, she had been given as an obligation to the abbey, accepted by Father Lucas and Mother Kazi, and she'd been needed as a healer, was needed now at Houska, but never in her life had Mouse been wanted. Not like Ottakar wanted her. Being wanted was the first step to belonging. She belonged with him, and the joy of it overwhelmed her. But her responsibility to Father Lucas and her commitment to keeping the demons in the pit hung heavy on her. Was she being arrogant, as Ottakar suggested, to think that it was her task alone to guard the pit as some God-made warrior? A normal life, married with children, a simple life—had she rejected these because of her pride, convinced that God had made her special to do some grand deed? Mouse shook her head, unable to see past what she *wanted* so she could see clearly what she *ought* to do.

She would write again to Father Lucas and wait for his response before she made any final decisions. In the meantime, she would get Ottakar settled at Hluboka, savoring the time with him, knowing it might be all they had together if Father Lucas summoned her.

"Seems we will enjoy the spring together, my Lord," she said, smiling.

⁓

Her first glimpse of Hluboka came on a small rise as they rode in from Prague. The castle was all loose stone and scaffolding. Ottakar was pleased, though, at the completed battlements, the moat with water redirected from the Vltava and circling around the hill that held the fortress and the four towers that anchored the corners of the wall around the keep.

"A proper stronghold," he said as he took a slow walk around what would be the bailey. "It may not look it now, but it will be a work of art, too, Mouse." He took her hand, and as he talked of what would be, she began to see it, too—the high peaked roofs, the spires, the polished stone, the grand windows that would fill the hall with light, the ornate archways at the great doors, the graceful sweep of the flying buttresses. "Come, I will show you the drawings I made."

"They will be in the East Tower, my Lord, with your master carver. Ludolf set himself up there to get some quiet, he said." Vok laughed and Ottakar joined in—Mouse could already see the tension in him uncoiling. He loved this place.

They also settled in rooms in the East Tower since the keep was still under construction. Though much smaller than the accommodations at Prague, Mouse loved her little room that rounded at the far wall. From the arched sliver of a window, she could see out over the forest that stretched down to a lake, water sparkling in the sunlight.

Besides Gitta, no other ladies had traveled from Prague. Lady Rozemberk, at Ottakar's request, had stayed to keep an ear to the gossip of court. At the break of winter weather, many of the nobles had left for their own estates, but a few stayed at Prague, and despite filling key positions with his own men and leaving his own guards to make sure his father stayed imprisoned in his rooms, Ottakar wanted a less official ally sensitive to temperament as well as keen to political strategy.

And so they lived simply at Hluboka—food cooked over an open fire in the bailey and eaten with the German craftsmen and servants in the open air as the weather allowed or in the unfinished lower hall of the keep. Raw as it was with wood unpolished, glassless windows, and bare walls, the room was stunning. The intricate carvings of faces and animals and creatures of folklore ran along the sills, columns, and the curved beams at the ceiling; they seemed more alive in the unstained wood. Mouse could not keep from touching them, half expecting them to laugh under the tickle of her fingers.

"You like my work, Lady Emma," Ludolf said one afternoon.

"They seem alive to me."

"To me as well. The wood, too. It tells me what it wants to be, and I work to make it so."

"May I watch you sometime?"

He studied her a moment, the pause awkward as she had expected an easy yes. "You are an artist?" He asked the question but acted as if he already knew the answer, nodding before she spoke.

"I draw and paint. Nothing so beautiful as this."

He nodded more vigorously. "You are an artist. I would be honored for you to watch me carve, my Lady."

But he did better than simply let her watch his work. He brought her a carving knife and scraps of wood, showed her how to let her fingers listen to the wood.

"Close your eyes," he told her, putting the piece of wood in one of her hands. "For the real artist, we see by touch, like the blind. The wood talks to your fingers, see?" He ran her other hand softly along the grain in the wood. "It tells your mind its secrets. Who it is. What it wants to be."

"I see it," Mouse said.

"Yes, yes! I knew you would." The German clasped his rough hands, torn by splinters and callused by labor, over her small, smooth ones.

Mouse opened her eyes, smiling, taking up the knife ready to carve the image she had seen in her mind. And then she saw Vok watching her from across the bailey, where he and some of the knights were at swordplay; he looked grim, displeased, and she tried to think of what she might have done, but then she'd always been a source of displeasure for him. With a shrug, she turned back to Ludolf and began to shape the wood.

∾

"Here you go," she said playfully as she gave a wooden figure to Ottakar weeks later. Her hair spilled out on the grass, and the faces of the violet sword lilies turned down, looking at her. Beside her, propped on his elbows, Ottakar separated her long tresses into locks, coiling them into castles surrounded by walls of more hair.

They had gone out for a ride with the knights and Vok, and they had stopped by the side of the lake to picnic. The air, now almost-spring warm and heavy with the scent of pollen, lay on them like a blanket, and many of the men stretched out under the trees and slept. Vok walked along the shoreline, picking up rocks and skimming them across the water. Mouse thought it odd to see Lord Rozemberk, usually stiff and formal, toss the stones so gracefully; he looked almost like a little boy, all ease and joy.

Hluboka had been good for all of them. Ottakar slept in his chamber alone, though he still kept a candle burning in the lantern for when the nightmares came. Mouse slept lightly, always half listening for his screams, but they came less often now. A letter from Father Lucas telling her that all was well, telling her to stay with Ottakar and promising to write to her if he needed her, had freed Mouse to enjoy herself and to dream again about a different kind of future.

"My Mouse has gone wandering," Ottakar said, pulling her attention back to the moment.

"And so I did. I am sorry. What do you think of my first efforts?" She nodded at the wooden figure he toyed with in his hand.

"It is my childhood hound, Sharpsight." He sounded odd.

"Do you like it?"

"He looks just as he did, as if you had known him. His lop-sided ear, the scars on his face just where they should be, his paw lifted as he sits just as he did when he lived."

"You told me about him, remember?"

"Yes, but all those details? And on your first carving?" He shook his head.

Mouse grew still, her voice too steady. "Ludolf called me an artist, a natural." But what she heard swirling in her head as

Ottakar studied her was *witch*. "Do not keep it if you do not like it."

She grabbed at it, ready to fling it into the lake, but Ottakar was stronger. "I did not say I did not like it." He pulled back, rolling over and taking her with him, and they wrestled, laughing. He lay back, holding her arms against his chest. "You just keep surprising me, my odd little Mouse."

"Good."

He slid his hand to the back of her head and pulled her to him. She had grown used to his kisses, though they still made her heart race, her face flush, but this one was different. Hungrier. He wrapped his arm around her waist, pressing her body against his.

"A summer storm nears, my Lord. Perhaps we should make our way toward the keep." Lord Rozemberk hadn't even cleared his throat to announce his approach.

Mouse spun upright, pressing the back of her hand to her mouth, embarrassed.

But Ottakar only laughed. "As you will it, my Lord Rozemberk."

∽

"You are too intimate," Vok said to her on the ride back.

"Excuse me?" Though a little ashamed at Ottakar's growing appetites and her confusion about how to manage him or whether she even wanted to or not, Mouse was not prepared to be lectured on modesty.

"My Lord the King says you are a daughter of Aragon."

That explained Lord Rozemberk's recent change in behavior; he seemed more tolerant, less disdainful, if still critical. Mouse had thought it might be a sense of gratitude or even respect for her part in freeing him, a consequence of her seeing him tortured and helpless. But she saw now that it was merely an acknowledgment of her suspected noble blood.

"Your familiarity with the servants, with the craftsmen, with Ludolf—"

"And Ottakar," Mouse added.

Vok's mouth was a thin line of disapproval. "How the King chooses to interact with you is his business, not mine."

"But?"

"But the way you talk to the servants, like they are your equals, and the way you let Ludolf hold your hands like—"

"He was showing me how to carve! And besides, he is old enough to be my father."

"And for all we know, he could be."

Mouse's face stung. Turning her back to him, she leaned low against the horse and whispered, "Run."

Ottakar thought it a race and so it was. They raced back to Hluboka, all of them laughing and windswept by the time they reached the keep.

All of them except Vok and Mouse.

TWENTY-THREE

The beginning of the spring marked the end of everything else.

Gitta pulled Mouse out of bed before dawn. "We
must go make the witches, my Lady!"

They had slipped between the old linden trees, massive
roots arching above the earth and entwining like fingers, the
woods thick with mist. Mouse had come to love this forest that
stretched out from the keep; she took long walks through the
pathless wood, often with Ottakar but sometimes alone for
the first time since the attack that had left Luka blind. Here
she could climb the low branches and nestle herself among
the limbs that held her like a hand. She could wonder at being
descended from kings in a faraway land she had never seen or
twist her loose hair as she thought about who her father was
and where she might find him. She dreamed about her future
with Ottakar, which, in her mind, centered here at Hluboka.
Ottakar planned to call the castle Deep. Mouse wrapped herself in the joy of days spent hidden from the world with him.

The morning music of the song thrush greeted Mouse and Gitta as they broke into the clearing where the other girls— some servants at the castle but most from the little village near the Vltava—sat among the tall grass, skirts encircling them like blooms. They were weaving in the dawn light.

"Let me show you, my Lady," one of the village girls said as Mouse dropped onto the ground beside her. "You take a handful of grass, see?" The girl gathered a bunch in her hand and cut it. "Fold it over with a bit of loop at the top. For the head, you understand?" The girl nodded to her own question. "And then grab a bit more of the grass and wrap it around the witch's neck so. Tie it and let the ends hang loose." She held up the grass witch for Mouse to see. "You got a head and some arms and once you fluff it a bit, a skirt." She handed the figure to Mouse. "A witch. For burning. Now you make one."

No one at the abbey had celebrated Walpurgis Night. Some of the lay brothers and sisters might go down to the fires at Teplá, but Father Lucas never allowed Mouse to go. Tonight would be her first time to dance around the flames that drove out the dark and celebrated the coming spring, full of light and life.

Mouse sunk her fingers into the tall grass, letting it slide along her palm, grasping it and then cutting through the thick bottom stalks with her knife. As she ran her hand along the strands, smoothing them, a blade of grass sliced her finger; when she bent the stalks as the girl had shown her and tied it off and fluffed the skirt, a smear of blood lay just below the witch's neck.

"What do I do with it now?"

"You toss it on the fire later, at just the last bit of darkness before the spring starts to rise."

"And I get my wish?" Mouse asked skeptically.

"No, no wishes, my Lady. But the straw-witch soaks up whatever darkness has clung to you over the year and the fire burns it up, you see? Then your light shines like the spring sun."

∽

At sunset, they gathered at the river. The water caught the reflection of the bonfire and the nearly full moon and the shadows of the couples dancing around the flames; Mouse and Ottakar were simply black shapes among the others, hands entwined as they huddled by the fire. The darkness and the wild wood, the gentle hum of the river, the touch of moonlight and the music mixing with the sounds of the night animals lifted them all from the mundane into something magical. Mouse understood why the Church frowned upon such festivals—not only because they anchored the people to the old ways and pagan tradition, but because they effaced the boundaries of positions and titles as rules and expectations blurred into the communal reverie of the night.

They stopped only to eat and drink, throwing themselves onto the benches that ringed the edge of firelight.

"Sing for me," Ottakar said, his breath tickling the back of her neck.

"Not in front of all these people," she answered, half turning to him.

He rested his chin on her shoulder, mouth grazing the exposed skin. "I want you to sing."

Mouse felt like someone else, careless and bold, as she skipped to the musicians and then around the circle gathering all the maids. She whispered to Gitta, who, giggling, whispered to the girl next to her. The women all held hands, the bonfire at their backs, and they danced, weaving and bowing, loose hair bouncing along their waists.

And Mouse sang.

"'May, sweet May, again is come, May that frees the land from gloom.'" Soft and low, her voice slid out into the darkness and touched the men, touched Ottakar. She became part of the magic. "'Every branch and every tree, Ring with her sweet melody.'"

Ottakar sat straighter still.

And then the women joined in the chorus: "'Sing ye, join the chorus gay! Hail this merry, merry May!'"

"'In a joyful company, we the bursting flowers will see,'" Mouse sang. Ottakar leaned forward, elbows on his knees, watching her. As the girls spun, she saw Vok watching them, too, and she blushed at the desire in his face, wondering about the object of his gaze. Gitta, perhaps? "'Our manly youths— where are they now? Bid them up and with us go.'"

A chaotic mix of squeals and laughter erupted as several of the men answered the song's invitation and ran to the circle, grabbing at the girls, who scattered into the woods. Mouse ran with them and Ottakar joined the chase.

The moonlight barely pierced the canopy; only splinters of light lay on a bush or branch here and there. The woods were full of curses as people stumbled on roots and bracken, then shrieks of glee as someone was caught. Mouse could hear footsteps behind her, tripping and then plodding more carefully. She eased between the trees, never stumbling because she knew the woods; she could see in her mind the layout of trees and stumps and fallen limbs. Mouse could easily have escaped, but she wanted to be caught.

When his hand grabbed her arm, she coiled into his chest. He was breathing fast from the run. His mouth was on hers before she knew that something was wrong. This was not Ottakar's heartbeat or scent. These were not his arms squeezing her so she couldn't breathe, not his fingers clawing at the laces on her back.

Mouse turned her face away. "Stop, Vok! Let me go!" Even in her panic she was careful to keep her voice clear of power; she would not be responsible for maiming or killing another person, no matter the consequence to herself. He must be drunk anyway, she thought, though she could smell no signs of it, but a sober Lord Rozemberk would surely not have touched her for all the world.

"The King has shared his women with me before," he said, shoving her against a tree and sliding his hand down her back to pull at her skirts. "He will not mind if I have a taste of you."

"Get your hands off me!" She pulled her knee up hard against his groin and pushed him back as he doubled over. Losing him in the dark woods was easy enough now that Mouse didn't want to be caught; she hid in the cleft of a linden tree until she heard him pass, and then she walked silently back to the bonfire. Many of the couples sat on the benches again, some were dancing, some had stayed in the woods. Ottakar stood looking out over the river.

"You hid too well," he said as she joined him.

"I did not mean to hide at all." Her mind raced, trying to make sense of what had happened; Vok's words came back to her, and an unwelcome thought pushed out all the others. "Did you come looking for me?"

"Of course I did." He slipped his arm around her waist, pulling her close and kissing her.

But Mouse was wrestling with doubt. She could not imagine the formal and loyal Lord Rozemberk committing such an indiscretion without permission from his king. Yet even Ottakar controlled his desires when he was with her, respectfully letting her dictate the boundaries of kiss or touch. Mouse might not belong to the Church, but her abbey upbringing and the thought of disappointing Father Lucas kept her own lust in check. She would not be the King's Mouse, as Father Lucas had said, until the King had given her his name.

"I thought you might want to be found," Ottakar said.

"I did. By you." It made no sense that he would offer to share something he himself had not yet enjoyed; Vok must have lied or misunderstood something the King had said.

"Would you like to play again? Slip off into the woods and I will come after you."

Vok's behavior might make no sense to her, but the seed of doubt he had planted about what she meant to Ottakar gnawed at her.

She shook her head, looking back over her shoulder at the woods.

"What is it? Did something happen?"

"Just a mistake, I think. Someone—"

"Someone stole a kiss, is that it? Like as not, it was no mistake. Watching you dance, your voice running over a body like warm water—you make any man want you, Mouse. Like I want you." And he pulled her to him again, kissing her.

"Dawn is coming!" one the women cried out, and couples came from the benches and the woods, straightening clothes and combing leaves from their hair, to stand circle around the fire, straw-witches in hand.

Mouse pulled two from the small bag tied at her waist. She had made Ottakar one, but she kept the first, smeared with her blood, as her own. She toyed with the witch in her hand, her thumb running against the red. She knew the potency of blood in a spell; even if no one here chanted words, there was magic in the dance and in waiting for the first of the spring light and in throwing a sacrifice onto the flame. If the witch did soak up the year's darkness to let a person's light shine bright and strong, what would happen if a person had no light? Like Mouse.

Would she burn up like the witch? What if she was a witch?

"Here comes the sun!" someone cried.

And all the others answered: "Burn the witch! Burn the witch!" Their faces played upon by the firelight, streaks of glowing red and deep fissures of darkness. "Burn the witch!"

Trembling, Mouse stepped back from the circle, knowing now why Father Lucas had kept her from Teplá's Witches' Night festivals. The people there knew something of her oddness; some of them even called her witch. Caught up in the fervor of the night, might they have laid hands on a little Mouse and thrown her in the flames with her straw sisters?

Mouse held her bloody witch to her chest, tears sliding down her cheeks. She would not sacrifice the poor thing. She would keep her mounting darkness to herself—at least until she was sure of her own light.

As morning came, she joined the girls dancing, weaving in and out, braiding ribbons that wrapped around the Maypole, but she was terribly conscious of how she moved; she did not sing as the others took up the May Day song again. Ottakar's assumption that the other men looked at her as he did and his lack of care troubled her and fueled the doubts Vok had seeded.

⚫

Those first days after Walpurgis Night, Vok had said little to anyone, jaw and arms clenched tight, his nostrils flared, but eventually he eased into his typical aloofness. Mouse wondered if he'd told Ottakar about the kiss; she hoped not. Ottakar had said nothing about it, and it stung to think he might know but not care.

The letter came weeks later, when the strips of colored linen they'd draped in the trees hung in tattered shreds, ripped by summer winds and bleached by the sun. The messenger arrived when they were down at the lake, the handful of Ottakar's knights splashing and dunking each other, Ottakar and Mouse cooling their feet in the shallows near the shore. Vok had stood alone under the shade of some oaks.

Ottakar accepted the letter and read it quickly. "We are needed in Prague," he said, already on the move back to the castle. Mouse and Vok turned at the sharpness in his tone.

"Why?" Mouse asked.

"My aunt writes that my father is ill and asks for me."

"You cannot trust him," Vok said.

"He is my father, Vok. What would you have me do?"

"Let him die."

Mouse found herself uncomfortably on Vok's side. "He tried to kill you, Ottakar. More than once. How can you trust him?"

"I do not trust him. I am not a fool. But he is my father. I do not expect you to understand what that means," he said to Mouse and then turned to Vok. "But you should."

"What duty you owed him died when he locked you in that box the same as mine died when my father asked to have me broken on the wheel," Vok spat back.

"I do understand," Mouse said, her eyes stinging. "He may not be my natural-born father, but I have a Father all the same. I know duty." She swallowed the bitterness as she thought about her own choice to stay with Ottakar rather than return to Houska. "Sometimes other needs outweigh that duty. Your people, you owe them protection and sound leadership. You owe them your life, do you not? How can you risk it then for someone who has done you and them such ill?"

For a moment, Ottakar considered what she said as he lowered himself to the grass beneath the trees, but then he found his argument. "My father's plotting was part of the sickness in his mind. My aunt seems to think he has come back to himself, his mind healing even as his body grows weak. And I do trust her."

Vok sighed with disgust. "They should have both hung, your father and mine, for what they did to us and to Damek. He was certainly innocent in all this, whatever crimes we may have committed as sons."

"And I believe we might lay another innocent life at your father's feet, Ottakar, and one that smells of malice rather than insanity." Mouse spoke softly, unsure of how he might react to her suspicions and unsure of her own motives for sharing it; she liked having him to herself here in Hluboka, and she hoped her selfishness was not blinding her.

"What do you mean?" It was Vok who asked it.

Ottakar was staring out at the lake.

"I see you already suspect it," she said to Ottakar.

"Say it anyway," Ottakar answered.

"Watched as closely as she was, how could your mother get your father's hunting knife unless it was by someone else's intent? And where did she find such will to act? A grieving woman who had not even enough determination to get out of bed on her own? How could she summon the courage to kill herself?" Mouse knelt beside him, laying her hand on his arm. "And why would she? Her only living son—a son she had raised to protect the weak, to fight for honor following the code of the knight—was riding, victorious, to claim his throne. She knew you would never do harm to your father; you are too good for that. If she was aware at all, Ottakar, she was proud of you! Why would she kill herself unless someone preyed on the weakness of her mind and convinced her that you were doomed, that she would live to see another son dead, perhaps at the hand of his own father? Perhaps by the man who slipped her his own knife to do the deed he bid of her."

"Have you any proof, Mouse?" She heard the hope in his voice.

"No."

"Nor do I, though our thoughts run the same." He looked up at her. "Would you have me believe that my father bears the mark of my mother's blood? How could such a truth console me? She is dead. He is all I have left."

"The truth might not offer consolation, my Lord," said Vok, "but it will keep you on your guard."

The King looked up and his eyes were fierce. "I will never drop my guard again, Vok. I swear it now as I swore it to Damek's widow and orphaned son. I will surely again lose men in battle under my command, but I will not take another life from my own stupidity." He sighed. "A show of reconciliation with my father will serve to heal the damage we have done to the country. And it will make my rule easier. Besides, I must return to Prague at some point. I cannot hide away here forever. We will leave within the week."

Despite her misgivings, when it came time to leave, Mouse was more than ready. She'd had her own unexpected letter from Father Lucas. This one was filled with quotes, but not as part of their usual game. He worked them into the body of his letter, making them seem natural—admonitions for her spiritual well-being, Scripture, the words of St. Norbert, lines from St. Francis. But they were anything but natural; they were code. It took her less than an hour to decipher it, though she was sure no one else would have been able to do it—just as she was sure someone else had read the letter before her.

Father Lucas was in trouble.

He seemed to think that she might be in danger as well. His message warned her: Tell no one about what happened at Houska. Tell no one about the code she had broken or the books they had read. Tell no one about her gifts. Show no one what she could do.

She wondered if Bishop Bansca was still at Houska and if he was the source of danger. Mouse felt safe enough from the reaches of Rome—what would they care about some no-name girl—and surely her connection to Ottakar offered some protection. It was Father Lucas who was truly in jeopardy; the Church saved its Inquisitions for its own. Had they found the *Book of Enoch* and the Watchers' book with Father Lucas? Books denied by the Church—would that be enough to accuse him of heresy?

Mouse meant to get answers from Bishop Miklaus and then travel to Houska as soon as possible.

TWENTY-FOUR

They rode out early one morning later that week. They spoke little. A chill rain began to fall as they came over the hills and saw the dark shapes of the towers and town. Vok kept rubbing at his forehead as the water collected in his hair and dripped onto his face.

They had reached Prague after nightfall, so immediately after Mass the next morning, when Ottakar went to see Vaclav, Mouse visited Bishop Miklaus to demand permission to go to Houska.

"Why would you want to go there?" he asked as he settled himself in his chair.

"I want to see Father Lucas."

"But he is not there."

"Where is he?" Cold dread ran through her.

"With Bishop Bansca, I imagine."

"And where is Bishop Bansca?"

"The last I heard from him, he was at Houska, but he wrote of plans to travel on elsewhere. That was some weeks ago."

"Travel to where?"

"I am sure I do not know."

"You are lying, Bishop." She had seen the dart of his pupils, heard the skip in his heart. "Now tell me where Father Lucas is."

"Or what? What will you do?"

The fear in his face and curiosity in his voice put her on her guard. He knew something. He had been in the hall when she quieted the bear with a word and a touch, but what else did he think he knew?

"Did I tell you that Brother Jan has been named abbot at Teplá?" he said, smirking.

"That is Father Lucas's position." She willed her trembling body to be still. If Brother Jan was the bishop's source of information, she and Father Lucas were in serious jeopardy. Brother Jan would most certainly talk about them breaking the law of cloister, but what else did he know? Like everyone at Teplá, Brother Jan knew about her general oddness, but he had never seen her use any of her gifts.

"Father Lucas forfeited his position so he could continue with his travels. He felt guilty that the abbey was left so long without leadership." He was lying again, and Mouse was done playing games.

"What I will do, Bishop Miklaus," she said, "is ask the King to pursue this with you. If you will not give me the information, I am sure you will give it to him."

"My Lord the King has little purview in matters governed by Rome."

"I will be sure to tell him that you find allegiance to his sovereign rule to be in doubt, Bishop. And what interest would Rome have in the doings of a simple Norbertine like Father Lucas?"

"As you well know, things are never as they seem, my Lady."

When Mouse found Ottakar in the bailey, his high spirits did not match her own mood; worry ate at her. If anything had happened to Father Lucas, the guilt of it lay on her shoulders: she should have gone back to Houska.

As Ottakar hefted sword and shield, training with his knights, she could see no sign of the damage done to him here just months ago. In some ways she wished he had more than the scars on his fingers to remind him of what his father had done, especially when he started to speak so happily of Vaclav's recovery.

"The rest has done him well. He speaks plainly, his mind sharp."

Mouse thought a sharp-minded Vaclav sounded more dangerous than ever, but she kept the thought to herself. She needed Ottakar's help and didn't want to risk offending him. "I am happy for you."

"Are you?"

"I wish him no ill, Ottakar. I only want you to be safe."

"I know." He took her hand. "His body is ill, though. The physicians here have done him no good. Would you be willing to look at him, Mouse?"

The request caught her off guard. "I . . . I cannot imagine that your father would want me anywhere near him."

Ottakar let go of her hand. "I am sorry I asked."

"No, please. I will gladly see if there is anything I can do for him, Ottakar, but have you asked him if it is what he wants?"

"I want it. He will agree." He stood. "Now I must return to training."

"I had something I would speak with you about, too, if I may?"

He stopped to listen but did not sit.

"I cannot find Father Lucas."

"Is he not at Houska?"

"Bishop Miklaus assures me he is not, but he will not tell me where they have gone."

"They?"

"He believes the Father is with Bishop Bansca."

"Well then, you have your answer." And sighing, he turned to go.

"But he will not say where they are. Could you ask the bishop? He might answer you."

"I will try to remember to ask when I see him next." He took a few steps toward the ring of knights still at swordplay, but then paused, turning back to her. "What do you mean he *might* answer me?"

"He implied that it fell outside your purview as it was a matter of interest to Rome." She waited.

"What matter? Not just Houska?"

"It seems not."

"I will make inquiries, Lady Emma." He bowed and went back to the fight.

Mouse couldn't shake the sense of foreboding that had settled in her skin. She had not been Lady Emma to him for a long time.

⁓

Ottakar had no answers for her when she saw him at mealtime in the Great Hall—and apparently no time for her, either. She still sat to his right at table, but his attentions were focused on the noblemen on his other side. Not long after the third round of food was served, she stood, meaning to slip off to her room, but Ottakar, whom she had thought was engrossed with some baron's land dispute, reached his hand out to stop her. She liked that he was still tuned to her presence, connected even if he had other obligations to manage.

She stepped closer to his chair, and he turned to her once the baron finished airing his grievance.

"Ah, I have missed you today," he said.

"I have missed you, too, my Lord." The formality hung between them for a moment.

"Where are you going?"

"To bed. I am tired from yesterday's ride and more accustomed to our hours at Hluboka." She saw the memory of their dawn rides and early evening walks play across his face.

"Are you too tired to go see my father? I told him we might pay him a visit this evening."

It wasn't what she wanted; she wanted to slide into bed, where she could worry over Father Lucas and the changes already happening to Ottakar and then cry herself to sleep. But as she looked down at his face, softened by the candlelight, all she felt for him surged, burning her inside; she had given herself to him that first day at Teplá, woven her life with his for good or ill. However he might change, despite her responsibilities to Father Lucas, regardless of the circumstances, she was anchored to him. She could feel the tether as it stretched between them; she closed her eyes and could see it sunk deep in Ottakar's glowing soul, and though she could see no light in herself, her end of the binding must be attached to something, too, because it held fast, unmovable. It gave her hope that she had a soul, even if she could not see it.

"I am yours to command," she said playfully as she pulled Ottakar up with her.

As they climbed the stairs together, Ottakar kept stopping to pull her to him, kissing her. In the dim corridor leading to Vaclav's room, he stopped suddenly, tugged her into an alcove and pushed her up against the wall, his lips finding hers in the dark. One arm wrapped around her waist, pressing her hips against his, while the other moved slowly up her side until it cupped her breast. His kisses were gentle but when his knee slipped between her legs, his hand pulling hungrily at her skirts, she pushed softly against his chest, and he stopped. He laid his forehead against the wall next to her ear.

"I would have you, Mouse."

"But for how long?"

"What do you mean? I want you. What do you want?"

"I want you, Ottakar. It is just—" She took a breath trying to push down the knot in her throat. "Despite having no name, no mother, no father, no family that wants me, even knowing that the Church does not want me, I—" Her voice broke. "No matter how many times someone bows and calls me Lady, I am nobody and I have nothing. But that makes it even more important that I value myself. Because no one else does." She was shaking. "I want to be with you. In every way, but—"

"You want a promise."

"I have no future, Ottakar, except the one I make."

He sighed. "And mine was laid out for me the moment my brother died." He looked at her sadly before taking her hand and leading her back down the hall. A quiet somberness had settled on them by the time they entered Vaclav's sickroom.

"My Lord," Mouse said, bowing as she neared the bed where Vaclav sat propped against pillows.

He looked a different man, gaunt and pale, but his eye still blazed and his voice was still sharp. "Have you come to work your magic on me?"

Father Lucas's warnings and Bishop Miklaus's insinuations left Mouse wary of the perception about what she could do. "I have no magic, my Lord, only the skills Mother Kazi taught me at the abbey. I hope they may be of service to you."

"To hear my son speak, you have the skills of Raphael himself. Turn around. Show me your angel wings."

Mouse felt the barb, but she spun playfully, refusing to do battle. "No wings, you see. Just a girl."

"You said that to me the night you saved my life. The first time." Ottakar's voice was thick with remembering. "And you are more than just a girl."

Mouse was anxious to be done and gone. "Shall I examine you, my Lord?"

At Vaclav's nod, she bent to listen to his breathing. She already heard the rapid, irregular beat of his heart.

"Have you thought more about Austria, son?" Vaclav asked.

"Austria?" Mouse looked over her shoulder at Ottakar.

"They are without a clear line of succession. Some of them have asked that I come for a visit. My father wishes it as well."

"It is our best chance for a foothold there. Imagine Bohemia with Austria under its heel! And Styria would surely follow. We could rival the Holy Roman Emperor himself."

"It will take more than a visit from me for us to find ourselves rulers of Austria, Father, and I am not interested in leading us to war."

"As I already told you, there are more ways to acquire what you want than force, but, yes, it will take more than your charm. That is just the key that opens the door. Find the right—"

"And I told you I do not want to discuss it." Ottakar cut his eyes toward Mouse.

"But duty must come before your wants, and, besides, you can have both. Eventually."

Mouse interrupted. "Have your physicians made a diagnosis, my Lord?"

"Not really. Just one sickness after another. One in the gut, the next in my chest."

"They have been letting blood?" She ran her hands along the grisly scars at his wrist and elbow.

"Regularly."

Mouse turned to Ottakar. "They must stop. They have taken too much and made him weak. He needs—"

"No." Vaclav cut her off. "They bled out the ill humors in my mind. I will not lose myself again. Not even if it means I must die."

Mouse felt sorry for the pain she heard in him. "My Lord," she said gently, "rest and quiet and prayer have helped ease the sickness in your mind, not the bloodletting. Have you tested yourself? Have the bells rung since Christmas?"

He held his lips in a tight line.

Mouse shrugged her shoulders and turned back to Ottakar. "I would have him out walking in the sunlight and clean air. I would have him eating more eggs and fish, more grain. There are herb teas I could make or a poultice—he has some tightness in his chest when he breathes. I would burn coltsfoot at night. I would take no more blood. And I would be sure to shelter his mind—nothing demanding, no decisions to make, no plots to hatch, no lands to conquer. Let him read books."

Vaclav hissed. "She would have me dead, if she could, and you under her foot."

"You are wrong on both counts. I wish you well and I want nothing from your son except his happiness." The last was not fully true. She wanted his love and to give him hers, openly; she hoped that would make him happy.

Ottakar stared down at his father, his face unreadable, even to her. "Thank you, Lady Emma. We will consider your advice. You may leave."

As the heavy wooden doors closed behind her, anger chased embarrassment, searing Mouse's face and waking the power that had slept during their months at Hluboka. She spun, laying her hand on the door's pull, wanting to go back in and demand an apology, wanting to let her fierce will humble their own petty ambitions. But as the feel of her power, fueled by righteous indignation, filled her, she remembered the demons feasting on the hollow-eyed children in the pit, their faces distorted by hunger; she imagined her own visage looked much the same—hungry for something and powerful enough to get it.

She took a deep breath and walked to her room, but the thought of what she could do, of what she wanted to do, squirmed in her chest. When she was a child and had wrestled with temper or desire, Father Lucas taught her patience and control. He busied her hands and mind until the anger abated, the power quieted. Once, when she was particularly angry, he had had her count the petals of a meadow full of hyacinths; another time, he had scattered a sack of grain in the herb garden and asked her to gather each kernel, one by one.

But now, Mouse could think of nothing ample enough to count her way to calm. She took a piece of wood she had brought with her from Hluboka, running her fingers along the grain, and then, eyes closed, she took her knife and began to carve. The sharp jaw first, the nose, the deep-set eyes; she imagined the color of the wood would be a good match for his hair as she cut swirls of curls into the grain. As she carved, she saw Ottakar in her mind as they had been that spring.

It was hours later, the sculpture nearly done, when the scream rang down the hall. The blade sliced her thumb as she jerked at the sound, but she was out the door before it had begun to sting.

He had stifled the cry as soon as it woke him, so Mouse was not surprised to find him sitting up in bed, arm wrapped around his bent leg, head hanging. The candle had been lit, but his servant was gone. Ottakar must have sent him away.

Mouse eased herself onto the bed beside him. He turned, grabbing her around the waist, and buried his head against her; it was wet with sweat. She held him and sang until he was calmer.

"I am not fit to rule, afraid of the dark like a child."

"You are not frightened of the dark, Ottakar." Mouse leaned over and blew out the candle on the table beside the bed. He sucked in a sharp breath. She took his hand, working to keep her own steady and her voice free of the fear that also consumed her.

"Here. Feel. No metal coffin." *And no demons*, she said to herself.

"Just dark," she said. *Just dark.*

"You are not afraid of this." *I am not afraid of this.*

They sat there, Ottakar gripping her hand, using the other to reach out and touch the open air. Mouse strained her eyes to find the faintest sliver of starlight on the windowsill, willing the visions of the demons away.

"I am sorry," he said finally.

"For what?"

"My father." He was quiet for a moment. "I hate him, Mouse, but I am scared for him to die."

"Why?"

"Because I am not ready."

"Yes, you are."

TWENTY-FIVE

Eventually, Mouse had gone back to her own bed and lay there past morning, leaving Mass to the faithful and the Great Hall to those who belonged. In the afternoon, she went to gather herbs and made a tea and poultice for Vaclav. She gave it to Gitta to take to the King's chamberlain, not wanting another awkward encounter—not with Vaclav or his son. She waited to see if Ottakar would come seek her out. He didn't. Reluctantly, Mouse went down for supper, but when she saw that Ottakar was not there—a delegation of Austrian nobles had come to Prague and they were deep in council— she walked in the solitude of the night woods and then went to bed.

And so she passed each day, mostly alone, often in the Queen's garden pulling weeds and cutting back dead things, nursing her hurt feelings and loneliness. It was here one day after a few weeks that Ottakar finally came to her.

She was singing softly as she pulled at the dead stalks of the moon daisies that had been left to run wild in the garden.

"I have missed that," he said, smiling at her song.

"And I have missed you," she said as she turned. He looked tired, his face taut. She regretted having left him alone so long.

He lowered himself to sit on the path beside her, careless of his fine silk mantle. "Caught you hiding in your Mouse-hole, did I?"

"I did not realize I was hiding," she lied. "I have been tending your mother's garden."

"I see that you have." He looked around at her work, his face softening.

"I am getting it ready for the winter. It looks barren and butchered now, but it will be beautiful come spring. I have only pruned and cleared, not planted anything new, so it will be your mother's garden again." She looked down at the brown, curled petals of the daisies. "I thought you might like to have a place to come to, quiet and simple, some place where you might feel closer to her, to draw strength from her."

"And from you."

He sounded sad. Mouse studied him, trying to understand.

"These past weeks, I thought you were cloistering yourself like some pious nun, angry with me because I asked for something I had no right to. And you were right, I was arrogant. Too much like my father, thinking that just because I wanted something I should claim it." He laid his hand on hers; she had been running her finger along the embroidery of hounds and horses on the hem of his cloak. "But here you have been working still to heal me of my grief and my fear. You always surprise me. You shame me and teach me."

"You think too much of me," Mouse said, leaning into him playfully and using his own words against him. "I *was* hurt and feeling sorry for myself." She shrugged. "But no matter our differences, no matter what you do, I am always on your side, Ottakar. I will always be ready to do anything to help you." She pressed her lips together quickly to keep from telling him that she loved him. He didn't need to hear it to know it, and she couldn't afford the gamble of what he might say, or not say, in turn.

"Always saving me, you are." He leaned down and kissed her on the forehead. "And now my father owes you his life, too. Your teas and poultices have worked magic. Even he is convinced enough of your skills that he has stopped the blood-letting for a while. Thank you."

"I am glad he is better. But you seem very tired."

"As I suspected, playing courtly games with Rome and the rest of the world is far more demanding than managing affairs at home. The Austrians want much and offer little." He ran his hands through his hair. "But that is not why I sought you out. I wanted to ask you, as a personal favor, to attend the feast in the hall tomorrow."

It took Mouse a moment to realize which feast it was; she had been measuring her time in tasks, not days, and had lost track of where they were in the calendar. She shuddered as she thought about the last Hallows' Eve.

She didn't want to spend her birthday overwhelmed with the bitter gossip of the lords and ladies in the Great Hall. She had grown accustomed to solitude again, days spent interacting with only Gitta. But she could not deny him and so gave him a nod.

"Have you heard anything about Father Lucas?" she asked hesitantly. Her daily visits to see the bishop always ended in closed doors and no answers, and, despite her constant worry, she had been too proud to seek out Ottakar's help again. But now that he had come to her . . .

"I wrote to Bishop Bansca myself and am waiting for a reply. I will tell you as soon as I learn something."

"Oh, thank you," she said, throwing her arms around him in relief and kissing him.

She could still feel the warmth of his breath on her face when she turned back to the dead flowers after he left.

∽

Gitta had a new gown for her when it came time to dress for the feast—a deep red silk covered in gold sparrows, the colors and sigil of the house of Aragon. Ottakar had ordered it made for her. Her bracelet was back, too. Mouse felt odd in the new clothes, as if she wore a mask like the mummers in the Church plays, another uncomfortable reminder of last year's haunting of the hollow-eyed children on All Hallows'.

But Ottakar thought her beautiful when he came to take her down to the hall. "All you need is a crown, for you are every part a queen."

"I doubt—"

He laid his finger on her lips. "I will allow no argument this night. I mean to compliment at will and you must simply suffer in silence. Am I understood?"

She nodded, but when he gave his next gift—a round brooch made of delicate gold leaves and a vine with a mouse, standing on its hind legs, engraved in the center, its emerald eyes looking out on the world—she laid her hand on his, stopping him from pinning the brooch in the fabric gathered at the hollow of her neck.

"I do not deserve this, Ottakar."

"You promised no argument." And he kissed her.

"But you know what people will think." It's what she also secretly hoped—that the brooch was a promise of more promises to come—and even though his behavior since they'd come back to Prague made such hopes seem foolish, she could not let them go.

"By the saints, I care nothing of what other people think! Not tonight." His eyes narrowed. "And I will not let you worry about it, either. We are going to have a good time, free of the burden of state and futures. We will be like we were at Hluboka. Will that suit you, my little Mouse?"

"It will make me very happy."

They entered the hall side by side, and all the people stood. The minnesingers played the songs Mouse loved. She and Ottakar danced the carols together. They spent most of their time talking despite the hovering presence of the Austrian nobles. When it was almost time to leave for the vigil at St. George's, Ottakar stood, waiting patiently until the Great Hall grew silent.

"Many of us find ourselves wrestling with ghosts on this All Hallows' Eve as we think about this time last year, about those dark days in Prague, days plagued by torment and cruelty and illnesses of the mind," Ottakar began. "I am sad for what we all suffered, but we should keep those days as a talisman to strengthen our resolve to do right even when it demands that we stand against those above us or those close to us." He pulled himself up straighter. "There were three here who did just that, who did not cower in the shadows from fear. They used their wits and courage instead of swords or battleaxes, but they fought as soldiers all the same, and they led us back into the light with a father and son reconciled, both healing from injuries or illness."

Mouse heard the strain in his voice. He took a deep breath and continued. "Our country is whole again, ready for the bright days to come, and we owe a debt to these three who made it so. First, my aunt, Mother Agnes, whom you all know for her work with our sick and poor. She could not be here tonight, as she holds vigil with her Sisters. To her, I have committed to build a new wing for her convent and a new chapel, too." The men and women pounded fists on the tables in approval. "Second is Lady Rozemberk, to whom I grant a small estate near the lake of Landstejn, which shall be under her sole management and be her own property until the time of her death, when it will revert to her younger son, Lord Rozemberk. The elder Lord Rozemberk has been stripped of his title and privileges, and his estates default also to his younger son." Again, the people sounded their pleasure. Ottakar cut his eyes toward Vok, who sat like stone; Mouse knew he had petitioned to have his father labeled a traitor, but Ottakar had refused.

"We thank these women for their service, but it is to one other we owe our deepest debt. With the bravery of a knight, she sought relentlessly to right the wrongs she witnessed, and so we bestow upon her this night a special honor: the rights of a knight." He held out his hand to Mouse, pulling her to stand beside him; she was sure her face was as red as her dress. "Lady Emma, you will keep vigil this night in the Chapel of All Saints and on the morrow make your oath before me and God and be knighted as a protector of Bohemia."

The Great Hall stood silent. Mouse's heart thundered in her ears. No woman had ever born the title of knight in Bohemia, and it seemed the lords and ladies did not wish it to be so. Mouse chewed at her lip and was about to tell him that she did not need such accolades when Vok began pounding his approval on the table. Ottakar's men quickly joined in and then finally the others in the hall did, too.

Ottakar bent, his lips cool against the heat in her cheek as he whispered, "You do have value, Mouse, not lent you by parents or a family name, but a worth all your own."

∽

After the others had gone to St. George's to keep the Hallows' Eve vigil, Ottakar and Mouse slipped into the Chapel of All Saints. Mouse cried a little when she knelt before the altar as

Ottakar laid sword and shield on it. Bishop Miklaus offered a stilted blessing and then left quickly.

"They were mine when I was a boy. My mother had them made for me," Ottakar said as he knelt beside her, nodding to the sword and shield. "We called them Long and Broad."

Mouse smiled; the old Bohemian folktale had been a childhood favorite of hers.

"They are yours now," Ottakar went on. "Like the hero in the tale, you broke into the tower. You defeated the evil sorcerer. You told me you were a soldier; I believe you. And every knight must have a blade and shield, though I am not sure when you might use them." He looked over at her. "Do not imagine that I mean to take you to war, knight or not."

"Are we going to war?" she asked, suddenly serious.

"No *we* are not, but I am sure I will lead men to their deaths on the battlefield at some point. Each day I learn how much more twisted and tangled are the politics of the Church. And how far-reaching. I must keep this pope a friend, and I am sure he will have people he wants me to bend to their knees for Rome." He sighed as he made the sign of the cross. "But this night those troubles rest elsewhere. Tonight, we must clear our minds and cleanse our souls so we are pure to take the oath tomorrow."

Mouse bowed her head; she counted her breaths and then her heartbeats, methodically sifting through the swirl of emotions until she was calm. But she still worried about being brave enough to try to cleanse a soul she wasn't sure she had. She couldn't help but look at Ottakar's glowing soul as he kept vigil beside her. It seemed different somehow; though as she studied it in her mind's eye, she could not easily tell what had changed. She finally resolved that it was not smaller but tighter, more rigid. And she was troubled.

He left her for a little just before dawn. Against her better judgment, she turned her special sight inward, looking again for a flicker of light, some sign of a soul to cleanse. In the quiet of the chapel, the wind whipped around the windows like a creature seeking a way in to the sanctuary; the candles at the altar flickered as its tendrils snaked in between the loose panes. Mouse shivered.

"'I will declare what God hath done for my soul. I cried unto Him with my mouth.'" As she whispered Father Lucas's favorite Psalm, his face flared up in her mind like a warning. "'Verily God hath heard me; He hath attended to the voice of my prayer,'" she said over and over, trying to make the sense of foreboding that pressed down on her slip away like smoke from the candlewick.

Mouse heard the door to the chapel open and ease shut, Ottakar's footsteps coming down the aisle, the rustle of his silk mantle as he stopped beside her. He helped her rise, and she felt the heat in his hand, longed to lay it against her cheek, to kiss his palm. The flush of desire felt as odd as the rush of fear had moments ago. He led them to a bench beside the altar.

"So how will you knight me, then? Am I to be Sir Mouse?" she asked playfully, trying to force herself back to normal; she felt as if she were dipping and soaring like a bird on the wing.

"I think Lady Emma will do, but you will always be Mouse to me." He tried to match her tone, but he avoided her eyes, playing instead with the ribbon around the cuff of her sleeve. She knew him well; he was wrestling with something.

"If it has to be told, Ottakar, then best be done with it." She whispered the words, almost hoping he wouldn't hear.

"You are stronger than I am." He spoke softly in the voice he saved only for her, unburdened by expectation and free of command. He kept twisting the ribbon of her sleeve where her hand rested on his thigh. She bent to look in his face, tucked a strand of hair behind his ear so she could see his eyes. They normally reminded her of the hyacinth-covered hills near home, but tonight they were clouded.

He jerked away from her and stood, gripping the balustrade, his shoulders hunched.

"When you look at me like that, I cannot think about anything but—" His words came thick and fast. Mouse wanted to go to him, but she couldn't move, frozen by a sudden, terrifying hope.

She was sixteen and she knew what she wanted for her life. But it was impossible—he was impossible. Then he was beside her again, his breath hot against her mouth, his lips pressing on hers. Her mouth parted for him, ready to give him what he wanted, what his body craved, as he was about to give her what her heart desired—a name, a place to belong, a life with him. His hand slid behind her head, the other around her waist, supporting her as his lips opened into her own. Mouse felt dizzy and alive, but then he pushed himself away from her.

As he turned back toward the altar, she lifted her hand to her cheek, cooling the tender skin his stubble had chafed.

"I am sorry for that," he said.

"I am not."

"I think you know how I feel about you, though neither of us has said it. I can keep nothing from you anyway, even if I tried."

She smiled at him, confident and comfortable with the openness they had always shared.

"But it does not matter what I feel. I am King and you are . . ." He shook his head. "By the saints, Mouse, a wayward mother, even if she claims connection to the family of Aragon, and God only knows who for a father? I swear I would give Moravia to find him a noble and ready to claim you, but despite all my efforts I can discover no evidence of him. It is like you were sired by the wind." He clenched his jaw, and then his face softened as he looked at her. He sat beside her again, took her hand.

Mouse's body coiled as the sense of foreboding seeped into her again.

"You told me yourself that in order to be a good king, different from my father, I must put the needs of my people above my own desires. The time has come for me to do my duty. I must craft battlements to shield Bohemia from the threat of an ambitious pope. I am elected duke of Austria, Mouse. We will announce it tomorrow."

"I am sure your father is pleased," she said coldly.

"This is none of his doing."

"He has always wanted to claim Austria. When he saw he could not do it for himself, he used you to get it for him. He has been working on you ever since we returned to Prague. He has infected you with his ambition."

"No, Mouse. This is my decision. And in order to be Austria's duke, I must appease their nobles. I am to marry Margaret, Henry's widow. And you will—"

Mouse didn't hear what else he meant to say. She saw now that the hope she'd clung to this night had been desperate and false. By choosing duty over her, Ottakar breathed truth into what had been uttered in spiteful missives by the ladies of the court and hinted at in the longing stares of Ottakar's men. She was and always would be—nothing. Here in the flickering candlelight of the chapel, Mouse finally believed it.

The cold of the marble pew seeped into her hips and legs, numbing her. She wanted to run away, but she had nowhere else to go.

"I love you, Mouse. I will always take care of you. And you will marry Vok. He will make a good husband for you. You will want for nothing and—"

"What?" she asked as the words finally registered. "Vok?"

"You will marry Vok."

"No."

"He wants you. He will make a good husband and—"

"It does not matter."

"It matters to me." He sounded sad.

"I do not want to marry."

"You would choose to be a nun? But Mother Agnes said—"

"No. The Church is not for me. Just let me go."

As she said it, she knew he would refuse. She had no family. She could not return to the abbey. Mouse had nowhere to go; she was trapped. She trembled as she thought about the reality of what her life would be now.

She stood to leave, but Ottakar grabbed her arm.

"There is more. I would not give you so much to bear, but I feel you would want to know."

Mouse felt as if she were in a dream.

"I have a letter from Bishop Bansca. It came today." His voice sounded far away, hollowed, and the scratch of the parchment in his hand, too loud. "He speaks of Father Lucas."

She froze.

"Would you like to read it?" He held out the letter to her.

Her hand moved slowly, the fingers numb as they closed over the broken seal. She meant to nod, meant to open the letter, but her arm dropped slowly down to her side.

"He is ill," Ottakar said.

The words thawed her; she quickly turned to him, too quickly after hours on her knees. The image of St. Wenceslaus in the stained glass swayed and Ottakar's arm wrapped around her waist to steady her.

"I must go to him. Where is he?"

"You cannot help him, Mouse."

"I am a healer. I will make him well." She took comfort in the arrogance of her tone.

"He is beyond healing."

"What do you mean?"

"Bishop Bansca says it is leprosy."

"No." She would not let it be so. "I will go see for myself. This comes from Bishop Miklaus, yes? He and Brother Jan want to discredit the Father, to get him out of the way so Brother Jan can have the abbey. They—"

"The letter comes directly from Bishop Bansca, Mouse."

"I do not know this man. I do not trust him. And besides, if it is true, if Father Lucas has—" She choked on the words. "I can still tend him, ease his suffering." She was weeping.

Ottakar pulled her to his chest. "And risk the disease yourself? Do you think I would let you do such a thing?"

"I never get sick." She sounded like a child. "And he will be sent to some cruel place with no one to care for him. No one here wants me. Please let me go to him. Tell me where he is, Ottakar," she sobbed.

"I do not know."

"Then find out!" She dug her hands into his tunic; she would make him answer if she had to.

"I think your Father anticipated such a response, Mouse. He writes to me at the end of the bishop's letter. See here?" He took the letter crumpled in her hands and unfolded it.

She read the short lines, clearly in Father Lucas's hand though oddly scripted as though he'd had difficulty holding the quill— "Tell my little andílek to let me rest where I am glad to go."

"No," she cried, her legs giving way beneath her. Ottakar carried her back to the bench.

She cried until she had no more tears.

An hour later, she stood as if dead and let Ottakar knight her in front of the people who had crowded into the chapel; none of it mattered.

In her room, the morning sun pouring through the window too brightly, she let Gitta help her undress.

When she got in bed, she did not care if she ever woke.

TWENTY-SIX

Visions of Father Lucas, grisly lesions covering his face, his hands gnarled, fingers bloated and black with infection, finally drove her from the numbness of half-sleep she'd lingered in for hours. Mouse sat at the edge of the bed trying to find the will to do something. All she wanted to do was run, though there was nowhere to go. But her body would not stay still. The power in her coursed through her like fire, feeding on her despair and reminding her that she had the power to make Ottakar change his mind or to force Bishop Miklaus to tell her where Father Lucas was.

Mouse had sent Gitta away, so she dressed herself and headed to see the bishop. Last night's wind had brought a bitter cold, and she bent her shoulder to it as she wove between the icy puddles in the bailey. She was glad for the warmth of the bishop's house, though the reception of her was as chilly as the weather; Bishop Miklaus would not see her. Too busy with Church matters, his man said. So Mouse kept watch from the shadows of St. Vitus's, where the freezing rain had formed uneven fangs along the eaves of the church. The bishop would leave his house sooner or later, so Mouse lay in wait, teeth chattering.

When the door finally opened and Bishop Miklaus headed down the path, Mouse followed him, not wanting to confront him where there might be witnesses. He pulled his cloak around him as he walked toward St. George's. The freezing rain, now mixed with pellets of stinging ice, had driven almost everyone indoors; the back bailey was empty. She had assessed the bishop as he walked, noticed how he lurched leftward, his leg dragging a little in step. He was weak on that side. The growing sheets of sleet would help her, too. He was sure to take the narrow path between St. George's and the outer wall for the bit of cover it would offer and the break against the biting wind.

Mouse slipped around the front side of the church ahead of him and pressed her body into the dark of the wall, willing herself to blend with the shadows as the hollow-eyed children had done.

He did not see her as he passed.

She slipped her foot in front of his left leg as it dragged; his right knee buckled when it took his full weight, and his body spun as he lost balance, slamming into the church wall. Mouse was on him before he could he cry out, one hand on his chest, pushing him hard against the stone, and the other shoved tight against his throat.

"Tell me where Father Lucas is." She could barely speak, her voice thick and hoarse from the cold, her mouth nearly frozen.

"I do not know."

Mouse's fingers tightened against his throat, digging deep into the flesh and curving around his windpipe; she could feel the heavy and rapid beat of his heart where her thumb pushed against his artery. His eyes grew wide, panicked.

The power grew in her, drunk on the rage that burned in her like blasts of hot air from a fire gone wild. What did she care of oaths made? Why should she keep faith with God, who had never claimed her, or Ottakar, who tossed her aside?

"Tell me where Father Lucas is!" she commanded.

"I do not know," the bishop gasped.

"Then tell me where Bishop Bansca is." Mouse squeezed her hand even tighter about his throat, her fingernails cutting into his skin.

"Rome."

"What?" She felt the cartilage in his throat start to give, his eyes bulging and then rolling back in his head. But it was the hopelessness of his answer that doused the anger and the power so suddenly.

If Bansca had gone back to Rome, he was beyond her reach. And if he was the only one who knew where Father Lucas was, then Mouse would never find him.

Bishop Miklaus slumped as she let him go.

Horror rushed to fill the emptiness in her, and she crouched, frantically laying her ear against his chest. His heart beat, irregular and faint; he was still alive. But it was only luck that had saved him; it was not her conscience that had stilled her hand.

Mouse ran through the sleet to the Black Tower. She told the guards the bishop had collapsed, and then, as they tended to him, she slipped through the gate and into the woods. Numb again, not from the cold, she wandered without purpose or thought between the ice-coated trees. They tinkled like glass as branches brushed each other, moaned as the wind rubbed limb against limb. As she walked down to the river, she could hear the voices of the Sisters, carried down from the convent, praying for All Saints. They did not call her back or send her on her way.

There was no one to watch her step into the swirling water.

In her mind, Mouse imagined the warm shallows of the Teplá back home; she could barely feel the sharp teeth of the nearly frozen and much deeper Vltava. She was thinking of that day last year when she'd gone into the water unsure of her future, afraid that her dream of adventure—made flesh and bone with the arrival of the wounded Younger King—was dead. She had thought Ottakar was leaving the abbey without her, and, as she'd laid her head back in the gentle waters to rinse away his blood, her disappointment had led to a wish that the river would carry her away to someplace new, an unseen future. As the violent currents of the Vltava pulled at her skirts, Mouse made the wish again.

This time, the river heard her.

With a vicious swirl, the water snatched her feet out from under her, and she sucked in a panicked breath just as her head plunged beneath the water. The river pulled her to the bottom, dragged her against the rocks and debris. When something sharp jabbed into her leg, she cried out, but the sound floated away in a bubble and water rushed in to take its place. Mouse clawed her way to the surface, spluttering and coughing, and then sucked in another quick breath before the Vltava took her again.

It did not let her go this time. Her chest burned with the need to breathe, but as she tried to push herself up, the riverbed dropped away and her head slammed against a rock, and the darkness swallowed her.

⁂

Mouse tried to move but something had her pinned. She opened her eyes, expecting the sting of river water, but it was dry, cold air that drew tears to her eyes. She couldn't tell where she was. Everything was dark except for an eerie glow in the distance. Just like in the pit.

Fear drove her to a frenzy.

She pushed hard against the surface under her. Ice cracked and fell around her like slivers of glass. Her clothes, frozen stiff, ripped as she shoved herself up, and her skin burned where it peeled away from the icy ground. As she rolled onto her back, Mouse could see now that the glow was only the moon behind the clouds; its faint light glistened on the ice that coated the trees. Her feet still dangled in the river.

She grabbed at a nearby tree and pulled herself up. *I should be dead*, she thought as she stumbled through the woods toward the keep. She must have been lying on the riverbank, soaking wet and freezing for hours. *Why am I not dead?* But her mind was as numb as her body and gave her no answers. Her skin was bluish in the dim light, her heart sluggish from the cold.

She thought the guard at the tower asked her something, but she couldn't hear over the high whine that filled her head. Only when she tried to speak did she realize that the whine was coming from her. As she silenced herself, she fell to her knees. It hurt when the guard picked her up, his hands burning her through her clothes, which crackled as he shifted her in his arms. She saw blurs of color, heard bits of sound.

She squirmed as she was laid on the bed, someone's hands tugging at the thawing clothes, the warmth already beginning to drive needles into her. As the pain mounted, she pulled herself inward, back to the abbey where pain was for a purpose; she could take the agony of the knives running through her, the throbbing in her leg, the burning in her chest if she knew it was for a purpose, penance for something she had done.

And then Ottakar was with her, whispering in her ear. "You are a soldier, Mouse. Fight!" But she didn't care about fighting; she had done something wrong, but for the first time in her life, she couldn't remember, her mind too full of pain.

"Please, Mouse." He sounded like he was crying, and she felt sorry for him, but she was too close to finding what she had lost to help him. As the bishop's face, bulging eyes and gaping mouth, flared in her mind, she felt her stomach clench. Someone pulled her to her side, lifted her hair from her face as she retched up river water and bile.

"I love you," he said as he wiped her face with a warm cloth. It hurt too much, so she let go of the pain and the penance it offered and fell asleep.

✍

Ottakar was not so gentle in the morning when it was clear she would live.

"What did you do?" he demanded.

"Went for a walk, fell in the river, dragged myself back to the keep." She looked him dead in the face as she lied. She had woken midday and wrestled for a moment with guilt and fear and then moved on to trying again to figure how she had lived, but after an hour with no plausible solutions, a recklessness had settled on her.

Mouse just didn't care anymore.

The river had most certainly offered her a prophecy, and she was smart enough to understand the lesson: Just as she had no soul, she had no future. She had been a fool to think herself made for a purpose, wasting all that time trying to figure out what she was meant to do. She was meant to do nothing. There was no path laid out for her, no destiny. Just as her parents hadn't cared enough to give her a name, God had not cared enough to give her a soul or a purpose in life; she was like the chaff, discarded waste left to burn or not at God's whim. She could get pulled under and spit out at his whim. She would live or not at his whim. Suffer or not at his whim.

So Mouse decided then that she would live in the moment, day to day; she would not consider tomorrow or harbor the past. She would not care about rules or opinion; she would do as she pleased and lie when it felt right.

"I promise, Ottakar. It was an accident. I am not so lovesick as to risk eternal damnation." She sounded convincing even to herself.

"I love you, Mouse," he said more softly. "No matter who claims the title of husband or wife, no matter the demands of country or Church, I will always love you."

"And I you." The truth of it almost pierced her newfound callousness.

∽

When she went down to supper for the first time days later, she tried to drink herself drunk. She was surprised no one had questioned her about Bishop Miklaus, but when she opened her mouth to ask about him, she silenced herself by tossing another glass of wine down her throat. She reminded herself that she didn't care—not about whether he had recovered or if he had named her as his attacker.

"So you fell into the river?" Mouse heard the disdain and doubt in Vok's voice. She was now seated beside him as his betrothed; he sat between her and Ottakar. They had been at table for more than an hour, and these were the first words he had spoken to her.

She shrugged in answer to his question.

"It was an unlucky day, then. The bishop also had a bad fall. Hit his head, it seems, though he cannot remember what happened."

Mouse swallowed the wine in her mouth.

"I mean for us to marry soon. You have no family, and the only one of mine I care to be present is already here," Vok said.

In the corner of her eye, she saw him nod toward Lady Rozemberk, who sat on the other side of the King.

"Whatever pleases you, my Lord," she answered, and, in her mind she kept telling herself that none of it mattered. She had no future. Only now.

"I also mean for us to leave immediately for my castle in the south. My older brother threatens to claim what is now rightfully mine. I want to establish myself as lord there quickly. And we need no feast to celebrate our marriage, do we?"

She didn't bother to answer and instead drained the cup of wine and kept her eyes on the couples dancing the carol.

She sensed Vok stiffen, offended at her refusal to acknowledge him.

"Tomorrow then." And he turned to speak with Ottakar.

She tried to deaden herself to the sting. Tomorrow she would be Vok's. She would leave Prague. She would not see Ottakar. She could make herself not care about the first two; the last brought tears to her eyes. Ottakar would leave for Austria just after Martinmas, but that would've given them several days to spend together—not now, though.

The sound of Ottakar's voice from the other side of Vok interrupted her reverie. "Tomorrow? You need not rush, Vok. I will not change my mind. I swear it," the King said.

Clearly Ottakar was not ready to say good-bye so soon, either. It made the knot in Mouse's throat burn more. She announced that she was not feeling well and slipped from the Great Hall to seek solace in the small walled garden.

The weather had warmed a little, making the evening almost pleasant. But the gentle sounds of horses and the hounds and the sight of the stars and the half moon angered Mouse. Signs of God's goodness, the rightness of his world, they salted her wounds. By the time she reached the fountain, her tears were dry and her tongue sharp.

"I will not come to you again for comfort as I did the other night," she hissed to the heavens. "Why should I? What do I get for all my good works, my obedience and long suffering, my faith? Nothing. You break me. You take everything from me even though I have so little." She closed her eyes against the beauty of the night sky and saw again the darkness in herself. "Yet still you do not claim me. You give me no soul. No future. No hope. What good are you to me? You close your Church to me, hide your face from me? Well, so be it." She was yelling now. "I close my heart to you. I turn my back on you. I swear it!"

She spun quickly toward the path to leave, but a wave of nausea sent her to her knees, her stomach awash with acid and wine. She lowered her head against the stone bench, the coolness settling her queasiness. In the quiet, visions of the days spent here with Ottakar as he healed played out like ghosts before her and then, more vividly, images of the book she had made him—the illumination of Siegfried and Kriemhild's wedding night.

Mouse knew what she wanted.

She would give herself over to her desire in hope that it would drive out her anger and sadness. She would save those for tomorrow and think only of tonight.

She found him talking to the Austrian nobles and slipped her hand in his. With just the slightest pull, Ottakar followed her. She led him to All Saints Chapel where, just days earlier, he had killed her hopes of becoming his wife. But Mouse would have what she wanted, one way or another. If he could not be hers, then she would be his. Before God, if not man, and whether God liked it or not.

"Send the guard away," she said.

He did as she told him.

"What are you doing, Mouse?" Ottakar asked, his voice already thick with longing.

"I want you," she said simply, and she took his hand and wrapped it around her waist.

He pulled her against him and lowered his mouth to hers. His beard stung her skin like tiny needles. Her jaws hurt as he pressed his mouth against hers, forcing her lips to part. And then he pulled away.

"Not here. Come." He pushed her toward the back of the chapel to a small door that she knew opened to a hallway. He would have her in his own bed. In secret.

"No, Ottakar. Here. Now."

She would not be just another of his conquests. She would not have him remembering her tangled in his blankets, stained with his wine, her hair spilled across his bed like so many others. Mouse was not a fool. She knew what this night was. It was not a promise or a future. She would make herself a wife now and think of herself as a widow in the morning when Ottakar left her. No one else would ever know.

Except God.

Mouse pulled Ottakar's face back to hers and slid her hands behind his neck. She opened her mouth for him this time. He ran his fingers along the front of her gown and tugged at the corded belt that hung low on her waist. He moved his hands to the laces at her back, and she shivered when the cold penetrated the loose linen underdress as her gown fell away. His hand ran along the linen edge, tracing her collarbone, pulling the underdress gently over her shoulder until it, too, fell away.

"By the saints, Mouse, you are lovely." He bent to kiss her neck, pressing himself into her, and she could feel the hardness of him. Feel his desire. "The most beautiful woman—"

She put her finger against his mouth. This was not his seduction; it was hers. And this was not about romance. This was not the beginning of something. It was the end, a final act of rebellion. She lowered her hand to touch him. He groaned. And then he had no more tender words for her, just the grunts of his desire, which he'd leashed for the year she had been with him. His hands pulled at her body, the rings on his fingers cold against her back, her buttocks, her breasts. His own clothes, shifted but not removed, billowed around her, slapping against her face, smothering her as his weight pressed down on her, again and again, until he cried out and she lay beneath him, shaking, her lips bruised, blood on her thighs.

"I am sorry. I meant to be gentle." He wrapped her in his mantle as he pulled her head to his chest, trying to warm her. "Next time will be easier, Mouse." He kissed the top of her head. But Mouse knew there would not be a next time. Tomorrow she would marry Vok.

TWENTY-SEVEN

T hey rode for five days in heavy snow, Mouse and Vok and Lady Rozemberk dragging a long tail of men and carts filled with supplies. Ottakar did not mean to march into Austria with a horde of knights like a conqueror, but rather with the pomp and show of a newly elected duke. And so he'd given care of the larger portion of his men to Vok to have at the ready should circumstances take a less congenial turn. Ottakar would collect them when he came back to Bohemia with Margaret in the spring.

Those had been the last words he spoke to Mouse on the day she left Prague—a promise that he would see her again. He had bent to kiss her but then pulled back quickly, the muscle in his jaw twitching, his nostrils flared.

"Be well, Mouse," he said as he helped her onto the horse.

He had said those same words when she left with Father Lucas for Houska; she'd promised him then that she would come back to him. Now she felt sure Rozemberk Keep would be just another kind of pit with its own demons, and she made no promises this time—except to herself. She would look no further forward than the moment in which she lived, nor linger on the past.

She allowed herself one look back as her horse pranced in step to follow Vok's through the South Gate. She did not want the last time she set eyes on Ottakar to be the moment he had bound her to Vok. At midday, she'd stood in St. George's with Lord Rozemberk at her side, one hand on the small of her back and the other wrapped like a vise around her arm as he claimed her. Only Ottakar had served as witness. The deed was done in three words: "I marry you." Vok's had sounded like a branding; Mouse's were a sacrifice. And a lie. She had already given herself to Ottakar.

The night they reached the keep at Rozemberk, exhausted and half frozen, Vok came to her room. Mouse tensed when she heard his steps outside her door and looked helplessly at Gitta, who had begged to come with her from Prague though Mouse felt sure she did so at Ottakar's bidding. As Gitta neared the door, ready to open it should Vok knock, he walked away. Mouse sighed, relieved. She knew the day would come, but she was glad it had not come just yet.

Waiting ambivalently for Vok to decide when their married life would begin, Mouse settled into a dull routine and kept mostly to herself. Vok spent most of his time training the men and dealing with the estate affairs now that he was officially the Lord of Rozemberk. But there was nothing for Mouse to do, as Lady Rozemberk managed the keep; it had been her home, after all, and Mouse's experience as first lady at Hluboka hardly qualified her to see to the domestic details of Rozemberk Castle. Mouse simply tried to stay out of her way. Lady Rozemberk did not approve of the marriage—she even refused to attend the wedding in an effort to sway her son. At first, Mouse wondered if her sketchy family history or her familiarity with Ottakar caused the objections, but the Lady's continued whispers of "witch" and her muttered prayers against evil gave Mouse a more likely answer. There would be no rekindling of friendship with her mother-in-law. So besides Gitta, Mouse found herself in solitude once more.

She walked as the weather allowed, but the keep sat on a narrow finger of land with the Vltava twisting around it. The sounds of the river followed her wherever she went, taunting her. On her first walk through a small grove of trees between the river bends, she ran into the outer castle battlement, which was guarded by Vok's men.

"Can we do something for you, Lady Rozemberk?"

It took Mouse a moment to realize that the guard was speaking to her; she was Lady Rozemberk now.

"I wish to pass."

"I am sorry, my Lady, but his Lordship gave orders we were not to let . . . anyone beyond the walls."

She heard the lie; Vok's order was not for anyone but for her alone. He must be worried that she would run away. Mouse was trapped. And angry.

"I only want to take a walk in the woods. Surely there can be no harm in that."

"Still trying to slip beyond your boundaries, my Lady?" Another man, unseen farther back on the wall, spoke. "And you and I both know what harm can come from a walk in the woods."

Mouse knew the voice, and it laid on her another heaviness of spirit.

"Hello, Luka," she said, shielding her eyes from the sun as she looked up at him. He did not need to cover his eyes as he looked out on her; they were as milky blind as they had been the last time she saw them—in the woods after she had taken his sight. "How are you?"

"I am well."

"You serve as guard?" The men laughed, and Luka laughed with them. Mouse wasn't sure if it was a bitter laugh, but it felt harsh to her ear.

"No, I am Lord Chamberlain here. I was simply checking on the men. And how are you, my Lady?"

"Happy to see you well," she said with a sigh as the guilt pulled at her.

"And I you." He smiled and the men laughed again.

Mouse could not make herself join in; she bit back words of apology and turned away quickly. "I should return to the keep. Good-bye, Luka."

Once she was clear of their view, she leaned against a tree, weeping, not only for the reminder of what suffering she'd caused but because she knew she could this very moment give Luka back his sight as she had the minnesinger. And why shouldn't she? She wasn't supposed to care anymore. She slammed her fist against the tree and spun back toward the guards. But she couldn't make herself take a step. Digging her hand into the bag that hung at her waist, her fingers played with the woven grass witch she'd made at Hluboka. If she healed Luka, she might as well build a fire and throw herself on it. Mouse was too afraid. The fear of what waited for her after death compelled her silence now.

As she wrapped herself in the lackluster nothingness of her days, Mouse dismissed her tiredness, her inability to recover from the journey, as general malaise. She used it as an excuse to keep to her room. Vok had come to her once, drunk, and kissed her roughly and pawed at her but then left again suddenly. She wondered what stopped him. Fear of Ottakar? Or a sense of guilt? Whatever the cause, she was happy to be let alone.

It was when she started vomiting that Mouse suspected she was pregnant. She heard the first faint heartbeat a week later, and she was afraid. Vok would most certainly know the child wasn't his; he would just as certainly know whose it was. But that wasn't what scared her.

What frightened Mouse was the baby itself.

For days she let worry gnaw at her, until finally at the Angel's Mass at midnight on Christmas, she found the courage to close her eyes and look within herself. What she saw crippled her with joy. For the first time in her life, Mouse saw the spark of a soul in her; God had not turned his back on this child as he had Mouse. This child had hope, and, for the moment, that meant Mouse had a future.

She began planning. She filled her days with necessary sewing until Gitta, sworn to secrecy and with even more solemn oaths that she would not write to Ottakar, had taken over the task. Mouse turned to a more enjoyable chore and started carving bits of wood until the windowsills filled with the likenesses of people she knew and an army of animals and figures from stories. When she started to carve a face for Father Lucas, the softness of his eyes and the sharp cut of his nose, a longing awakened in her to share her new joy with someone who loved her. Even ill, Father Lucas would enjoy hearing about the baby.

Mouse wrote to Mother Agnes in Prague and asked her to inquire with others who might know Father Lucas's fate. She also wrote to Mother Kazi at Teplá, asking if she knew where the Father was and begging her to come to Rozemberk in the summer when the time of delivery neared.

A letter came quickly from Teplá—Mother Kazi was ill and could not travel; they had no word of Father Lucas. But Mouse was still waiting for answers from Mother Agnes when Ottakar came back to Bohemia with his new bride.

She heard the horses as she worked in the garden she was planting. The last of the March sun was resting on Mouse's back, but she shivered and laid a hand on her rounding abdomen.

"It will not show, my Lady," Gitta reassured her. "But he will see it in your eyes if you are not careful."

Mouse held the words as caution when she bowed before Ottakar later that day in the Great Hall as he made introductions for his Queen. Margaret was far older than Mouse had imagined, much older than Ottakar himself. Any lingering jealousy vanished, and pity took its place as she saw how unhappy he looked. He smiled and kissed her, but his eyes were dark with worry and disappointment. Listening in on his conversation in the hall revealed the source of his disappointment—the politics in his new kingdom were more tangled than he hoped and the pope was planning a new crusade. Mouse saw more worry in his face on the few occasions when Ottakar looked at his wife. Margaret might have given him Austria, but it was very unlikely that she would give him an heir.

Mouse almost placed a protective hand on her belly.

Out of fear of giving herself away, she worked to disconnect from the people around her, focusing on the food passing in front of her, nibbling at bits of bread or fruit, smiling blankly but trying not to hear the conversations. She tuned her ears on the minnesingers Ottakar had brought with him, troubadours he had taken with him to woo his Austrian wife. Mouse let her eyes flicker toward Margaret once more to quiet the sudden bitterness; she seemed as out of place as Mouse felt.

"Will you dance with me?"

Lost in her own thoughts, she had not noticed him come up behind her.

"Vok, you do not mind, do you?" Ottakar asked, looking over her shoulder.

"Not at all, my Lord." It did not take Mouse's special gifts to hear the lie, and as he took her hand and held it out to the King, the flash of anger in Vok's eye promised consequences.

For a moment, she thought of refusing Ottakar, but the nearness of him—his smell, just as it had always been, floating down to her as he bowed, and the blueness of his eyes which lost their worry as they gazed at her—kindled the old feelings. She found that still she could not say no to him.

Ottakar took her hand formally from Vok, but as they moved past the table, his fingers slid to lace between her own. The steps of the dance brought them close and then apart again, hands touching and then not. Anyone watching could see in their faces how they felt about each other. Time had healed no wounds here.

No sooner had Mouse sat down, breathless, heartbroken, and ready to find some excuse to retire to her room, than Vok roughly grabbed her arm, pulling her back to her feet.

"My turn," he hissed in her ear.

His fingers dug into her waist as he moved her into the circle of dancers and pushed and pulled her through the movements. When the dance finished, Vok yanked her toward him, crushing her against his chest and kissing her hard on the mouth. She knew better than to push him away, so she let him put on his show for Ottakar.

The King's grim look as they returned to the table seemed proof of something to Vok, who called loudly for more wine, clapped Ottakar on the shoulder and began to talk about the hunt he had planned for the morrow. Mouse could not tell if he was pleased or angry.

She got her answer in the middle of the night.

When she had announced her intention to go early to bed, claiming a headache from too much sun in the garden, Vok had boasted his intent to see her later. She knew he meant it for Ottakar's ears more than her own. He'd quit coming to her bed weeks ago after he'd burst into her room again, mostly drunk, and stared at her for the better part of an hour without saying a word before slamming his fist against the wall. Mouse had heard the bones crack, but when she had gotten out of bed to help him, he had pushed her away and left.

So when she woke with a start from a dream of dancing with Ottakar to find Vok standing quietly over her, she lay still and waited for him to leave.

He didn't.

"I will not let him have you. I mean to claim what is mine!" He snatched the covers away from her, leaving her exposed in her thin linen undergown to the chill air and his eyes, which slid slowly from her face along her breasts and finally to the roundness of her stomach.

"What is this?" He spoke so quietly she barely heard him. She gave no answer.

He grabbed her forearm and jerked her up, pulling her off the bed; she landed hard on her knees against the wood floor.

"Tell me who did this," he said. She kept her eyes on the floor. He grabbed a handful of her hair and yanked back, forcing her to face him. "Tell me."

"You already know," she said as softly as she could with her throat stretched taut.

"I want to hear you say it."

She tried to swallow. "Ottakar."

"He said he had never had you. He lied so I would take you off his hands."

Mouse realized that it was not her betrayal that hurt him.

"He did not lie. It was the night before we married. The one night only. And it was my doing, not his."

He let go of her.

She had closed her eyes and so did not see his fist before it slammed into the side of her head; she half caught herself but not before her mouth hit the arm of the chair beside her. She heard him moving, pulling his foot back as he prepared to kick her, but she yanked the chair around to catch the blow and then scrambled to her feet.

"Stop!" she ordered. Vok stood still, panting, his hands balled into fists at his side. The power surged in her chest and the baby rolled, kicking violently. She laid her hand on her stomach, worried that the power might have affected the fetus, and breathed slow and deep until she was calm—the baby and the power both quiet.

"If you hit me again, if you endanger the life of this child, I will kill you," she said resolutely. "Now get out of my room."

The bruise and split lip kept Mouse in her room for the rest of Ottakar's stay, and though she longed to see him, she knew it was better this way. When he left for Prague, Vok went with him.

Mouse enjoyed a peaceful spring, almost as pleasant as last year's at Hluboka, despite her longing for Ottakar. The garden thrived and now that Luka was in command of the keep, she took long walks in the woods beyond the wall, although as her belly grew and the heat of summer descended, the walks shortened. When she could no longer hide her condition, Lady Rozemberk took a fresh interest in Mouse.

"You must take care with Vok's heir," the Lady cautioned as she insisted on mornings in bed for Mouse and restricted activity—no more gardening, no more walks beyond the bailey. Mouse wondered why Vok had not told his mother who the baby's real father was; she wondered if he had told Ottakar.

When the letter came from Prague in the rainy days of July, Mouse took it with shaking hands, sure it was from Ottakar setting claim to his child. But it was not his seal. It was Mother Agnes's, and it bore ill news.

Father Lucas was near death at the monastery in Sedlec.

TWENTY-EIGHT

*S*edlec, she thought as she hurried to the stable. It drummed in her mind, driving out all reason. *I must get to Sedlec.*

"I want a horse," she said thickly as she took the stable boy by the shoulder and pushed him to a stall.

"Which horse, my Lady?"

"I do not care. Just ready a horse!" She paced as she waited, bits of questions sifting past the sense of urgency. Mother Agnes wrote in haste, explaining nothing but that the news had come from Ottakar. But why would they take Father Lucas to Sedlec? There was no leper colony there. If he had not been among lepers, where had he been?

"Help me up," she barked when the boy had finished saddling the horse. Her belly made her clumsy, but once mounted, she wasted no time prodding the horse into a trot past the keep and toward the only gate out. She hoped Luka was not there.

"Let me out," she called to the guards as she neared the wall.

They did not move. Her horse, sensing her nervousness, pranced and scurried side to side.

"Let me pass." Mouse worked to soften her tone. "I am riding down to the village. It is too far for me to walk in my condition." The lie slipped easily from her lips.

The guards looked at each other hesitantly. "I am not sure—"

"I need cloth from the weaver."

"Let me fetch what you need from the village, Lady Rozemberk. You should not be riding. What if the horse were to slip and—"

"I thank you for your care, and I will take great caution, I assure you, but I do not know what I want. I must see what he offers." When they still did not move, she added, "Perhaps I should find Luka, then? I believe he has given orders on this matter already—that I am free to go where I please when I please—but I am sure he will not mind having those orders questioned. Let me fetch him." She turned the horse back toward the keep.

"No, my Lady. I would not bother the Lord Chamberlain. I only meant to caution you." He nodded to one of the other guards. "Let Lady Rozemberk pass."

Mouse kept to the village road until she was sure they could no longer see her from the tower and then turned her mount northward, weaving him between the trees until she reached the road toward Kaplice. She closed her eyes, envisioning a map Ottakar had shown her once during the early days at Prague, and settled on a route to the Sedlec Monastery.

She ran the horse at a steady canter until neither she nor he could stand it any longer. It was enough to give her a comfortable distance from Rozemberk Keep. When it grew late enough that she was sure to be missed, Mouse steered the horse into the woods, deep enough that anyone riding the road would likely not see her but close enough to catch occasional glimpses of the track to be sure she was still heading in the right direction. The pace slowed as they wove through underbrush and bracken, leaving time for her mind to race and her body to complain. Would she get there in time, she wondered as she straightened, trying to stretch her back. Her shoulders and eyes sagged with exhaustion and grief.

Images of the dismembered squirrel clawed at her mind and she jolted awake; the horse had stopped in a small clearing, munching grass. The stars were out. Mouse led the horse back to the road, her hand pressed into the small of her back, trying to push away the pain stabbing at her in waves.

They stopped at Trebon in the late morning so Mouse could buy food for them both. Every part of her screamed the need to hurry, to get to Sedlec before it was too late, but the tired horse could do little more than trot, and the baby protested every jolt. Mouse worked to keep her mind on the promise of finding Father Lucas alive.

It was dusk the next day when she saw the spires of the monastery bell tower. She asked the horse to run, but he could not, any more than she could when she dismounted, her legs leaden. She walked stiffly toward the infirmary, but as she passed the church with its doors flung wide, she saw him laid out on the table at the back of the chapel.

Her knees shook, muscles quivering with the onslaught of grief; she wrapped an arm under her belly trying to lift some of the weight to ease the burning in her back and then forced herself down the aisle at a creeping pace.

"No," she whispered, laying her trembling hands on his chest. He had been dead awhile. No one had even washed him.

"I am sorry, my Lady. Are you family?" The monk came from the altar to stand beside her.

Ignoring him, Mouse walked slowly around the table, her hands running along Father Lucas's body. She shook her head, not wanting to believe.

"Who did this to him?"

"Did what, my Lady? I understand he was ill."

"These are not the marks of leprosy." Her voice ran cold with rage.

"Leprosy?" The monk took several steps back from the table. "I . . . I do not think he had leprosy, my Lady. They would not have brought him here."

"No. He did not." But she was not talking to the monk; she was mumbling to herself, her voice hollowed from the shock at his condition and the rage at what had been done to him. "There are no sores, no signs of infection." She stopped, laying her face against Father Lucas's bare feet, her hair falling over them like a curtain.

"Come away. You should not see him so." The monk put his hand on her back.

She snapped upright, grabbing his arm and looking him in the eye. "Who did this?"

"I think you are confused. He was ill."

She pulled him toward Father Lucas's feet. "See here? The bottoms of his feet are nearly black."

"It happens when the flesh is left—"

"No! His skin is darkening with decay, but his feet are much darker. Bruised before he died. And his toenails—do you see? Cracked and peeling back from the flesh." She spoke rapidly, breathlessly and dragged the monk beside the table. "And look here—his thumbnails cracked just the same." She felt along Father Lucas's hands and fingers, silent tears running down her face. "Broken, crushed. Torture leaves such wounds. Not illness."

"Torture? Who would want to torture a sick, old man?" The monk pulled his arm free. "I . . . think you are overtired."

"Where was he before he came here?"

"I do not know. Please come with me to see the abbot. We will find a place for you to—"

"Leave me." Looking down at the Father's habit, which was tattered and soiled with blood and urine, she listened to the monk's fading footsteps. When she knew she was alone, she sank to her knees.

"Oh, Father, I am so sorry." She held his shattered hand against her cheek. "I should have found you." She gritted her teeth. "I swear I will find who did this to you." But she couldn't sustain the heat of revenge against the heaviness of her loss. The power in her snaked its way up and whispered a clear truth.

Come forth, Lazarus.

Her body shaking violently, Mouse pulled herself up to stand beside Father Lucas again. She stared down at his bloated face. And she understood why Jesus wept before he resurrected his friend. Like Mouse, he had come too late and lost the friend he loved. Mouse felt the pain of that failure burn her throat. Jesus could have his friend back and be free of the guilt of having come too late. Raising Lazarus was good for everyone, for Mary, Martha, Jesus, God—everyone except Lazarus. And that was why Jesus wept.

Just as Mouse wept as she bent to kiss Father Lucas.

His head wobbled oddly as she leaned against it to whisper in his ear. Slowly she looked down to his neck, pulled back the folds of his mantle, and saw the jagged flesh.

His head had been twisted and ripped from his body.

Mouse thought of the squirrel, its arms and legs never joining quite right, its shredded flesh hanging at odd angles. She bent double, retching, and then pulled herself up onto the table next to Father Lucas, her pregnant belly resting against him, her head touching his. She could not put him through the suffering of resurrection, not for her own selfish reasons, not when she knew he was finally at peace. So she would suffer instead and let him rest where he was glad to go, just as he had commissioned in his last words to her.

Mouse looked up to the mural on the ceiling of the apse—John baptizing Jesus in the Jordan, a dove hovering over the haloed Christ, the hand of God poised in blessing over his son.

"You could have left him whole." She closed her eyes. "I hate you for this," she hissed.

She slept, waking only when the monks came to take the body.

"Go away."

And they did.

But they came back in the morning. They tried to pick her up, but she screamed until her throat was raw and she spewed them with spit. They came back on the third day, masked against the smell, and took the body. She followed them outside and slid down the wall of the church when her legs would not hold her.

The fire crackled and danced in the early morning air. Mouse bit into her tongue as the Brothers lowered Father Lucas into the cauldron of boiling water, and she gagged at the smell of cooking flesh. When the Brothers took the last of the bones, gleaming white, from the cauldron, and carried them to the ossuary where they would be used as a candelabra or pulls for the vestment cabinet, Mouse folded in on herself, sobbing.

Someone came to squat beside her, but she didn't care. She had maggots in her hair; she reeked of death.

Strong arms lifted her.

"Time to go, wife."

On the way back to Rozemberk Keep, Mouse's water broke, trickling between her legs onto the horse in a warm wash. She did not cry out and none of Vok's men noticed. It was raining; everything was wet. Vok rode at the front.

He'd had nothing to do with her after that first day when he had carried her to the monastery guesthouse, had bathed her and washed the maggots from her hair himself because he did not want to wait for a woman to come up from the village, had sat with her until she ate, sat with her while she slept.

"Why are you doing this?" she asked.

For a long time, Vok had just looked at her, something he rarely did, but she was too tired, too consumed with grief to read him. He had finally shrugged and said, "You saved my life that day in the prison. You held the water, gave me a moment of peace, gave me hope." He rubbed his hand absently across his forehead. "A deed for a deed," he said and then he left.

The next morning he put her on a horse. And now Mouse was in labor.

Pulling her mount a little closer to the man nearest her, she asked, "How long until we reach the keep?"

"We could be there tonight, my Lady, but for the weather. See?" He pointed to the south. Mouse had been shrouded in mourning and had not noticed the massive towers of dark clouds that climbed over the hills. "We will likely make camp soon, and if the weather breaks by sunup, we will be home before midday."

Mouse chewed at her lip. She could ask Vok to make for home despite the weather, but she had understood him all too well when he said "a deed for a deed"—he had paid the debt he felt he owed her, and he was done. She certainly did not mean to beg a favor or to obligate herself to him in turn. She urged her horse on and hoped that the storm would hold off. Mother Kazi had told stories of women who had been in labor for days with their first child; Mouse hoped that might be the case for her.

Both hopes died an hour later as bright flashes of lightning crashed down on the hills around them and Mouse felt the contractions pull her stomach taut. Vok led the men to a some-what sheltered nook in the foothills and bid them make camp. She leaned against a rock, swaying, as they put up her tent.

The wind whipped at the flaps as she tied them shut and rain ran under the edges of the tent as she stripped down to her linen undershirt, which was stained with blood. She paced as she could and squatted or knelt against the camp bed when the contractions built to a peak.

"Can I bring you food or wine, my Lady?" the guard called at her door.

"No, thank you," she hissed through gritted teeth, her hands gripping the bed covers as she laid her head against the low frame.

As the storm passed, Mouse smiled to herself, her fear abating and her confidence growing as each contraction came and went. In the intervals, she closed her eyes and checked the baby's heartbeat, strong and steady. But in the deep of the night, another line of storms rolled in, more violent than the first, the wind screaming as it pushed past the hills, the canvas tent popping at the gusts.

Mouse was on all fours, her fingers and toes digging into the saturated rug, sweat dripping from her hair as the contractions came fast and hard until finally she cried out, moaning with the wind.

"My Lady?" someone called out at the tent door.

But she could not answer. The last contraction had left her shaking, curled up on her side, trying to catch her breath before the next one came. She wanted Mother Kazi or Gitta. Father Lucas. Someone. Anyone. She was scared.

Hail pounded the roof of the tent, tearing a rent near the seam along one wall. Little white pellets bounced on the rug.

And then the next contraction took her. She pushed herself onto her knees again, rocking with the pain, breathing fast and shallow. She tried to listen for the baby's heart, but all she could hear was the scream of the wind and her own high whine; she tried to look for his tiny glow, but all she could see were bright flashes of lightning and of her pain, running in angry red streaks against the blackness of her closed eyes.

Someone ripped the cords that fastened the doors, letting wind and rain and hail rush into the tent. Mouse turned and saw Vok standing over her holding a lantern, its candle flame dancing in odd rhythm with the candle near the bed. A guard stood at his back.

Mouse whimpered, shaking again as the contraction let her go for a moment, comforted that at least someone would be with her through the last of it. Vok would deliver the baby.

But he turned, stepping back out into the storm.

"Leave her be," he shouted to the guard over the wind and rain.

"But my Lord, she needs—"

"She will live or not as God wishes. Leave her be, I said." And then he was gone.

The guard tied the frayed ends of the flap back, shutting out some of the storm.

Mouse was alone.

"I will do this. I will live, whether God wishes it or not." She pressed her head to the floor, hands wrapped in her wet hair, as her belly locked up, tight as stone. She barely had time to breathe as it left before she felt the next one coming.

"No, please, not again," she moaned, rocking herself, and then she slammed her fist against the ground.

Again and again through the night, she battled the contractions until she thought they would never end. She was afraid to die, sure her soulless state and the curses she'd flung to God would condemn her, but it was want, not fear, that ultimately drove her onward. She wanted to meet the little life she had carried, the soul she had nurtured and shared; she wanted to leave a legacy of goodness to balance the evil she had done. She could die, but not until the baby was born, alive and well.

And so in the middle of raging storms, alone, she pulled herself to a squat, legs trembling, and gave herself over to the urge to push. She chewed her cheeks raw rather than give Vok the satisfaction of hearing her scream, despite the searing pain when her body ripped as the baby's head pushed free and then his shoulders, and then the whole of him. Her son lay bloody and crying, curled on the sodden rug.

Mouse worked quickly to cut the cord and tie it off with a bit of thread she'd already prepared. She wiped the baby clean and wrapped him in the bed linen before the pains began again and she delivered the afterbirth. When it was done, she lay in the bed beside him, exhausted, and brought him to her nipple, letting it play along his lips until he latched on. She sang him a lullaby—the one her mother had sung to her, held note for note in Mouse's perfect memory and her only proof that she had been loved. It was her first gift to her son.

"On t'aime, mon petite. On t'aime. Le bon Dieu, au ciel, t'aime. On t'aime, mon petite. On t'aime. Ta mère, à jamais, t'aime," she sang. "You are loved, little one. You are loved. By God in his heaven, you are loved. You are loved, little one. You are loved. By your mother, forever, you are loved."

TWENTY-NINE

N o," Vok said when she came out of the tent pale and so sore she could hardly walk but alive and with a new understanding of love swaddled in her arms. She had asked about the baptism first thing. She was determined to claim for her son all that she'd been denied— membership in the Church, God's blessing, and a name. Love she could give him in abundance, but the others required quick thinking on her part. Vok would not want Ottakar's bastard to bear the Rozemberk name, but Mouse meant to steal it if she could.

"A baptism can wait. We ride straight for the keep," he ordered.

"I will stop in the village myself then."

In a few long strides he was on her, towering over her, his shame and anger flashing in his eyes. "You will obey me, wife."

"I will, Vok." She spoke softly so none of the men would hear. "In every way, I will be what you expect in a wife. Once this is done."

"No. You will do as I say. Now. And I will not give your bastard my name."

"Everyone assumes he is yours, and they need never know otherwise unless you announce it with your words or your actions. Claim him and you have a son to bring you honor. Refuse and you open yourself to their scorn." She nodded to the dozens of men breaking camp.

"By the saints!" He drew back his hand; she would not flinch. "I said no."

But when they rode down the hills, the tower of St. Nicholas Chapel peeking over the treetops, Vok sent a rider ahead. Gitta and Luka were waiting beside the priest at the altar to become godparents, and so Mouse gave her son a name: Nicholas, for the secret gift-giver, Lucas, for the Father she lost, and Rozemberk because she had no other. As they left the church, she felt the power of being part of a family for the first time, and a new determination settled on her to make peace with Vok, to make them a family in more than name only.

Her hope was short-lived.

Vok stayed for less than a week. While Mouse kept to her room recovering, mourning for Father Lucas, and reveling in her new joy, Vok would come crashing in unannounced, sometimes before dawn, other times in the middle of the day. Scowling, he would watch her nurse the baby or stand staring down into the basket where little Nicholas slept. It frightened Mouse; she could see the hurt in Vok's eyes, could hear the heavy, hard thud of his heart. He would rub at his forehead and then turn to look at her, sometimes like he was pleading with her, sometimes like he hated her.

She was glad when he left.

As the leaves turned scarlet and the wind carried a promise of the coming winter, Mouse's heart filled completely for the first time in her life. She belonged to someone. She and the baby spent their days learning each other. Nicholas would reach his hand up to play with her face as he nursed, gently tracing the line of her jaw, the shape of her nose, the curve of her mouth, which seemed now to always be smiling. She would play with his toes, lift the fine, tawny curls from his face, and sing to him. And Mouse would laugh. Nicholas would laugh.

She told him stories to help him fall asleep and lay beside him on the bed so when he dreamed and startled, hands and legs flung out in panic, she was there to put her hand on his chest, whispering to tell him he was safe, to sing their lullaby—"You are loved, little one. You are loved."

Ottakar sent Vok home on St. Andrew's Eve. Mouse stood with Lady Rozemberk and Luka to greet him. He kissed his mother, clapped Luka on the shoulder, and walked by her without even a glance as he went into the hall, asking someone to bring him a cup of warm ale. Mouse tried to talk to him at supper, to ask about Prague and Ottakar's new acquisition of Styria, but Vok kept his back to her.

She was playing on the floor with Nicholas when Vok came to her room the next morning.

"And how does the sheep go, my smart little boy?" she asked Nicholas as he played with a wooden lamb she'd carved.

"Da-da-da-da." The baby mumbled then stuck the lamb in his mouth, gnawing it with swollen gums.

"No, no," she said as she took it away from him. "You do not eat it, silly. And a sheep says 'baa, baa,' not—"

"Ottakar wants you in Prague," Vok said from the doorway. Mouse noticed the lack of formality, no "my Lord," no "the King." Just Ottakar.

"Da-da-da," Nicholas said again as he turned to look at Vok.

Mouse watched Vok's eyes soften as he took a step forward, but then he stopped short and his face drew up like a withering flower.

She sighed. "Why does he want me in Prague?"

"He says his father is ill again."

Mouse looked down at Nicholas's blue eyes and gold hair. It would darken as he grew older, like his father's, but even now anyone would notice the resemblance if they saw them together. The gossipers at court would surely spare no ill word in making the connections. Mouse shook her head. She had no interest in opening fresh wounds either—not for Vok, not for herself or for Ottakar.

And Ottakar would know Nicholas was his. He would love him as she did. He would want him for his own.

"No," she said. "Nicholas is too young to travel, and I will not leave him."

Vok shifted. "You would defy me still?"

Mouse stood, wrapping Nicholas in a blanket. "Gitta, will you take the baby for some fresh air?"

Vok wasn't angry because she didn't want to go Prague; he was angry about Nicholas. Mouse was afraid of what he might do to the baby and so gave him another target instead.

"You want me to go?" she asked as Gitta closed the door.

"I want—" He shook his head, gritting his teeth. "I will not be made a fool!"

"No one thinks you—"

He scrambled toward her. "You are my wife, not his. Mine. This body," he grabbed her waist, put his other hand roughly on her breast, "is mine to do with as I please."

"So do as you please," she said, holding her arms out to the side and looking him in the eye.

He leaned down, his mouth covering hers, and then pulled back. He waited a moment. "By the saints!" he swore. "They say you are a witch. Even my mother speaks in fear of how you spelled a raging bear. What have you done to me?"

He shoved Mouse's hand to his crotch, and she understood now why he had come so often to her room but left without touching her.

"I have done nothing to you, my Lord." She kept her tone level and her eyes on his.

His hand snaked around her wrist. "You think yourself brave. You are just stupid. I can break you without even trying."

He squeezed.

She looked at him.

He squeezed harder, twisting her arm between the vise of his fingers and thumb.

Mouse used all of her unnatural control to hold her face still; she knew what would happen, could feel the bone bending, but she'd made a new deal with God a few days after Nicholas was born when she woke from a night filled with dreams of him dead by disease or at Vok's hand or, horribly, dead by command of her own careless words. She swore she would not use her power so long as God protected her son, not only from death but also from her own fate. Every day she watched for signs of unnaturalness, of "gifts" in the baby; she saw none. And every night she looked for the glow in him, found it, and fell asleep smiling and content or crying with relief and longing.

As long as God kept up his end of the deal, she would keep hers, and so she stood waiting until the bone cracked with a sick pop.

Vok let her go. She cradled her arm against her chest.

"You broke me. Now what?"

He left without a word.

But he came to her every night. After the first night, Mouse sent Nicholas to sleep with Gitta in a nearby room, close enough so she could nurse him if he woke but safely out of Vok's awareness.

Vok came to her hungry, wanting her body and her fear; she was willing to forfeit the first, but his own body continued to fail him, and Mouse refused to give him her fear. Every night he left her bruised or broken, but he also left dissatisfied. When he saw how quickly her wounds healed, her bruises faded, he crossed himself against her, but rather than scare him off, it seemed to fuel his determination to mark her as his in some lasting way.

Near dawn on Innocent's Day, before he left to visit the other keeps and townships under his command, he slammed her door open and went straight to the fire in her room. He took the fireplace forks, twisting the logs and stirring up the flame. He was drunk.

Mouse slipped out of the bed and moved toward the door, but Vok was closer. He grabbed her arm, spinning her toward the fireplace and then pushing her down onto the floor.

"This is not what you want, Vok," she said, her voice forcibly calm but her breath ragged, her body eerily still as she waited.

"Burn a witch," he slurred as he turned. "Make her mine."

Mouse felt the heat long before it burned through the linen and into her skin. She blacked out as the pain grew, Vok raking the scalding fork across her back, but in her mind she could see the image he burned—the five-petal rose of the Rozemberks—and she could hear him sobbing.

Still on the floor when she woke to Nicholas's hungry cries, her back stinging, Mouse knew something was going to have to change. Vok was going to kill her, and then Nicholas would be alone in the world just as she had always been. Even as she watched Vok ride away later that morning while Gitta rubbed a salve against the blistered rose, Mouse knew he would come back again. She needed to be ready.

She and Nicholas had the spring and early summer to themselves. They celebrated his milestones—sitting up, crawling. They spent most of their time outside in the little garden or in the woods with Gitta and Luka, Nicholas beheading the flowers, handing them to Mouse with a full-faced grin, or cackling as he gripped her fingers and waddled along the paths, giddy with his newfound mobility. Even as she lost herself in the warm days and sweet smells and joys of her son, Mouse's mind worked constantly to find a way out for both of them.

But as many paths as she traveled down, she could not find one where Vok would leave her alone—or Nicholas either, if he was with her. If she went back to the abbey, if Mother Kazi let her, or to Mother Agnes's convent at Prague, Vok would come for her. Even if she sold all she owned or stole what she needed, she had nowhere to go, and, though she was more than willing to risk herself traveling alone, she would not risk Nicholas. Once again, Mouse could find no future for herself and Nicholas.

As the days grew hotter, Nicholas must have sensed his mother's foreboding. He screamed for her, his little body trembling, whenever she left his view. He would crawl after her, calling, "Ma-ma-ma-ma," and pull himself up by her skirts, reaching for her until she picked him up, and he would kiss her on the cheek, openmouthed as if he were taking a bite, happy that all was well with the world again.

And then Vok came home just before Nicholas's first birthday.

At first, he seemed reconciled, at peace, but as Mouse watched him interact with others in the hall or the bailey, she noticed that he never smiled and rarely looked at anyone even when he was talking with them; he either yelled or spoke in a hollow whisper, ate less and drank more. He rubbed constantly at his forehead. Mouse wanted to help him, but he had ignored her since his return, and she was scared of drawing his attention, scared for both herself and for Nicholas.

It was only a matter of time before Vok came to her, stone sober and in the light of day. Nicholas had been laughing as he walked the perimeter of the table, his hands holding the edge for balance, but he stopped at the sight of Vok's unfamiliar face, dropped to the floor and crawled as quickly as he could to Mouse. She picked him up, and he planted his face against her shoulder and played with her hair.

"Send him away. I want you," Vok said.

"Gitta, will you—" Mouse leaned toward her, letting Nicholas's weight help pull him free, but he grabbed a handful of her hair and a fistful of her tunic and let out a high, panicked wail.

Mouse pulled him close again and he quieted. "Nicholas, you and Gitta are going for a walk in the woods. I will come find you."

He shook his head, the curls, bleached nearly white from the summer sun, falling into his face. "No, no, no," he said as his lip quivered. He put his hand in the little dip at her collarbone.

"Would you like some berries? You and Gitta can go to the kitchen for them and bring them right back."

"No, no, no—"

Vok grabbed Nicholas from behind. "Get rid of him, I said!"

The baby screamed. Mouse reached for him, but Vok spun. "Be quiet!" he yelled as he shook him.

Frozen in fear, Mouse saw in her mind how it would all play out so that as it actually happened, everything seemed too slow, hazy as if she were watching through wavy glass. Nicholas's head snapped back; she could see the shock on his face, heard him suck in air, stifling his cries.

"Stop, Vok," she said as he moved to shake the baby again, but the power that had slept in her for nearly a year did not wake. And then her fear transformed into a mother's fury.

"Stop, Vok!" The voice was not her own, deeper and laced with an animal-like growl.

Vok froze, a silent Nicholas dangling from his outstretched arms.

"Hand me the baby."

He lowered Nicholas into her arms; the baby wasn't breathing, but as he took in his mother's face, he breathed out, crying.

"Shhh, shhh," she whispered as she laid Nicholas against her chest, and he quieted. Mouse bit her lip.

She chose her words carefully. "Vok, you want to go hunting. This afternoon with your men. Go." And then she pulled the power back into herself. Vok left without a word.

Mouse sank to the floor, weak, the power roiling in her until she vomited. Nicholas would not leave her arms, and they were both covered in spit and bile. She rocked the baby until finally he slept.

"Gather what we need, Gitta. It is time." Her voice shook, but Mouse had planned for this.

∽

And so they slipped through the woods and along the riverbank until they saw the boats where the Romany clan had set their watery camp. Back in the spring, the gypsies had wandered down from the Sumava Mountains that towered to the west of the Rozemberk lands. But the village would not have them so they had moved down the river, taken some trees, and crafted barges. They poled goods for trade up and down the Vltava, but mostly they kept to themselves—until two of the children caught the fever, and the Romany remedies failed. When the patriarch had raced to the village in the night, pleading for help, the priest had sent them to Mouse.

"Hanzi, are you there?" Mouse called out as she and Gitta and Nicholas stood by the river.

"Ah, my Lady, you are well this day?" A man, thick as a barrel, stepped out of a tent on one of the barges, dark hair hanging and slapping against his back as he jumped to the shore and embraced Mouse.

"I wish I could say yes."

"Ah." He let his hands rest on her shoulders, but his eyes ran back along the riverbank. "The trouble we spoke of has come?"

She nodded.

"Then tonight we move on."

"The trouble might follow us. Are you sure you want to take the risk?" She looked at his wife standing with two little girls just outside the tent.

He put his finger on her lips. "You gave me back the life of my children. For you, I would face any trouble."

Hanzi lifted Mouse onto the boat as she held tightly to Nicholas. Gitta followed.

As they walked unsteadily toward the tent, Hanzi tugged at the rope tying them to the bank. "*Avree! Avree!*" he hollered, and two teenage boys came running from the woods and jumped onto the other tethered barge. "Away!" he said to them; one pulled loose the rope and the other took up a long pole, spearing it hard into the river and pushing. Hanzi did the same until the current took both barges and sent them on a quickening jog down the Vltava.

THIRTY

T he spires of the castle loomed in the distance as they
reached the faster waters of the Devil's Stream and
Hanzi pushed the boat toward the shore. Mouse stepped
out of the tent, the early morning air cool against her skin, but
she could not make herself step onto the gravelly bank. She was
back in Prague. But this was not her home any longer.

"You come with me," Hanzi said to Mouse as he stood beside
her, arm draped over her shoulders. "Be my family."

"Oh, Hanzi, I would." She wiped a tear from her eye. "But I
have already put you and the family in danger. If Lord Rozemberk discovers that I left with you, he will hunt you. And if I
go with you now, he will never stop hunting. It is best that you
move on as we talked about."

"As you say. But we will stay here for a little while in case
you need us."

Mouse hugged him and let him help her off the boat. She
took Nicholas in her arms and headed up the path with Gitta
behind her.

As they walked, Mouse saw the towers at the castle take shape, dark against the lightening sky, like four fingers of a hand with its thumb still hidden under the trees. She worried that once she stood in its grasp, those fingers of the castle would curl down on her and she would be crushed.

The guards knew her and let her pass after playing a little with Nicholas, who was both fascinated and frightened by their armor and their swords. Mouse walked alone with the baby toward St. George's; she sent Gitta with a note into the keep.

Mouse waited as the first of the sunlight scattered like colored spears through the stained glass window. Saint Ludmila's painted eyes watched Mouse sway in the light, rocking the baby on her hip. His hands tugged at the strings of pearls dangling on her bodice. She would not lift her eyes from the baby's face, his curls, his blue eyes, his round mouth where a second tooth was just beginning to break through. When she heard the clack of boots against the stone staircase, she tightened her grip on her son.

"Mouse."

She felt like a stranger in what had once been home, but as he said her name, she felt a flicker of belonging. No one called her by her name anymore. She was "my Lady" or odder still, "Lady Rozemberk." But to Ottakar, she was still Mouse, and some part of him was still hers. She could hear it in his voice, feel it as he laid his hand on her back, see it in his eyes as she turned, finally, to greet him.

As much as she loved him, she also hated him for what she had to do. But it was her fault, not his.

"You are well?" she asked, looking away.

"Always looking after my health, you are." He smiled. "Well enough. And you?"

She shrugged. She did not smile.

"What is it?" he asked.

She shook her head. "Ottakar, I want—"

He sighed. "I have missed that. Even my wife calls me 'my Lord King.'" His eyes darkened for a moment and then he held his arms out. "May I hold your son?"

She nodded, unable to speak; she could never undo what she was about to do, and the weight of it crushed her.

Nicholas went to him willingly but turned quickly to be sure Mouse stayed where she was. Ottakar laughed as the baby tugged on his beard and put the edge of it in his mouth, made a face as it pricked and tickled, and then started giggling. Mouse found the courage she needed.

"Ottakar, this is Nicholas—your son." Quick and sharp the words came, like the thrust of a sword.

"Mine?" Behind the confusion, Mouse heard the hope and joy.

"He cannot—" She tried to make herself breathe. "He cannot stay at Rozemberk. Vok knows that Nicholas is yours." Her heart withered at what she had done. But she would not watch her husband strangle her son in some drunken fit of jealousy.

"How does he know?" he asked. "How do you know?"

Her face reddened as if he had slapped her. "I know. Vok knows. There can be no doubt."

He studied her for a moment, and then he wrapped his arm around her waist and pulled her to him. "Mouse."

"Stop." She pushed away from him. "Will you take him? I have brought Gitta to stay and care for him. She . . . she loves him, too." Her voice pitched high with tethered emotion. "And there are people, friends, down at the Devil's Stream. Vok may be looking for them. They could be of use to you at Hluboka. Could you—"

"Stay with me," Ottakar said. "I can send you and Nicholas to Hluboka, too. Come visit you there."

"And Vok?"

"I am his king."

"And Margaret?"

"She is sick. She is not . . . a proper wife." He laid his hand on Mouse's shoulder. "We can ride horses in the summer and picnic at the lake like we did before. We can raise our son together. He will rule after me. There could be other children." He talked quickly, nearly breathless with wishing.

For a moment, Mouse shared his dream, but she knew the truth. Vok would not care that Ottakar was his king. Ottakar had added much land and wealth to Vok's estate and given him power second only to the crown; Vok would prove a dangerous enemy, though she doubted she could ever convince Ottakar of that. So Mouse gave Ottakar another truth instead, a truth he would understand and believe.

"And what would be thought of me?" she asked. "I would be seen as a whore waiting for you to come to me at your pleasure. You could do nothing for Nicholas then. You would anger Margaret's nephew in Germany. The Church would not allow it. You would lose your crown. This pope is like the Innocent before him. He thinks himself your master, does he not?"

"They always do." He sounded tired.

Nicholas started to whimper; he reached out to Mouse and she took him. Sleepy from a restless night on the boat, he laid his head against her chest and ran his hand along the skin at her collarbone. Mouse swayed and hummed the little lullaby.

"You sang that for me once," Ottakar said.

She buried her face in her son's soft hair and breathed in his smell.

"Are you sure, Mouse?"

She could not speak, so she nodded. She could see no other way to keep her son safe.

Ottakar reached for her hand. "I will take care of him. I will love him. I will tell him about you."

Mouse reached into the bag at her waist and pulled out a wooden figure she'd worked on during the spring and summer when she knew what must happen. Whenever Nicholas slept, Mouse stayed awake carving the figure. She shed her tears on the wood, rubbed them into the careful notches she made, smoothed the grain with them.

"Will you give him that?" The words came out deep, heavy with her loss. The figure was of her nursing Nicholas, his hand on her face, her mouth open in song. Along the bottom, she had carved the words of the lullaby.

Ottakar kissed the top of her head. He took the figure and then a sleeping Nicholas from her arms.

Mouse dropped to her knees as the weight of her son left her. Ottakar turned and stepped into the nave.

Nicholas woke. "Ma-ma," he called, wanting and then panicked. "Ma-ma!"

The sound of his screams pierced her. She dug her fingers into the grooves of the stone floor to keep from running after him. Her wails tore her throat before they traveled up into the vaulted ceiling and fell down on her again. She lay prostrate at the foot of the crucifix, her face buried in hands that still smelled like her son.

THIRTY-ONE

Mouse slipped from the horse's back and landed in the hay. Her legs were numb from riding—three days from Prague in the rain back to Rozemberk Keep. She had not eaten. She had not stopped to sleep, but sleep had claimed her, and she'd lain across the horse's neck until the dreams woke her. She was calling out for Nicholas, and then she remembered. Nicholas was gone.

Not long after Ottakar had taken the baby, Gitta had found Mouse and taken her to her old room in the castle and put her to bed. She didn't know how long she had slept, and she didn't care.

When she woke, Gitta tried to make her eat. "My Lord the King will be back in the morning, and he will be angry if you are still not well."

"No." Mouse's tone was dead, like she felt, but her mind was clear again. She was certain that she had done what was right for her son—and also certain that she could not be here when Ottakar returned. "Bring me clothes," she said. "A man's clothes."

"Please, my Lady—"

"I am not your Lady. Bring me clothes or I will find them myself."

Gitta had done as she was told, and Mouse had left Prague within the hour dressed as a man to ride alone back to Rozemberk. She'd had to show herself to one of Vok's guards at the gate of the castle. He had watched her pass with wide eyes, shocked by the masculine clothing and the wild look in her eyes.

She now untangled the sleeve of the rough gardcorps as she grabbed at the stirrup to pull herself up from the ground. She threw her arm across the horse's back to support her weight and give the blood a chance to return some feeling to her legs. Mouse laid her head against his wet coat and let the smell of sweat and rain draw her back to the world.

The stables were empty. Mouse assumed everyone was in bed until she heard the footfall behind her.

"Where have you been, wife?"

Mouse jerked her head around. "Vok—"

He stumbled into her, pinning her against the horse. "Off whoring with gypsies, I hear. Just like your mother, you are, like a rutting animal."

"You are drunk. I will not talk to you this way. I am tired and—"

Even though she saw it coming, Mouse did nothing to avoid his backhanded blow. The horse whinnied and shifted, but Mouse was silent.

"Where is your bastard?" he asked, eyes darting around the stables as he grabbed her chin roughly.

"Gone. That is all that should matter to you." She saw the surprise dilate his eyes.

"You went to the King?"

"Yes."

He shoved her hard to his left. Her head slammed into the cold dirt floor of the stables before she could break her fall; the horse shied and Mouse quickly pushed herself away to avoid the heavy hooves slapping the ground.

"He sent you away, then? Of course he did. Now that he is king, you are nothing to him." He spit the words, wet with drunken slaver. "He has had you already. He has many other women to fill his bed. Women better than you. And now he's left me burdened with his leavings."

As she tried to raise herself from the ground, he put his foot on her back and pressed her down. Her tunic shifted, revealing a sliver of skin above the top of the tight-fitting braies. He yanked it up, exposing her back, and hissed.

"I marked you, wife. Where is the scar?" He pinched the smooth skin at the base of her back where he had branded her with the Rozemberk rose. Her power had healed her as always. There was a small scar, hardly visible even to Mouse, but her keen senses could detect the bit of waxy flesh as she ran her hand along the skin. She would not give him the satisfaction of admitting it.

"I have never been yours. You do not have the power to leave a lasting mark." She meant to bait him, her misery driving away care.

In the year of their marriage, even when he was hard with longing and came to her bed, his manhood had left him. He was sure it was her doing, but now his desire throbbed in him, refusing to be denied. "Your witchcraft might magic away a scar, but there is a way I can make you mine. I will get what I want. Make your belly grow with a son of my own." He slid his boot to the ground and shoved his knee into her back as he ran his hands up the inside of her thighs.

Mouse pushed up hard against him, her mouth dry with panic. But he was too heavy, too strong. Bits of straw and the smell of wet hay rushed up her nose as he shoved her face back into the stable floor. As he dug at her leggings, she spat the dirt from her mouth.

When Vok leaned back to loosen his belt. Mouse saw her chance. She moved her arms under her again, lifting herself and turning this time, throwing him back and off balance. She smiled at the shock in his face.

She knew exactly how he would move, and she was ready. When he lunged, she did, too, and brought her knee up into his face. He spun toward her again, blood dripping from his chin. The horse reared, distracting Mouse as she moved back, and giving Vok the chance to swing around to her side. He threw his weight into her. As she caught herself against the stable wall, his weight and hers bent her hand back onto her forearm, and she heard her wrist snap where he had broken it before.

Instinctively, she hunched, grabbing at her wrist, and Vok folded over her. It gave Mouse an unexpected advantage. She bent at the knees and threw herself back against him, slamming her head into his already broken nose. He let go, grabbing his face as he screamed, and stumbled backward toward the horse, which was pulling frantically against its tether.

Mouse saw what would happen.

She did nothing to stop it.

She watched the horse throw its weight onto its front legs, kicking backward in defense. The hoof hit Vok in the side of the head. Bone shards jutted up out of his scalp and through his hair with a gush of blood. He was dead by the time he landed on his back in the already scarlet hay.

Mouse watched the horse's tail swish through the red as it mixed with horse urine and a puddle of rainwater in the middle of the stable floor; it looked like an artist swirling his brush in the water to clean away the paint.

She picked up a horse blanket, draped it over her head and torn tunic, and took the servants' path up to Rozemberk Keep. She was surprised to find a fire lit in her room; no one had been expecting her. Shadows danced around the room, making everything seem unfamiliar. She sat down heavily on the bed.

She knew she could not stay. Without Nicholas here, this was not home and never could be. She should never have come back.

And then something else erupted in Mouse, full grown and blossoming with glee, as she realized what Vok's death meant for her. Maybe God had not forsaken her; maybe, like Job, she had finally proven herself worthy and God had shaped a future for her. Mouse could stay here, as Vok's widow, and live a comfortable life. With Nicholas. She could have her son back. The joy of it choked her, and despite her exhaustion, she jumped up ready to dress and ride back to Prague to find Ottakar and reclaim her son.

She had not noticed the bundle until it slid to the floor with a dull thud. Mouse almost didn't stop to pick it up. She was eager to start the new life that God had just opened for her, but she knew that would have to wait until morning. She needed to sleep and to change. She would have to deal with the consequences of Vok's death. And then she would travel as his widow to bring home his heir.

So she moved to a chair closer by the fire and laid the bundle in her lap. Firelight sparkled on the silk threads of the rich fabric as she unwound the ribbon. On top lay a note and, underneath, the leather satchel that held Mother Kazi's medical tools. The note was from Sister Kveta at the abbey. It said simply, cruelly, that Mother Kazi was dead. There was no explanation for the medical tools, but Mouse understood. They had been dear to Mother Kazi, her only treasure and a means of empowerment in a world governed by men, her secret identity hidden behind her veil. And Mother Kazi would have wanted Mouse to have them.

Tears spilled onto the leather, staining it, as Mouse grieved for her Mother. She opened the satchel and ran her hands gently along the bone and metal tools inside, neatly tied with leather straps. Mouse had sewn these straps herself, a gift for Mother Kazi, to replace the ones that had been broken and worn.

Mouse was alone in the world now. Except for Nicholas. But he would be enough. She would bring him here and live a quiet life. She would not be special, no one's angel, not a saint, not marked by God with gifts to do wonders. She would just be a mother. She would watch her son grow and tell him about Mother Kazi and Father Lucas. It would be enough.

And then she saw it—at the top of the leather satchel, poking out from the binding where the seams had torn, was Father Lucas's breviary. He had read the Psalms to Mouse from that little book, had bid her memorize them and seemed overjoyed when she did it so quickly, after just one reading.

As Mouse opened it, a letter fell into her lap. The portrait of herself she'd given Father Lucas as a girl, its edges worn from handling, slid out as she unfolded the parchment. The girl in the drawing was wide-eyed, and bits of unruly hair swept across her face half-hiding a soft smile.

Mouse turned to the letter. Though the script was shaky and difficult to read, she knew Father Lucas's hand at once. It was addressed to her.

> *My little andílek,*
> *Forgive me. I have burned the books.*
> *Bishop Miklaus writes that Rome is sending someone here to Houska soon, before Easter. This troubles me.*
> *As I watch the ancient covers curl and turn to ash, I confess that fear drove me to lay them in the fire. The*

bishop from Rome will have questions. He will want what answers I have. If the books are not here, he will not ask about them.

I pray he will ask nothing at all.

But the Psalmist warns me—"For thou, O God, hast tested us; thou hast tried us, as silver is tried." I know what is coming and I am ready.

And so must you be.

You must know who you are so you may guard yourself against the dangers without. And within.

That night at Houska—before I died—I started to tell you about your father. But I am a coward. I wanted to keep you as my own for as long as I could.

Please, little one, keep me in your heart as Father despite what I am about to tell you. And I beg you, do not turn your back on what is right and good. Do not turn away from who you are—for you are good, little andílek, though you may not believe it.

Consider what others would have done with your power, how they would have used it for gain. But not you. You have only ever wished to be just a girl. You fear what you cannot find in yourself, that glow of a soul you see in others, but I tell you: I see your light shine bright and pure every day. You think of others first and yourself last. You are a healer of body and spirit, a ministering angel.

You are my child as sure as anyone's.

And you belong to God.

Even though it was His enemy who gave you life.

Some call him Semjaza or Satariel. Others call him Abaddon, the Destroyer. The Father of Lies. Satan.

This is what sired you. This is your father.

But this does not frighten me. I am frightened by what

others would do to you if they knew. What makes me tremble is what I fear you will do to yourself now that you know.

Please, little one, protect yourself from harm. Guard yourself against the darkness that will come.

Remember what the Psalmist tells us, even in the fires of torment—"Blessed be God, which hath not turned away my prayer, nor His mercy from me."

For my sake, little andílek, be strong and believe in your goodness as I do.

Your loving Father.

Mouse's hand curled around the edges of the little girl portrait of herself; she crushed it and tossed it on the fire.

She hated that girl and her naïve love of the world and all she met in it. She hated her for her hope and her belief in herself. That girl who shriveled in the flame was a lie. Mouse was a lie. The daughter of the Father of Lies. She was not an angel, not gifted by God as she had always believed.

Father Lucas might have kept faith; Mouse had none.

Her life made sense now. She was an abomination like the children born of the Watchers in the *Book of Enoch*; evil spirits, God had called them, demons. Of course God would hate her.

Mouse thought of Nicholas and bit her tongue to keep from crying out. That future was dead to her now.

Her hands shook as she put the letter back in the book and the book back in the case—just as it had been, as if it would undo what she'd read. She wrapped the satchel carefully in the bundle again, sliding her fingers over the soft silk of the ribbon, and then shoved it into her bag. She bound her broken wrist with linen she ripped from the bed, pulling it tight against the swollen skin, making it hurt. Then she went down the hall and into Vok's room. It was empty.

She found his hunting knife on the table by his bed and sat on the floor before the fire. She sat there for a long time twisting the knife in her hand and watching the flames dance along the blade. She was too dead to mourn anymore.

Finally, she lifted a handful of her long hair and began to saw at it with Vok's knife. After she was done, she gathered the pile of hair and threw it in the fire. The bitter stench made her gag as she watched the strands undulate in the heat like a mass of snakes.

Shorn and dressed again in men's clothes, Mouse walked past a sleeping guard at the gate. She walked beyond the edge of the castle grounds. And then, just as the sun lifted over the low rise of hills behind her, she stepped into the black of the Sumava forest.

THIRTY-TWO

Mouse sat on the shore of a dark lake, clenching her teeth as she dug a knife into the rotted flesh at the heel of her foot. Like the Israelites, she had been wandering in the wilderness. The Sumava forest belonged to bears and wildcats and the rare wanderer looking for the same thing Mouse had been looking for—someplace to disappear. Her hair, once shaved, now hung in matted ropes over her shoulders and down her back; this wasn't the first time her feet had bled and blistered and turned foul.

Mouse had been wandering the woods for more than fifteen years.

After reading Father Lucas's letter, her only thought had been to run—away from the truth of what she was, away from anyone she might hurt, far enough away that Nicholas and Ottakar would seem impossibly out of reach. She hoped distance would quell her want of them. It didn't.

During those early years in the forest, Mouse found herself sliding always north and east toward Prague, as if her little golden-haired boy pulled at her like some primal force calling her home. "Mama!" But then the woods would grow lighter, and she would smell the hearth fires and the livestock or hear the calls of the farmers to their wives. She would scurry like a wild thing back deeper into the Sumava. Like a leper, she needed to keep herself isolated so she would not spread her curse to anyone else, especially not to Nicholas.

But to think of him daily, to know that he lived and yet not be able to see him or hold him or sing to him—it was more than she could bear. She feared that sooner or later she would give in and drag herself, cursed or not, to plead at Ottakar's feet to be reunited with her son. To keep Nicholas safe, Mouse needed him gone from her as if he were dead. She tried to trick her mind into believing it, torturing herself with imagined details of tragedies that could have befallen her little boy. She imagined what his dead weight would feel like in her arms, the pallor of his skin, his mouth gone slack. She wore her grief so well, it began to feel real to her.

She also returned to the discipline she'd learned at the abbey: solitude, silence, suffering. These were easy in the Sumava. Avoiding the trade paths, she saw no one. A stone on her tongue helped her turn from the temptation of speaking out loud when she was so desperate to hear a human voice that even her own would do. And the wilderness offered plenty of suffering—bare feet abused on rough terrain and in bitter weather, broken bones after a fall, piercing cold and frostbite, the hollow ache of nearly constant hunger.

A chunk of dead flesh fell from the knife at her foot, bright red blood flooding the wound. Thoughtlessly, she bound her heel with a strip of cloth. It would heal soon enough with or without her ministrations, and then it would be time to walk again. After fifteen years, Mouse was sick of walking. She was sick of gathering berries and gnawing the flesh from the back of a piece of bark to silence her hunger, sick of seeking shelter from the storms. These things she did out of habit, like an animal—which was what she was. Anything human in her had been worn away by her years in the woods. She was tired. Tired of trees. Tired of skies. Tired of climbing up mountains and tired of stumbling back down them. She wanted it all to end.

Mouse looked around the dark lake at the spruce and fir that bent themselves down, their tips reaching out over the water like penitents praying to some god at the center. The tops of the mountains stretched up around her, a giant hand holding her and the water in its palm. This would be a good place to die.

As night fell, she lit a fire on the stony shore. The lake looked like it was full of stars, their twinkling lights reflected in the still water and bringing the impossible close to hand. Mouse drifted off, wondering if God would stretch out her life and keep her wandering in her wilderness for forty years like the Israelites. She wasn't even halfway there. This did not make her sad; Mouse didn't think she could feel anything anymore—not anything but tired. A last thought came to her before sleep: Perhaps God would have mercy.

When Mouse woke the next morning, she knew immediately she was not alone. At the edge of the thick fog that lay over the lake, she could see a dark mound on the shore. The smell of the thing had woken her—a wildness made pungent in the wet air. She shifted her head slightly, trying to get a better look without alerting the thing that she was awake and aware of its presence. But it remained shapeless and unmoving. Convinced that whatever it was, it was likely dead, Mouse started to push herself up. At the first low snarl, she jumped to her feet, crouched and ready for the thing to lunge at her.

She tensed as the mound turned and amber eyes glared at her through the heavy mist. A wolf. Its muzzle drew back with another snarl, revealing sharp fangs, the growl rumbling deep in its chest. Mouse's heart raced, her instinct screaming at her to run before it attacked, but something stopped her. Perhaps her thoughts had been heard last night. Perhaps this was God's mercy.

She took a step forward, swallowing as she pictured the wolf ripping out her throat. But she held her ground, closing her eyes when she heard the ping of scattered rocks as the wolf moved. Soon. It would be soon.

A whimper interrupted the low growl, and Mouse opened her eyes. The wolf sat on its haunches, teeth still bared, watching her warily. It was nearly starved—Mouse could see the skin sinking between each rib—and its front leg was badly broken. As she crouched, trying to study the injury, the wolf flopped onto its side, its eyes still on Mouse, but its mouth open, panting. It was done. It, too, had come to the lake to die.

A few more days of suffering, she thought numbly, and it would all be over. She wondered if she should take mercy on it, put it out of its misery. She looked up from the wounded leg and into the wolf's eyes. She expected the pain she saw there, but it was something else that made her catch her breath. The wolf was looking at her with hope. It wanted healing, not mercy.

And Mouse was a healer.

The truth of it slipped inside her and twisted, bringing tears to her eyes—the first in a long time.

The wolf watched her cautiously as she headed into the woods, her stride purposeful and her gaze determined. When she came back, he didn't even raise his head. Mouse pulled the linen strips from her own feet and scattered them with the crushed herbs she'd gathered. The wolf snarled again as she took its injured leg in both hands, feeling where the bone jutted out and where it was supposed to fit underneath the skin; she

326

turned it, sliding it back in place, as the wolf yelped. Mouse splinted the leg and wrapped it with the cloth.

They stayed by the lake, Mouse bringing him berries and bugs to eat, changing his dressing, brewing teas to fight the infection, until the wolf was able to put weight on his leg. He limped up the mountain after her, both of them stopping so he could rest, until they reached the shallow cave she'd found in an outcropping. She slept in the darkness of the cave, while he slept at the mouth, half inside, half out.

The more he healed, the more Mouse expected him to be gone when she woke. Weeks later, when she removed the splint, he ran for the first time, not fully nor far and with a gait still favoring the leg. The next morning, he left at the sound of other wolves in the woods. When he had not come back by sunset, an unexpected regret settled on Mouse. Despondency and despair quickened in her as the sun dropped below the tree line, throwing a last shard of light onto the smooth water. In a few hours, the moon would rise and resurrect the lake in silver light, but Mouse didn't care to watch alone.

Later, when she felt the wolf's warm body wriggle under her arm in the cold night, she wondered if this was her manna, her *bohdan*. A gift from God.

❧

Mouse smiled as Bohdan flopped down on the ground near the lakeside fire, his thick tongue lolling over his muzzle.

She and Bohdan had survived two winters together, Mouse providing the heat and shelter, the wolf feeding her with squirrel and rabbit when her supply of nuts and berries ran out. Mouse had quit wondering how long he would stay or why he stayed; she was just glad he did. His acceptance of her had come at no cost with no expectation and no judgment; Mouse once again belonged to someone who loved her without fear or awe, loved her just as she was, like Nicholas had as a baby. Bohdan's love proved a powerful healer, and Mouse came to heed Father Lucas's last wish for her—that she not let the name of her father define her, that she believe in her own goodness. Bohdan thought her good regardless of whether the light of a soul shined in her or not. Mouse was working to see herself that way, too.

Another part of her had also come back to life. She had started to carve again—mountain cornflower and monkshood, capercaillies and lynx; the artist in her found limitless inspiration in the primeval woods. She left her masterpieces scattered through the mountains, a half-smile playing on her lips as she imagined some traveler discovering them long after she was dead. She had even carved life-sized statues of the archangels—one for each of the seven peaks surrounding the lake—though she wasn't sure if she meant them to be guardians watching over her or prison guards, Enoch's Watchers made of wood.

But despite her recovered skill and practice, her hand shook now as she pressed the blade against the thick log that lay between the fire and a sleeping Bohdan. It had taken Mouse days to drag the wood back to their camp. Already debarked, it was ready for her hand to shape it, but it took an act of courage and hope for her to make those first cuts, to peel away layers of the tree's life and give birth to her art. Mouse wanted this to be her greatest work, the only marker she would leave as a testament to her own life—a statue of a little boy made of golden aspen.

She worked by firelight through the night, Nicholas's face emerging from the wood by the time she lay down her knife and rubbed her sore fingers. She hadn't thought about him this way in a long time; after so many years of picturing him dead to harden her heart, it was difficult to think of him happy and still hers. She tossed a handful of shavings onto the fire and then took a longer limb to stoke the flame. The sun would be up soon, another beginning. And an ending. Tonight was Walpurgis Night and Mouse meant to burn a witch. She had carried the straw-witch she'd made at Hluboka with her all these years. Still smeared with her blood, it was shriveled and gray with age. The grass doll had come to signify everything Mouse hated about herself, and tonight she would rid herself of it.

As the first pale light slid over the mountain, she tossed the straw-witch on the flame, not to burn away the darkness so much as to destroy her fear of it. The fire curled and blackened the skirt and arms, and Mouse's eyes stung with sadness for the little doll. Then, as the flame licked at the blood-stained chest, she cried out in pain. Bohdan woke with a yelp as Mouse fell, arms wrapped around herself, writhing on the ground like she was burning, too. The power in her, quelled by Mouse's discipline during the years of wandering, twisted and reared as if it were in the throes of death. Bohdan circled her frantically, whimpering, until the straw-witch turned to ash and fell apart and Mouse grew quiet.

She woke to the cry of a falcon fishing in the lake and the midday sun in her face, the fire doused by the dew and Bohdan sleeping beside her.

Mouse felt clean at last.

∽

Streaks of bright orange and yellow and red wove though the dark evergreens around the lake as Mouse and Bohdan prepared for their third winter together. While Mouse spent her days foraging, the wolf would hunt, but Bohdan was always waiting for her at dusk as she came back lugging the baskets she'd woven from the mountain matgrass, full of the forest's offerings. He would jog down the path to greet her, running his head under her hand so that her fingers raked the fur along his neck and spine.

But one day, heavy with clouds that crawled from the far north promising the season's first snow, Bohdan wasn't there as Mouse rounded the lakehead and turned for home. She was late, the sun already set. She knew the path well enough to walk it in the growing dark, but an uneasiness quickened her step. The scream still caught her off guard. She raced up the path, basket slamming against her hip and sending showers of nuts rolling madly behind her.

As she crested the rise, Mouse saw near the mouth of the cave a memory come to life again: The deer strung up on a tree. The poachers in Ottakar's woods. The man who'd tried to rape her. The man she had killed.

Then another scream ripped the air.

It came from the deer that was not a deer. It was Bohdan. His front legs were bound and jutting oddly over him as they held the weight of his body which dangled from the tree. His head hung down like the crucified Christ, eyes open.

Gathered around him were things that were not men, not animals. They were not natural creatures—too thin, rib cages sticking out like skeletons, a slick skin like tarnished silver stretched taut over them. The two on either side of Bohdan crouched on all fours, but the one in the middle stood upright like a man, hips strangely angled. It reached up and pulled its claw down the side of Bohdan's chest, tugging at the wolf's coat until it tore from the body, skinning him. Bohdan screamed again.

Mouse screamed with him.

The creatures holding the wolf's legs let go, startled, and they all turned to look at her.

She acted without thinking, rage driving her. Still screaming, she ran at them but turned at the last, thrusting the bottom of her basket into the fire. The dry grass caught fire quickly, and Mouse swung the basket in front of her as she made her way to Bohdan. The silver demons slid back. She grabbed her knife from where it hung at her waist and reached up to slice at the rope above Bohdan's head.

One of the demons slashed at her, claws raking her leg as she swung the basket of flames at it. It squealed in pain, blisters bubbling on its silver skin. Remembering the hollow-eyed children, Mouse doubted that the fire would kill these demons, but as long as they held their physical form, they were as vulnerable to pain as anything else.

She lunged at the other two, driving them farther back into the shadows as she cut through the last of the rope and Bohdan dropped to the ground at her feet. He didn't move. Mouse didn't wait. She grabbed the rope still wrapped around his legs and ran toward the cave, dragging him behind her.

She heard the demon coming before it landed on her back, claws digging into her shoulder. Mouse turned to swing the basket around, but the flame had eaten through the grass and it fell apart in her hands. She could feel the demon's breath on her neck, and she knew it was about to bite. She threw herself toward the cave.

As they crossed the threshold, the demon on her back cried out, and Mouse felt scalding liquid run down her spine. She spun, crawling to grab the rope and pull Bohdan into the cave with her. She saw a pool of silver bubbling on the other side of a dark line running along the mouth of the cave. When she and Bohdan had decided to make the place their home, out of habit Mouse had crafted the protective spells Father Lucas had taught her all those years ago. She never thought she'd need them.

The other two demons paced silently at the edge of the firelight, but Mouse wasn't watching them. She bent over Bohdan. And what she saw broke her. His mangled skin lay twisted under him, shredded muscle and sinew glistening in the fire-light. He opened his eyes as she ran her hand along the top of his head. He looked at her the same way he did when they first met. With hope. He wanted to live. He wanted to stay with her. But this time there could be no healing.

Mouse buried her face in the fur at his neck, tears running as his blood ran, both of them weeping. She looked back into his eyes, shaking her head. And he knew. She could see the hope leave and another want take its place.

Mercy.

Mouse gripped the knife, brought it to his neck. One jab and it would be over in seconds. Her body shook. She bit into her cheek, trying to use the pain to summon her courage. But she couldn't. She wanted those last minutes with him. She flung the knife away and curled herself around him, her head resting beside his.

"I love you." Half whisper, half cry, her voice thick and cracked from disuse, they were the first words she'd spoken in nearly twenty years, and at the end of them, he was gone.

But she had little time to grieve.

"What are you?" The demon breathed in rather than out to make the sounds, so the words all ran together in an eerie monotone.

Mouse sat up and looked out toward the dying fire. The light glinted off the silver bodies of the demons as they slithered back and forth in front of the cave.

"You are not like the others," it squealed. "Look what you did to our brother." It dragged a claw through the silver liquid that puddled at the mouth of the cave.

Her grief gave way to anger. "I'll do the same to you," she spat. She wondered if she could. "Come here," she commanded, waiting for the power to awaken in her, watching to see if her compulsion would work.

The demons stilled but they came no closer. The one who had skinned Bohdan pulled its lips back into a sneer, black fangs dripping with saliva, and let out a long, dry, scratchy laugh like sand grinding on stone.

All the better, she thought, as her mind filled with how to kill them slowly so they would suffer as Bohdan did. Teeth gritted, Mouse took a step toward the mouth of the cave, but her foot brushed against Bohdan's body. She dropped to her knees again, breaking under the weight of what she had lost, her rage transformed. "Why did you do this?" she asked.

"We want it."

"Want what?" she asked, but she knew the answer to her question before they gave it.

"The power. We felt it. We want it." They called out in that sick, uneven drone of inhaled words.

Mouse understood. Walpurgis Night. Her blood on the straw-witch. She'd felt it, too, as the witch burned and released that power. The demons had come because of her, just like the hollow-eyed children all those years ago.

She felt the despair caving in on her, but as she turned back to Bohdan, she thought about what he had given her—healing, love, hope. To give in to her rage or despair would undo the years they'd shared, all that he had done. She couldn't let that happen. What years were left her she would live as a testament to their time together.

Mouse carefully pulled the tangled skin out from under Bohdan, gently smoothing it in place. She gathered her needle and the vine she used to mend her clothes and began her work. She could not heal him, but she could make him whole.

She stopped often when the tears came too thick to see. She ignored the taunts and screams of the demons. As the morning light broke over the mountains, she looked up to watch them slink away. She carried Bohdan up the mountain opposite the lake—Raphael's mountain, she called it, because near the summit stood her statue of the archangel of healing carved from a seven-foot tall shaft of sycamore that had been struck by lightning. His arms were held out wide as if he were blessing the lake and valley below.

Mouse lifted Bohdan up into the angel's arms. She built a mound of kindling at the base of the statue and lit it.

"Carry him with you as you go. Heal him on the way," she said as the fire took wolf and statue together. Lifting her head higher as she watched the tendrils of smoke join the clouds overhead, flecks of snow drifting down white and pure to burn in the flame, she spoke to God for the first time in years. "Do not turn him away because he was my friend. He was better than me. He has a soul. I saw it."

Mouse did not cry, but she stayed until there was nothing but ash, and then she started her long journey out of the woods.

THIRTY-THREE

N ow where did you come from?" asked the old woman pulling up a bucket of water from the far side of the Otava River.

Mouse had been walking for days, doubling back often to check that she wasn't being followed—she didn't want to lead the demons to anyone else. But the silver demons had been drawn to the power, not to Mouse, and if the power was gone from her, there was nothing to lure them. She had certainly seen no sign of them or anyone else as she traveled the woods.

And yet Mouse never felt alone. She found herself looking for Bohdan out of the corner of her eyes, expecting to see him weaving between the trees beside her. She would lower her hand, fingers spread, waiting for the cold, wet nuzzle and then the soft fur of him raking his head under her palm. She would reach out for his warmth in the night and though he was not there, the memory of him was and it offered a bittersweet comfort. With her sadness came the realization that he would be with her always like this. There but not there.

This feeling of his presence gave her the courage to come to the river and speak to the old woman even though every part of Mouse wanted to bolt, frightened like a wild animal by the smell and the sounds of anything human.

"The lake," Mouse finally answered, pointing back toward the snow-covered woods. Words still felt foreign in her mouth.

"Devil's Lake?" The woman shook her head and crossed herself. "There be dark things living in them woods and water. My dear Bernd tried to cut wood up near the lake many years ago, and he come running home, afraid for his soul. God be with you if you came through there, girl."

The woman squinted and leaned a little out over the water. "How you come to be out in them woods? You wander off? Lose your man, maybe?"

Mouse couldn't answer, couldn't look the woman in the eye, but she managed to shake her head. She was trembling now, not from the cold but from fighting all her instincts to run.

"Trouble find you, girl?"

Mouse nodded.

"Best come home with me," the woman said and beckoned Mouse to cross the river. "It ent deep here, though it is sure to be cold. But home is just up the rise. Come along, now."

Mouse was wet to the waist when she stepped onto the shore beside the woman and bent to pick up one of the buckets of water.

The old woman nodded. "I near took you for a ghost so thin you are and dark about the eyes." She smacked her lips and shook her head. "You need food, girl, and I could use some help seeing after the workers boarding with me. They come to build up the new town for our Gold and Iron King." The unexpected mention of Ottakar ran like ice through Mouse, chilling her far more than the river had. The Gold and Iron King—it was the title she had given him years ago.

For her, he had become like a character in some minnesinger's tale of heroes, a part of her life so long gone that despite her perfect memory, she never fully trusted her remembrances. She had pushed those memories away so often that Ottakar was more ghost than man, just as Nicholas had become more dream than reality. But now she had come back to the world of men, and here was Ottakar. She wondered about Nicholas.

"I be Enede," the old woman said. She waited a beat for Mouse to give her name, but when nothing came, Enede started rattling on more about the new town they were building and the old one they were tearing down. Hoping she might say something more about Ottakar, waiting foolishly for a mention of Nicholas, Mouse followed Enede's voice until they reached the tiny cottage.

She balked at the door, the closed space and smells too unfamiliar. A few sheep and goats and chickens were penned on one side, a wooden table and a handful of stools stood at the other, and a thick patch of straw ran along the front wall. Simple and bare like the homes Mouse had visited with Mother Kazi back in Teplá, tending the sick or birthing babies. Mouse knew this life. She had lived this life once before. She could live it again. She stepped over the threshold and closed the door behind her.

That first day, Mouse ate little, not trusting her stomach to real food after so long, but the warm, yeasty bread in her mouth tasted like joy. She kept herself busy so she wouldn't think about where she was—the walls surrounding her, the stifling human smells, the loud voices of the half dozen men who paid to eat Enede's food and to sleep on her straw. It was hardest when they talked directly to Mouse. She felt too visible, too much among them. Fighting the panic squeezing her chest, she would grab the buckets and go down to the river where she could breathe and be alone just long enough to calm herself. The men learned soon enough to ignore her.

They talked instead about the work of building the new town. And about the king who had ordered it. These craftsmen, who had come at Ottakar's bidding from Germany, loved their Golden King. And Mouse loved hearing them talk about him.

"By the saints, you stink, lass!" one of the men, a new boarder, spat as she bent over him, refilling his cup. She had been at Enede's for the better part of a week and had learned to control her fear and nervousness though it never really left her. She felt her face flush now as the men all looked at her. Enede, too, seemed to be studying her, and Mouse was suddenly aware of her ragged, soiled clothes and the ends of her filthy, matted hair that dangled as she bent. She put the bronze ewer on the table, wine sloshing from the spout, and walked back to the fire.

"Hurt the child's heart, you have," Enede reprimanded the men, who were laughing as they traded crude jokes about filthy women. But as they left for work, one of them laid his hand on Mouse's shoulder, "We meant nothing by it, girl."

His touch, the first human touch she'd had in nearly twenty years, plucked something lose in her. She spun toward him. "I am not a girl!" She turned to Enede. "Nor a child, either." Her voice came out as a quiet croak rather than the forceful shout she intended. The man didn't even turn back to look at her.

But Enede had heard. "Right you be, a woman you are, though to my old eyes you still look a child. I be fifty years old come my name day." She chuckled. "And sadly, to most men, every woman's a girl until she's in his bed. Wrong they were to tease you so, but the truth be that you need a bath and a hair washing. Go fetch us some water."

Mouse lingered at the river, buckets in hand, her eyes turned up toward the lake as she tested herself. Living among people was hard. Alone was better—though maybe not alone without Bohdan. She sighed and turned back toward the cottage.

The bathwater had turned dark with grime by the time Mouse had scrubbed herself clean. She stood now in an old kirtle Enede had pulled out of the bottom of one of the trunks along the wall. The dress clung to her damp skin and her wet hair pulled heavily on her neck. She smelled fresh, the wildness washed away.

Enede smacked her lips and shook her head as she tried to comb through Mouse's ratted hair, which stretched well past her waist. "There be nothing for it but to shave it off and start again," the old woman said and took a razor to Mouse's head. The hair coiled in long dark ropes around her feet as it fell, and something quivered in Mouse as her eyes carefully studied the black tresses. It took her a moment to realize what was wrong. There should be gray in the hair of a woman almost forty years old, but her hair lay there as dark as ever. Her head jerked forward as Enede cut a large chunk of hair from the back, freeing her from the weight, and Mouse bent down, running her fingers through the mass of cut hair.

"Young as you be, it will surely grow back," the old woman said soothingly.

Mouse started to shake. Young. Girl. Child. She looked into Enede's eyes trying to see herself in them.

"Calm yourself, child. I promise it will grow back as thick and beautiful as it must have been before the dark times befell you out at Devil's Lake."

Mouse pushed past Enede and grabbed the bronze ewer from the table, flipping it upside down, wine splashing red against the straw-covered floor. The smooth bottom of the polished brass made a looking glass, and Mouse saw herself for the first time in many years. Enede had not yet finished, so part of her head was shaved bald and the other had clumps of frayed hair sticking out from her scalp at odd angles. The bones jutted from her face, her eyes sunk back in dark holes. But these were to be expected from the years of hardship in the Sumava. These did not scare her.

Frantically, she ran her hands along her jaw, around her eyes. It was all the same as it had always been. Mouse looked just as she had twenty years ago when she went into the woods. She had not aged.

She looked up at Enede, terrified. The old woman reached out to her. Mouse grabbed her hand. She held her own against it. Enede's hand, not ten years older, sagged and wrinkled with age and wear. Mouse had the hand of a young woman, smooth and spotless.

She paced, her hands rubbing her rough scalp, trying to understand. Enede tried to calm her, but Mouse didn't hear; her mind was racing. It *had* been almost twenty years; she knew it. Her unnatural mind kept perfect awareness of the days—she had always known when it was Nicholas's birthday, she knew Walpurgis Night, she knew the Saints' Days, though she did not honor them. And besides all that had been the seasons. She could count them—the fourth winter when she broke her leg, the ninth autumn when she watched the wolves trap the deer and she could not save it, the summers with Bohdan, the springs.

Twenty years and not a mark on her to show it.

Mouse felt the anger that had flared earlier that morning come back to life. At first she meant to lay this at God's feet— he had indeed extended her life to prolong her wandering, to punish her. But then she thought of Bohdan, her manna from heaven, her peace offering. She was not at war with God. She was at war with—

"Him," she hissed, shocking Enede into silence. "His doing. Always him."

"What him, child? Him who mishandled you out in them woods?"

Mouse stared at the woman blankly, slowly shaking her head as she let the pieces fall into place. A prolonged life, her not aging, they were like the other marks of her birth—unnatural senses, rapid healing, a quick mind and perfect memory. Mouse knew her enemy.

"My father." The truth ran through her like her tainted blood.

Still holding Enede's hand, Mouse folded to her knees, weeping. The old woman held her, crying with her.

"Your father? He what done this to you?" Enede ran her hand gently over Mouse's shorn head. "Shame on him. God curse him. But don't you let him keep hurting you." Mouse sobbed. "That's better, girl. Let it out and then you can heal. Then you can move on."

ϖ

When the men came back to the cottage that night, Enede met them at the door, whispering warnings at them. Mouse heard it all, but she was still grateful when none of them said a word about her now fully shaved head.

Drained from the day's revelations, she wove between them listlessly as she filled bowls with stew and cups with wine. Her ears pricked when the talk turned again to Ottakar.

"Eh, the nobles don't like him because he cares about the likes of us more than filling their bellies full. But they cannot touch him."

"Maybe they can now that he got the ban put on him by the emperor," the new man added.

"What you say?"

"I heard word of it before I left Prague. The Holy Roman Emperor has named the King an outlaw of the Church. Anybody can kill him now and not hang for it."

Mouse walked to the fire, hiding her face from the men, afraid that it would show too much.

"Ent nothing holy nor Roman about that Rudolf. God be with our good King," said Enede, crossing herself.

"God may not have much to do with it," the man answered. "Heard the King done been excommunicated."

Mouse stepped outside, not wanting to hear more. A fresh snow was falling. Ottakar an outlaw, the doors of the Church closed to him. Just like her. He was alone.

As impossible as it might be to help him in his troubles, Mouse could not silence the voice screaming at her to go to him, that he needed her.

And so she went.

THIRTY-FOUR

Whatever Mouse expected of an outlaw king, it wasn't the swarm of tents spilling out beside Wroclaw, hoards of oxen, horses, and goats framing the swirl of white spires circling around the scarlet pavilion at the center. Here was Ottakar. And he was certainly not alone.

Leaving the old woman's house, head shaved and dressed in a stolen monk's habit, Mouse had made for Prague first. Ottakar wasn't there, but slipping in and out of monasteries along the way as she played the traveling monk, Mouse had gathered the pieces of his story, of what had happened to him while she was wandering the Sumava. She learned that many of the Bohemian nobles had failed to support him in his earlier bid to thwart the Holy Roman Emperor's grab for land and wealth. Ottakar had built a mighty empire, overflowing with riches and filled with German craftsmen and Jewish tradesmen protected by his just laws—laws that revoked the unbridled power Vaclav had granted to many of his nobles. When the emperor came calling, besieging Ottakar in Vienna, those nobles gladly took the opportunity to seek revenge on their king and only a few of them sent knights to Ottakar's aid.

Ottakar had come home defeated—shunned by Rome and betrayed by many of his own, as well as the Austrian lords who had once begged him to be their king. But he was determined to protect his people from the emperor's ruthlessness. And so Ottakar had gone looking for help elsewhere.

As Mouse now looked down from Mount Ślęża, beyond the fields already white with the first snowdrops of the spring, it seemed clear that Ottakar had found his army—thousands of loyal Bohemians and Moravians as well as Silesians and Poles afraid that a hungry Rome would not stop at the Krkonose Mountains.

Mouse slowly made her way down Ślęża and meandered between the tents and the edges of fields where the soldiers trained, wondering what she would do when she found Ottakar. She could hardly just introduce herself; she looked exactly as she had when Ottakar last saw her twenty years ago. But something kept pulling her closer to that scarlet tent in the center of the camp.

"Name?"

Mouse took another step toward the tent before the guard's hand came down on her shoulder.

"What is your name, Brother?"

"Herman," she said. It was the best she could do in the moment, German for "army man."

"You have business with the King?"

She tried to think of some reason a poor monk would need to speak with the King, but as the possibilities of being near Ottakar again played out in her mind—of looking him in the eye, hearing his voice, saying his name—her courage fled. Panicked, she shook her head and slipped quickly out of sight behind a tent opposite Ottakar's. And from there, she watched.

Every time the flap of his tent lifted, she held her breath; each time it was someone else who came or left, she went back to chewing at her lip, waiting.

When, near twilight, they brought horses to the front of the tent, Mouse knew she would get her glimpse of him, but still she wasn't prepared. She held the moment, outside of time like she had when she first saw him at the Teplá River all those years ago, and she drank in the sight of him—the white along his temples and in his beard, which softened the tawny hair of his youth, the dark circles at his eyes, the wrinkles as he squinted to look off into the distance. Her heart raced with wanting to go to him.

But it was the young man who came out of the tent just after the King that broke the spell.

"Nicholas," she called out before her hand clamped her mouth shut.

He spun around, but Mouse had ducked behind the tent.

He looked so much like his father—same nose and eyes, the way he held himself—but his hair had gone dark like hers, his mouth was shaped like hers, and his skin was light like hers. He was her son. Fear chased her joy, and she trembled at the thought of what his likeness to her might mean. Mouse closed her eyes quickly, hoping for the first time that one of her gifts was still there. She sighed as she saw the glow in Nicholas, steady and full.

And then they were on the horses riding off toward the city.

Mouse sat relishing the gift. She had buried him in her mind, never dared hope to see him again, and even as she sought out Ottakar, she'd not considered that Nicholas might be with him.

Seeing him here filled her with joy and terror. It was as if he had come back to life. And she could think of herself as his mother again. The joy of it swelled in her until she could barely breathe, but with it came the worry of what might happen to him, since he had clearly allied himself with his father against Rome. Her fear for him brought with it a fierce desire—to be with him somehow, to protect him in any way she could.

And so Mouse found a new purpose. She went to war.

During the week before they broke camp, she found it easy to lose herself among the sea of soldiers. Wherever men gathered, there was illness even if battle had not yet come to make the wounded. Mouse gathered herbs on Mount Ślęża and made teas and poultices. She moved among the sick, who were laid on cots or blankets or bare ground depending on rank. She tended them and pretended to pray with them when they asked.

"Little Brother," they called. "Come say a word to God for me."

And she would bow, silently. She felt helpless then, but many of them lived anyway.

Every day, Mouse looked for Ottakar and Nicholas. She allowed herself only one glimpse each day and never close enough to catch their smell, never close enough that she might be tempted to speak. But then the son of one of the Moravian lords fell from his horse and was trampled and someone mentioned the healing skills of the Little Brother.

Mouse blinked as the soldier guided her into the dark tent, a sense of déjà-vu running through her as she knelt beside the boy who was struggling to breathe. He looked to be about the same age as Ottakar when she first met him. She laid her head against his bloody chest. She cut him quickly, slipped the cannula in and stepped back from the rush of blood. It turned her feet scarlet.

"What have you done?"

Mouse froze, unable to turn around at the sound of Ottakar's voice asking the same question he'd asked her all those years ago. He stepped beside her, took her by the shoulder and spun her to face him. It was Nicholas; he sounded just like his father, though his eyes were a softer blue.

"Brother, I asked what did you do? The lad breathes better."

She lowered her face quickly and shook her head.

"The Little Brother does not speak," said the guard who'd brought her to the tent.

Mouse knelt again, bending to see in through the cannula, her hand gently probing the boy's belly. The horses had crushed his innards; his ribs were not simply broken but smashed, slivers of them embedded in the organs. There was no hope for him.

She eased the cannula from his side.

"He will live now that he can breathe?" Nicholas asked.

Mouse could hear the care in his voice.

"A friend?" she asked softly, breaking her silence with a wish to comfort her son.

Nicholas nodded. "Will he live?"

Mouse could not stop her hand as it reached out for his. Surprised, Nicholas looked at her, a gaunt and grimy monk in his eyes, but he did not pull his hand away.

"The horses have crushed him inside. There is nothing to do." Her voice was thick with a mother's love.

Nicholas nodded again, his mouth pulled tight. "Will he suffer?"

"He does not have to."

"Will you help him?"

"If you wish it."

Nicholas squeezed her hand. "Wait," he said as he lifted the tent flap.

He came back with two men: the boy's father and his own.

Mouse lowered her face quickly, her heart pounding. She need not have worried. Ottakar watched her crush the hemlock seeds and mix them with wine, but he did not see past her shaved head, her habit, her stained fingers, her grim face. Ottakar did not know her.

She held the cup of wine to the dying boy's mouth, then stepped back to let his father and Nicholas kneel beside the cot to say good-bye. As she stood beside Ottakar, she breathed him in, relieved she could be so close to him yet hurt that he did not recognize her.

Mouse closed her eyes and watched the boy's soul lift and leave. As Nicholas wept, she reached out to lay her hand on his shoulder just as Ottakar did the same; their hands touched for a moment and the feel of his skin on hers burned through her.

With a gasp, she slipped quickly from the tent; her hand covered her mouth to hold back the words she wanted to say, but she was unable to stop the tears. When she reached the cover of the woods at the foot of the mountain, she spun around like she had as a little girl in Adele's arms, like she had the night she danced with Damek at the castle in Prague, and then, dizzy, she sank to her knees and lifted her face to the ribbons of light filtering through the trees. Mouse was swirling with joy and sadness—sad for the boy who died, sad that she was dead to Ottakar and Nicholas, but she was also bursting with the joy of being with them again. Such joy and loss woven together that it left her shaking on the forest floor. Mouse didn't rise until the trill of the nightjars echoing in the trees around her announced the coming darkness.

THIRTY-FIVE

When the army set out on the slow crawl to battle, Mouse felt as if she were in the wilderness again, only this time surrounded by an endless forest of men. The column of horses and soldiers and oxen pulling wagons never changed; the same clanking armor, squeaking wheels, snorting animals, and complaining men week after week. She spoke to no one. She got no glimpses of Ottakar or Nicholas, who rode at the front and then sequestered themselves with the other lords behind tent doors in the evenings while she wove between the men who called out for the Little Brother to treat festered blisters and twisted ankles, and, after days of walking in the spring rains, rotting feet.

Mouse only slept in stolen naps shuffling along with the men, and she was often disturbed by short, violent dreams in which Nicholas died, a vengeful God standing over his body. She woke with his words in her ear—"You reap what you sow."

At the Moravian Gate, a gentler pass between the Sudetes and the Carpathian Mountains, Ottakar's outriders came back with stories of a mounting Hungarian army. As his own army continued toward Austria, Ottakar and a small guard rode off not long after passing into Bohemia and came back days later with thousands more men. Apparently some of the vengeful nobles liked the idea of an arrogant king better than a foreign tyrant.

Ottakar laid siege to Drosendorf at the border and took the city and castle with little bloodshed. Except for a few Imperial guards, the people welcomed Ottakar as their rightful king, refusing to acknowledge some Swabian prince even if he called himself the King of the Romans, the Holy Roman Emperor.

Ottakar left a few men there and moved the army on to Laa. They suffered their first casualties when Cuman warriors rained down on them from the castle high atop the Great Mountain at Staatz. The Cuman, who had slid like glaciers from the Yellow River into Europe and wandered from country to country until the Hungarian king gave them land in exchange for military services, followed no code of battle. They wore no armor and carried no shields; like ghosts, they could swiftly and silently steal up from the rear in ambush, flinging arrows as they raced.

Following the attack, Mouse dug out arrowheads shaped like narrow pyramids with jagged barbs, Cuman-crafted to pierce armor and tear flesh both on the way in and as they were yanked out. The barber-surgeons' arrow pulls, made for broad flatheads, would not work. Mouse sketched Galen's diagrams of the body in the dirt, showing organs and arteries, and taught the surgeons how to guide the arrow through and out, just as she'd done for Ottakar all those years ago. Still, the work was bloody and many men died. She lost two herself, her hands buried in chest and gut as she heard their hearts stop; she closed her eyes and watched their souls spill out of them, the light dissipating in the air and the ground, until it was nothing.

BOHEMIAN GOSPEL

After a second attack just before the army reached Laa, Nicholas moved his cavalry to the rear.

Mouse slept no more.

She walked at the edge of the men, eyes searching for signs of trouble at the front with Ottakar and ears tuned behind her for sounds of horses or arrows, listening for death coming for her son.

The siege at Laa proved more difficult than Drosendorf. Hungarian knights protected the castle, but Ottakar's men rallied. Felling trees in the nearby woods, they built catapults and flung mighty rocks against the walls surrounding the town, biting at the stone and sending shrapnel flying into soldier and citizen.

Like Jericho, Laa fell on the seventh day, and Mouse wondered if God was also with Ottakar. But then outriders came with the news that Rudolf had ridden from Vienna, afraid that the Viennese would rally at Ottakar's return like Drosendorf; the Imperial army now waited in the Morava basin. Ottakar's men marched quickly to meet them, stopping after twilight when they neared the Morava River so the soldiers and horses could ready themselves for battle.

Mouse readied herself, too.

Staying with the barber-surgeons and the infantry would mean staying in camp during the fight. She would be no use to Nicholas or Ottakar there; she needed to be close so she could get to them if they were wounded. She snaked through the men, many of whom were sleeping, some who called to the Little Brother to pray with them, but Mouse ignored them. The guard around Ottakar's tent was heavy, but she didn't need to be close.

She leaned her back against a willow tree, the long slender limbs hanging like a curtain between her and the wall of Ottakar's tent. Nicholas was there, too, with the Silesian and

German lords, planning for tomorrow. Mouse let her body sink into the dips of the willow trunk, closed her eyes, breathed in the warm, damp air, and focused on listening past the chirp of the crickets and the rattle of the armored guards until she could hear Ottakar's voice and pick Nicholas's heartbeat out from the others. She nearly broke with remembering that heartbeat, faster, growing in her belly, and the glow of a soul she'd had for a few months.

"Rudolf will keep all but a few of the Austrians to shield himself. He will let the Hungarians do the early fighting," she heard Ottakar say, bringing her back to the moment.

"They have mostly light horse cavalry. They will be vulnerable against our barded chargers," one of the lords commented.

"But they will be faster, Lord Rozemberk," Nicholas answered.

Mouse stiffened and strained to hear the other man's voice.

"I think I know more about war than you, boy," he said. Not Vok—he was dead. And his father would long be dead, too. This must be a brother, then, who inherited the estate and the title.

"Mind your tongue, Vitek," Ottakar barked. "My son is right. Our heavy armor will take its toll on the men in this heat. We must prepare them. The Hungarians will also be fighting for revenge against me," he added. "It will feed them." Ottakar sighed. Mouse could hear the weariness in his voice. "The less they see of me, the better. And I want Rudolf."

"I will take the left, Father, and destroy the Hungarians as you did here years ago. Let them wish revenge on me hereafter." Mouse shuddered at the arrogance in Nicholas's voice; he was his father's son. Yet, despite her misgivings, she smiled when she heard chain mail clink against chain mail and imagined Ottakar embracing Nicholas.

"You do me great honor, son." His words vibrated with emotion. Ottakar had been true to his word—he loved the son Mouse gave him.

She wrapped herself in the moment, and as the men continued to talk war, she let her mind drift until the voices grew softer, gentler, and then faded away.

∽

She jolted awake, never having meant to sleep. The sun sent spears of light through the low trees to the east. The back end of the cavalry was riding down the hill toward the river.

Mouse ran, sucking in the hot, humid air; sweat ran underneath her wrapped breasts by the time she caught up with the men.

"Down! Down!" The echo pealed up from the Morava riverbed below.

The clearing filled with the high whine of feathers slicing the air and the thumps of broadheads as they bounced off shields and landed in the dirt. Iron bodkins squealed, metal on metal, as they pierced the hauberks and bit into flesh.

Then the screams started.

Full-throated and shrill, they tore from the horses as they rolled in the dirt, trying to stop the stinging pain of the shafts dug deep in their haunches. Muffled and ghostly screams came from the riders crushed underneath. Men wailed as they clawed at the arrows in their backs or jerked in the last throes of life while they fingered the blood-soaked fletchings.

With her unnatural senses, Mouse could hear all of it. Not as a chaotic symphony of war, but as individual sounds—the crack of arrows as they hit their mark, tearing flesh and shattering bone; blood falling like soft rain on thatch, turning the dirt into scarlet mud; last breaths bubbling in the mouths of dying men.

She threw back her hood, trying to calm herself with a clean breath, but the sour sweetness of bowels voided from the dead men and horses mixed with the sharp taste of blood in the air, and she gagged. Shoving her fist against her stomach to stop the heaves, she, too, ran toward the riverbed. By the time she reached it, the living had moved on toward the battlefield; the dead dammed the river.

Where was Nicholas? Where was Ottakar?

Mouse weaved through the bodies and waded into the water.

Blood swirled in the current. She pressed her lips together tightly as the water rose nearer her head. Mouse could feel the anger swelling in her, chewing at her. Anger at all this needless loss. Anger at men and their ambition and pride. As her anger grew, the river began to churn with heat, rolling in angry swirls around her and slapping against the shallow wall of corpses a foot upriver. She froze at the thought that it was because of her—that her wrath had become the river's wrath.

The churning Morava finally drove its way through the crooks of the dead men's elbows and knees, disentangling the unlucky dam. The gush of water swept Mouse downstream among the corpses until she tangled her foot in the fronds of quillwort on the river bottom, anchoring herself as the bodies flowed past, and then she climbed the riverbank. Cresting the hill and using a birch tree to push herself upright against the heaviness of her soaked robes, Mouse got her first look at the battle of Marchfeld.

Everywhere men and horses. Hacking and stabbing. Screaming. Rearing.

She raked her fingers across her bare head. "You God-damned fools!"

All of them under pretty banners whipping in the stifling air as army ran up against army. All of the flags red, decorated with fanged lions or eagles, their wings spread wide and talons sharp.

Bohemian. Moravian. Silesian. Hungarian. Austrian. Imperial.

She thought she saw Nicholas's red-and-white banner on the far side of the field, but she could not see Ottakar anywhere.

She ran along the hill at the edge of the fighting, searching for him. And then she saw him with a small group of knights moving behind the front lines toward an oncoming Rudolf surrounded by Imperial forces.

As she ran toward the battle, she watched Ottakar's knights fight boldly, cutting through line after line of enemy soldiers.

And then—"All is lost!"

Mouse turned toward the sound and saw a man holding a shield decorated with a five-petal rose—Lord Rozemberk. He was near the edge of the field not far behind her; he was already turned and riding for safe ground. "Ottakar flees! Save yourselves!" he cried.

Mouse saw the smile play along Lord Rozemberk's lips; Ottakar was betrayed.

Others looked up, confused, and saw their King riding away from the main battlefield. Just as planned, Ottakar was heading for Rudolf, who had held back from the front lines. Lord Rozemberk knew this, but the soldiers didn't. He preyed on their doubt and made them think that their King had abandoned them.

"No!" Mouse yelled. "Ottakar rides for the emperor. Fight on!"

But no one heard her. Some of Ottakar's men continued to fight, but in the chaos, the Hungarians washed over them like blood gushing from a slaughtered beast, and many of them broke ranks and followed the traitor Lord Rozemberk, racing for safety.

The screech of sword on sword spun Mouse back around to where Ottakar and his men pressed on toward the emperor. She watched as Ottakar charged, slashing at Rudolf; the horse fell and Rudolf with it. Ottakar's knights raised arms in victory unaware that the battle behind them had already been lost. Their fellow soldiers ran for their lives as a fresh corps of Cuman warriors, hidden by the deceptive emperor against all codes of honorable warfare, broke through the Bohemian flank and raced to Rudolf.

A curtain of Cuman browns and blues closed around Ottakar.

Mouse screamed as she ran, ducking and weaving as she tried to see through the wall of shields and horse legs, and then the circle of Cuman warriors grabbed Rudolf and rode off to regroup at a safer distance.

Suddenly, like an undertow, silence swallowed the sounds of the army and Mouse stopped. She could hear her own breath, her own heartbeat as she watched Ottakar's knights make the sign of the cross, and then, one by one, they peeled away and raced back into battle.

Ottakar was alone by the time she reached him.

She lifted his head into her lap and pressed her hand against his chest, trying to stop the blood, but knowing there was no point.

Mouse felt the anger coiling in her again. If the power still lived in her, she could save him with a word. Even as she turned her focus inward, desperately searching, not for the glow of a soul this time but for some sign of that dark power that was her father's legacy, she felt nothing.

Ottakar screamed and twisted in agony.

She laid her cheek against his forehead. "Please, please," she begged, but she knew no one would answer her. Because of who she was, what she was.

"I am here, Ottakar. You are not alone." Her tears joined the rivulets of sweat running along his jaw. "I am here."

"Mouse?" He mouthed the word. It was the first time she'd heard her name in more than twenty years.

Grief closed around her throat, but it was rage that tore at her, that came in hot bursts of breath. She was burning up with it.

She lifted her eyes to God. "Take him then! Damn you! You blind, absent God! What kind of Father are you? Not mine! Not mine!"

Sorrow shredded what was left of her, and she lowered her head to Ottakar's ear.

"I love you. Be at peace. Go now." She took a last ragged breath. "Die."

And she felt the power erupt.

It took her last word, meant only for Ottakar, and surged forth after all the years of being beaten down and smothered in her; she understood now that it had just been waiting. She saw the eerie glow of it pulse from her and spread outward completely beyond her control. Gently, like a kiss, it touched man and boy and horse, and it drank. They dropped, one after the other.

Mouse fell forward, drained of everything; she saw the blades of maidenhead grass wither, and then she saw nothing.

∞

When she woke, Mouse heard nothing. No buzz of insect. No whinny of a horse. No birdsong. As she opened her eyes, she saw why. Everything was dead. The grass. The trees. The armies around her. Ottakar in her lap.

She had killed them all.

She scrambled up, letting Ottakar's body roll to the ground. She walked over body after body, cataloguing each slack mouth and vacant eye. *Not Nicholas*, she thought as she passed each face. *Not Nicholas*.

Ten thousand dead.

She finally spotted Nicholas's banner flapping weakly in the slow breeze; his men, dead, lay all around. She could not make herself search for his face. She had no hope that he would have been spared. God was not merciful.

She wove her way through the corpses back to Ottakar. Her hand closed around the hilt of his sword and she pulled it to her. She was too weak to lift it very far and so she crouched. Dirt stuck to the viscid blood on the blade. She heard the first of the carrion crows flying in from the river as she pulled the sword across her throat.

THIRTY-SIX

What have I done, Mouse wondered, cowering at the back of the crypt as the monk laid the first stone. She could hear the Brothers singing her Requiem Mass. But she had thought herself dead several times since the battle at Marchfeld.

She had woken in the field, her clothes stiff with her own blood and the deep slit at her throat sealed, a thick grisly scar the only proof that she'd taken her own life—a last mortal sin to damn her. Careless, dead in mind and heart if not body, she started walking aimlessly, though some intangible pull drew her north toward home, across the border back to Bohemia.

Despair had taken her again, and she'd strung herself from a tree along the Thaya River, but the fabric of her makeshift rope had frayed and broken, and she woke again.

She threw herself from a cliff in the Brdy Mountains; she felt her back break against a rock, limbs tore at her as she broke through the canopy of trees, and the darkness took her.

But Mouse had woken again.

And now she could not sit still as she listened to the monk press the stone into the gritty mortar as he built the wall that would finally close her off from the world. *Inclusus*, the Church called it—a punishment for heresy and a death sentence for many.

Mouse had begged for it.

The Brothers of Podlazice had found her at the pond lapping water with the goats. Strings of algae hung from her fingers, and she was covered in filth. It looked like she'd crawled there; she was too weak to stand and unable to speak. She moaned as they lifted her and carried her into the monastery. Dressed in a habit and with her head shaved, the monks thought her one of them. She'd found it difficult to remember who she was—whether she was a boy or a girl, human or a mouse. She thought she had been all of these things at some point. She was a Mouse but not quite human. She was a girl but had made herself a boy.

They had fed her and given her clean water, but she refused to let them touch her, to bathe her. One of them sat with her during the night and whispered last rites. They were surprised in the morning. A miracle, they'd said.

Mouse knew otherwise.

She cleaned herself and ate again. She couldn't remember eating since Marchfeld. She asked to see the bishop. He bartered for her redemption.

"*Inclusus*?" The bishop studied the gaunt face of the Brother before him.

"The solitude is necessary, Father," Mouse answered.

"For what purpose? What can you have done that requires such a sacrifice? To be walled away?" Though the young monk gave no answer, the bishop saw the pain and guilt in Mouse's face. "I do not even know your name, Brother."

"Herman," she said blankly. "And I can give you something in exchange, Father." Mouse saw the man's doubt, but she would make any deal to get what she wanted: to be dead to the world so she could not hurt anyone else. "I will make you a book. It will be like none other. I promise. It will hold all we know in the world. A wonder."

"Impossible." But the bishop's ambition had been whetted and Mouse saw it.

"It will make you famous, powerful. You will see."

And so the Brothers had walked her down to a cell in the crypt. She leaned her head against the closed door and listened as they turned the key. She could smell the hot wax as they poured it in the lock, heard the splatter as drops landed on the stone floor and the squeak of the bishop's ring as he pressed his seal.

Panting, Mouse paced back and forth from wall to wall of her tiny cell. *What have I done?* she asked at each step.

She laid her head against the door; the metal of the monk's trowel chinked against the wood and then scraped the stone with a squeal. The wall was nearly done. A happenstance tomb like Christ's own.

She took several quick breaths, fighting the panic of the close space, but the sour smell of the mortar stung her nose and throat, and she stepped back again. Someone pushed jars of ink through the small slot near the floor at the side of the door; like liquid ants they inched in a line toward rows of candles and a stack of parchment. The bishop meant to get his book.

Mouse would give it to him, every scripted letter a penance for a soul she had taken, every bright illumination a pouring-out of anything good left in her, until she emptied herself and hopefully withered and turned to dust.

I must write the book, she thought over and over, trying to anchor herself against the torrent of fear building in her chest and crawling up her throat as she watched the last bit of light seeping between the crack of door and frame waver and go out as the monk wrested a final brick in place.

And he rolled a great stone to the door of the sepulchre and departed, she quoted silently.

And so Mouse was left alone in the dark cell lit with a single, flickering candle. Entombed. She whimpered as the shadows closed around her. Her breath came fast and shallow.

The Book. She knelt quickly at the parchment, picking up a quill and dipping it in the ink, her hand shaking. She could not think where to start, her mind too full of ghosts to remember words.

"In the beginning," came a voice from the dark.

Mouse spun toward the back corner of the cell, but she saw nothing. No hollow-eyed children pulling themselves out of the blackness. No demons from the pit. No slinking silver creatures.

"It starts 'In the beginning,'" said the voice again, light, almost laughing.

"Who is there?" Mouse barely had the breath for a whisper.

"Greetings, daughter." The voice chuckled. "I thought it was time we met."

EPILOGUE

Present Day

"I t was once considered a wonder of the world, the largest book of its time, containing the breadth of medieval knowledge—the Latin Vulgate version of the Bible, a surprisingly extensive collection of medical information as well as Bohemian history." Professor Jack Gray looked out at the stony faces of his fellow historians and tried to decide if they were bored or just disapproving of their young colleague. Taking a gamble, he clicked the button on his remote and changed the PowerPoint slide.

The scholars in the room shifted nervously in their seats as they saw the image that stared down at them: a figure with clawed hands raised and split tongue flicking out between rows of sharp teeth.

"The Codex Gigas is better known as the Devil's Bible thanks to this full portrait of the man himself and the mysterious legends surrounding the making of the book. Yet, despite hundreds of years of study, we still cannot answer the most basic question about its production. Who wrote it?" He paused for effect. "Was it the Devil, as legend claims? Did poor Herman, the monk, walled up in his cell, eventually admit the impossibility of his penitent task—to write a single book containing all the world's knowledge—and call on Satan to rescue him?"

The room chuckled, and Jack Gray knew he had them. His first book, *Who Wrote the Devil's Bible*, lay waiting for them in pretty little stacks on a table in the lobby. But he wanted more than book sales; Jack Gray wanted to make his career.

Dropping his smile, he said more seriously, "I think we've been looking in all the wrong places for the author of the Devil's Bible." He paused a moment, distracted, as a young woman stood and made her way to the exit at the back of Vanderbilt's Sarratt auditorium.

She let the double doors ease shut, drowning out Jack Gray's voice as he continued his lecture. She leaned against the cool brick in the lobby and took a steady breath, forcing her heart to slow. Mouse wondered if seven-hundred-year-old ghosts had finally caught her at last.

ACKNOWLEDGMENTS

As my first acknowledgments page for my first novel, I wondered if I should start my thanks at the beginning—parents for conceiving me, older brother for not smothering me, and second grade teacher, Mrs. Covey, for convincing the librarian to let me check out any book I wanted (Hello, *Moby-Dick*!). But out of concern for your time, I've decided to limit myself to folks who actually helped with this book.

Early readers are vital to a writer's process because they have to be people she can trust—both to handle the story with care and to offer honest feedback. Leanne Smith loved Mouse like I did, and she helped me find my way when I wrestled with doubt. Jamie Blaine helped me see how to tell some of the harder pieces of the story more gently, and Tessa Hoefle gave me the perfect gift of clarity to untangle a tricky bit of Mouse's journey. Other early readers who helped me see what was working and what wasn't were Rachel

Craddock, Rebecca Smith Crimmins, and Chris Nelson. Paige Crutcher read at a later but crucial time when her enthusiasm sustained me.

I am also immensely grateful for the encouragement Clay Stafford and the people at Killer Nashville gave me. The Claymore Award was a game changer for Mouse. It led me to Iris Blasi, my awesome editor at Pegasus Books. The excitement she and the rest of the staff (especially Claiborne Hancock, Katie McGuire, Becky Maines, Charles Brock, Linda Biagi, Mary Hern, Maria Fernandez, and Michael Levatino) expressed about getting Mouse's story out there for others to read, and Iris's tireless investment in guiding me through my first foray into publishing, defied everything I had heard or read about publishers. The people at Pegasus are special and I am thrilled to be working with them.

My agent, Susan Finesman, has been a stalwart champion and friend who traveled with me through the dark places—rejections and illness—and she did not give up. I am so very pleased to be on this journey together.

I am thankful that my little brother, Shane Chamblee, knows things that I do not and is generous with his time and his computer skills. I owe him (although I think all the times I dressed up and played Rambo in the backyard ought to count for something).

My sister in life, Beth Spencer Cummings, fills my well with creative energy, guides me with her wisdom, and shares the pain and joy of writing and life like only a soul-sister can.

My husband, Greg, read the novel first, last, and dozens of times in between. He could probably recite it at this point. That kind of tireless reader is invaluable to a writer, but it was another gift he gave me that I cherish most—a safe harbor. He held the chaos of life at bay so I could write. He let me try out crazy ideas and write bad sentences without judgment.

He refused to let me give in to self-doubt or to berate myself with mommy-guilt. He is my safe harbor.

And the mommy-guilt was all self-inflicted. The kids never complained (well, not about the writing at least). Instead, they started writing their own stories and novels. They inspired me and reminded me that the journey should be fun. They kept me dreaming. They still do.

ABOUT THE AUTHOR

DANA CHAMBLEE CARPENTER is the award-winning author of short fiction that has appeared in *The Arkansas Review*, Jersey Devil Press, and Maypop. *Bohemian Gospel*, her debut novel, won Killer Nashville's 2014 Claymore Award. She teaches creative writing and American literature at a university in Nashville, TN, where she lives with her husband and two children.